VOYAGE EMBARKATION

ZACHARY BONELLI

VOYAGE
ALONG THE CATASTROPHE of NOTIONS

VOLUME I
EMBARKATION

ILLUSTRATIONS BY
AUBRY KAE ANDERSEN

FUZZY HEDGEHOG PRESS

First published by Fuzzy Hedgehog Press
Seattle, Washington USA
www.fuzzyhedgehogpress.com

ISBN 978-1-62802-071-7

for my father

Contents

EMBARKATION

Illustrations

Prologue

Multiple Realms in the
Milky Way Galaxy
17,916 BCE

W HEN IT HAPPENED, my body had grown to occupy one thousand and twenty-nine distinct universes. At first, I had no idea what had transpired. I had to watch their world fall apart before my eyes. I had to watch them suffer and die by the thousands. And I couldn't do anything but stare. Not because I chose inaction, but because I hadn't caught up yet. I hadn't had enough time to process what I was seeing. It all flew by in a fast-forward blur, so that by the time I was able to comprehend what I'd done, my victims were already two years dead.

I hesitated before the devastated rocky orb for a moment, waves of frustration and self-loathing and guilt washing over me. Unable to stand it, I tore myself away from that little planet at the edge of the galaxy, and I ran. I headed directly for the galactic core, knowing what I sought would most likely be there. I weaved through the peripheries of systems whose names I neither knew nor cared to know. There would be no going home, no more tolerating my peers' chuckling scorn and the adults' condescension. I saw only one path, one way out. I had made a decision. I was going to follow through this time.

Nearing the galactic core, I found what I was looking for: a pair of gravity wells that were present in the exact same spot in all one thousand and twenty-nine of the universes I inhabited.

A wave of fear washed over me. I took my universe number eight hundred and sixty-five body, the one who shared the reality of my victims, and gave it a quick shove into the space exactly halfway between both gravity wells. I felt that body being wrenched and then torn. I was stretched all out of proportion until I could hold myself together no more. I was dispersed on that universe. My former constituent parts drifted, inert, falling toward one gravity well or the other. That me was dead, and I now occupied one thousand and twenty-*eight* distinct universes.

It was not enough. Those horrible emotions coursed through me more deeply than ever, overriding fear. I pushed another dozen of myself into the gravity wells, then another two dozen. I writhed and reveled in their destruction. The pain only strengthened my resolve. I'd show them. I'd show them all!

Another one hundred of me fell away and were torn apart. I seized up across all the universes of myself. My breathing quickened. I felt dizzy and nauseous. And that was as it should be. I was the stupid being who had killed all those people. I was the stupid being who *always* screwed *everything* up.

No more adventures. No more exploration. The only recompense I had left to give was the cold, dark end of all of me. Another two hundred of me disappeared into the void.

A white haze formed over my field of vision, and I stumbled closer to the gravity wells. Another push like that last one, and all that was left of me would wither away, painfully, without any help from the gravity wells, as I would completely compromise my natural regenerative abilities. I paused. I could feel myself becoming less and less aware of my surroundings. This piecemeal approach was too traumatic for my system. What if I went unconscious? I supposed one gravity well or the other would eventually pull me in and finish the job, but that would not be a fitting enough end for Id, the destroyer of worlds.

I steeled myself. I prepared to throw all the rest of me into the abyss.

"Id, stop!" a pair of voices called out.

I couldn't believe my eyes. "You two? Come to gloat?"

"No, no, dear boy. Nothing of the sort," the Mythos one said.

"You need to stop this. Now." The Ethos one was resolute.

"Why? So you can tell me what an idiot I am? How I should have listened to you?"

"No, that is not why we're here," Ethos said.

"Actually, we have a job for you," Mythos said.

"A job?" I giggled. "Do I look like I'm in *any* position to do a job? *I'm trying to commit suicide.*" I remember wondering at the time, how they could be so stupid as to need such an obvious thing explained to them.

I tossed another two of myself into oblivion. "You want this useless hunk of matter and energy to do a job for you?"

"Want nothing, Id! Your presence is required! Five half-rotations from now."

Ethos's booming voice resounded throughout all of me, harmonizing among each of my remaining quantum selves.

"Why? What happens in five half-rotations?"

"You will have the opportunity to save many more lives than were lost today. You have work to do, dear boy," Mythos said.

I hadn't expected that. I remember, it was the moment that the notion of my self-inflicted demise first soured. My rage collapsed, replaced by curiosity and intrigue. I steeled myself once more through blurred vision and nausea, and despite lingering resentment and self-loathing, I had, at least, one glimmering hope—the renewed sense of purpose Mythos and Ethos offered.

"Step away from the gravity wells," Ethos said, "and we'll explain what you must do."

Setting Sail

Realm #4663, "Felis"
May 22, 2178

KAL TUGGED at the strap of his goggles. The nanobubble over his right eye kept letting the water slip through. He rubbed at it, trying to nudge it into place, but he knew that trying to fix it here would be futile. Some buggy code, most likely. He'd tinker with the program when he got home.

For now, it was enough to gaze into the deep blue of the underwater realm that dissipated to black as the lakebed fell off into the distance, an inaccessible abyss.

He dove deeper. In the archive, Kal had found a program for underwater breathing. He'd enhanced it, and now it offered protection from the forces of unseen currents as well.

He felt his ears pop. His nanites couldn't pressurize the air any further. This was as deep as he dared go.

A school of fish swam past him. They were long and grayish green with navy blue stripes. Kal wondered, as they flitted away, if this species of fish existed in the Lake Michigan of Earth or not. Perhaps the fish there were navy blue with grayish green stripes. Maybe they didn't even have stripes. His pad would have the answer.

He squinted, another few drops of water leaking into his right eye, and found himself tugging at the strap again. He took one more look around, noting the contours of the lakebed, its rocky surface weaving downward and away. What wonders lay hidden down there, behind that impenetrable veil of darkness?

Kal turned his head upward, put his hands together above his head, and kicked until he burst through the surface of the lake. He turned, found the beach, and swam for the shore. Small waves rocked him up and down, surging through him and guiding him back to land.

When Kal reached the shallows, he stood, water rushing down off him as he pulled off his goggles. A bright and hot day greeted him, the heat and humidity common in Northeastern Illinois. If humans had ever lived here, they would have called it just that: Illinois. Or maybe they would have called it something else. Kal could only imagine the multitude of possibilities, and even his imagination probably couldn't do justice to reality.

He rubbed at the back of his neck. Thoughts of leaving this place and having adventures filled his mind.

The sand turned dry and hot beneath his feet. Kal ran across it toward the beach's edge, where the sand gave way to grass and rocks. He was nearly there when he stopped and stared. A large dust devil, half Kal's size, passed over a mound of sand. It dissipated, and then a second followed along what looked like the same trajectory as the first. He gazed at the dune for many moments, then shook his head. It was probably just some trick of the light combined with his angle of approach.

The sand burned into his feet, driving him onward toward the grass where his pad lay waiting for him. Kal picked it up and held it in his left hand, positioning his thumb on an indentation in the pad's edge.

At his touch, the device came to life, and a colorful, three-dimensional holographic interface formed over its surface. Kal touched a few icons, and with a hiss and a small pop, a flurry of nanites evaporated all the water from the surface of his body.

The ground shuddered, and Kal smiled as Higgs and Bjorg ran up to greet him. The cats belonged to the pride that claimed this territory as their own. Higgs was a gray tabby with pointy ears, and Bjorg a splotchy mix of brown and white. They were biologically similar to Earth's house cats, *felis catus*, but for the fact that they were roughly the size of Earth's elephants.

Higgs dragged his bristly tongue over Kal's entire right side, and the auto-defense nanites on his skin sizzled in mild exertion.

Kal smacked away Higgs's enormous whiskers. "Higgs, quit it! I just dried myself."

Bjorg smashed his head into Kal. "Mrrr... mrrrow."

Kal dropped his pad and climbed over Bjorg's face. He righted himself on Bjorg's neck and scratched him behind his ears. Bjorg's engine-sized voice box rumbled happily in response.

Before long, Kal felt Higgs's teeth pulling him from Bjorg's neck. Kal swung onto Higgs's neck and began scratching behind his ears, while Bjorg mewled in complaint and head-butted Higgs.

When his arms grew tired, Kal slid down from Higgs's side, grasping one tuft of fur at a time until he was able to jump the last meter to the ground. He picked up his pad and jogged toward his treehouse at the edge of the forest. He passed Daisy and Engrie, curled up into one another on the grassy plain. Charles sat hunched on the ground, looking up into the sky as though he were ready to pounce at the small tufts of passing clouds.

Kal reached his tree and climbed the rope ladder. He stepped onto the balcony, took off his swimsuit, and threw it onto the railing. He then put on his T-shirt and shorts, which lay waiting for him on the balcony's hammock.

He pushed a button on his pad, and the invisible nanite forcefield guarding the doorway disappeared with a light whoosh. Kal stepped inside, and a second whoosh announced the forcefield's reinstatement. The room's interior was cool and dry, a pleasant change from the hot and sticky weather outdoors. Kal set his pad down on the table at the center of the room and walked to his bookshelf. Just as he began scanning the rows for a particular volume on biomolecular data encryption, a wailing cry erupted from the forest.

"Muuuuuurrrrow! Mrrrrrrow-row-row!"

Kal rolled his eyes. He snatched up his pad from the table, undid the doorway forcefield, walked out of his treehouse, and descended the rope ladder.

Kal shook his head as he strolled into the forest toward the howls. Such events occurred with some frequency, often twice within the same week.

Boson, a tall, brown-furred cat with a fluffy mane, batted idly at the enormous, bushy-tailed rodents that inhabited the trees, unconcerned with the tortured cries from deeper inside the forest. Like all the other cats, he had become apathetic to these antics long before Kal had arrived. Kal remembered, years ago, when he had first heard the belabored yowling. He had raced into the forest, wondering what horrific fate had befallen one of the cats.

Kal walked into a clearing. Max, a fat, orange tabby, lay on the ground, his large bulk pinning down the top half of a small tree. Max loved to climb trees. Unfortunately, the trees didn't love him back. Not a single tree in the forest was capable of supporting his massive weight, and when Max would reach some critical altitude, sometimes not higher than a few meters, the tree would collapse and bring Max down with it.

"Muuuuurrrr... Murrrrrrroooow!" Max cried out.

"Max, you're bigger than the tree."

"Mrrrr... Mrrrrow-row." *But it'll hurt if I get up.*

Kal furnished Max with a sigh. His pad in hand, he activated the interface and executed the usual program. He touched his hand to the tree's base, and an invisible cloud of nanites streamed silently off him and engulfed it. The program created a force that pinned the tree to the ground, preventing it from snapping up and hitting Max if and when he decided to move.

"Mrrrr...?"

"Yes, you can get up now." Kal grinned.

"Mrrrrrrrrrr." *I'm not so sure.*

"It's really okay, Max. The naughty tree won't hurt you."

Max sprang up, his lardy bulk sloshing backwards, and he galumphed off into the forest. No matter how many times Kal did this, Max was still convinced that the tree was a force to be reckoned with.

Kal initiated the second phase of his program. His nanites relinquished their restraint gradually, bringing the mangled tree slowly upright once more.

The program's final phase scanned the tree for structural damage and attempted repairs. Kal watched as the tree's chips and bruises vanished before his eyes. Smiling at another job well done, he walked back to his treehouse.

Now his real work could begin.

Kal swiped his hand through the holograms, and they flickered out of existence. He looked out the window at the lake. There was just enough light left for one more swim. It was tempting, but stubborn preoccupation drove his mind back to the task at hand.

There had to be a way to make this work.

He took a deep breath, leaned forward, and pushed gently at his pad, which lay flat at the center of the table. The holograms, an enormous projection of Kal's brain, reappeared. Holographic neurons flickered, representing the buzz of electrochemical activity inside his head. The four implants were also visible: two just below his cerebellum, and two more where his neck met his shoulders. The metaxic nodes were his only

way off Felis, world of the enormous cats, and out into the metaxia, that strange and wonderful alternothing that separated each quantum universe from all the others.

Kal flicked an error notification hologram out of existence.

"Okay," he said. "If I try an encryption pattern with a *thirty-two* character base, and if the lockout mechanism releases twenty-three seconds after five failed tries, I will only have to run the program for…"

Kal typed out some arithmetic on the number pad of his holographic keyboard.

"Four years." He slammed a fist on the table and threw himself back in his chair.

"Although," he sat up straight again, an idea forming. "A dictionary attack… I could limit the lexicon to phrases in my personal journal."

"It'll get through that in—" more number crunching "—just over eight hours."

Kal smiled.

It was worth a shot. If the password hadn't been based on him, he'd be no worse off. He'd just have to try a different lexicon or switch to the brute force method—the four years method. He leaned back in his chair and frowned at the thought of being stuck on Felis that long.

He grinned again, thinking of the unlock protocol he'd written. His metaxic nodes were supposed to go into lockdown after five failed access attempts. Kal had written a program that was able to crack the lockout after twenty-three seconds, meaning he could try alternative passphrases as many times as he wanted.

Kal scanned over his program once more and hit the button of projected light that would execute it.

His treehouse shook.

"Mrrr…"

"Meow!"

"Meooooow!"

Kal realized that he had not only forgotten to feed the cats, he'd forgotten to feed himself. His stomach growled at him indignantly.

He turned off the pad and walked to the kitchenette in the corner. A holographic display emerged from the wall above the sink, and he scrolled through its menu. For himself, a turkey sandwich. For the cats, a couple dozen immense hunks of turkey meat.

The sandwich materialized on the table while roast turkeys the size of small boulders shimmered into existence on the floor wherever there was space.

The tree shook again as Kal lowered the forcefield of his room's window. Humid air rushed into his apartment. He grabbed the hunks of bird meat and heaved them outside. The usual thumps and thuds of feline feeding ensued. Max and Daisy, Jumper and Engrie, Charles and Bjorg, Higgs and Boson all seethed about, anxious to sink their teeth into their mock prey.

The entire pride consisted of fourteen cats, one of which, Catface, had been born just last year. Kal had named them all.

When he had first begun exploring Felis, he'd been wary of the cats. They had, after all, made numerous attempts at his life with flailing paws and gnashing teeth. After that followed a period where they avoided him, regarding him warily as the strange being from another world, whom they could not hope to injure.

With time, he had become their protector. Kal fed them, cured them of illnesses, and provided them heat in the winter. He was theirs, and they were his. Was he a member of the pride, maybe? Well, not quite.

Kal heaved the last two turkeys out the window and turned the forcefield back on. His nanites returned to scrubbing the heat and humidity from the air.

He looked at the sandwich on the table and then out the window. Yeah, one more swim would probably feel pretty good.

He stripped off his clothes, put on his swimsuit, and grabbed his pad off the table.

∽◌⟋◌∾

Kal had programmed his window and door forcefields to block sunlight between the hours of four and nine a.m. Even though the sun rose over the lake and should have shone directly through his treehouse windows, the room's interior remained dark.

His treehouse shook.

"Mrrrr... Murrrrow!" Max called out.

Kal rolled over.

"Mrrrr... Mrrrrr... Muurrrrr-row!"

I'm going to ignore him.

The treehouse rattled again, and Kal rolled into the wall. More unhappy mewling sounded from below.

"Mrrr......"

"Meow-yow-yow!" Max demanded, rocking the treehouse violently. Books fell from Kal's shelves.

"Fine!" Kal stormed out of bed. He pulled up the menu, found the biggest hunk of fish his computer could create, and watched it coalesce on the floor. He grabbed it up, hauled it to the window, and slammed at its control panel. A burst of sunlight assaulted Kal's eyes, and Midwestern summer air congealed around him. He hurled the load outside.

"Now leave me alone!" Kal shouted, but Max was already nose-deep in the enormous hunk of fish.

He pounded blindly at the windowsill until the forcefield reactivated, returning the treehouse interior to darkness, and collapsed back into bed.

As he tried to make himself comfortable again, he felt a tingling at the edge of his consciousness that made the hairs on the back of his neck stand on end. He was not drifting back into sleep but becoming more and more awake with every moment. Something was... different. Something should excite him.

It struck him all at once. Just as he had picked up the fish. On the table. His pad. The hologram. Kal bolted out of bed, stumbling toward his table in the darkness and rubbing his eyes.

Three words hung in the air above his pad: "encryption decode successful."

Kal let out a small, disbelieving laugh. He rubbed his eyes again, expecting to see his interface reverted to its usual state of "access denied." But the success message remained, bouncing every few moments over the holographic representation of his brain.

He activated the interface inputs and released the light-dampening nanites from their duty, allowing the morning sun to splash in over him.

His hands peeled over the holokeyboard, and he struggled with his still-adjusting eyes to consume the newly unlocked data from the depths of the technology rooted at the base of his brain: the metaxic coordinates of known inhabitable worlds, metaxic coordinates of less-than-habitable worlds, programs for quantum-locking bubble creation, and there! The program for automated nanoexploration of the metaxia.

It was too good to be true. Kal pored over the code, his hands trembling. Line by line, he pieced together its behavior. The program would first tag his nanites, and then it would activate the nodes in his neck, sending each one through the metaxia to an alternate Earth. They would scan their target planet's atmosphere and geological state before returning home. Worlds determined to be too dangerous, or worlds from which the nanites never returned, were locked out immediately.

Kal executed the program.

The code vanished from the display, and an empty field replaced it.

At first, he wondered if anything had really happened. He ran a hand over the back of his neck. Was he supposed to have felt something? Maybe the nodes had been damaged or physically disabled after he'd arrived on Felis.

His fears were soon allayed. A point of light labeled "Earth 0001" appeared at the center of the table. Other dots sprang up around it, Earth 0002, 0003, 0004, 0005. Faster and faster, points lit up in clusters forming tendrils of alternate worlds, branching off the Earth dot. Upon reaching 9,999 visible worlds, the program terminated.

Kal glanced down to a pop-up window at the bottom of the field containing an exploration report. In its search for the 9,999 visible Earths, 105,386 nanites had been lost to worlds with destructive environments.

His gaze returned to the twisting clusters of lights branching off Earth, each one of them also Earth, but a completely different Earth. Each would have its own history, its own culture, perhaps even its own topology. He even spotted Felis, which his computer had labelled #4663.

At the edge of the field hovered a big, glowing button, one that he could press to take himself to any of those ten thousand tiny lights. Each one represented an entire universe of adventures and possibilities. All he had to do now was choose.

"We need to have a talk," a deep, booming voice resounded from the doorway.

Startled, Kal stumbled away from the table and backed into the wall behind him.

Outside the door to his treehouse stood two men. One was short and plump, wearing deep purple robes, and held a wooden staff with an ornate, spherical metal head. The other man stood tall, resolute and aggressively thin, wearing a suit and tie, both pitch black. He held a clipboard with a pad of paper and pen attached, though not a light pen, but an antique, one of those ancient mechanisms that utilized either ink or graphite, Kal couldn't remember which.

The two men entered his apartment, their forms passing directly *through* the doorway forcefield.

Kal leapt forward and snatched up his pad, then scrambled back toward the wall.

"Who are you?" Kal asked, eyes wide and heart racing.

"My name is Mythos," the one in the purple robes said.

"Ethos."

"You're here from Earth... come to shut down my nodes?"

They both shook their heads.

"What do they call it again... that, um, program, for living things? Was it lifecoders?" Mythos said quietly to Ethos.

"No, you're thinking of 78963 by 64." Ethos smiled wryly. "This one's home is Earth, 78964 by 63."

Ethos's gaze returned to Kal. "Run your bioscanner."

Kal found his hand slowly rising toward his pad, and he hit the bioscanner icon. As he set Mythos and Ethos as the program's targets, his mind swam with thoughts of how they knew his name, how they knew of Felis, how they could move through nanotech forcefields, where they were from if not Earth, and a million other questions.

Kal balked as the data streamed in.

"What are—"

"Your Fermilab representatives referred to us as 'quantum life forms'," Ethos said.

Mythos chuckled. "Not our least favorite designation, anyway."

Calming, Kal suddenly became self-conscious, realizing that he was wearing only the pair of underwear he'd woken up in. Not taking his eyes off the strange duo, he sidled toward his dresser.

Mythos nodded encouragingly while Ethos stared out of the treehouse window, impassive. Kal wondered if he had any hope of protecting himself from entities that apparently inhabited not one universe, not every universe, but *in-between* them. Probably not.

"You've been to Earth?" Kal asked, pulling on his shorts.

"Oh yes, beautiful world," Mythos said.

"I was pleased to see that you developed nanotechnology when you did," Ethos said. "As you will discover shortly, Earth is an island, a sea of nano-destruction on one side, and a sea of eco-destruction on the other. And yet, Earth managed to avoid both catastrophes. Just the right mix of technological and social development. Fascinating culture."

Kal had taken his hands off his pad just long enough to slide on a T-shirt, then snatched it up again. His heart no longer pounding quite so quickly, he sat down at his table, and gestured, offering Mythos and Ethos the opportunity to sit. They accepted.

"Then, you're not going to stop me from exploring the metaxia? Are you going to tell... anyone on Earth?"

"Oh no, dear boy," Mythos said. "It's not our job to interfere."

"It is our job to observe," Ethos said. "With one exception. The metaxia is more fragile than it may appear from your perspective. Every traveler who passes from one plane to another pokes a tiny hole in it. Now, the metaxia can recover from a handful of intermittent pin pricks. But those nodes in your head, Kal, they are a powerful technology. If misused, they could rip the metaxia apart."

"Our species does not tolerate metaxic damage," Mythos said. "Just as your ancestors fought to save their ecosystem from destruction, we will fight to save our home realm if it is likewise threatened."

Kal nodded. "I understand."

There was a pause. Mythos and Ethos shared a glance.

"Kal," Mythos said. "You do have more questions, don't you?"

Kal opened his mouth, hesitated, and closed it again.

"It's okay. You can ask us anything."

"You're metaxic organisms... you live in the metaxia?'

Ethos nodded, raising his eyebrows, and Mythos gestured impatiently.

"Why come here now? Why tell me these things?"

The duo shared another momentary glance. Ethos raised an eyebrow, then turned to Kal. "Whenever a uniquantum organism, such as yourself, is about to embark on metaxic travel, we make a brief appearance and set the ground rules."

"You, dear boy, are a unique case," Mythos started to say before Ethos shot him a piercing glare. Mythos paused. "I mean, we've already spoken to the friendly Fermilab scientists on your Earth, but they never told you about us. They probably didn't expect you to go exploring."

Kal put his hand on his chin and leaned into the table, wondering how much more information he should try to get out of them. He'd finally shed the rules and regulations that had been restraining him for the last four years and wasn't in the least anxious to be shackled by new ones. "Are there more quantum organisms in the metaxia? How will I know if I'm using the nodes too much?"

"Mythos and I are assigned to this metaxic intersection. From your perspective, that is about 250 quindecillion alternate universes, Earth and Felis included. Unless you venture far outside that group of universes on your computer, it is unlikely you will meet any more of our kind."

"As for the resiliency of the metaxia," Mythos said, "if you do not enter or leave a universe more than, say, a couple dozen times a day, the metaxia should be just fine."

Kal had begun idly poking around on his pad while they spoke, and he looked up now that they had stopped. Mythos's friendly expression had vanished, and Ethos, if possible, looked even sterner.

Mythos sighed. "I understand you're anxious to go exploring, but do me a favor first. Pull up that map, that 'grid' of worlds you made."

Kal gestured over his pad, and the field of snaky light-point tendrils shimmered into existence above it.

"Those points of light do indeed represent wonders you can't yet imagine," Mythos said, waving his hand through the map, the hologram distorting around it.

"Notice though," Ethos pierced the small window at the bottom of the display with his pen. "In order for you to discover ten thousand relatively healthy worlds, you had to sacrifice over ten times that many of your nanomachines to the dangers of the unknown. On some Earths dwell forms of life that will either not care or not notice when they accidentally snuff you out of existence. In others, Sol is not a yellow dwarf, but a red giant. And in others still, there is not even a planet where Earth should be. Those nodes in your neck are not just capable of ending the metaxia if misused, Kal. They can end you."

Kal gulped.

Mythos and Ethos looked satisfied and stood up. Kal found himself doing the same. The grid hologram flickered away.

"Be careful, Kal," Mythos said.

"I will."

Mythos and Ethos walked out the door of the treehouse, directly through the forcefield once more.

"Oh, Kal." Mythos turned to face him. "Are you sure there isn't something you'd like to do before you leave here? Something you've maybe forgotten?"

Kal scratched his head. He had his pad, he had the grid, he had functional nanites, and he had protective nanite programs.

"No, I don't think so."

Mythos and Ethos looked at each other. Ethos raised an eyebrow, and Mythos shrugged. They nodded at Kal, and then their humanoid bodies blobbed and morphed into two writhing, spheroidal blue masses. The globs wobbled briefly in midair before flashing out of existence.

Kal stood motionless, staring at the space where they'd been. He blinked a few times, then walked to the doorway and pressed his palm flat against the forcefield. It shimmered where he touched it, repelling his hand.

He shook his head and returned to his preparations.

Kal took a deep breath. He had heard that breathing deeply could help calm you. It didn't seem to be working.

He had dreamed of this moment for so long. Kal had been through the metaxia once before, on his trip from Earth to Felis, but he had been unconscious the entire time. The descriptions he'd heard from others had fueled fantastic dreams of traveling to other worlds. But the ecstasy of each dream would turn bitter the moment he awoke to the yowling of a cat and discovered he had not actually traveled anywhere at all.

Kal held his pad out in front of him now, gripping it tightly. He took another breath. The button sat in front of him, the button that would activate the nodes, and this time his nanites would not be the only ones to enter the metaxia.

He tried to push the button, but his hand wouldn't move. He then tried counting down from ten, but when he reached one, his hand still refused to budge.

Come on, Kal. Get a grip.

He took another deep breath.

His hand moved tentatively forward, his pointer finger sticking out toward the button of light.

He jabbed at it.

The air crackled around him, arcs of blue electricity bursting forth and obscuring his view of the treehouse. He tensed up, and his heart raced. The static haze encompassed him, forming a sphere. Inside it the air stood still, but outside it great gusts of wind erupted throughout the treehouse, rattling the furniture and shaking the whole tree from side to side. All of the books he had returned to their shelves this morning toppled back onto the floor.

The coruscating blue silently dissipated, and the view of his treehouse twisted and rippled away, crumpling into a sea of swirling, azure eddies. Brilliant, cerulean streaks pulled and sheared themselves every which way — rippling, swirling, merging, advancing, and retreating, like the sheen of oil on water, but in three dimensions. Shimmering blobs composed themselves into shapes that seemed almost recognizable, before twisting chaotically into some new configuration.

Kal stood and watched it for many moments, his mouth agape.

Then he caught a glimpse of something in his peripheral vision, but when he turned to look at it, it had vanished. His gaze managed to catch another, a view of a forest that flickered into and out of the blue. A battlefield strewn with bodies rippled into, and then, just as quickly, out of existence. He glimpsed other bits of realities in the metaxia: a field of volcanos spewing lava and ash; a city like Chicago but with yellowish, stone architecture; a navy fleet sailing an ocean where there should be land. So many different worlds, all rushing around him, around the bubble of real space that the nanites had pushed here with him inside.

He stuck his hand out cautiously in front of himself. Although he couldn't see anything but the blue streaks, he felt his fingers touch the edge of the bubble, and he retracted sharply. He tried again, this time pressing his hand fully against the invisible boundary, not terribly unlike a forcefield, the edge of his chunk of reality. He gazed out into the swirling void of all-possibility that lay beyond it.

"Alright," Kal said, rapping his fist on the bubble wall. He turned his attention back to his pad. "Where to go first?"

ಜ⟨⟩ಣ

"Mrrr... Muuurrrow-row-row!" Max called out.

Night had fallen. The other thirteen cats sat beside him, gathered around Kal's treehouse, their food untouched. They sat expectantly in the dark, having elected Max to call out for their friend. Max had always been the most talkative of them, so it felt appropriate for him to give voice to their sorrow.

"Mrrrooow!" Max cried.

He received no reply.

Longing

Realm #5941, "Ydora"
June 7, 2178

THE SUMMER AIR of Felis swirled about Kal, replacing the climate-controlled interior of the metaxic bubble as it peeled away. The cats, for all their fur, seemed no worse for the muggy weather. They lay in clumps around the treehouse, their sides rising gently up and down under the moonlight. Many hadn't even opened their eyes at the disturbance created by the bubble's unpeeling. Such events had become commonplace.

Kal climbed up into his treehouse and threw his pad onto the table. The interface lit up and erupted into numerous slowly filling bars, indicating the progress of the data sync to the treehouse computer system.

He glimpsed his bed, and a small shudder ran through him. He searched the room for something to occupy himself with, anything that would keep him awake.

He walked to the window and looked down at the mess of bird meat strewn across the ground. He smiled, glad that the computer program he'd written to feed the cats in his absence was working as intended.

Weariness overcame him in a wave, and he tried to fight it off. He thought of things he could maybe program, or notes he could write up. On the last world, he'd climbed into an enormous crater for a view of a swirling Lake Michigan. On that Earth, it was not really a lake, but a massive, perpetual whirlpool fed by hundreds of gushing rivers. He had enjoyed the trek, but the effort of mountain climbing had drained him.

Somehow, against all conscious effort, he found himself shuffling into bed, clothes and all, and he shut his eyes.

∞⟨⟩∞

Kal clung to a ladder made of wood and vines. Chirps, buzzes, hisses and squawks sounded from all around him, greenery encroaching from every direction. The ladder continued upward another ten meters or so. The ground lay at least three times that distance below.

Below. He didn't like thinking about that direction. He clutched at the ladder as a wave of vertigo spilled over him. He clenched his eyes shut and jammed his chin into his chest. When it subsided, he looked up and focused on the opening that led into the bottom of the large, oval, wooden structure. The bauble hung suspended from the branches of two mammoth trees on either side of him. It pulled at him, commanding him upward, and so he forced himself to keep climbing.

Just one hand carefully over the other, he repeated to himself. He kept his head facing up and focused on the rhythm of the climb.

A breeze burst through the leaves, swinging the rope ladder from side to side. Kal was glad that his hands and feet had been firmly planted on the rungs when it had happened. He waited for the wobbling to cease, then breathed deeply and continued his ascent.

Before long, he reached the hole in the bottom of the structure and climbed through it. He flung himself from the ladder onto the floor, gasping heavily and glad to feel something solid beneath him once more. The interior was enormous, but it was also very dark compared to the bright jungle outside, and his eyes would need time to adjust.

He pulled off his backpack, got out his pad, and stood up. He stood at the bauble's edge, near the wall. A single open portal at the center of the roof cast a beam of midday sunlight down onto the floor. A vast conglomeration of intricate, papery hexagons lay illuminated below it. They wrapped and twisted around one another, spreading out in contorted tendrils, shaped eerily like the map of alternate Earths on his pad.

He readied his pad and put his nanites on alert.

Fist-size insects began emerging from the hexagons. They crept slowly at first but soon accelerated, swarming forward toward him. Some scuttled over the wooden floor while others flew.

The clattering of their claws against the floorboards and buzzing of their wings became deafening, but he stood his ground, certain that his nanites would protect him.

Just as they were about to reach him, the leading edge of the insect swarm seized up. Their deep green exoskeletons began to shrivel and brown, peeling off their bodies. The fliers plummeted to the floor, their wings melting off. The entire swarm began to slow, then turned, limping away from Kal as fast as their sickly limbs could take them.

His pad indicated the cause. Each of Kal's tiny robots produced a small quantity of nanogenic radiation. While it did not affect most organisms, the radiation had triggered a terribly damaging reaction in these insects, and all Kal had done was try to scan them.

They huddled now, shivering in their hive. Some had lost most of their exterior and were barely anything more than sinewy, goop-covered limbs. Kal deactivated all his nanotechnology except for the auto-medical and auto-defense systems, which were programmed to remain either in or on his body.

When he was close enough, he peered inside one tendril of the hive. A group of three insects lay curled up together. Underneath the decay, a new, more resilient frame was growing atop their limbs.

His eyes widened and shot down to his pad, the interface abuzz with new information. The insects did not just have an aversion to nanogenic radiation, they also had within their genes the ability to adapt to it, to overcome the aversion.

He sent his nanites at the insects, each one ready to scan their genetic configuration.

Data began streaming into his pad, and Kal whooped in excitement as sequences of DNA burst into view on the interface.

oe⟨⟩oo

"I found it! I can—" Kal shouted triumphantly and sat up in bed. The sounds of the jungle had vanished. He sat in his treehouse on Felis. He was sweating, and the wave of realization rushed over him, washing away his euphoria.

His eyes teared up. This happened every time. It always felt real. Kal punched the wall, then his bed, breathing heavily.

It was still night. Daisy let out a long wheeze directly below the treehouse.

Kal got out of bed, wiped his eyes, and sat down at the table in front of his pad. He opened up the DNA sequencing interface. An empty double helix spun in front of him. Above it, GC and AT compounds glowed, waiting to be placed.

He sat and stared at it. Finally, he turned the pad off and rested his head on the table. No matter how hard he tried to remember it, the most important detail of the dream—the configuration of those insects' genetic code—always eluded him. The rest remained crystal clear in his mind.

This was now the fifth night in a row that he'd had the dream, and although he could remember it clearly in his waking mind, in the dream, it was always as though he was experiencing the events for the first time. The insects' aversion and subsequent resilience to nanogenic radiation surprised and delighted him, but each time, he was torn away at that crucial moment, just as he began the genetic scan.

Kal took off his clothes, threw them onto the floor, and trudged back to bed. At least the dream had thus far spared him repetition within the same night.

∞⟨⟩∞

Kal awoke to Max's meowing and clawing at the tree. He groped blindly through his darkened room to the wall panel and ordered the cats' breakfast constructed. He went for his morning swim, and, after returning to the treehouse, ate his own breakfast, resolving to find out if a world existed that matched the jungle of his dream.

He turned on his pad and pulled up a container of still images, each corresponding to one of the ten thousand worlds his nanites had placed on the grid.

First, Kal filtered out the eighteen uninhabited ones he'd already visited. The display was still enormous, filling most of the room, and the pictures were tiny.

Munching cereal and typing at the same time, Kal programmed a filter that would get rid of all but the images that contained a high quantity of the color green since the trees in the jungle all had big, green leaves and vines.

There, that was better. The cloud of the images contracted to fit nicely over the table, and the pictures were a little bigger. Only about five hundred of them now. Kal scanned them over, but none jumped out.

He also noticed a lot of Earths that simply had green skies. He began flicking away the images that were clearly not matches. It was easy going until he got down to the last fifty or so. The morning dragged on as pored over the details of the remaining images.

Eventually, he narrowed the selection down to five candidates. He didn't see any wooden bauble structures hanging from trees, but that could have been because the nanites that had taken the pictures might not have been pointed at any.

He sent more nanites off to the five candidate worlds for more photos. Minutes later, they returned. Kal was able to throw out three more worlds right away.

And then he saw it. There they were beyond the tops of walls, the wooden baubles suspended from the branches. And people amongst them.

Kal gulped.

Until now, he'd been able to avoid worlds inhabited by humans. He had in his treehouse computer all the reports of the first metaxic travelers from Fermilab. He had read each of them dozens of times. They had traveled out to other worlds five years ago, just before Kal had come to Felis. Famously, all the members of Team Haskell had been murdered. The culture of the world they were exploring had seemed friendly and peaceful at first, and then the team had shown off their pads and nanotechnology. They were executed on the spot, their bodies molecularly disassembled by the powerful and deadly nanotechnology of that world. The pads of the dead explorers promptly disassembled themselves, returned to Earth, and composed a mechanical account of the events that had led to their owners' deaths.

Of course, that had been just one of fifty inhabited worlds the Fermilab teams had explored, and many other teams had found beautiful, vibrant, and healthy human cultures. In the metaxia, healthy human cultures were the rule, and unhealthy, self-destructive cultures were the exception. The theory was that the unhealthy ones didn't stick around for very long on their way to mass extinction. But Kal wasn't a quantum life form or a huge team of experts. He didn't get to make metaxic mistakes. It would take only one dangerous world to end his adventures permanently.

Kal thought about his dream. He thought of its implications and about the possibility of having it every night for the rest of his life.

He sighed, picked up the pad, climbed down the tree, and walked to the small hill by the beach, the place he'd designated as his metaxic takeoff point.

His computer prompted him for a target, and he input the designation for the jungle world.

ഗഉ⟨⟩ൟ

Kal stood in his bubble, the metaxia swirling around outside. A holographic document hung suspended in the air.

"One," Kal read aloud. "Initiate the construction of a translation matrix for your target world. You can find the controls under the main menu of the linguistics program. The nanites will travel to the target world, and begin sampling the language of its inhabitants."

He opened up the interface of the linguistics program and found the appropriate menu while an Earth with an industrial-era Chicago peeled in and out of view in the metaxia beyond his bubble.

"Do not unravel the bubble until the translation matrix reaches a felicity rating of seventy-five percent or greater."

He watched the linguistic database's felicity rating tick upward.

"Two. Enter your age and gender into the sartorial program and activate it." Kal did as the document instructed and continued reading aloud. "When the red indicator turns green, activate the next phase of the program. The nanites will make the necessary adjustments to your clothing."

A few moments later, the red button on his interface did indeed turn green, and he pressed it. His T-shirt and jeans shimmered away, and he balked at his new attire.

Instead of pants or shorts, he wore a small thing around his waist that resembled the racing suit he'd worn when he was on the swim team on Earth. On his feet were some kind of moccasins, and a sash about as wide as his palm lay across his chest, running from his left shoulder to his right hip. All three garments were made of the same synthetic material, and they itched terribly.

"What the hell?" Kal looked down at himself. He pulled up the images his nanites had taken of the jungle world and looked more closely at the people. Before he had only noted their presence, not their clothing. Looking at the pictures more closely now, he could see that he was indeed wearing suitable attire for the jungle.

He gazed moments longer at this image. Some of those residents had rather appealing physiques. He shook his head, reminding himself of the dream, and turned his attention back to the document.

"Three. Run the secondary cultural analysis program. If any warnings pop up with severity four or greater, it is strongly recommended that you abort the mission and return to Fermilab."

Kal ran the program. A huge list of cultural vectors appeared before him, but all of the danger ratings hovered near zero, with only a few spiking up toward one. Kal breathed a sigh of relief, but reminded himself that the program wasn't perfect. This was the same software that had reported extremely low numbers for the world of Team Haskell's demise.

He pondered Team Haskell and stared at the pad. An idea formed, and he turned his attention back to the photos. A young man in the picture about Kal's age had on a kind of backpack. It was barely anything more than a synthetic sack with cords to sling one's arms through, but it would do. Kal programmed the nanites to construct one for him.

He noticed something else. On his grid, the label for the point of light that represented the jungle world had changed. Previously, it had read "Realm #5941," the ID of the nanite that had originally explored it two weeks ago. It now read "Ydora." Curious, Kal pulled up the linguistic database and discovered "Ydora" was the word for "Earth" in the jungle Illinois.

Kal took a few deep breaths. He typed one final command into his pad and stuffed it into his backpack. The blue swirling of the metaxia dispersed, and the bubble wall flashed, then peeled away, the blue whorls coalescing into the deep green hues of the Ydora jungle.

∂℮⟋∂℘

Kal walked through the jungle for ten minutes before coming to the edge of the city he had seen in the stills. From the jungle floor, he could just see over its walls. The wooden, ellipsoid structures were tied with thick vines to the branches of absolutely massive trees.

It was even hotter here than it had been on Felis, and the heat made the high humidity even more oppressive. Kal realized that the clothing he had, just ten minutes ago, been so reluctant to wear, was actually quite amenable to this climate, and the idea of covering himself more seemed ridiculous. The itchiness that he had felt while in the dry, climate-controlled bubble had disappeared once the humidity of the Ydoran jungle had engulfed him.

Kal spotted a tall man standing near the city gates. He was gazing into the jungle, and Kal's first instinct was to turn and flee. Too late. The man spotted him, smiled, and nodded. Kal tensed up. He forced himself to exhale slowly and relax. Somehow, he managed to smile back. He commanded his legs forward, and they brought him to the city gates.

"Welcome to the hermitage of Shik'wa," the man pulled a pad of paper from his belt. "How long a residency would you like?"

Kal pondered this briefly. *Nothing extreme, then. Not too long, not too short.*

"One week, please," Kal said. The border guard didn't seem disturbed by this number in any way that Kal could perceive.

"Your name?" the man's voice sounded officious but calm.

"Kal Anders."

The man scrawled on the pad with an implement that looked like a quill. It had a long stalk with hairs protruding from it. Kal wondered if it had actually come from a jungle animal or if it was synthetic, like the clothing.

The border guard tore off a slip of paper and handed it to Kal. He then opened the gates and motioned for Kal to enter. Kal hurried inside, and the guard closed the gates behind him.

Kal slowed and gazed around himself, finally seeing the baubles and the rest of the city properly. Shik'wa had two clear levels: one on the ground where he stood, and another that consisted of elevated platforms, bridges and terraces, connecting the wooden baubles that hung overhead.

Unpaved soil thoroughfares divided up the ground level into plots of short, pruned grasses. Teachers instructed groups of young people at some while artists busily hacked, glued and welded at others. All of the art pieces were abstract. Geometric shapes sprouted from one another in various hues, some with frames of metal and others of wood.

Kal chose a dirt path at random and began walking down it, trying to appear normal.

The crowd grew denser, and the sculptures gave way to doctors tending patients, craftsmen offering their services, and merchants hawking their wares. There didn't seem to be any currency, just barter. And in the case of food, the hunters and farmers freely gave away their crops and game. What was important, Kal noticed, was a person's permit paper. Anyone involved in trade examined their partner's permit prior to the transaction.

Shik'wa's residents wore the same kind of clothes Kal's nanites had constructed, although children younger than about four were allowed to go either completely naked or diapered. Among the adults, women and men wore the same thing, except that for women the sash was reversed, running from the right shoulder to the left hip. After many minutes, he had to amend that distinction, when he spotted some men and women with "flipped" sashes. Also, some women, particularly the ones carrying weaponry and freshly killed game, wore a kind of tube top. The garments came in a variety of colors and patterns, and although everything appeared to be made of the same material, no two person's outfits looked exactly the same.

He walked the streets for some time, trying his best to study all the details without appearing too inquisitive. Many of Shik'wa's residents seemed too absorbed in their own business to pay any attention to him. He mentally patted himself on the back at a successful first attempt at blending in.

Eventually, Kal worked up enough confidence to climb one of the vine and wood ladders to the hermitage's upper level. Alighting at the top, he leaned over a vine railing and gazed down over the lower level. The thoroughfares formed a network of their own, weaving together the two distinct districts, one of art and one of craft.

Feeling even more confident, he decided to give communication a try, and approached a middle-aged woman.

"Excuse me, could you tell me where the library is?" Kal prayed the nanites' linguistic program would correctly render his words.

"Sure," she smiled. "The archive is just down Mesh'ga Canal Street. Take that bridge and follow it for about a kilometer, then turn left. It's the biggest bauble in that part of the hermitage. You can't miss it."

"Thank you!" Kal beamed at yet another success and took off down the bridge network in the direction she had indicated.

Fifteen minutes later, he reached Mesh'ga Canal Street. The actual dirt path lay meters below him, and an equally bustling network of bridges stretched out on either side of him, spanning the upper level.

However, an even more impressive sight commanded his attention. Kal walked to the edge of a terrace. Before him, the trees broke away, and he could see Lake Michigan, or rather, Lake Mesh'ga. The sand was grainier and yellower than on Earth or Felis, and he could see people swimming in the lake and playing games on the beach. The waves looked higher, and he spotted a group of young men about his age, surfing on long hunks of wood. Further out, he could see wooden ships, both large and small. A port to the south harbored many more.

Clearly the residency paper didn't confine a person to the hermitage's interior. People could come and go as they pleased. Kal wondered what would happen when a permit expired. And what was the upper limit on residency length?

He looked out at the surfers, who looked friendly enough, and fought the urge to join them. He sighed, looking out at the lake one last time, and then hurried down Mesh'ga Canal Street as quickly as he was able.

It didn't take him long to find the 'archive bauble' the woman had spoken of. Its massive size, at least twice the circumference of the others, indeed set it apart.

Kal walked through the archive's vaulted entryway and entered a hall of shelves that extended left and right, sloping ever so gently. The hallway was missing its back wall, a railing in its place. Kal walked to it and gazed out into the bauble's hollow interior. The shelves of books wove around the edge of the structure in one continuous spiral hallway. Kal smiled at the sight. Ydora was no Earth, but from this brief glimpse of their culture, it seemed like a place that would be worth exploring in depth. At least so far. The weight of the pad in his backpack reminded him that he had yet to determine their attitude toward more complex forms of computer and robotic technology.

Kal wandered the aisles, passing through row after row of books, his nanites helpfully translating their titles to English before his eyes. He came to the end of one row, and was awestruck to discover a meticulously drawn map of the world. The people of Ydora, it seemed, had mapped their entire planet with a high degree of precision, despite having no apparent computer or satellite technology.

The map depicted astounding differences between Earth's and Ydora's respective topographies. East Asia and Australia looked more or less the same, but further west, the similarities degraded. India was an island continent, and Europe was jammed into Africa with no sea between them. South America was fatter with no isthmus leading off it. And as for North America, well, it was mostly recognizable, except that it seemed to be missing everything east of Texas and south of the Ohio River. According to the map, the Atlantic Ocean lay just two hundred kilometers south of Shik'wa.

Kal stood physically at the same latitude that Chicago lay on Earth, but powerful ocean currents fed this region with hot, wet air, creating the tropical climate.

He tore his gaze from the map, reminding himself that he was here to investigate his dream. He wondered if the enormous bauble with the insects was part of a hermitage. That seemed unlikely since the dream experience had been so solitary, a stark contrast to the bustling crowds of Shik'wa.

He leaned against a bookshelf and sighed, thinking how unlikely it was that he'd be able to connect the dream's details with a physical location on his own. Asking for directions to an archive was one thing, but, "Oh excuse me, can you direct me toward an enormous building filled with giant ants and bees?" was another matter entirely.

He continued his research despite the odds. He eventually turned up a tome that was something like a regional atlas and paged through draw-ings of Shik'wa and other hermitages, grinning at the familiar names – Rok'fwo, Miil'wak, Mids'no, Mno'ols, Diit'roy and more – but none of the pictures matched the vivid locale that had visited him for the past five nights.

After hours of leafing through artists' renderings of hermitages, Kal became aware that the archive was nearly empty, and he should probably leave. He'd also neglected to feed himself again and resolved to find a meal and a place to sleep for the night.

∞∂⊲⊳∞

"I found it!" Kal sat up in his bed, sweating and gasping for breath.

He glanced around and realized he was not alone. Tired, annoyed eyes looked up at him from the room's other beds. His emotions rushed quickly through disappointment and anger before giving way to embarrassment. He tried to fluff his pillow nonchalantly, then rolled onto his side.

Great, he thought. *First night in an alternate Earth youth hostel and my dream causes a scene.*

He tried to relax and opened his eyes briefly.

Across the room, he saw a young woman, about his age, with long, dark braids, gazing back at him. When their eyes locked, she tapped at her head, then pointed at her eyes with her index and forefinger, and then pointed both fingers at Kal.

Kal repeated the gestures slowly and methodically.

She raised an eyebrow sharply, then shook her head and rolled back onto her side, facing the wall.

Well, crap. That hadn't been an appropriate response now, had it? Kal inhaled and exhaled heavily, then rolled over and closed his eyes.

Lake Mesh'ga shone brightly with reflected morning light. Kal sat on the terrace outside the hostel bauble eating a breakfast of fruit and some kind of dried, mashed grain bars. They were stiff and flaked to pieces at the slightest touch but tasted good nonetheless.

"Hi."

Kal looked up to see the young woman from the hostel standing at his table. He saw her clearly now, in the morning light. She was tall, had dark hair and skin, and a friendly smile. She wore a backpack like his own strapped over her shoulders and carried a breakfast tray.

"Hi." Kal smiled back.

"Can I join you?"

"Sure."

She set her tray on the table and sat down in front of him, smiling intensely.

"I'm Sprig'g," she said.

"Kal." He almost offered her his hand and then reminded himself that customs could differ too. She nodded at him, and he returned the nod, hoping it was appropriate.

"So, how long have you been traveling?" Sprig'g asked.

Kal blinked. Was she another metaxic traveller? How did she know he'd been exploring? "A few weeks. How long have you been traveling?"

"Weeks?" Sprig'g's eyes grew wide. "You've been having the dream for weeks?"

Kal nearly choked on his food. He managed to swallow, coughing to clear his throat. "The dream?"

Kal felt so confused that he wasn't sure if it had been a statement or a question.

Sprig'g waited patiently for Kal to stop coughing, her eyes radiating intensity. "It's a huge bauble. You climb and climb that ladder that leads up into it, and there's a breeze that hits you when you're almost there.

You feel dizzy and pause. Then you climb inside. There's a beam of light down the center and a pedestal underneath it. An unknown artistic master's book of the lost works and notes sits at its center, and then just as you open it up and begin reading—"

"You wake up," Kal finished for her. The orange-hued, half-eaten pear fell out of his hand and clattered against the tray, and he fumbled with his plate, trying futilely to make the behavior seem natural.

"Hasn't anyone told you about the Sejjh?" Sprig'g asked.

Kal shook his head. "I never told anyone about the dream. I thought… I thought they might think I'm crazy."

"You're not crazy." Sprig'g clasped his hand with hers. "It's okay. You can tell anyone about it, but kids don't know any more than us, and the adults won't tell you anything except to go to the Sejjh."

"Is that what the bauble in the dream is called, the Sejjh?"

"I think so. I'm not sure. The adults all insist that the answer is there. That's where we have to go to make the dream stop."

Kal furrowed his brow and bit his lip. "Our dreams are different though."

"Oh?"

"Yeah. Well, the beginning's the same, but in mine, there isn't a book, it's, um—" Kal hesitated.

"It's okay. What do you see?"

"Insects."

Sprig'g scratched her chin and looked away, pondering this a moment. "Now that's interesting. The dream is the same except for the thing we find. You like insects?"

"Not particularly, but these insects are… they're special. It's like someone knew exactly what I'd want to find and put it in my dream."

"Same with me," Sprig'g said. She tapped her fingers on the table. Her food sat on the plate in front of her untouched.

"I've been looking for help getting to the Sejjh," she said finally. "I've got permission to tag along with a hunting party going to Rok'fwo, and the riverboats can take me to the Chasmedge, but there won't be any hunters going out from there."

"What do you need hunters for?" Kal was immediately sorry he'd asked the question, and cursed himself at getting so worked up in the excitement of finding a person who understood his plight so completely.

She gave him a weird look, blinking a few times. "Because the jungle isn't exactly safe."

Kal raided his memory for something he'd learned in the archive bauble to cover up this blunder. "I mean, I grew up around Bauz'tun, so we didn't have to worry about such things that much."

Sprig'g smiled again, seeming to buy it, and Kal was immediately glad he'd spent the previous day researching instead of surfing.

"Well, you're welcome to come with me as far as the Chasmedge. I'm sure the hunting party won't mind."

They both stood, Kal taking note of how tall she was. Sprig'g stuffed the food that was supposed to be her breakfast into her rucksack and threw it back over her shoulder.

"I have to take care of some things before we go," she said. "The hunting party leaves at the next bell. From the west gate."

Just as she spoke, the tolling of bells erupted from many directions all at once. He'd heard them yesterday too. They sounded at roughly two hour intervals.

"I'll be there," Kal said. Sprig'g did the greeting nod again, apparently also a nod of parting, and took off into the hermitage.

Kal smiled, thinking how fortunate he had been, and looked out over the lake. He glanced down at his backpack on the bench beside him and noticed the rectangular outline of his pad, visible through the synthetic material. The fate of Team Haskell came to mind, and he rearranged the sack's contents as discreetly as he could.

∞⟨⟩∞

The hardest part of leaving Shik'wa was the revocation of his residency paper. He'd learned in the archive that one should always stay a resident roughly the same amount of time as declared on entrance. Although it was a bit unusual for him to leave early, it wasn't unheard of. The border guards gave Kal a lecture about respecting the residency system and proper educational planning, but in the end, they agreed to stamp the paper as revoked.

"I guess I didn't think I'd find help so soon after arriving in Shik'wa," he said to Sprig'g once they were away from the Shik'wa gates.

"Don't sweat it," she said.

The hunting party was a group of two men and a woman, all of them much older than either Sprig'g or Kal. They were built like Sprig'g, lean and muscular, and he realized that they must do this their whole lives. He wondered if their protection came with a price tag.

"Where did you have residency before the dream started?" Kal asked.

"Miil'wak," Sprig'g replied. "How about you? Did you walk here all the way from Bauz'tun?"

So Sprig'g was a native after all. But that left the mystery of the dream. And had he walked here from Bauz'tun? That was a good question. He had yet to see a single vehicle on Ydora.

"Yeah," Kal guessed. This prompted no adverse reaction from Sprig'g, so Kal decided to press forward with his questioning. "How long have you been having the dream?"

"Five nights now, every night. I woke up in the hostel screaming just before you did. It's absolutely infuriating. Each time is like the first, even though I remember the dream when I wake up. I can't imagine this going on for weeks." Sprig'g shook her head.

"Maybe the dream's difference is important. What's significant about the artist's book for you?"

Sprig'g didn't respond. Instead, she shook her head and marched forward along the jungle path. Kal wondered if, like the insects for him, her desire for the book of the artistic master was a touchy subject.

The hunters stalked through the jungle in front of Kal and Sprig'g, their crossbows ready.

A few hours into the morning, Kal slowed to rub at rashes that had formed at his ankles. Pal'mno, the female hunter, dropped back and gave him an impromptu lesson in plants he should avoid brushing up against. Soon, he could recognize the chemically aggressive ones by the shape of their leaves. Kal nodded his thanks to Pal'mno, wondering if he'd done anything right in this culture at all.

At midday, the group stopped for a lunch break. Kal had made the assumption that the merchants, farmers, and hunters would not be interested in the artistic endeavors he'd witnessed in Shik'wa. He was surprised to see Ben'lorr, one of male hunters, set down his crossbow and produce a sketchbook and charcoal from his sack.

Sprig'g displayed an immediate interest and began asking him about the hermitages he'd studied at. They discussed art for some time before the hunter asked about her background. Sprig'g reluctantly revealed that she was training to be an artist at something called a mastery in Miil'wak. Ben'lorr's eyes lit up, and Sprig'g did her best to answer the rest of his questions politely.

After lunch, they resumed their trek.

The jungle grew not just thicker but also noisier the deeper they travelled into it. The chirps, squeals, hisses, and squawks grew into a cacophony.

Later in the day, Kal discovered the price of the hunters' protection. They gave Kal and Sprig'g each a sack. Periodically, two of the hunters would run off through the trees, leaving the third to watch Kal and Sprig'g. They'd come back carrying freshly shot prey, which Kal and Sprig'g added to their respective sacks in turns.

"How can they tell when an animal's nearby?" Kal asked Sprig'g after the second such kill.

Sprig'g shook her head. "It's something to do with changes in the sounds of the jungle. If the jungle ever goes quiet then you're in real trouble, because it means a predator is either pissed off or insane and is about to attack. I learned the basics in first-fourth year. I thought I was going to be a hunter because I got high marks on the physical evals, but then I tried using a crossbow and found I couldn't hit a mark to save my life."

"How'd you get into art?"

"I didn't really. It's just something I've always done and enjoyed doing."

Like programming for me, Kal thought.

Sprig'g's and Kal's bags steadily filled up with carcasses.

When the light began to fade, the hunters stopped and set up camp. Kal and Sprig'g threw down their sacks. Sprig'g took out her knife, pulled out the carcass of a fox-like creature, and began ripping its body open. Kal gazed transfixed at the gore, instantly losing the appetite he'd been developing all afternoon.

"Could you get the hydromesh from the hunters?" She tore through the canine's innards.

Happy to get away from all the blood and guts, Kal found Ben'lorr and asked him for the hydromesh. The hunter pulled two bundles of blue, foamy cloth from his sack and unrolled them. Each was about half a meter square and a centimeter thick. Kal took them back to Sprig'g, who greeted him by slapping a bloody hunk of raw meat into his hands. She looked at him expectantly, and he found he could only return her gaze with his mouth agape while the gore ran down his arms.

"Oh, you're—I see. I respect your values, but we have to do our part for the hunters in return for their protection. I promise to do all the cutting if you do the drying."

He realized she'd mistaken his nausea and confusion for some kind of disapproval of animal meat. "No, no, it's just I've never—"

She took the bloody limb and placed it between the two sheets of hydromesh, then slapped the whole bundle onto the ground.

"Press." She motioned for him to apply pressure to the top of the hydromesh sandwich.

He did as she had instructed, and the foam constricted, a long whoosh of moist air bursting up off it. The outline of the meat contracted.

When the burst of air had subsided, he tore off the top layer of hydromesh to discover... jerky. Sprig'g grabbed it and slapped another wad of bloody muscle onto the blue foam.

They finished just after the sun went down, their work lit by the fire the hunters had set.

After dinner, Kal talked with Pal'mno. He found out she made a hobby of chemical research, which she had become interested in it through her sister, who worked at an oil well in the south, near the ocean.

The Ydorans of this region, it seemed, were deeply interested in chemistry, and also in human and animal cells. They were aware of DNA but only at the chromosome level. The biggest research hurdle for them was generating enough electricity to power scientific instruments. As he talked more with Pal'mno, he noticed that she seemed to worry more about electricity being misused than the scarcity of its supply.

Kal glanced over and saw Sprig'g talking to Ben'lorr again. She was asking him questions about his artwork, but when he asked about hers, she deflected the questions, steering the conversation back to his techniques.

So, she's sensitive about her talent, Kal thought to himself. *Why?*

The second day of their journey proceeded much like the first. Although he had swum two or three kilometers every day for the last two years, nothing could have prepared him for the pace Sprig'g and the hunters kept. His legs ached, and now he had a bag of dried meat as well as a bag of dead animals.

The third hunter, Keit'n, paused and insisted on helping them. Kal looked at Sprig'g, not sure how to respond.

"There's too much burden for you two alone," he said. "Time to spread it around some. We already have more food than we need for Rok'fwo."

Keit'n hitched his crossbow onto a loop at his waist, and Kal and Sprig'g each gave him one of their bags. He carried them as though they were filled with feathers.

Just when Kal thought his legs and arms might give out completely, he realized that the sounds of animals had dropped off, the jungle had become less dense. Half an hour later, and with less than an hour of light left in the day, they arrived in the hermitage of Rok'fwo.

Kal and Sprig'g thanked the hunters, nodding respectfully. They each applied for single-day residency papers as quickly as they could, then took off into the hermitage, heading directly for Rok'fwo's youth hostel. They gobbled down dinner and then crashed onto their respective beds, falling immediately to sleep. Kal had his dream again that night and woke to hear Sprig'g shouting too.

They looked at one another through gasping breaths, and after a few moments, their tension evaporated as they realized where they were.

Kal gulped, and threw himself back onto the bed to escape the inherent awkwardness of the situation. He heard Sprig'g do the same before he drifted back into slumber.

The morning seemed to wash the episode away, and they ate breakfast together amicably, refreshed.

Curious, Kal decided to try finding out more about her version of the dream from a different angle. "You're an artist?"

Sprig'g sighed. "Just training. That hunter, Ben'lorr, his stuff is really good. Did you see any of it?"

"Yeah, I saw it. What about you? Do you have a sketchbook?"

"I paint mostly. All my work is in Miil'wak." She fiddled with one of her braids.

No good. Sprig'g simply got too anxious when he tried to talk about her artwork. He decided to let the subject drop for the time being.

"I have a friend here in Rok'fwo," Sprig'g said. "Her name is Mel'anii. She taught me math, physics, and chemistry when my family had residency here four years ago. I think there's a good chance she'll tell us about the Sejjh."

"Because she's your friend?"

"That, and I know she's been there."

After breakfast, Kal followed Sprig'g down into the Rok'fwo thoroughfares. Just like Shik'wa, Rok'fwo had the two levels. It wasn't as big as Shik'wa though, and instead of sculptures, it was chalkboards and chemical experiments that filled the city's grassy patches, which were here burned out and ragged from being splashed with corrosives.

From reading in the Shik'wa archive, Kal had learned that most hermitages specialized in one particular subdiscipline of either science or art, though apparently the word in their language was "scienceart." They conceived of the two as a single endeavor, not just related, but fundamentally the same.

Wait a minute, Kal thought. He stopped and squinted, inspecting something that looked out of place among the landscape of scientific experiments.

"That looks familiar..."

"Where?" Sprig'g said.

Kal pointed.

"Oh no..." Sprig'g's expression fell, then gave way to irritation. She seemed to forget Kal and strode toward the statue he had spotted.

"Ni'ero!" she shouted.

Kal ran to keep up with her.

"Ni'ero! What the plunder is this?" Sprig'g stood, fuming, beside a statue of herself. Its skin resembled papier-mache. It was life-sized and depicted Sprig'g with her paintbrush held forward. Kal hoped that the expression on the statue's face had been intended to seem deep and mystical. Unfortunately, owing to its sculptor's skill level, the visage made Sprig'g appear more tired and drunk than anything else.

A young man about Kal's age, presumably Ni'ero, stood behind the statue, massaging its head, the only incomplete portion. At the sight of Sprig'g, he stopped what he was doing and rushed down off his stepladder. He had long, wavy hair and was just a little shorter than her.

Ni'ero embraced her, getting plaster all over her back. She stood frozen, gaping in shock, then snapped to her senses and shoved him away.

"What have you *done?*"

"It's my tribute to you!" he beamed.

"How dare you!"

"I love you, Sprig'g. I had to build it. I just— I just had to. You don't like it?" Ni'ero's face filled with desperation.

"You can't do this, Ni'ero. This is a hermitage for chemical engineering, not sculpture!"

"Who cares what the stupid rules are!" Ni'ero shouted. "To plunder with them! I can't believe I wasted my time on this! And on you!"

He turned his back to her and clenched his fists. Bits of plaster oozed off them and fell to the grass.

"Fine," he said. "Just... fine."

Ni'ero staggered toward a sack at the base of his work area and produced a device that consisted of a spout attached to a long tube. He ripped the synthetic cover from the spout, pointed it at the statue, and pulled a trigger at its base. Fire burst forth from its nozzle, and the statue of Sprig'g burst into flames.

Kal watched Sprig'g's face closely, unsure if he should try to comfort her, or say anything at all. She covered her mouth with her hand, her eyes wide.

Rok'fwo residents rushed the plot, shouting wildly. Ni'ero tried to escape from the ensuing chaos, but two adults grabbed him by the arms and held him fast. Kal and Sprig'g continued backing away from Ni'ero's work area as other residents cordoned it off. The statue of Sprig'g burned to the ground. First its arms fell off, giant black embers, then its head, and finally the whole frame crumpled and collapsed into smoldering wreckage.

A team of a dozen men and women wearing headbands rushed up with large buckets of water and doused it.

"I loved you, Sprig'g, I really did!" Ni'ero blathered through tears as the Rok'fwo adults hauled him away.

"I don't love you!" she shouted back and stormed off in the opposite direction.

Kal was running to keep up with her again.

"I'm... I—" she stuttered.

"It'll be okay, Sprig'g. We're just here for a little while to find Mel'anii, right?"

Sprig'g nodded solemnly, still rushing away as fast as she could.

⊶⟨⟩⊷

Mel'anii, Sprig'g, and Kal sat around a table on a terrace overlooking the tumultuous Rok River. Mel'anii was about as tall as Sprig'g, but with a leaner frame, slightly lighter skin, and a dozen or so metal rings adorning her wrists and ankles. Kal had seen residents of Shik'wa and Rok'fwo wearing them, but this was the first time he'd seen so many of them on one person.

"He did *what?*" Mel'anii balked at Sprig'g's story of Ni'ero's scene.

"He burned it." Sprig'g sighed. "Just pulled out a glowtorch, ripped off the cover, and burned the whole thing to the ground."

"Just... wow." Mel'anii smiled weakly. She sighed and scoffed. "I honestly don't know what you ever saw in him."

"I guess that makes two of us," Sprig'g tapped her fingers furiously on the table.

"He isn't... dangerous, is he?" Kal tried.

"I doubt it." Sprig'g said with a chuckle.

"Rok'fwo's criminal rehab is top notch," Mel'anii said. "Setting fire to an illegitimate craftwork... that ought to get him... what do you think? A couple of years at least, right?"

"Hopefully longer," Sprig'g said through clenched teeth, and a protracted silence ensued.

"Mel'anii, Sprig'g told me that you'd been to the Sejjh," Kal said.

Mel'anii's face lost its color, and she bit her lower lip.

"You can't tell us, can you?" Sprig'g said.

"Sprig'g, you know I would tell you if I could."

"Really? You too, Mel?" Sprig'g leaned forward into the table and glared at her.

Mel'anii, though clearly disquieted, gazed back resolutely, grasping her teacup with both hands. "Do you remember An'do?"

"Don't change the subject."

"I'm not."

Sprig'g crossed her arms and sat back again. "Yes, I remember him. I remember him and Y'rem doing their best to turn your class into a circus."

"He was here just a few days ago. Same journey as you—he was having the dream. You just missed him."

Sprig'g rolled her eyes. "Funny, I always imagined those two going feral together."

"No. I saw it even then, An'do especially. The immaturity was a smoke screen to draw attention away from his insecurities. He's studying Ro'kel functionalisms in Mno'ols."

Sprig'g's eyes widened. "An'do got into the Mno'ols mastery for *functionalisms?*"

Kal couldn't help but think that if he were on Earth right now, he'd probably be at a university studying microcomputers. He pushed the unhappy thoughts away and refocused on his conversation with Sprig'g and Mel'anii.

"Mmmhmm," Mel'anii sipped her tea, smirking as she set the cup down. She set her hands on the table and looked directly at Sprig'g. "If it were in your best interest for me to tell you what's at the Sejjh, I would tell you. But it's not. No explanation can compensate for the experience of going there yourself. I remember the isolation and the loneliness of the journey and worrying that everyone's in on some kind of grand conspiracy against you. Please believe me when I tell you that it's really not like that."

Kal felt a little relieved hearing this, but Sprig'g seemed nonplussed. He was now more curious than ever to discover the Sejjh's secrets.

Sprig'g nodded deeply at Mel'anii, managing to hide her obvious despair, at least a little. "I'll come see you when I get back then."

Mel'anii stood and nodded back.

"Nice meeting you," Mel'anii said to Kal. She took her teacup and walked off.

Kal and Sprig'g sat in silence for a minute or so.

"What do we do now?" Kal finally worked up the nerve to ask.

Sprig'g stared at the table. "We go down the river to the Chasmedge."

"You were really sure she'd spill the beans, huh?"

She curled up her lip.

"Damn it!" She pounded a fist on the table. Then she exhaled heavily. "Yes, that's what I'd hoped."

"Hey, we'll figure this out together, okay?"

That seemed to cheer Sprig'g up, just a bit.

"How do we get down the river?"

"A riverboat. There's a harbor. Come on." She stood up and grabbed her pack. "If we hurry, we might be able to get the overnight one."

Kal and Sprig'g arrived at the harbor where the riverboat crew was prepping for departure. It was a huge, wooden, multi-level craft, and Kal watched as workers loaded it with enormous vats. Fuel, Kal guessed. He wanted to pull out his pad and run scans on their contents, but thought better of it.

Sprig'g went off to pick up tickets from a woman standing near the river's edge.

Kal noticed a group of guys his age swimming in the river. Their sashes and moccasins lay in piles on the riverbank. The water crashed around them, and a number of them were letting the currents briefly sweep them away before fighting back with strong, upstream strokes. It looked dangerous and therefore exciting. Kal wished he could join them.

He turned, realizing that Sprig'g was standing beside him, watching him watch the swimmers.

"You swim?" she asked. She was grinning too widely.

"Oh, ah, yeah. I swim. A lot. You?"

"Mel taught me track and field. I've never been a very good swimmer. Couldn't get the form right."

There was a lengthy pause.

Sprig'g nodded in the direction of the river. "You know, it'll be twenty minutes at least before the riverboat's ready."

Kal dropped his backpack and threw off his sash and moccasins, grinning.

"I'll be back in time." He started toward the river.

"Kal'and," Sprig'g said.

Kal stopped and turned around. "Yeah?"

She leveled a knowing gaze at him. "Boys will be more likely to notice you back if you wear your sash like I do."

Kal smiled. "Will do. I guess there's a lot about these western hermitages I don't know. Thanks, Sprig'g. See you soon."

She smiled back, and Kal took off for the river.

Kal made it back just as the riverboat whistle erupted.

There was nothing to dry himself with, so he rubbed at his hair, shaking the water out. He picked up his sash. Recalling the shoulder thing, he threw it over to his left shoulder. Or had it been on the left before? He fumbled with it, trying to set it right, but now he couldn't remember which side was which. In his hurry, he threw it over one shoulder or the other, snatched up his pack, and ran for the riverboat.

No one seemed bothered by the fact that he was soaking wet, so he boarded still dripping river water. The bell from Rok'fwo rang nine times, announcing evening just as the final whistle sounded the boat's departure.

Kal found Sprig'g at the bow of the ship.

"Have fun?" Sprig'g asked.

He grinned. "Yeah."

"Have you ever been over the Chasmedge?"

Kal had seen it on the maps in the archive. An enormous gorge ran from the northwest edge of Illinois diagonally southeast through the state, ending near the border between Illinois and Indiana. The Rok River flowed directly into it.

"No," he said.

"We're going to have to cross it. How do you feel about heights?"

"They've never bothered me except—well—for some reason they bother me in the dream. It's weird. I've been up tall ladders and mountain paths before and never had any problems."

"It's the same for me," Sprig'g said. "It's almost like it's someone else's dream, not mine. I've wondered if the Sejjh is some kind of dream transmitter. That'd be horrific though, don't you think? Not the kind of thing Mel would think is a good reason to run off into some lawforsaken part of the vastness. Someone would have dismantled it by now."

Kal frowned and nodded. He agreed that such a device as she had described was completely out of sync with what he'd seen of their culture. "Mel'anii did say that we'd understand when we find it."

"And I trust Mel," Sprig'g clutched the railing at the boat edge. "None of this makes any sense."

Kal shrugged and smiled, leaning back against the railing with his arms crossed.

"We'll have a problem at the Chasmedge," Sprig'g said. "There won't be any hunters going to the Sejjh, and we didn't find anyone else having the dream in Shik'wa or Rok'fwo. We'll have to wait at the Chasmedge for someone with weapon skills."

"I can keep us safe," Kal said.

"Oh?"

"I have a new kind of technology that protects me from harm. I can use it to keep you safe, too. Is that okay?"

"What hermitage developed it?"

"Bauz'tun."

"Hmm. Sure." Kal watched her eyes. At least part of her was suspicious.

Sprig'g yawned and stretched against the railing. "I'm going to turn in."

"Night," Kal said, and watched her disappear into the boat's interior.

He stood a while, watching the currents of the river fade away in the waning light. He waited until the sun went down. The windows of the boat became little beacons in the dark, tiny spotlights passing across the pitch black jungle.

A couple near the edge of the forward deck eventually retired to their room, leaving him alone. Kal pulled out his pad, turned it on, and began programming.

⁂

The riverboat was still surging steadily down the river when Kal awoke. He and Sprig'g ate breakfast on the deck, and she told him they would reach an outpost called Orr'jen within the hour. It wasn't a hermitage really, just a way point for hunters and artisans. It had few resources and residents, but its location atop the Chasmedge drew a huge number of visitors.

"Have you ever been here before?" Kal asked Sprig'g as they were preparing to disembark.

"Nope. I've only heard stories from others."

Kal had heard that the Grand Canyon was widely considered to be the most beautiful natural wonder on Earth's North American continent. He'd seen holorenders of it and wondered if the Chasmedge would be similar.

He and Sprig'g joined the crowd of people shuffling across the narrow gangplank off the boat.

Once they were free of the crowd, Sprig'g motioned to Kal, then took off through Orr'jen. He followed her up a ladder, and they arrived atop a plaza of platform terraces overlooking the Chasmedge.

Kal looked out at it in wonder. Below the platform, the ground merely ended and fell away so far that the rock just disappeared into darkness.

The other side of the Chasmedge lay in the distance, and it was clearly much lower than Orr'jen. Kal had read that a geological disaster had occurred on this part of Ydora thousands of years ago. The ground had been wrenched open, and the slab of land southwest of them had dropped about two hundred meters in elevation.

The Rok River gurgled to his left. Kal turned and saw it spilling over into the Chasmedge, dispersing into a cloud of mist and disappearing into the dark haze below.

To his right lay Orr'jen's two way stations. One consisted of dangling seats that looked similar to ski lifts. The other was an array of zip lines. Kal spotted a man strapped into a harness attached to one of the zip lines and watched as he was launched away from Kal's side of the Chasmedge and hurtled down toward the other.

Sprig'g grinned at him. "Hope you were telling the truth about heights."

The way station technician moved around Kal, strapping him into various harnesses, but his mind was elsewhere, jumping amongst past experiences that had made him nervous. None came close to his present situation. There had been particularly tense swim meets, when he'd worked hard to psychologically set himself up to swim as fast as he could or faster. His heart raced with a similar intensity now, but emotionally this was very different. He gazed out into the abyss. A thrill and a shudder worked through him simultaneously. Shortly, he knew, he'd be launched over that void, a thin rope the only thing preventing him from plummeting to his death.

Another technician was strapping Sprig'g into the neighboring zip line ten meters away.

"You ready for this?" she called out to him.

"Ready as I'll ever be." Kal shouted back. "You?"

She gave him a reluctant smile. "Couldn't be better."

"Belay on," a technician called out from his left.

"Belay on," Sprig'g and Kal's technicians announced.

He felt a pressure at his back and flew out over the Chasmedge, Sprig'g alongside him. There was a moment of tenseness and extreme anxiety, which quickly dissolved into euphoria. The hot wind blew up against his face as he was falling and flying and holding on for dear life. He let out a whoop of excitement, and he heard Sprig'g do the same.

Kal looked around at the sky and the birds and even down into the hazy black pit below him. Blue above and black below and the adrenaline rush mixed with the blissful blur. Not a single experience in his life could compare.

The lower side of the Chasmedge rushed up to him, and he lurched to a halt. He found himself wishing he could do it all again.

"That was awesome," Sprig'g shouted to him as technicians ran up to release them both from the harnesses.

"Incredible!" he yelled back.

Kal saw the technicians grinning at each other, and Kal realized that they must do this at least once or twice a day, up and down, back and forth. He marveled at how such an extraordinary experience could become commonplace, and hoped that such wonders would never cease to amaze him.

oᴐᐸⳁᴐo

Kal and Sprig'g meandered around the way station for some time, inquiring whether or not others were headed toward the Sejjh, but nearly everyone was headed south along the main way, to the distant hermitage Pe'o.

They would be on their own.

One of the technicians approached them, grinning. He handed over a map of the Rok Valley, the portion of the river that had been terminated when the Chasmedge had opened up. It was overgrown now, lush jungle where the river had once been.

The man drew a circle on the map, highlighting a great hill, once an island in the river. It lay twenty-five kilometers southwest of the lower Orr'jen way station. Seeing Kal unarmed, he offered to give Kal his crossbow and a knife. Kal initially refused, but the technician insisted. Kal balked at the idea of killing a living thing, but at least Sprig'g seemed happier once he'd accepted the weapons.

She dawdled at the edge of the way station and kept looking over her shoulder, watching the zip line with hopeful eyes. Eventually, she sighed and hurried off with Kal into the wilderness. The animal noises and thick foliage resumed almost immediately outside Orr'jen's walls.

Sprig'g seemed more furtive, tense, and alert than she'd been on the first part of the journey. She held her crossbow ready and kept her hand near the knife in the pouch at her side.

They traveled for hours without talking, just listening to the sounds of the jungle. Kal strode casually at first, but as he watched Sprig'g, he realized that each little squawk, hiss, and growl set her on edge, and her eyes darted through the vines and scraggly ferns. Her nervousness was infectious, and Kal found himself stalking through the jungle as well.

Hours of travel passed, their muscles and attention relaxing with each passing hour.

In the middle of the afternoon, they reached a small glade, and Sprig'g suggested they break for a snack. They sat across from one another on a rocky outcropping and pulled food from their backpacks.

"Sprig'g," Kal said, "there's something I've been meaning to talk to you about."

She looked at him curiously.

"We've talked about the parts of our dreams that are the same, but we've both been avoiding talking about the parts that are different. For me, the insects are something that I'm a bit— That it makes me uncomfortable to talk about. Something about that art book... is it the same for you?"

Sprig'g looked away and nodded.

They sat in silence a few moments more, not making eye contact.

"Alright." Sprig'g threw up her arms. "But this is just between us, okay?"

Kal nodded.

"I've never felt confident in my abilities as an artist," she said. "Growing up, I loved sports. Everyone told me I'd be a hunter. When it turned out I wasn't very good at that, I tried all the other skilled professions – medicine, trade, farming. I was all right at some, but none *felt* right.

"I've been painting as long as I can remember. Mel and others encouraged me to submit my work to the Mil'waak mastery, and I got accepted. Everyone's nice. They compliment my work, but... I guess I feel like I don't really belong there. Like I'm not... not good enough.

"I imagined once that if I found a book of some hermit artistic master no one had ever heard of, then I could just learn her style, and everyone would always love it. I wouldn't have to worry about feeling this way anymore, and I could get through the apprenticeship. I know how incredibly disingenuous that would be. I wouldn't really do it, even if it turns out such a book actually exists."

Sprig'g crossed her arms and leaned back. "What about you? What are those insects of yours all about?"

"Well," Kal breathed in deeply. "In my dream, I'm able to analyze the insects' DNA."

"How? Is there scientific equipment in the bauble?"

"Yeah," Kal said, careful not to slip his white lie. "I need to see that DNA. The insects got sick when they got near me. But then they got better. If I can find that DNA, I might be able to go—"

Sprig'g gestured for him to be quiet. Both of them searched the jungle with their eyes. The jungle had grown quiet. Kal jumped to his feet, fully alert.

Sprig'g pulled out her crossbow and loaded an arrow while Kal fumbled with his own.

A tiger-sized canine with maroon fur jumped from the brush, all thrashing claws and fangs. White foam dripped from its mouth. It leapt at Sprig'g, and she ducked to avoid its first attack.

Kal's heart raced. He was filled with one emotion—fear—but from two conflicting sources: the animal's ferocity, and the thought of revealing his pad. He felt jumbled, torn between conflicting choices.

The animal twisted around itself and prepared to leap again. Sprig'g fired at it and missed.

"What are you waiting for?!" Sprig'g shouted.

The crossbow wobbled in Kal's hands as he pulled at the trigger ineffectually. It wouldn't fire. Kal cursed and threw the useless contraption on the ground.

Sprig'g pulled out her knife as the beast fell upon her with gnashing teeth. She flinched and braced herself, but her skin shimmered where it bit at her, its teeth and claws not impacting her skin.

Kal's heart sank. There was no hiding the truth now. He tore off his backpack and opened it up.

Sprig'g gazed at herself and the wild animal. She seemed unsure if what was happening was real. The beast bit and scratched at her, but the nanites on her skin absorbed all the force of its attacks.

Kal pressed a button on his pad, and the dog hurtled a few meters back.

It righted itself and turned its attention to Kal, lunging at him.

Kal pressed the button again, and the animal lurched backward once more.

Unfazed and lost to the frothy delirium, it waved its head about, eyes wild and bloodshot. It reared back, preparing to lunge at Sprig'g yet again.

Kal sighed and tapped a few holographic buttons. Medical program… Pathogen removal… Setting nonhuman animal target.

Just as the beast lunged at Sprig'g, Kal pressed the final button. Fury left the dog's eyes. It scrambled to a halt on the ground and turned to its side, coughing up froth. It looked momentarily confused, then scared, before loping away into the brush.

Slowly, the ambient noise of the jungle resumed.

Kal could only look at Sprig'g with pleading eyes while holographic readouts danced on the interface. He swallowed the lump in his throat, then turned the pad off and lowered it to his side. His eyes remained locked with Sprig'g's.

"What is that?" Sprig'g stood, glaring at the pad.

Kal opened his mouth, but words wouldn't come out.

"What is it?" She stomped toward him.

"It's a computer."

"Mistech." Sprig'g spat the word. "And what did you do to me exactly? Why couldn't the aard'og hurt me?"

"You asked me for my protection, and I gave it." Kal's heart raced.

"No, you used some kind of mistech on me without my permission, and it stops now!"

He looked at the ground and knew that she was right. She hadn't really given her permission.

"I don't know what kind of hermitage is developing this crap, but the whole of Ydora is against you. *We* have ethical standards."

Kal felt himself tense up. He was afraid and regretful, and he felt more alone than he had in four years. Part of him wanted to tear himself away from Ydora, go back to Felis, and forget about metaxic travel forever. Sprig'g had turned away and was marching deeper into the jungle without him.

"I'm not from Ydora!" he shouted at her back.

Sprig'g turned and marched back to him. "You want me to believe you came here from outer space?"

"No. Right here. An Ydora with a different history, different culture... different timeline. You called this mistech. I don't even really understand what that is. To me, this is normal. It's just a computer." Kal's voice wobbled.

Sprig'g eyed him warily for several moments that seemed to stretch on into eternity, and Kal imagined all the secret, horrible technologies the people of Ydora used to punish mistech users. He'd be a Team Haskell of one.

Sprig'g narrowed her eyes and tapped her foot on the ground, just watching him.

"Come on," she said finally, her voice calm but stern. "Let's get going. We're almost to the base of that hill. Oh, and whatever you did to me, undo it. You can undo it, right?"

Kal nodded vigorously. He wasn't sure exactly what he was feeling. Relief and desperation mixed with fear and panic. He programmed away the nanites on her skin and ran after her through the jungle.

☙⟨⟩❧

They reached the base of the great hill at sunset and made camp. They ate their dinner in silence. Sprig'g insisted on keeping the first watch. When her back was turned, he pulled out his pad and programmed a defense perimeter around their camp as quickly as he could. Sprig'g had asked him to remove *her* defenses, but she hadn't said anything about any other programs he might write.

When he had finished, he lay down and stared up into the vines and long leaves, the light of their fire dancing across them. Eventually, he closed his eyes, just listening to the sounds of the jungle, finding it hard to fall asleep.

Worry seeped into his mind about what Sprig'g was thinking and planning. He jolted up and grabbed his pad, making sure that it was both locked down and that an alarm would sound if anyone touched it but him. With that done, he lay down once more and let weariness overtake him.

When he woke from the dream, Sprig'g remained motionless at her watch. He gathered himself, and they exchanged roles wordlessly. Kal wondered if he'd completely botched their friendship or not.

He had to admit, their culture had an elegant logic to it. Earth's history had left him well versed in the myriad wounds that improperly utilized technology could inflict. He thought back to his lessons on their last two hundred years of history: nuclear proliferation, nuclear war, the great climate change of the twenty-first century, and the huge technowaste cleanup that had taken nearly two generations' worth of effort.

And then, through the harsh struggle for survival, he had been told, the remaining cultures of Earth had grown up. They'd stopped working against one another and started working together. Though even in the modern day, with all their technological and social success, there was always the nagging worry that one rotten dictator would appear, and it would begin all over again—poverty, exploitation, and injustice.

If Kal guessed right, Ydora had avoided the problem completely. Instead of creating rules and regulations to limit harmful technological application, they merely had a cultural imperative against its abuse. "Mistech."

In the morning, he and Sprig'g cleared their camp and began trudging up the hill. The steep hike once again pushed his legs beyond their limit.

An hour later, they reached the summit. Kal knelt, panting, on the flat summit that stretched out before them, a field of small ferns and grasses. Two absolutely enormous trees towered over the plateau, their thick branches holding at least fifty meters aloft the largest bauble Kal had seen on Ydora. A rope ladder led from the ground up into an open portal at its edge, just like in his dream.

Sprig'g sat down beside them. Both of them sat there for many minutes, looking up at it. It felt so surreal, finally seeing this place in his waking life: the Sejjh.

Kal broke their daylong silence. "What do you think we'll find inside?

Your dream or mine?"

"Perhaps both. Maybe neither. Come on."

◦℘⌇℘◦

The climb up the rope ladder was nothing like his dream. Kal had been alone, and Sprig'g was above him now. He felt no rush of vertigo.

The breeze from his dream was also mysteriously absent, and the air was very still. Not a single gust of wind disturbed the trees. And the sun was in the wrong place—morning instead of noonday.

Kal looked up and watched Sprig'g enter the bauble. A few rungs more, and he too climbed inside.

Unlike his dream, this bauble had a completely open ceiling. Sunlight dappled the room in patches, having passed through the leaves and branches above.

At the room's center stood a granite statue of a man holding a cane. Sprig'g stood a meter in front of it, just staring at it, her back to Kal.

"Sprig'g?"

She didn't move or speak.

"Sprig'g!" Kal started toward her.

Something, some kind of wave, passed through him, and he slowed, coming to a halt. He still stood in the bauble, but his perception had become hazy, as though a grainy, blurry filter had been placed somewhere between his eyes and his brain. The air felt thicker, and the sound of his feet on the floorboards took on a twangy echo.

"Hello, Kal'and."

The statue had become a real man, who stepped down from his pedestal. He was old, maybe about sixty, and he was adorned with dozens of bracelets and anklets, even more than Mel'anii. His cane, formerly stone, was now made of wood, and rapped on the floorboards as he strode forward. Although Kal's view of the bauble's interior had blurred, the man with the cane appeared to him with crystal clarity.

"Hi," Kal replied, though his eyes darted about, searching for Sprig'g. She had vanished.

"My name is Lorr'enz. I built this hermitage."

"My friend—"

"Is fine," Lorr'enz said. "I'm talking to her too."

"What *is* this place?"

"Many years ago, I helped develop a new technology. I learned of radio waves and brain waves, and eventually I got to wondering if the latter could be transmitted in the same way as the former."

"Telepathy?"

"That was the goal. My research consumed my life, and after many years, I did find some success, but only with dreams. It never worked with waking thoughts. We struggled for many more years to find a practical application for this technology and failed. All the while, I was assaulted by those who suggested my research to be mistech, saying it could cause mental disorders and insanity."

"Then the dream isn't mine. But that doesn't make sense. It had the insects. No one on Ydora could know that I would want to find them so badly."

Lorr'enz smiled widely. "Yes, that which you desire greatly. You see, it's also possible, once a dream's pattern is recorded, to 'poke holes' in it, so to speak, to leave parts out that the host mind must fill in."

"So my unconscious mind made up the insects and added them to the dream?"

Lorr'enz nodded that deep Ydoran greeting nod. "The statue I built broadcasts the dream to a specific mental profile—ambitious, talented young people, like you and Sprig'g. When I reflected on my own youth, I came to believe that I might have grown wiser faster if my ambition had been tempered by a greater understanding of my yearnings, the deep desires that I dared not share with anyone."

Kal's heart sank, and he felt his face flush with anger. "No insects... No cure! It was all just a ruse."

Lorr'enz pointed his cane at Kal's chest. "What would finding that cure do for you, Kal'and? Is it truly critical for your development as a human being?"

"Critical for my development?" Kal crossed his arms. "I'd be able to go home, to Earth! It's where I belong."

"Is it now? Then tell me, Kal'and, isn't there something you've forgotten to do?"

Kal glared at Lorr'enz.

"When I was young," Lorr'enz continued, "I just assumed that the point was to reach the goal or find the solution. But it's not the destination that matters, Kal'and, rather the journey and the decisions you make along the way. That's why I created the Sejjh the way I did, out here in the vastness. To give you a journey."

Lorr'enz sighed and laid a hand on Kal's shoulder. "There are times in life when you will only get one chance to do things right. Reflect on your desires, or they will rule you from the shadows of your mind and corrupt every decision you make."

Kal thought of what he'd done to Sprig'g with his nanites, and indeed, he regretted it deeply. "I think I see what you mean."

Lorr'enz nodded resolutely and returned to the spot at the center of the room, rapping his cane on the pedestal.

"You may dismantle this statue if you believe it to be mistech. But if you feel you have learned something from this experience, please leave it in place for the next group of ambitious young people to reflect upon."

"Wait, I—"

Everything went black.

∞⟨⟩∞

Kal opened his eyes. His vision was still blurry. He stood in the Sejjh bauble, and Sprig'g stood in front of him, shaking his shoulders. The statue was behind her, once more made of stone.

He looked up. The sun had traveled to the opposite side of the ceiling. The waking dream had taken, what, six hours? His stomach growled in affirmation.

He glanced at Sprig'g, who exhaled in relief and caught his gaze only momentarily before turning to the statue of Lorr'enz. Kal looked it over too. An odd mixture of emotions surged through him, anger and awe both. He'd wanted to find those insects so badly, and yet, somehow he had become suspicious of that desire. What if Lorr'enz was right?

"Mistech?" Kal asked, though still unsure if his guess about what the term meant was correct.

Sprig'g shook her head. "I don't think so."

They stole one last look at the statue, so calm in the red and orange glow of evening sunlight, patterns of leaves moving over it in the breeze.

Sprig'g broke their trance, moving quickly for the ladder, and Kal followed. They descended quickly and quietly, but the character of their silence had changed. Kal couldn't stop thinking about what Lorr'enz had said in the waking dream, and he imagined Sprig'g must be pondering her interaction with him as well.

They made camp at the base of the hermitage and ate slowly beside the fire.

"Why did you take me the rest of the way?" Kal asked, staring at his food. He wasn't sure he would like the answer.

"Because you're not an enthusiast," she replied, calm and sure of herself.

He looked up at her, pleading with his incomprehension.

"You really have no idea what it is, do you?"

Kal shook his head.

"Okay, mistech is a technology or use of technology that creates an inappropriate power relationship between two humans or groups of humans. Equality above all else. So, if I take this crossbow and kill an attacking animal, it's just a crossbow. But if I point it at you, it's mistech. And, of course, there are technologies so powerful that they corrupt any person who touches them."

She waited for Kal to nod before continuing. "An enthusiast is someone who learns, makes, or uses mistech anyway. You're a riddle, Kal'and. You have a mistech device, your computer, but instead of using it to hurt me or manipulate me, you used it to protect me. Tell me, what brought you here from your alternate Ydora?"

Kal looked at his feet. "I'd hoped to find a way to go home."

"If you can travel between these alternate worlds like you say, what's stopping you? Did you get lost or something?"

Kal took a deep breath. "No. My Ydora is called Earth, and I know exactly where it is.

"Six years ago, I was on the West Chicago Junior Swim Team. We had a meet, a, um, kind of race, an important one. I jumped into the pool and started swimming, but I didn't reach the other side. I have a... genetic disorder, a kind of allergy. I'm sensitive to the radiation that nanites make. Too much of it causes my lungs to stop absorbing oxygen. I passed out in the pool and slipped into a coma."

Sprig'g shook her head, confused. "Nanites?"

"They're the tiny machines I told you about. On Earth, they're everywhere. The ground, the air, the water, they're in and on everything.

There's nowhere on Earth where I'd be conscious, much less safe, so my parents found scientists experimenting with travel to alternate Earths, and they were able to convince them to help me."

"They brought you here?"

"No, to a different world, one with no nanites, no people at all, actually. I sort of took off on my own. The insects in my dream were hurt by the radiation at first, but then they adapted to it. If I can find a real organism that can do that, I can study it, and I might be able to apply its adaptation to myself somehow."

"How many other worlds are there?"

"Pfft. Infinite. Or near it anyway."

"Sounds exciting."

"Dangerous, too. Like I said, cultures are all different. You never know how people are going to react to this." Kal held up the pad.

Sprig'g nodded.

"What about your art?" Kal asked. "Do you still want to find that artist's book?"

Sprig'g gazed up into the trees and then shook her head. "No. I think I was always judging my own work by someone else's standards. I wanted to make the best art the residents of Miil'wak had ever seen. But I think I've been missing the point. I think, from now on, I'm going to challenge myself instead. I've been giving up too quickly, holding myself up against others' expectations. No, I should make the best art *I've* ever seen."

She opened her backpack and produced a roll of papers, a brush, and a small bag that made tiny, glass clinking sounds.

Sprig'g grinned. "You said you wanted to see my work, right? Well, I've just had an idea."

oꝎ⧸ꝏ

The next day, they began walking back to Orr'jen. They started out silently. Sprig'g seemed lost in thought, and Kal was hesitant to bother her. Eventually, she began prodding him about Earth.

"Electricity and machines that do human work—does everyone just use them to hazard?" Sprig'g ended the question abruptly, appearing to wonder if she'd made herself properly clear. "Without limits or restrictions?"

"Yes and no. We are free to do whatever we want within certain limits."

"Interesting. And your society is stable?"

"Funny you should ask. We used to be a lot more carefree, 'to hazard,' like you said. But we had a lot of environmental and political problems because of it, and had to start regulating technology a lot more. We came up with limits based on our experiences of what was and wasn't healthy and sustainable."

Sprig'g hopped across the rocks in a little stream cutting through the trees. "We've believed for a long time that growing dependent on technologies like those would lead to sloth in the short term and destruction in the long term. Are you saying that's not the case?"

Kal thought about this as he balanced on the slippery stones. "It's hard for me to disagree. History tells us we were on that track for a while and came close to destruction. But then we invented the nanites, and, well, we fixed our environment, but now we *have* to be both careful and responsible. Nanites are the most powerful invention we've ever created. If we screw up now, there won't be any recovering from it."

Sprig'g smiled. "So you understand 'mistech' after all."

Kal leapt onto the solid ground beside Sprig'g, pausing with a pang of regret as he thought about his own behavior on Ydora.

"I'm sorry," he said, looking at the ground. "I used my technology on you without your permission. Well, without your explicit permission. It's a mistake I won't repeat."

Sprig'g stopped and put a hand on his shoulder.

"Apology accepted," she said, and they continued onward.

An hour later, the animal noises started to fade, and Kal could tell that they were approaching the lower Orr'jen waypoint. He stopped her.

"I have to go," Kal said.

"To... another Ydora?"

"Yeah."

Much to his surprise, she turned and hugged him. "If you get lonely on those other Ydoras, you come back here and find me, okay?"

Kal found himself hugging back. They let go, and he took a few steps back, producing the pad from his backpack. He nodded deeply, the nod of departure.

Sprig'g nodded back.

He activated his nodes. A sphere of cobalt blue electricity crackled around him, and Sprig'g's awestruck face peeled away along with the rest of Ydora. Kal's clothes shimmered, returning to his T-shirt and jeans. He sat in his bubble for five, then ten minutes, just thinking. He opened the backpack, removed a roll of paper, unfastened a clasp, and unfurled it.

The painting he held depicted Kal and Sprig'g in the center of the Sejjh. On the left, behind Sprig'g, the walls shimmered with landscape portraits and murals while on the right, behind Kal, stood the twisty, hex-agonal chambers of the green-shelled insects.

He looked over the work, then rolled it up, refastened the clasp, and returned it carefully to his bag.

He input the coordinates for Felis. It was time for a very, very long swim.

Just a Game

Realm #1384, "Spele"
June 16, 2178

Kal SWIPED through the pictures, trying to reconcile the disparity between them and the world around him. They depicted a technologically advanced cityscape teeming with people, but he stood instead in a forest. Oaks and pines, aspens and birches, all with typical bark and green leaves, loomed over grasses and prairie underbrush. There were no flame-spitting fungi or crystalline ferns. No, this forest could have easily passed as one of the parks he'd visited on Earth as a child.

He programmed a nanite to enter the metaxia and return to realm #1384. He waited, and his pad registered the nanite's return. Kal shook his head. He was indeed standing on the world that the pictures had come from. But no city, lake, nor people presented themselves. Just the forest.

Kal latched his pad onto his white suit pants and furrowed his brow. In that moment, he realized just how much he hated the clothes he'd adopted for this world. They felt too stiff and formal, not at all appropriate for an Illinois summer. He wondered why he should even bother with them now. He pulled up the sartorial program and, a few button presses later, his clothing shimmered and reverted to the T-shirt and shorts he was used to wearing on Felis. Having the air against his skin felt much better.

He felt a pin prick against his neck and heard the familiar light buzz of nanite activity. A wooden arrow with a metal tip and bright red feathers clattered to the ground.

Kal grabbed up his pad and reached instinctively for the auto-defense control panel. He maximized its interface and jacked the sensitivity all the way up to its highest setting. He heard the whiz of another arrow and, though he felt nothing, glanced a splintered tangle of wood as it fell to the ground.

"Hello?" Kal tried.

Two more arrows struck him and fell to the ground as crumpled masses.

"I'm willing to talk," he called out.

A young woman leapt out of the underbrush at him wielding an axe. She lunged forward and slammed the weapon into his chest. Instead of slicing into him, the weapon writhed out her hands, distorted and twisting, then fell to the ground as frayed, wooden shreds and metallic dust.

The young woman jumped away from Kal, her facial features twisted up in panic. He eyed her suspiciously, perplexed at her behavior.

She was about his age. Her hair was a tangled mess, her clothes hardly anything more than tattered, gray rags. Her eyes darted at him, then across the prairie brush, then up into the trees.

"Kill me!" she shrieked.

Kal covered his ears. When it seemed she would not scream again, he tentatively pulled his hands away from his head. "Why would I kill you?"

"Why?" she asked, as if the question were absurd. "Who are you?"

"My name's Kal. What's yo—"

"Rakan!" She leapt up onto the nearest tree branch, not pausing before scurrying further upward and away. She had started mumbling something to herself, but Kal couldn't hear what it was before she was out of earshot. She scaled the tree with incredible speed and ferocity. Kal spotted a bow and full quiver attached to her back as she receded into the foliage.

Kal sighed and turned his attention back to his pad. Maybe he'd glossed over some crucial piece of information his nanites had gathered about this world's supposed culture. He doubted he'd find out anything more talking to Rakan.

The city he'd seen had exhibited all the signs of an advanced and stable culture, not violently insane savages.

Rakan jumped down beside him and attempted to grab his pad. The nanites pushed her hand gently away from the device. Rakan's face twisted up at the sight of her own hand being propelled backward against her will.

Kal grinned. He'd never seen the auto-defense system's highest setting before. Just as expected, the nanites were repelling living things while their crushing and grinding force was reserved for inanimate, high-velocity projectiles.

"What is that thing?" Rakan asked.

"It's called a computer pad," Kal said, still reading Spele's cultural report.

"You're going to have to kill me, you know."

"I don't *have* to kill anyone. And I certainly hope that you don't think you have to either."

"Oh, I have to kill." Rakan nodded. "I have to kill them all."

Kal turned off his pad's display. "All of who?"

"The other players."

"What other players?"

"Of the game!"

"What game?"

Rakan laughed loudly–too loudly, like a small child. When Kal didn't respond, she stopped and tensed up her face.

"The adults make us play," she said. "They put us in here. They hide weapons, then we use them to kill each other until there's only one of us left."

Kal frowned, worried that she might actually be telling the truth. "Why on Ear— Why would any of the adults want to do that?"

"Entertainment."

"What?!" Kal gaped at her.

"That's right." She pulled at her quiver, swinging it around it in front of herself, and began counting the remaining arrows. "They put us in here with weapons and make us kill each other, and then there's what the birds see. Up there. In the trees. It's what the birds see."

Kal raised an eyebrow at her and blinked a few times. "Sorry. Lost you. Horribly unjust and ruthless social system of adults oppressing children. I'm with you there. And then there's what the birds see?"

Rakan nodded as though this should be perfectly comprehensible. She unhitched the empty axe sheath from her belt and discarded it nonchalantly.

Kal gulped.

"How about we team up?" Rakan said. "You can draw the others out since weapons don't hurt you. Hey, can that computer make it so that weapons won't hurt me either? The killing would go *so fast* if we were both immune. What do you say?"

"Uh, no." Kal wanted to retch just thinking about what she had proposed.

He eyed her with disdain, turned his attention away, and continued poking around his pad. Just then, a thought occurred to him. This was the only person he'd met here. Maybe there was some truth buried beneath the many layers of her sociopathy.

It was clear that the story she had told him about a game and adults watching children kill each other was utterly ludicrous. His computer's cultural analysis programs were imprecise, but not that imprecise. A culture as horrifically degenerate as the one Rakan had described would have to be degenerate across a huge number of social vectors, ones his programs should have reported, but hadn't.

Where was the city he had seen? Were there doctors there? Did they have an advanced understanding of genetics? Which was right, Rakan or his computer?

Kal turned back to Rakan, who'd taken up counting her arrows again. "Actually, I think that we should work together. I'll protect you from harm, but only if you promise not to hurt or kill anyone else."

Rakan nodded vigorously in agreement, a manic grin plastered across her face.

"Good." Kal pulled out his pad and made the necessary adjustments, putting Rakan under the protection of his nanites. "We'll send a message to the adults that we're in control."

Kal marched after Rakan through the woods, always considering what question to put to her next. Some she answered, others she deflected with a twitch of her head. He learned that fourteen other young adults of varying ages were left alive in the game. She also told him that a forcefield surrounded the woods and that anyone who touched it would explode. She told him these things between bouts of needing to "see what the birds see." On such occasions, she would rush up the nearest trunk and descend a few minute later.

During one such excursion, Kal pondered the forcefield she had described and sent a contingent of his nanites out looking for it.

Rakan jumped down, landing at his side.

"Orra's nearby." She pulled out her bow.

Kal grabbed its frame. "Who is he? Or she?"

"He's one of the other players." She pulled the bow out of his grasp.

"What do you know about him?"

"He's got a mace. Weak though. Easy kill."

"No, I mean, do you know anything about *him*? What's he like as a person? Can we appeal to his sense of right and wrong, justice and morality?"

Silence. A blank stare.

Kal calmed his growing internal frustration and resolved to try again. "Does Orra hate the adults?"

"Dunno." Her head twitched twice to the right.

Kal grimaced, feeling he might be on the verge of developing a twitch himself. At least they had something in common now. He turned to ask her another question and realized that she was no longer beside him. He felt hands on his shoulders pulling him down into the brush.

"There he is," Rakan whispered, pointing through the thicket.

Orra, the boy in the distance, could not have been more than thirteen years old. He stumbled through the forest, holding a mace he could barely lift.

Kal stood up. "Over here!"

"What are you doing?" Rakan hissed.

Kal ignored her and walked out toward Orra. The boy spun around, hefting the weapon up over his head, and rushed Kal, the mace wobbling in his hands.

Kal sighed and shook his head.

Orra approached and heaved the spiked ball into Kal's neck. His auto-defense program crushed it like an eggshell.

Kal smiled. "We just want to talk."

Orra backed away, breathing heavily. His mouth opened and closed awkwardly, like he was trying to talk, but couldn't.

Kal furrowed his brow. "Do you understand me?" He took a step closer, his right hand extended.

Orra glared at him and staggered away, his mouth still opening and closing.

Kal looked him over. He wore the same tattered clothes as Rakan, had the same frizzled hair. His facial features were similar to hers, like he and Rakan could be siblings.

"Is your name even Orra?" Kal asked.

Orra's neck exploded in red, gushing up a fountain of blood as his body toppled over. The red spray gurgled from his neck and mouth, forming a pool on the ground. Crimson dots lay splattered across the green grasses.

Kal blinked, gulped, and then turned and lurched into a tree, throwing up everything he'd eaten for both lunch and breakfast, maybe more.

"Rakan!" he managed to shout between heaves. "Rakan, what the hell was that? I thought we agreed—"

He heaved again at the thought of what she'd just done. Though ill, he held his pad tightly and programmed away the nanite defenses he'd set on Rakan between gasps and bouts of retching. "I thought we agreed..."

She popped up from the bushes beside him. "We have to kill them. It's the rules."

"To hell with the damned rules!"

"There are only seventeen left, anyway. With your help, we'll be through all of them soon enough."

"Wait, what? I thought you said there were fourteen..." Kal trailed off. Rakan was already on her way up a tree, mumbling to herself about what the birds see.

Fine, Kal thought, *if you won't help me get the adults' attention, I'll get it myself.*

Later that day, the nanites Kal had sent out to the explosive forcefield returned from their expedition. To his disappointment, he discovered that they'd never reached their target. In fact, they hadn't even reached the forest's perimeter. They'd traveled fifty kilometers then made a complete circle around his current location before giving up and returning. They'd found no signs of any forcefield, man-made structures, nor even other people, just the endless tracts of trees, ferns, and grasses. Kal puzzled over this, and wondered if Rakan had been lying about the forcefield's existence, or if she believed some lie she'd been told.

The sky glowed orange and red through the trees, the daylight waning.

"Where have you been sleeping?" Kal asked.

"On a tree branch." Rakan nodded vigorously. "It's so I can see—"

"—what the birds see." Kal finished in unison with her, sighing deeply.

At that, realization seemed to strike Rakan, as though the birds were something she'd long ago forgotten and only just now remembered. She rushed away, scaling the nearest tree.

Her mantra had shifted from annoying to unbearably tedious a few hours ago. At this moment, Kal was half-considering sealing her mouth shut with nanites. Every damn thing the two of them talked about seemed to come around to ' what the birds see,' regardless of their topic of conversation.

Kal hitched his pad to his jeans and began gathering up fallen twigs and branches. He piled them up, encircling the makeshift fireplace with stones.

Rakan jumped to the ground just as Kal pushed the button on his pad that ignited the pile of wood.

"Fire?" Rakan gazed at Kal. "No, no, no. The others will see the smoke and come attack us."

"I'll be fine." Kal flicked a finger into his left shoulder, his auto-defense nanites shimmering in mild exertion.

"Need a tree farther away…" Rakan mumbled, letting her gaze sweep across the forest.

"How do you sleep on a tree branch without falling off?" Kal asked.

Rakan unhitched two long, ragged, leather straps from her waist that Kal had thought were belts and presented them. "I strap myself in."

Kal pondered that a moment, wondering how it was even possible. Even "strapped in," shouldn't she slide off the branch the moment she went unconscious? Kal watched her refasten the straps and decided it wasn't worth the trouble asking.

"Will you at least stay at the fire long enough to eat something for dinner?" Kal gestured to the growing blaze. "I can make anything you want."

She perked up. "Anything?"

"Sure. If you can describe it, I can make it."

"Hasparjat roll," she said, grinning. Rakan's excitement had lost its manic edge for the first time since Kal had met her.

"What are the ingredients?"

"Bread, torquin, potatoes, lettuce, menall, rezzik sauce—"

"Hold on, you're going to have to explain some of those in a little more detail."

She jabbered on, almost happily, telling Kal all about the ingredients and how to combine them, not once mentioning the birds. Kal programmed the nanites to construct the roll she'd described, and it materialized before them.

Rakan's eyes went wide in amazement. He handed it to her, praying she would like the taste. He'd substituted a few Earth ingredients for those of Rakan's that were alien.

She took a bite, and her eyes lit up. She began gobbling it down.

"Do you know any of the adults who put you in here?"

Rakan nodded.

"Do the other players know the adults too?"

Another affirmative.

"Are all of the other players from the same city?"

She shook her head.

"Is there a city near here?"

Nod.

"Is this it?" Kal held up the holodisplay on his pad. Brilliant towers of glass and metal refracted the light of day, casting rainbow shards of light over the populace. People moved through the streets, and a modern, multi-level elevated train system wound between the buildings.

Rakan nodded again, just as she stuffed the last of the roll into her mouth.

"Tell me what you know about the adults," Kal said.

Rakan's face seemed to seize up, instantly forgetting the Hasparjat roll. Her mouth hung open momentarily, no sound coming out.

"Rakan?"

"The birds… the man with the birds… I thought he was going to take care of everything, but…"

"But what?"

Rakan gazed off into the distance.

"What the birds see!" She jumped up. "Your fire's going to draw the others here. And I have to go see what the birds see."

Kal put his head in his hand, and watched Rakan through his fingers as she ran to the tree she'd picked earlier and shimmied up its branches.

He slumped against the trunk of his tree and locked down his pad. He tended to his fire, drifting slowly into an uneasy sleep.

∞⟨⟩∞

Kal woke to Rakan whispering into his ear. He groped about for his pad. Finding it safe and sound, he clasped it tightly.

"He's close by," Rakan said. "You distract him, and I'll loop around and shoot him. Just like before, okay?"

Kal opened his eyes and yawned. She was gone before he could protest. He glanced around and spotted a boy darting between trees in the distance. He was older than Orra, closer to Kal and Rakan's age, but looked eerily similar to Orra, as though they could have been brothers. He held a bow very much like Rakan's.

Kal stood up next to the smoking fire pit and stretched his arms out. He yawned widely, and then turned on the pad. He opened up the programming interface and started typing, stringing together a few programs he'd already written but with some new targets.

An arrow whizzed through the interface, disrupting the projection only momentarily before crumpling and falling to the ground. He sighed deeply and focused on finishing his program. More arrows flew into him and fell to the ground as shriveled masses.

"What's your name?" Kal called out.

"His name is Zell!" Rakan shouted from somewhere above and behind them both.

Both Kal and Zell turned to Rakan, who wasted no time loosing an arrow directly at Zell's throat. It hit him full in the neck, but instead of piercing him, his neck shimmered. The arrow bounced harmlessly off him and shriveled into nothing.

Zell stumbled backward, not expecting the protection. He reached up to his neck, rubbing what he expected to be a wound.

An enraged bellow erupted from a nearby tree, and Rakan fired another futile arrow, just as Zell drew one of his own. The two loosed arrow after arrow onto one another, but Kal had applied protection to them both.

Kal hit a button on his pad. A platform with two swords on top of it materialized into existence a few meters in front of him.

"Come and get them," Kal shouted.

Zell and Rakan both ran for the swords. Zell, being closer, grabbed his up first, and hacked uselessly away at Rakan as she snatched hers.

Kal watched as the two of them thrust the metal blades at each other over and over, nanite interference deflecting each attack. An odd mix of emotions filled him. He was proud of his programming work. He'd gotten the defenses on Rakan and Zell to protect them from harm without shredding the swords. Still, no one in the forest seemed capable of considering any solution to their problems other than violent attack. And that fact filled him with despondence.

Both fighters paused, their faces turning to Kal and twisting up in rage at the unwanted protection Kal had bestowed.

Kal rolled his eyes and jabbed another button on his pad. Rakan and Zell froze in place.

"I'm putting an end to this!" Kal shouted into the forest. "Talk to me if you're there, if you're watching this. I can take this all away from you. No more killing wherever I go in the game! How would you like that?"

He stared up into the trees, just listening. A few birds chirped.

Kal turned to see Rakan and Zell, their expressions locked in mutual hatred. He crossed his arms and tapped his foot. He looked at his pad and sighed.

Then Zell moved.

It was barely perceptible at first: a slight twitch of his fingers, then a nudge from his arm. Zell gained more momentum and control with every passing second. Before long he was hacking away at Rakan again, although she remained immobile and protected.

Kal gawked and fumbled with his pad. He shook his head, regaining his composure. His hands darted over the interface in a mad quest for answers.

That's not possible. It's simply not possible!

The immobilization field that had surrounded Zell was intact. At least, it was intact in the spot Zell had stood moments before. Zell's body had somehow passed through it. He'd defied the nanites, and by proxy, every law governing physical matter that Kal understood.

Kal instructed the nanites to dissolve both swords. Zell lost his balance as the weight of his weapon dissipated, falling away to dust as he tried to swing it. He stumbled toward the still-immobile Rakan, then shot Kal an angry glare before running off into the woods.

Kal hesitated, staring at Rakan. He tapped his foot on the ground and twisted up his lips. He stared at her, grasping desperately at straws to find some shard of ethics that would allow him to leave her in the immobilization field.

His only moral choice clear, he pressed a button on the pad interface and released her.

Rakan immediately ran for him, her eyes brimming with rage, and slammed her hands into his chest. The auto-defense nanites shimmered. Kal didn't budge or feel it in the least, but she'd clearly intended to knock him over.

"Damn you!" she shrieked.

"Damn me? You were ready to kill that boy! What did he ever do to you?"

"For the last time, it's the rules of the game! The only way to survive is to kill everyone else!"

"Rakan, listen! Violence isn't the answer to your problems, and it never will be. No one can make you kill. No one. In the society you come from, people must have some concept of morality and ethics. Somewhere in your culture, *someone* must have suggested that violence under any circumstances is wrong, *right?*"

Rakan stood, her fists clenched, breathing heavily, her eyes ablaze. She made no attempt to answer his question.

"Fine." Kal shook his head. "You know what? Never mind. I give up. Go kill all the people you want."

He activated the pad and loaded the program to take him into the metaxia. Just as he reached to press the activation button, an arrow hit his shoulder. Not only did his nanites fail to crumple it, the arrow actually contacted him, and it did more than just sting. It went straight through his left shoulder. Shot from behind. The head of the arrow protruded a couple of centimeters, covered in his blood.

Kal yelled out in pain and heard his pad clatter to the ground. He fell to his knees, gasping. He gazed momentarily at the arrow shaft, transfixed. He felt dizzy and nauseous, and decided to tear his eyes away from it.

Gasping for breath, he cast his gaze wildly about. A group of two girls and two boys, one of them Zell, had appeared and were attacking Rakan. Something felt wrong. He glanced at Zell, then at the two girls, then at the other boy. Their physical similarities were uncanny. Were they all siblings? The boy alongside Zell was a dead ringer for Orra. And the two girls looked too much like Rakan for it to be a coincidence.

Rakan broke from the attacking horde and shimmied up a tree. She wasted no time finding purchase, and began picking them off with her bow. One of the girls hurled daggers at her, but Rakan dodged them with ease. She also seemed to have some protection left, although, like Kal's, its influence was diminishing. Still, the nanites gave her a huge advantage.

Rakan ran out of arrows and jumped down from the tree. She snatched up a dagger and hurled it into Zell's chest.

"Focus," Kal told himself. He smacked at his pad with his limp left hand. He even tried jamming the indentation on the pad with his right thumb, even though he knew that was useless. The security mechanism for the pad was simple—Kal's left thumb and only his left thumb could turn it on, a security measure he promised himself that he would change.

He looked up at Rakan and her attackers in the distance. Zell was nowhere to be seen, probably lying in the grass somewhere with the dagger sticking out of his chest. One of the girls had disappeared too. The boy who looked like Orra and the other girl circled Rakan's tree, darting through the grasses. The boy held a machete and the girl a spear.

There has to be some way this makes sense, Kal thought. His sight grazed the arrowhead sticking out of his shoulder, and he felt dizzy again. He fell into a nearby tree. Breathing heavily, he clutched the bark. His mind found purchase on its texture, and he opened his eyes, gazing up at it. Something about it...

It hit him all at once. This was the same tree he'd fallen against when he'd seen Orra killed, the tree he'd thrown up onto. But that tree must be kilometers away from here. They had definitely walked in a straight line from there to here, hadn't they...?

Kal dug his fingernails deeper into the bark, daring it to be unreal. He ripped a hunk of it off and gazed over the grit on his hand, the dirt and the sinuous strands of wood. He threw it onto the ground, more frustrated than ever.

Whatever this place was, Kal was convinced that there was, in reality, no game at all. But where was that damned city? Where was the real Spele, and how had he ended up here? Those answers were locked away, somewhere inside Rakan's twisted mind, behind those fearful, wild eyes. He had to reach her.

Rakan had retrieved some of her arrows and shot the Orra-esque boy through the neck, just like she had his doppel. That left only the girl, who limped away from her, haggard, winded, and bleeding from multiple open wounds. Rakan scurried up a tree, and Kal became certain, in that moment, that her opponent was doomed. He watched Rakan shoot the girl in the head, knocking her down.

Rakan scurried down the tree and picked up the spear Zell had dropped. She took it to where the girl lay, and Kal gasped as he watched her jab the weapon violently into the grass again and again and again.

Kal felt woozy, unsure if it was the loss of blood or the thought of what Rakan was doing to the poor girl whose name Kal had never even learned. His peripheral vision had faded, and he could only see a tunnel in front of him, one that contained Rakan running toward him with the bloody spear perched over her head. He tried again to grip the pad with his left hand. He tried so hard that he cried out in pain, whacking the useless appendage against the pad's inert surface.

Rakan closed in.

He felt something against his leg. Something metallic. He picked it up. A gun. It had a translucent hand grip, and an indentation for his finger. A trigger.

Kal stared at it in his hand. Then he looked up at the charging Rakan. He felt the urge to point it at her–a deep, primal, survival instinct urge.

He shook his head, ashamed of himself, and threw the gun back into the grass. He turned his eyes back to Rakan, so close now, clutching the spear over her head.

The point came down, and a sharp pain exploded through his chest. Numbness overcame him, and his vision diminished, the sight of Rakan's hateful eyes smearing away into black nothing.

∽❧∾

Kal awoke in what was clearly a hospital room. Machines beeped around him. His left shoulder and chest were wrapped in bandages. Breathing was agony. He could see the shapes of people moving through the hallway beyond his room through the frosted glass windows. On the opposite wall was another window, one to the outdoors. He saw the city he'd been searching for, the buildings of glass and metal and rainbow shards of light.

"Hello." A man stood in the door frame. Kal had been gazing so intently at the city that he hadn't noticed the man's entrance. He was middle-aged and wore white robes, not unlike doctors on Earth. He closed the door behind him. His voice seemed solemn, and Kal wondered if, despite waking, his life might still be in jeopardy.

"Hi," Kal said, finding his voice shaky. Talking hurt too.

"I'm Dr. Selar. What's your name?"

"Kal Anders."

"I know talking must be difficult, so let me explain. Then you can ask me any questions you want."

Kal nodded.

Dr. Selar sat down in a chair next to Kal's bed.

"Has the physician talked to you yet?"

Kal shook his head.

"I just spoke to him myself. He says you'll make a full recovery."

A wave of relief washed over him, interrupted by the searing pain in his chest. Dr. Selar winced.

"Would you rather I come back later?" Dr. Selar stood up. "I can explain when you're feeling—"

"No," Kal hissed. "Tell me now."

Dr. Selar nodded and returned to his seat. "I am the lead psychiatrist assigned to the girl you know as Rakan. She is, as you are well aware, a very disturbed individual. She was abused as a young child and later moved to a foster home. There, she latched onto the groundskeeper, but... there was an incident, and she killed him. In our culture, Kaal, killing is a terrible, terrible crime. We do not inflict it as a punishment."

Kal's eyes narrowed.

Dr. Selar shook his head and held up a hand, seeming to understand Kal's perspective. "Yes, I know. Hear me out. In circumstances where standard rehabilitation will not work, we put the criminal into a hologram chamber and run a program that is keyed to his or her psyche. For now, Rakan is still angry, hateful and dangerous, so those are the kind of characters the program creates. Eventually, we hope, she will tire of this. She will want something better for herself, and she will start to create emotional bonds with the holographic characters instead of killing them. At that point, we may be able to transition her to relationships with real people. But for now...

"Anyhow, everything she told you, the game, the killing, the adults who watch for entertainment, I assure you those are all elements of her delusion. Everyone in the simulation was a holographic projection, be-

sides Rakan and yourself."

"How?" Kal wheezed. "Holograms with physical substance?"

"Forcefield generators provide the illusion of physical substance. Even texture."

That explained why his nanites had seemed to stop working. Once the computer program generating the holograms had learned that it could move its projections independently of Kal's nanite forcefields, it had simply ignored them.

"The truth is..." the man paused, his lips tightening up. "The truth is that when you appeared, we thought that you were just another holographic person that Rakan's mind and the program had generated. We had hoped you to be a projection of some part of Rakan that wants to end her torment. We only discovered the truth after your trick with the swords. Of course, such chambers designed for criminals are not easy to exit... or enter. We regret it took so long to get you out and are deeply sorry for the injuries you suffered.

"I also feel responsible for telling you that Rakan's other specialists and I realize you possess metaxic flux technology and that it is how you came here. It is illegal in this country. If we release you from this hospital, our defence forces will likely arrest you. However, if you want to leave when you are better, we'll let you, so long as you do so discreetly."

Kal nodded. "May I have my computer?"

Dr. Selar retrieved the pad from a drawer in a nearby cabinet and handed it to him.

Kal reached out toward it, wincing in pain, moving his thumb into position over the activation button. Dr. Selar watched as the holographic interface appeared, nonplussed. He did, however, raise an eyebrow as Kal activated his medical programs. Kal coughed and began taking in deep, gasping breaths, his lungs regenerating in seconds. Selar nodded, thoroughly impressed, as Kal began ripping bandages from his shoulder.

"Thank you for explaining what happened," Kal said, his voice back to normal, talking no longer painful. "You said... you're Rakan's doctor. Do you think she'll ever get better?"

Dr. Selar shook his head solemnly. "I don't know."

"Give her my regards when she does. Tell her I don't blame her. Sounds like I won't be able to come back and tell her myself."

Dr. Selar regarded Kal quizzically as he stepped toward the door.

"Kaal?" he asked, stopping at the doorway.

"Hmm?" Kal pulled his T-shirt over his head.

"What do you call your Spele, your world?"

"Earth."

"There's something I want you to know. On Spele, this country in particular, we've had rather unfortunate interactions with metaxic visitors and our own metaxic explorers. I wish we'd had the opportunity to visit Earth. I think circumstances here might be different if we'd met you and your people instead."

Kal smiled weakly. "I'd liked to have known Spele, the real Spele, better too."

Dr. Selar smiled sadly and turned to leave.

"Oh, sorry. One more thing." Kal said. Selar turned and looked at him. "Rakan kept going on about the birds. What was that all about?"

Dr. Selar sighed, and his face fell once more. "The groundskeeper at the foster home I told you about kept a sanctuary for birds on the roof. Rakan walked in on him and a lady friend of his, in that sanctuary. She must have caught them together, and, well..."

Kal nodded solemnly. "I understand. Thank you for helping me."

Selar left the hospital room, shutting the door behind himself.

Kal looked out the window into the city. He watched two elevated trains weave around one another, crisscrossing, and he sighed.

Holograms with forcefields providing texture... Their technology could probably rival Earth's, even with their lack of nanotechnology. Was his genetic fix here somewhere, trapped inside a culture that would have nothing to do with quantum visitors?

He pulled up his pad and stole one last look out at the brilliant, alternate Chicago before he activated the metaxic nodes.

Tria

Realm #625, "Lehr"
June 20, 2178

KAL TOOK a step back from the table in his treehouse and looked over his work. He grinned as he typed out the last few commands and re-checked for syntax errors. His pad sat on the table, projecting a hollow, three-dimensional representation of his body. A glowing layer of auto-defense nanites covered the hologram's skin. Pop-up windows surrounded the figure, each displaying a chunk of code, all of them modifications Kal had made to the base program. Together, they would allow his nanite defenders to deflect even artificially generated forces, like those he had encountered on Spele.

Two of the cats yowled at one another below, probably Variable and Constant.

Kal smirked. *Another day, another cat fight.*

The light of the holograms danced about his apartment. Kal sighed, looking around the solitary room. His latest feat of programming expertise would go unnoticed, yet again.

He sat down in a chair and let his mind drift back to fourth grade.

They had been studying insects. He and three other students had been assigned an unconscious dragonfly in an immobilization field. They were given a list of measurements to take and anatomical features to describe. But the poor creature turned out to be at least partly conscious due to a bug in the immobilization field's program. He and his classmates struggled to do their work as the dragonfly convulsed sporadically against malfunctioning restraints.

Kal, tired of watching it suffer, pulled up the immobilization program on his pad. Of course, he knew better than to make any changes himself, so he typed his revisions into an empty document. Just five minutes later, he handed his corrections to the teacher.

Kal's teacher, a tall man with a big, furry beard, at first eyed the pad suspiciously. However, upon looking the program over, a smile spread across his face. The teacher ended up submitting Kal's revisions to the Council for approval without any changes at all. He congratulated him on a job well done, but reminded him that he should not really be writing any code before taking the high school preparatory classes.

Still, it was all Kal had talked about for days: the broken program, written by some adult, that *he* had fixed.

Kal stood now in the treehouse and looked over his work. Loneliness crept into him. If he sent any communication to Earth about his inter-metaxic activities, the Fermilab scientists might deactivate his nodes remotely, or worse, forcibly return him to Earth against his will. That would essentially be a death sentence.

He shook his head, returning to happier thoughts. He picked up his pad and activated the new program. The layer of auto-defense nanites on his skin shimmered ever so slightly, then became invisible once more.

Kal pulled up the stills of the next world he planned to explore. It was uninhabited (by humans, or anything else with speech), and therefore unnamed. Glancing through the stills piqued his curiosity further. *Something* was alive there.

"Interesting," he muttered to himself, reading over the collected data in more detail.

Kal made some food for the cats. Max whined and paced anxiously below the treehouse until Kal hurled his lunch out the window. Variable and Constant ceased their play and ran to get their portion. Other pride cats emerged from the forest, too.

Kal climbed down from his home, walked to his takeoff point, and entered the metaxia.

The buildings pulsed.

That's what it looked like, anyway. Translucent cords covered the surface of, well, everything. They lay across the facades of buildings, wrapping themselves around corners, through windowpanes, all the way up the tallest skyscrapers as far he could see. They lay across other architecture too. Miniature cords spiraled up a lamp post, all across a post box, a few abandoned cars and trucks, the billboards and street lights, even the struts and overhead tracks of the elevated rail line.

They came in various sizes too. The ones running up the buildings and rail lines were relatively small, no thicker than a light pen, but the one that lay through the adjacent intersection a block to the east stood two stories tall.

The cords pounded out a thumping rhythm, like a giant drum sounding from every direction at once.

Kal forced himself to focus on his pad, trying to shake the icky feeling that he was an invader inside an enormous organism, an organism that also happened to be an alternate Chicago.

He tapped a few more buttons.

Just a few more scans, he thought.

He took careful steps across the asphalt toward the throbbing wall of a nearby building and gazed at the cords more closely.

Their exterior seemed almost like skin. In fact, were the cords perspiring? He looked at his interface and confirmed that they were. The cords were cybernetic–organic, veins and blood mixed with some kind of fiber optic wire and metallic compounds he didn't even recognize. Did they insulate? Protect? No way to tell for sure.

Looking closer, Kal could see that the cords emitted a dull glow. The bright, midday sun had drowned it out from a distance. A clear fluid churned through their interior, alongside the outline of glowing fiber optic wire, illuminating all the rest.

He sighed. This was truly fascinating, but there was nothing about this organism or its DNA that was remotely related to his genetic aversion to nanogenic radiation. Time to get back to Felis.

A click sounded from behind him, and he turned. He saw nothing unusual, just the same empty street covered in cords.

He returned to his pad to make sure he hadn't missed something and promptly heard the same sound again, louder this time.

He turned back and still saw nothing out of the ordinary. Well, 'ordinary' for this city, anyway. It must really be time to leave. He prepped the program that would usher him back into the metaxia.

He looked around one last time for the source of the clicking and saw nothing. Listening carefully, he heard only the light, steady thrum of all the cords thumping in unison.

He shook his head. *You're losing it, Kal.*

Pain shot through his right forearm.

"Ow!" He shook it vigorously and felt something fall from his skin. He pulled his arm up to his face and ran his fingers over a long, thin red line of missing skin.

He looked down at the ground and squinted at a riot of blue and red squares that was now inching away across the pavement in stuttering bursts. The concussions of contrastive light erupted so intensely from it that Kal could look at it only through his peripheral vision without squinting.

He pulled out his pad and had the nanites run a full bioscan of his body. A window appeared, with the message "no pathogens detected." A small wave of relief passed through him, though the thought of something undetectable inside him brought on a wave of nausea. He breathed deeply through his nose to make it pass.

Kal turned his attention to the thing that had attacked him. He couldn't look at it, but he could certainly have his nanites scan it.

The form of a worm appeared before him on the pad's holographic interface. It was cybernetic, just like the cords.

The pixel worm limped spasmodically into the wall of a nearby building and stopped. Kal watched it as best as he could through nearly closed eyes. The creature curled up against one of the cords and began... doing something... biting into it, maybe? Bright, white sparks sprayed from where the worm bit the cord, the cord itself decaying into a black and brown bile.

The whole city rumbled and shuddered. The cords' pulse quickened. All of them, across every surface, retracted off all the artifices of human construction, spinning, wrapping, twirling and unwinding into a new configuration. The large cord a block away heaved itself upward and unraveled while new enormous cords appeared, laying themselves down into the other three adjoining intersections.

The ground shook so hard that Kal lost his balance and fell, catching himself just before he hit the pavement.

When the quake stopped, Kal grabbed his pad and hit the icon to initiate his escape. The familiar, circular field of blue electricity formed around him.

Without warning, the static sphere wobbled and collapsed partway inward. Blue sparks sprayed toward him, and Kal raised his arms to shield his face.

He looked up through the rain of sparks to see that more of the blue-red pixel worms had appeared on the walls of nearby buildings and were now leaping down at him, dive bombing his metaxic bubble.

His pad interface screamed bold, red warnings in multiple holographic windows:

'Quantum-locking instabilities detected!'

'Nanite activities impaired!'

Three buttons blinked helpfully into existence: 'abort', 'retry' and 'fail.'

He slammed the 'retry' button, but this only caused his computer to churn some more while the metaxic bubble continued to wobble precariously under subsequent attacks. The same three buttons reappeared.

Kal felt the urge to throw his pad at something, but decided instead to save that act for when he met the person who'd written the nodes' programming.

Kal pressed 'fail,' and the dysfunctional sphere of blue static dissipated.

An incandescent river of red and blue coursed over the top of the nearest building and surged toward him in an erratic, purple haze.

The cords clinging to the nearest walls tore themselves out of the ground and flung the majority of the worms away before they could hit Kal. It was the last thing he saw before he turned and fled through the empty city streets, away from the river of broken red and blue, and down the path that the cords had cleared during their reconfiguration.

∽๛◁◯๛

After what seemed like miles, Kal stopped to catch his breath and pulled out his pad. Just as the blue static haze of the metaxic bubble began to form, the river of worms surged around the corner.

He cursed, closed out the program, and took up running again.

The path between the enormous cords on either side of him took him east and slightly south. He emerged from between buildings, the cords guiding him across a street and into a grassy field. Kal turned another corner and discovered a building he recognized: the Art Institute of Chicago. He'd been to Earth's at least half a dozen times as a child. This version even had the lion statues and the great steps, though cords covered them as well as the entire building, making the whole structure throb.

Kal ran up the steps as quickly as his feet would take him. He glanced back and caught a glimpse of the worms crashing around the corner that the giant cords had created, flooding toward the steps.

He yanked open the doors to the Art Institute, ran inside, and slammed them shut behind him. He backed away from the doors, gasping for breath. His gaze fixated on the entrance.

Would it hold? Could the worm creatures eat through it as easily as they could knock out metaxic bubbles and sear through the layer of auto-defense nanites on his skin?

He got out his pad and began firing up the nodes again. Before the sphere of blue sparks could even form, the holographic interface flickered out of existence. His pad was dead.

Kal gulped and shivered. A bead of sweat dripped off his forehead onto its sleek, black surface. Kal jabbed at it, but it remained inert.

He jumped as the door shuddered, once, then twice more. They held fast.

A few smaller shudders and then silence.

Kal looked around him. Near the entrance, the typical vaulted ceiling stretched out overhead, but the further his eyes moved inward, the more alien the building became. The translucent cords were not laced over the building's interior, they *were* the building's interior. The grand entranceway lost its rectangular shape, forming into a staircase of cords leading down a tube.

No light fixtures hung from the ceiling. Instead, the cords' bioluminescence permeated the space, bathing everything in their soft, white glow.

Kal's heart sank. He kicked himself mentally. He shouldn't have let the building's familiar facade lure him inside.

He took a few tentative steps forward and lurched to a halt, gasping for breath. The bioluminescence of the cords had shifted, following him as he moved. Those stairs of cords were bright too, and they weren't pulsing like the rest of the room, making them easier to traverse. Someone or something was guiding him.

Kal pulled out his pad and tried to turn it on once more. It remained inactive. No escape.

His heart raced, and he wiped sweaty hands on his jeans. Slowly, he made his way down the stairwell tube. The cords that comprised it spiraled along its walls. That, combined with the throbbing, was more than enough to dizzy him.

Kal took deep breaths, forcing himself to remain calm.

At the bottom of the cord tunnel, he found an arched entryway that opened into a sterile, cubic, empty room with walls of gray metal. Lights hung from the ceiling in a grid. Kal walked very slowly to its center.

"Welcome home," a voice said directly behind him.

Kal lurched forward and turned to see a man in a black dress suit and white tie. He had light skin, blond hair, and blue eyes.

It was the last thing Kal registered before he fainted.

❧⟨❧⟩

Kal opened his eyes and blinked. He lay on the soft mattress of a bed, a white ceiling above him. A miniature Saturn passed over his field of vision. Kal reached up to touch the planet, and his hand went through the small orb. It cotinued on its path, traversing the space between the bed and the ceiling. Outside, birds chirped. A train chugged by in the distance, the sound of the train line just beyond his house.

Kal ripped the sheets off himself and lurched out of bed, and the holographic solar system on the ceiling shimmered out of existence. He grabbed at the mattress, then stumbled into his desk. He felt the grain of the wood, ran his hands over the sleek, black telescope by the window, and snatched up his school pad, the one he'd used for his sixth grade homework. It was all just as he'd left it.

This couldn't be. It absolutely couldn't be.

Earth?

He clutched at his chest. He didn't feel winded. He didn't even feel short of breath. Had they removed the nanites from the entire city? That couldn't be possible.

He jammed his hand into the interface at his desk, and the window forcefield dispersed, allowing a blast of humid, summer air to roll into his room.

This was Illinois, all right. His Illinois. But how did he get here?

A scream erupted from behind him. Strange—it sounded almost like his own voice.

Kal turned back toward his bed, but the bed was gone. Inky blackness spread across the room, consuming everything. Moments later, the entire room had been inundated, and the humidity and heat in the air dissipated.

There was only himself, the black void... and another Kal.

The other Kal sat huddled on the ground, but his arms were outstretched before him, and he was trembling.

"Hello?" Kal tried.

The other Kal screamed, and fell backward, shuddering.

"Are you... me?" Kal didn't dare take a step forward.

The other Kal shifted backward, his eyes radiating fear and his limbs shaking. "Who... who are you?"

"My name's Kal. What's your name?"

"Tria."

"How did you get here, Tria?"

"I don't know. I just know that I'm scared."

"Well, that makes two of us." Kal took a deep breath and exhaled. "Tria, can I come closer?"

Tria nodded hesitantly, still shivering. He wore the same clothes Kal had on. They could have been identical twins.

Kal took a few steps towards Tria and extended his hand. At this, Tria shook his head violently and squirmed away.

"Don't!" Tria shouted.

"Don't what?"

"Don't... touch me."

"Why?"

Tria gulped and looked at the floor. "I woke up in a bed, but when I tried to pull the sheets off myself, my hands moved right through them. I started sinking into the mattress, and... it was horrible."

"How did you—?"

"I— I got my feet onto the floor, and I stopped falling. But my hands passed through the bed and the desk and—" Tria shook his head, facing the floor. "There's something wrong with me."

Kal furrowed his brow and gazed out into the void all around him. Just him and Tria.

Kal sat down, face to face with his doppel.

"Do you know how this happened?"

Tria shook his head.

"Do you remember anything before now?"

Another no.

"Tria," Kal said softly. He waited until Tria had lifted his head up.

Those eyes were his own, and they were so incredibly scared. "Tria, I don't know how this happened to you either. But, you know what? There's something wrong with me too. I have this genetic aversion to nanogenic radiation."

"What's that?"

"There are these tiny robots called nanites. I can't go home because I'm allergic to the radiation they emit. But I'm searching for a way to go there safely. I might be able to find another organism with the same problem, or some other solution. I don't know. It won't be easy. But I'm going to keep trying.

"I think… maybe we could work together? We could search for a way to make you solid, too. We have a better chance of figuring all this out if we combine forces."

Tria reached out to Kal, and Kal reached out his hand, too.

They went through each other.

Tria recoiled, then reached out with his other hand. Clasping both his hands around Kal's, even though Tria's had no substance.

"You'd do this," Tria said, "for someone you just met? Someone with no memory, who doesn't even know who he is?"

"You look like me," Kal said.

Tria smiled. "Okay then. Let's try."

Kal's vision became blurry. Tria faded away.

Kal began to fall.

Kal fell and fell.

His descent slowed, the sensation of falling evaporating completely.

Something cold pressed up against his back.

His eyes flitted open. Before him lay himself, or rather, a clone of himself. The clone's eyes were closed, and he was naked.

Kal looked down. He was naked too.

"Oh, god. They cloned me." Kal fought back nausea and the overwhelming sense of violation.

A thought popped into his mind: *The clone has no physical body. And his name is Tria.*

…

How did he know that?

Kal jumped up off the metal slab, his feet hitting the cold floor. He was in the square room he'd seen before, just before the blond-haired man had appeared. The slabs were recent additions, but everything else was the same. Just an empty, gray cube with an array of lights on the ceiling.

Tria remained inert.

Kal scrambled around behind the slab, breathing heavily. His vision was going blurry. He felt gross and icky all over. What had happened to him? What had that man done to him? What would he do to Kal next?

His clothes lay neatly folded behind the metal slab. Kal pulled at them, anxious to cover himself. He'd just managed to get his jeans on when he rolled over onto the floor, the sickening feeling of having been genetically violated overwhelming him.

He'd heard stories from earlier in the century, horrible stories of countries who'd gotten their hands on nanotechnology before they were ready for it. They had altered humans, done horrible things to their DNA. Unspeakable things.

Kal pulled on his shirt, then grabbed at the slab.

Just find your pad, Kal. Find the pad and everything will be okay.

Kal gazed about the room. It wasn't on the floor, and there didn't appear to be any indentations or crevices in the walls.

There! His pad lay in a corner of the ceiling, fixed to the wall. Although there certainly wasn't any way to reach it, the fact that it was intact gave him some small comfort.

Tria's eyes fluttered open. He waved his head about, then looked at Kal.

"Tria..." Kal said. He still didn't know how he knew the name.

"Kal?"

"Yeah."

"I'm scared."

"Me too."

"Kal, where are we?"

"I don't know. It's an alternate Earth."

"What's Earth?"

"That'll take some expl—"

"Where are my clothes?"

Tria jumped down off his slab, then ran behind it and shrieked.

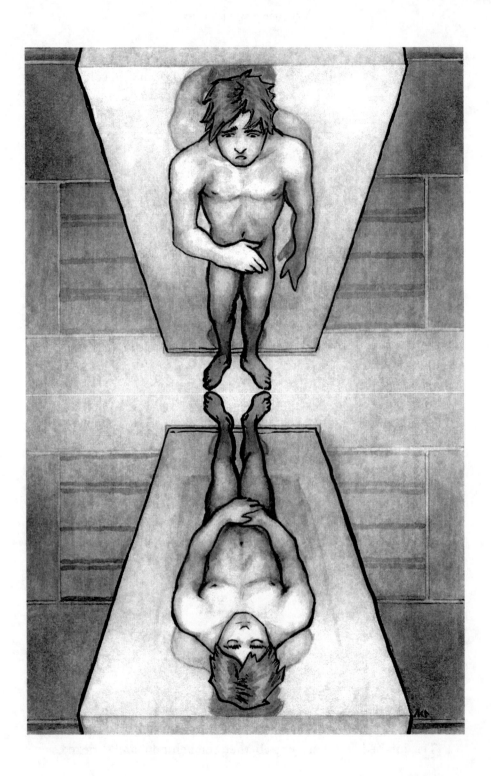

"Tria, you okay?"

He shrieked again, and Kal ran to him. "What's wrong?"

Tria was trembling, holding his hands out in front of him. "I tried to touch the metal, but my hand it— I'm not... I'm not real, Kal. I'm so scared. What's going on?"

"Don't worry." Kal somehow knew better than to try to reach out and comfort Tria with touch. Deja vu washed over him. "Everything's going to be alright. We'll work together, okay? We won't let anyone hurt us."

"Our designation is UsrLocal," a voice rang out from the center of the room.

Kal nodded to Tria, and Tria nodded back. They stood and slowly emerged from behind the metal slab.

The man in the black suit stood, grinning. Seeing them, he beamed with delight.

"How are you feeling, my lord?"

Kal and Tria exchanged another even more confused glance.

"Lord?" Kal asked the strange man.

"Of course. You are my... our god after all."

Tria's eyes grew wide.

Kal waved his hands. "No, I think you've got me confused with someone from—"

"*Homo sapiens sapiens*," UsrLocal said. "The species who created me... us, *Linaxia Gnopus.*"

"This is fascinating," Tria said, not looking fascinated in the least. "But I really just want some clothes... please?"

UsrLocal tilted his head mechanically, then reached up and snapped his fingers. Kal's pad shot down from the ceiling and swiveled around, stopping directly in front of him. It hovered there, Kal and Tria gaping at it.

"I've made some modifications to assist you, my lord."

The lighting flickered, and a crashing sound could be heard from somewhere distant above.

UsrLocal screwed up his face. "I'm so very sorry, my lord. If you'll excuse me."

His form shimmered and vanished. Another hologram.

Tria stared at Kal with wide eyes. Kal gulped and grabbed at his hovering pad. To his surprise, it came to life at his touch, and the interface had indeed changed. The main menu contained about a dozen new toggles and buttons. New programs had been uploaded into primary memory. And his sartorial program had been updated... for two.

Kal opened it. The new interface was easy enough. Tria's body shimmered, and his clothing morphed to match Kal's, except that Tria's T-shirt was blue instead of red.

More slamming noises erupted in the distance, and this time the room shook slightly.

UsrLocal shimmered back into existence. "My lord, I'm afraid we must leave immediately."

"Why?" Tria asked.

"You're in danger here."

"What's going on?" Kal crossed his arms.

"The Xplirir Contagion will shortly breach this structure. I... we believe they wish to render you." He turned to Tria. "No offense."

Tria just blinked at him. "I don't have the slightest idea what you're talking about."

"Me either," Kal said. "But if you'll let me use my nodes, I can leave this world—"

"No!" UsrLocal screeched, his eyes wide with terror. "We can keep you this time. Please don't leave us."

Kal shared a look with Tria. He was just as taken aback as Kal was.

"It's okay," Tria said. "Calm down. We won't leave you. Just help us understand what's going on. From the beginning. What are those noises? How did I get here? Who am I?"

UsrLocal looked up at Kal. "Is he... you really don't know? At all?"

Kal shook his head.

UsrLocal collapsed onto the floor, sobbing. The slamming noises grew louder and more frequent. The room shook again, more violently, and the lights flickered.

Kal knelt down and tried to put his hand on UsrLocal's shoulder, but it went right through. Kal nodded to Tria.

Tria reached out, and his hand contacted UsrLocal's shoulder. Kal and Tria shared a smile.

"What's wrong?" Tria asked.

"It's just..." UsrLocal said between sobs. "I thought you'd come back. It's been so long. I've... we've been so lonely. You have no idea how lonely!"

"How long since your humans left?" Kal asked.

"Eight—" he sobbed. "Eight hundred years."

Kal gulped. Another slam and the lights flickered off for a full second before returning to their normal illumination.

"Is that the worms?" Kal asked.

"Worms?" Tria turned to Kal skittishly.

"Before, when I first arrived on this world, there were these blue and red worms. One of them attacked me. Then there were hundreds or thousands of them in a giant wave. The cords rearranged themselves and guided me here."

UsrLocal looked up at Kal, smiling through teary eyes.

Kal gasped. "That was you! *You're* the cords, aren't you?"

"Yes, my lord."

More slamming. The lights flickered out again. One of the lighting appliances plummeted from the ceiling and exploded on the floor.

UsrLocal frowned and sobbed again, shaking his head. "You have to leave. For your own safety. The Xplirir Contagion will breach this structure."

"What will happen to Tria?" Kal asked. "Is he stuck here in your computer system?"

"No," UsrLocal said.

"Well, where *am* I then? Is my mind just a simulation too? Some artificial intelligence?"

"No." UsrLocal sighed. He pointed at Kal's head.

Kal clutched at his face, then looked at Tria.

"No… you didn't…"

"Our gods loved the mind clones." UsrLocal sniffled, wiping away tears.

"Tria's… in my brain?"

"I'm a hallucination?"

"No," UsrLocal said. "Not a dream or an illusion. A duplicate of Kal's mind cohabiting his brain. Tria, your form is projected by the pad's holographic emitters and your mind is your own, but you share Kal's brain. However, you are not limited by it! You can extend your consciousness into any computer with sufficient memory. Both Kal's pad and nanite technologies are adequately equipped."

"Make him a body." Kal crossed his arms.

"I can't. The gods taught us to clone minds, not bodies. We have tried to build artificial gods before. Not a single replicant lived for more than a week."

Another light slammed into the floor and exploded.

"I will fix Lehr for you," UsrLocal said. "I will continue my struggle against the Xplirir Contagion so that you might return to us."

Tria smiled and shook UsrLocal's shoulder. "That's the spirit."

"We'll be back then," Kal said as he began firing up the metaxic nodes. "We promise."

The slamming noises reached a peak and the room shook violently. The main lighting fell away, completely extinguished, and red emergency lighting flooded the room.

"Please do. We won't disappoint you. We've held together your cities, protected your computers. We will make Lehr a place you can inhabit again. I... we promise."

Kal smiled and nodded.

"Goodbye, UsrLocal." Tria waved as the bubble wrapped around both him and Kal. Lehr swirled away into the blue.

"Kal..." Tria said, gazing out at the eddies and fleeting glimpses of alternate Earths. "What is this?"

"The metaxia," Kal said.

"It's blue." Tria grinned.

"Yeah," Kal said, his expression falling. Tria didn't seem to remember anything. He was a clone of Kal's mind, but tabula rasa. No explicit memories. Everything was new to him.

"Hmm..." Kal pressed a button, and Tria's form shimmered out of existence.

Not funny. It was Tria's voice, but Kal heard it in his mind.

No way! Kal thought back.

Yes way, Tria thought. *I can see your filesystem, you know. This is a disaster. Don't you know how to organize?*

Kal grimaced. He hadn't expected this.

Leave my filesystem alone!

Kal had promised to get Tria a real body, hadn't he? He didn't remember doing that exactly, but he felt as though he had.

Wow, Tria thought. *This folder is taking up so much space. What do you need all these pictures and videos for? Oh, niiiiice—*

"Stay out of there!" Kal shouted. He took a deep breath. *That's very personal, private stuff.*

Geez, sorry. Just trying to bring some order to this chaos. Say, Kal, can I have my own personal, private folder like yours?

New body for Tria it was.

Corporeal

Realm #2140, "Vogg"
June 21, 2178

ZEEMZ FLEW Labshedd Seven low over the biofarm.

"Now!" he shouted back to Liza.

His eyes remained on the flight status monitors. He grimaced, not hearing the familiar sounds of the ejection pods opening as he guided the labshedd over the plot.

"What's going on back there?" Zeemz pulled upward and turned to loop back around.

"Sorry," Liza said.

"No problem," Zeemz replied, his tone carefully neutral. "We're coming around for a second pass. Be ready this time."

Zeemz completed the loop and lined the labshedd up with the empty row of the plot once more. He pushed forward on the controls, bringing the labshedd down.

"And... now!"

The concussive thuds of ejection erupted from below as the labshedd dumped out its cargo of genetically engineered plants.

"That's the last one, right?" Liza asked.

"Yeah," Zeemz said, looking over computer readouts. "Sorry Liza, looks like I screwed that last one up. You see it?"

The familiar beeps of the computer system sounded from behind him.

"I see it," she said. "Not your fault, actually. A gust of wind blew us off course just enough to put the last seven saplings out of alignment."

Zeemz grinned. Liza was too smart for this kind of work. If only she'd stop daydreaming. Her absentmindedness reminded him of his tradebrother.

"Heya," Nezim's voice burst out over the comm.

"I was just thinking about you," Zeemz replied into the mic. "How are those new plants coming?"

"Oh, great! There's—"

"Actually, is it alright if I call you back? Liza and I have to go outside and fix an alignment mistake."

"Alignment mistake? Forget about that." Zeemz could hear Nezim's childishly nefarious grin without having to see it. "You're going to want to come hear this. Murkwalker's back, and he's got a problem with his *brain*."

Zeemz rolled his eyes.

"Tell Murkwalker—" Zeemz paused. What had Murkwalker wanted to be called? Kazl? "Tell Kazl that I take my work seriously, unlike my ungrateful tradebrother—"

Nezim laughed loudly over the comm. He was currently far less society-indebted than Zeemz.

"And," Zeemz continued, "I have duties that require my attention before I can help Kazl with his… brain."

"Suit yourself," Nezim said. Zeemz visualized Nezim's signature shrug as others in Nezim's labshedd laughed over the comm.

"Zeemz out." He initiated the breaking stabilizers, bringing Labshedd Seven gently to the ground.

Liza had already moved to the rear of the craft, and was now pulling on the bright orange and yellow-green suit over her gray coveralls.

"You ever thought about bioengineering work?" Zeemz asked her as he pulled his suit out of the cleanser.

"No, not really," she said.

"My brother Nezim is on the bioengineering team for Labshedd Nine. If you're interested, I could have him show you the ropes."

Liza nodded curtly, then pulled her helmet over her head and fastened it as quickly as she could.

So, that wasn't what had been bothering her. He couldn't help but think of the rumors. Not liking those thoughts, he pushed them out of his mind and focused on suiting up.

They entered the labshedd's airlock. After eight seconds of whirring and hissing, the outer doors opened.

Zeemz and Liza stepped out into the Murk.

"I thought this was supposed to be an alternate Earth." Tria tried to kick a rock, but his foot went through it. "This doesn't look like the Earth you told me about at all."

Kal and Tria walked through an impenetrable, toxic haze that the people of Vogg called the Murk. It was so thick that everything more than a meter away disappeared into the sea of brown-green. Kal used his pad to navigate.

Both of them wore the bright orange and yellow-green suits that were crucial for outdoor survival. Kal absolutely despised them. They were stuffy, intrusive and claustrophobic, like being covered in a dozen layers of heavy canvas. The material crinkled and tightened with even the slightest of movements, as though it were threatening to collapse inward and suffocate him with every step he took.

He'd decided against wearing one on his first visit to Vogg, hating it completely and knowing his nanites would protect him from the chemical swill in the atmosphere. It had been one of his first big alternate-Earth social blunders. The locals were at first amazed to see him walking through the Murk without dissolving into a puddle of amino acids. But, it hadn't taken long for their wonder to turn into disdain and outright jealousy. They had begun pejoratively calling him "Murkwalker." None of his subsequent interactions, though positive, had let him completely shed that title. Tria had almost refused the suit as well, but Kal had insisted.

"Well, like I said, each alternate Earth has a completely different timeline," Kal replied. "Human cultures are very different across alternate worlds. All of these worlds on my grid split from Earth's timeline hundreds of thousands of years ago, some even millions. Vogg, for example, has over six thousand years of recorded human history. Earth has about twenty-five hundred, maybe three thousand depending on what you count as history."

"This place is gross," Tria remarked. Kal hoped that Tria's observations would become less inane, and he reminded himself that Tria was, after all, essentially newborn in many respects.

Kal collected himself and attempted an explanation. "Remember the late twenty-first century eco-disaster on Earth I told you about? Well, something pretty similar seems to have happened here. Except on Earth, we invented nanotechnology and were able to patch things up. The people who inhabited this planet three thousand years ago didn't, and their biome fell apart. The people of the Mobile seem to think their ancestors *let* things get this way."

Kal glanced around. Tria had vanished.

"Tria?"

"Over here."

Kal located Tria on his pad. He was a few meters to the right. Kal adjusted course, and spotted Tria's suited form next to a boulder almost a tall as he was. He had stuck his head inside it.

Kal sighed. Okay, he'd bite. "What are you doing?"

"Looking inside the rock."

"What do you see?"

There was a long pause.

Tria's voice crackled, light over the suit intercom.

"Darkness."

Then he erupted into a fit of laughter.

Kal bunched up his lips, closed his eyes, and took a deep breath. "C'mon. We need to get back."

"Okay, okay." Tria pulled his head out of the rock and ranked up beside Kal.

"How do they see through this stuff?" Tria waved his hands in front of his face. Kal rolled his eyes. He wanted to yell at Tria that he did not have physical substance, and even if he had, waving his hands around was certainly not going to help him see better.

Kal stifled a sigh and answered Tria's question. "They don't. Their suits have computers that network with the meteorolog. It's the biggest of all these dome vehicles. It projects images of everything in the environment onto the suit's visor. Trust me, you should be glad yours is fake."

"Have you worn a real one?" Tria asked, his voice brimming with excitement.

"Yes," Kal replied curtly, praying that Tria would catch the hint.

"What was it like?" Tria would have shaken Kal's shoulder if he could.

"The real suit is a pretty... invasive technology."

A moment of silence. "What's so bad about being invaded? I want to try being invaded. Can I try that when I have a body?"

"Sure." Kal started making a mental list of worlds with friendly cultures he could try to pawn Tria off onto once he got that body. He couldn't handle much more of this.

"Tell me more about the suits," Tria said.

"No." Kal said through clenched teeth.

Tria's odd curiosity only served to remind him of one the most unpleasant experiences of his adventure thus far. Kal still worried that the real suit he had tried on during his first visit to Vogg had done permanent damage. He'd only just strapped himself into it, and the thing had attached all manner of "equipment" to his body. Vogg's inhabitants had laughed at him, insisting that the suit's contraptions were only for waste disposal. Kal cringed to think of it even now.

Kal and Tria reached the meteorolog. Its gray, metal expanse curved out of view into the Murk on either side of them. The walls were covered in layers of thick brown-green tarnish and singed with black spots. Kal pressed the button next to the airlock hatch, and it hissed open. They stepped inside, and the hatch closed behind them, sealing shut. A cacophonous whirring filled the chamber. The Murk that had entered with them was sucked into large funnels that lined the airlock walls.

Kal counted out eight seconds. The interior door opened, and the two of them entered the meteorolog. They stood in an enormous domed room, dimly lit and lined with curving, weaving rows of computer consoles. An enormous screen adorned the wall-ceiling of the dome, immediately opposite the airlock, and depicted a map of the Midwest—Lakes Michigan, Huron and Erie.

However, unlike most inhabited alternate Earths, Vogg had nothing akin to cities. Those had been wiped out by environmental devastation long ago. Only putrid, barren land, polluted rivers, and cesspool oceans remained.

The meteorolog they stood inside was part of Mobile Ortie—what the locals called their nomadic collection of flight-capable domes. They were currently situated at the base of Lake Michigan, or Lake Mezg as they called it. But, the mobile could decide, even at a moment's notice, to fly the meteorolog and all the other shedds away to some distant locale. From what Nezim had told him, sometimes very distant. It sounded like they'd been all over their version of North America.

Kal took off his suit and dropped it onto the floor beside the cleanser. A native would have put his suit into the infernal, chugging machine, but since his was only for show, he left it on the floor, out of the way.

"Oh, right." Kal snapped his fingers and grabbed his pad, inputting the necessary commands.

Tria's suit disappeared, replaced by his now-signature blue T-shirt and jeans. Much to Kal's annoyance, Tria grimaced at having his holographic suit taken away.

"But I liked it..."

Kal inhaled sharply and continued forward into the lab, navigating the twisty rows of computers and the dreary-busy horde of jumpsuited people.

"Kazl!" a voice called out to him.

His friend Nezim stood at a computer console under the enormous map monitor. Nezim wore half his suit, with only the helmet and gloves removed. He was perhaps ten years older than Kal with sandy brown hair and bright, intelligent eyes. Like all the people Kal had met on Vogg, except the very young, Nezim's skin was pocked and wrinkled, making him appear older than he actually was. Something to do with minute exposure to the Murk over prolonged periods of time. But there was something about Nezim's eyes. They shone brightly in a way that most of the Mobile inhabitants' didn't.

Kal had decided that he liked Nezim very early into his first visit to Vogg. He seemed almost innocent and unsullied, at least in spirit, despite the rigors of his environment.

"How was your walk?" Nezim asked. "Did you get all of your questions answered, Zria?"

Tria's anxious gaze followed two men who marched mechanically past them, each with a tiny green implant blinking on their necks.

"I, um..." Tria's attention jumped back to Nezim. "Yeah, I think so."

"I've been looking over the specs for what you want to do, Kazl," Nezim said. "I don't know. We can grow the body, sure. That part's easy. But our psychological equipment, it's just not set up for this."

"Well, that's where my technology comes in. I'm sure that my nanites can help bridge my brain and the clone's brain," Kal said. He noticed several of Nezim's colleagues glance in his direction at his remark about the nanites, and he promptly lowered his voice. "With your brain mapping technology, your system should be able to distinguish my brain patterns from Tria's. Then, my system will map Tria's brain patterns onto the clone."

Nezim sighed. "It won't be that simple, Kazl. The human brain is incredibly complex. Six thousand years of human history and a genetic science that rivals even your nanotech-enabled Earth's and we still don't know how safe this will be or if it'll even work. You could suffer brain damage."

Kal had visited half a dozen inhabited world with relatively advanced technology and asked their medical professionals what they thought of his Vogg plan. None of them could give him any kind of estimation on what kind of risk he'd be subjecting himself to. Four had clearly been humoring him, probably convinced he was pulling their leg. The other two had put the odds of his described procedure succeeding on par with the flip of a coin.

Nezim raised his eyebrows, waiting for a response. Tria stood, hardly paying attention, moving his arm into the computer console and pulling it out again, back and forth, giggling to himself idly.

Sketchy alter-Earth statistics be damned.

"I'm in," Kal said.

∞⟨⟩∞

Nezim and Zeemz waited in the long line of the foodshedd, which followed the dome's interior wall, leading toward the growchambers.

"I'm worried about Liza," Zeemz said.

"I thought she was doing well."

"She is. Really bright, catches on quick. I wonder why she didn't sign up for bioengineering work."

"Could be anything. Do you know what her aptitude scores were?"

"No idea." Zeemz grabbed a tray, walked to an unoccupied growchamber, and picked some breadfruit and avocado from the undulating vine.

"Hmm. Why are you worried about her again?"

"She's been distracted lately. She misses planting cues, forgets to do simple things."

Nezim remained silent. It was no secret among the workers of Mobile Ortie that Liza and Razz were an item. He heard whispers. The next child born in the mobile would be Liza's. Nezim hated gossip like that.

Zeemz and Nezim sat down at an empty table with their trays of engineered food. Zeemz bit off huge chunks of his breadfruit.

"How'd the new plot go?" Nezim asked. "Did you get that problem all sorted out?"

"Yeah," Zeemz said with his mouth half full. He paused to swallow. "All in all, the work goes a lot faster with Liza on board. I try to reach out to her, you know, but she keeps me at a distance."

Zeemz glanced over at the table where the emotionally undead sat, green lights blinking on their necks. Their higher brain functions had been given over to the control of an AI in the meteorolog computer. Such individuals had not been able to psychologically endure life on Vogg for one reason or another. Not having the resources to incarcerate or rehabilitate, emotional undeath was employed instead. The green signalled that the AI maintained control. One hoped never to witness one of those lights go red.

"Hey," Nezim said. "What do you think about Kazl? He said if we help him he'll actually give us the nanotechnology. Can you imagine? Restoration could go from being millennia away to years away, maybe even in our lifetime—"

Zeemz swallowed another bite and put down his breadfruit, grimacing a bit. "You imagine too much."

Nezim returned his brother's glare. "Don't give me that line about Gluttony-tech. There was no Gluttony on Kazl's Vogg. It can't be Gluttony-tech if it comes from a—what did he call it? An alternate timeline."

"No, that's not it. I know that the nanites aren't Gluttony-tech," Zeemz said. "It's just..."

"What, then?"

"Remember when I asked Kazl about why some crazy person hasn't created a nanoplague or written a program to disassemble everyone?"

"Oh, right, the um, what did he call it?"

"Azla— Azlanz—" Zeemz sighed. "I don't know, Azl-something Nanoprogramming Ethics Council. And that's why he wouldn't give us the nanites on his last visit. Even though we wanted them. It was too dangerous. And our mobile agreed. Now, all of a sudden, he's willing to forget about his council, and he'll just hand the technology over if we help him. He seems different this time, don't you think? More nervous, less carefree."

More like most of us, Nezim thought.

Zeemz continued. "If he's willing to forget his Earth ethics to fix his... brain problem, what else is he willing to do? Do you remember how we behaved when we were eighteen? All the stupid things we did? If I understand Kazl's technology right... Nezim, he could wipe out every person on Vogg with the push of a button."

Nezim tossed his avocado onto his plate, horrified. "You think he'd do that?"

"No, of course not. I'm just saying, he seems desperate now, and it worries me."

Nezim exhaled and let himself calm down. It wasn't like his brother to worry without reason. Nezim picked the avocado back up and took a small bite.

"I have to admit," Nezim said, "the whole thing about the clone of him in his head without a body. That is pretty strange. But then so is a planet called Earth with green grass, a blue sky, and a Nanoprogramming Ethics Council, that's actually Vogg with a different timeline."

"And you probably forgot." Zeemz mouthed the next words silently. "I'm supposed to go see Hez this week."

Nezim frowned. If Zeemz stayed and helped Nezim get Kazl's nano-technology, he'd miss one of the few, brief reunions he'd ever have with his seven-year-old son. Like all children, Hez had been traded away to another mobile at the age of three. He was a member of Mobile Agarba now. Ortie, Nezim and Zeemz's mobile, was in close proximity to Agarba at the moment, but naturally, either mobile could move at any time.

"I wouldn't ask you to cancel," Nezim said.

"Tell me this," Zeemz said, his gaze stifling Nezim's propensity for sarcastic retorts. "I operate this stuff. I'm a pilot and a farmer and I'm good at it. Besides the basics, I don't really get nanites or genomes. So tell me, if we get our hands on these nanite things, is there a real chance of Hez coming of age in a world with a blue sky and green grass? With a horizon and a shining disc in the sky called the 'sun?'"

Nezim clenched his hands together. "If not Hez, then his kids, or at the very least, his grandkids."

Zeemz bit the last of the meat from his breadfruit. "Then I'll help."

Kal sat in a chair with a contraption of wires and blinking lights strapped to his head, clutching his pad. He was more unnerved than he thought he would be. He trusted his nanites to protect him, but this was the same equipment that the people of Mobile Ortie used to zap away a person's emotions and put a computer AI in their place.

The dome walls of Labshedd Five rose up to an apex above his head. Monitors circled the walls, their continuous loop broken only by the airlock.

Tria's hologram was off, his voice audible only to Kal.

"Let's start," Nezim said.

Kal's chair spun around to face a segment of the monitor ring.

"Zria, you need to close your eyes and ears, sing to yourself or something, okay?"

"Tria's good," Kal said for him.

"For this first one, just look at the images," Zeemz said. "Don't say anything. Here we go."

He pressed a button on his keyboard. A sequence of pictures flashed past Kal on the screens, alternating every second or so. After a few minutes, the images ceased.

"Got it," Nezim said.

"Okay, Kazl," Zeemz said. "Close your eyes and hum to yourself. Point the pad at the screens, and Zria, you watch through the pad's visual input. Can you see it?"

Kal tilted the pad in his lap in accordance with Tria's instructions, then closed his eyes and covered his ears.

He hummed to himself until Tria told him it was his turn again.

Nezim and Zeemz ran dozens of such tests. It seemed to drag on for hours, and when they had finally concluded, Kal felt as though he'd been mentally plowed over. He pulled the bundle of wires and metal off his head, lay down on the floor, and closed his eyes. Tria was silent too, probably just as exhausted as Kal was.

Hearing Nezim and Zeemz talk about getting lunch shocked Kal into opening his eyes. He couldn't believe it was only lunchtime.

"Hey Kazl, let me show you something," Nezim said as he walked to the edge of the dome, opposite the airlock. Kal picked himself up off the floor and latched the pad onto his jeans.

Tria cleared his throat in Kal's mind, reminding him to pull up his pad and activated Tria's hologram.

Zeemz remained at his computer terminal, poring over the display, a curious expression on his face. Kal started to ask him if something was the matter, but Nezim stole his attention away, calling for him and Tria again.

They walked to where Nezim stood. In front of them lay a tubular chamber, and inside it was a body, Kal's body—a real, completely physical clone. It lay inert, living only in the vegetative sense.

Kal smiled.

Tria laughed. "It's me!"

"You think this will work?" Kal asked.

"I sure hope so," Nezim said.

"Let's get some food," Zeemz called from across the room.

"Kazl," Nezim said, "maybe you can tell me more about nanites and how they manipulate matter. I'm particularly interested in how they—"

"No," Zeemz cut him off.

Kal and Nezim gazed at him.

"Nezim and I need to talk," Zeemz said.

Kal gazed at Nezim, but Nezim avoided making eye contact.

"I'll be back soon." Nezim squeezed Kal's shoulder.

He and Zeemz retrieved their suits from the cleanser, then entered the airlock, leaving Kal and Tria alone with the clone body.

Tria put his hands on the glass, pressing his nose into and through it. He pulled his face slowly in and out of the tube.

"This is going to be awesome." Tria giggled to himself.

Kal nodded with a reluctant glance at the airlock as it whirred shut.

∽∾⊰⊱∽∾

Kal made a meal for himself and ate at a small table near the wall of Labshedd Five. Tria sat on the floor, watching him eat.

"Does nanite food taste the same as real food?" Tria asked.

"Almost," Kal took a bite from his apple. "Everything's... duller, sort of. Little differences and inconsistencies show up in real plants. Nanite food is flavorful, but drab, in its own way. Too consistent."

"What about the mobile's food?" Tria asked. Kal stifled laughter, almost choking on a bit of apple. If Kal didn't know better... was Tria aware that he was worried about Nezim and Zeemz, and trying to distract his attention?

Kal finally managed to swallow. "Their food tastes like mashed cardboard. They've got a whole dome dedicated to growing the stuff. I had to pretend to like it."

Tria laughed, then a glint appeared in his eyes. "I can't wait to have taste buds. There are lots of foods I can't wait to try. Like kumquat. That's just a fun word."

Now it was Kal's turn to laugh.

"Speaking of names," Tria said, "What gives with ours? They call you Kazl and me Zria."

Kal swallowed a bite of his turkey sandwich and said, "Linguistics."

Tria looked up at Kal, his hands clutched together and his eyes wide.

"Linguistics..." he said slowly, as if tasting the word for the first time. "What's that?"

Kal put down his sandwich, surprised. "Well, these people aren't speaking English. They're speaking whatever language developed here. When the nanites construct their translation matrix, they can't make true analogs for proper nouns, like our names. So those come through as... well, whatever our names are in Nezim and Zeemz's actual language.

"But 'Kal' isn't an English word, it's just a name. Why can't they just call you that?"

"It's not that simple. Their language has different rules for constructing words out of sounds. They have to call me something that fits those rules. When I say my name, the nanites form it into something that fits all the linguistic sound rules of their language."

Tria looked askance. "But then, why don't the nanites translate our names back when Nezim and Zeemz say them?"

"Hmm..." Kal furrowed his brow. "Good question. I hadn't thought of that."

Kal picked up his pad and pulled up the linguistics programs. He dumped the source code into his programming environment and scanned over the lines. He searched for the handling of proper nouns, and... Aha!

Tria stood up and came to look at the interface. "What is it?"

"It was the linguist who programmed the translation matrix from the first metaxic exploration teams. He went exploring with them and wanted to hear what his name and all the place names sounded like in the source language. He wanted to hear everything 'au naturel,' and made it so incoming proper nouns wouldn't get translated."

"I'm glad he did that." Tria reached for the interface. "May I?"

Kal nodded reluctantly. "Sure... just don't run any programs."

"I'll be careful," Tria said, already scanning over the files.

Funny. This was the first time Tria had shown any interest in Kal's computer beyond the organization of his filesystem. And where had this sudden fascination with language come from? Kal had never found languages particularly interesting.

Kal's train of thought was interrupted by the thud of the outer airlock doors opening and the subsequent whir of the exhaust fans expelling the Murk. A figure entered, took off its suit, and stuffed it into the cleanser. It was Nezim.

Kal sat and waited. Nezim walked to the table, his expression blank. Kal found he couldn't read Nezim at all.

"Zeemz isn't going to be able to help anymore," Nezim said.

Kal started to say something, but Nezim began speaking before he could get a word out. "The meteorolog's detected an approaching storm. Zeemz works on the biofarms and has to make preparations. And he's having a bit of trouble with his lab assistant. I can still help you for the rest of the day, but tomorrow morning the mobile will leave."

Kal nodded. A believable alibi. Maybe he was reading too much into Zeemz's attitude, and Zeemz really was just worried about the approaching storm.

"Wait," Tria said. "I don't understand. Why's a storm such a big deal?"

"Vogg experiences huge, rolling electrical and acid storms," Kal said.

Nezim continued. "They're very powerful. Mobile Ortie will have to fly up to a safe altitude, or the storm will destroy the shedds."

"Tomorrow morning..." Kal shook his head. "That gives us only one shot at this. You told me once that your computer systems were designed for two people to be at the controls."

"One person *can* make it work..." Nezim sat down at the table, facing Kal. "Look, we can give this a go with just us. Or we can give up. It's your choice."

"Let's try." Tria nodded eagerly.

Kal nodded his consent, but inside, his hope that this visit to Vogg would mean freedom from Tria was crumbling.

oe૮✓ා౦

"No, no! That's not right!" Kal shouted.

"There's nothing else to do, Kazl!"

Kal's nanites ran in an invisible chain from Kal's head to the chamber across the room. They had been trying for three hours, but the clone had yet to even twitch in response.

"Integrity of the neural network is just too low." Nezim exhaled heavily and jabbed a button on his console.

The static hum of the shedd's computer systems faded. Kal's pad reported that the nanite chain had gone inert. He ripped the Vogg tech off his head and launched from his metallic seat. "What are you doing?"

"We've done enough. I'm tired."

"We had a deal!"

"I'm sorry, Kazl, but without Zeemz, there's just no way to do this properly." Nezim walked to the cleanser and pulled out his suit. "I'm sure no one will mind keeping this body in stasis for now. If you come back in a few weeks, after the storm has passed and the acid pools have evaporated, I'm sure we'll be able to try again. With Zeemz next time, okay?"

Kal nodded, and Nezim hurried off toward the airlock. It hissed shut, sealing Nezim away as it closed.

Kal slammed his fist into the table. He watched Tria's hologram appear on its own.

"Hey!" Kal said, startled to see Tria able to control his projection.

"I've been learning how to operate the pad." Tria nodded vigorously, his eyes wide with excitement. "It's cool. I can 'see' the interface in my mind. I've even been thinking... maybe we could make it so the pad projects a second interface for me to use when I'm being projected. And I have some ideas for making the linguistics programs better. You'll let me work on it, right?"

Kal's expression remained dour. "Yeah, that'd be fine."

"What's wrong?" Tria sat down cross-legged on the floor and looked up at Kal.

"Well, now that you have access to the pad, I guess it's time for me to give you the nanoprogramming ethics lecture. I don't really know if I feel up to it though."

"Why not?" Tria looked up with those inquisitive eyes.

"It's... It's what I'm planning to do."

Tria's smile fell to a frown. "What do you mean?"

Kal rapped his fingers on the table. "You know, writing a program that changes some wind patterns, that shouldn't be too hard. I could even program a sequence of pressure changes, really make it appear like the alteration in the storm's course happened naturally."

Tria looked up at Kal. His eyes had lost their spark of admiration. He seemed sad, even afraid.

"What's the worst that could happen?" Kal said. "A different mobile has to move out of the way? They do that all the time."

"I don't know, Kal. This just seems like a bad idea. Do you think that these nanoprogramming ethics exist for a good reason? Are they laws worth following?"

"I think so, but these are pretty exceptional circumstances, right?"

"Sure. I mean, I guess you know more about metaxic travel... but this doesn't feel right." Tria's voice carried a solemnity that made Kal even more uncomfortable.

Kal pulled out his pad and stared at the interface. A blank programming prompt appeared before him with a small holographic cursor blinking continuously atop it, awaiting input.

oა<ༀ

The next morning, Kal walked into the foodshedd calmly. The inhabitants of Mobile Ortie were rushing about, grabbing quick bites of food and gulping down cartons of water rations before hurrying back outside.

Kal took a tray, strolled through the quickly moving queue, and casually plucked a few pieces of fruit from a growchamber. He spotted Zeemz and Nezim sitting at a table in most of their suits, arguing. By their frowns and animated hand gestures, the debate was clearly heated.

Kal swerved through the bustle and sat down beside Nezim. Their conversation ended abruptly.

"What's going on?" Kal asked.

Zeemz glared at him.

"The storm has veered northward," Nezim said. "It'll hit further up the lake."

Kal watched Zeemz carefully. If Zeemz had seemed wary at their last encounter, his gaze was now unequivocally hostile. The idea of this man commanding a computer connected to his brain made Kal more than a little nervous, even with the protection his nanites afforded him.

He also became aware for the first time of a certain something gnawing at the pit of his stomach. He realized his discomfort had actually begun the night before, but something about Zeemz's gaze amplified the malaise into an unbearable sickening feeling.

"So, you're not leaving after all?" Kal asked.

"That's right. Although it's unusual for a storm to change course—" Nezim turned to look at his brother. "—it's not unheard of."

Zeemz ignored Nezim, keeping his eyes locked onto Kal, probing. Kal looked at the fruit on his plate. Although he had entered the food-shedd famished, ready even to down the mobile's mushy, genetically engineered fruit, his appetite had evaporated.

"It has happened before," Zeemz said. He glanced at his brother, seeming to calm a bit, before turning back to Kal. "We'll help you try to move Zria. Both of us. Okay?"

Kal smiled and nodded. The queasy feeling in his stomach didn't go away though. Instead, it got worse.

Kal— Tria began thinking.

Not now, Kal thought back. He fought to keep himself smiling at Nezim and Zeemz, pretending that everything was just fine.

Zeemz spent the morning with Nezim planning the next set of bio-farms. Nezim was checking over his most recent genetic alterations, and Zeemz was planning both the configuration of the plots and his flight plan.

Despite the name "biofarm," the mobile didn't plant anything edible outdoors. The growchambers in the foodshedd provided sustenance for the entire community. Instead, the biofarms consisted of genetically engineered plants the size of trees. Kal had seen some of them up close. They had huge vacuum tentacles designed to inhale Murk and convert it into oxygen and nitrogen. The people of Vogg were trying to take their planet back from a state of utter devastation, one atmospheric molecule at a time.

While Nezim and Zeemz did their work, Kal used his nanites to run a biological integrity scan on the clone body.

"Hey, listen to this," Tria said, sitting at one of the labshedd computer terminals.

Kal set down his pad and turned to Tria.

"What you said yesterday about Vogg having more human history than Earth intrigued me," Tria said, "so I started reading their history books."

"You got into the mobile's computer network?"

"Yeah. A lot of their literature is publicly available. As you can imagine, most of it's pretty bleak."

"I'll bet."

"I found this history book for ten-year-olds. Listen to the section titles: 'Part 1: The Ancient Era,' 'Part 2: The Edenic Age,' 'Part 3: The Mechanization,' 'Part 4: The Gluttony,' 'Part 5: The Modern Age.'"

"That explains 'Gluttony-tech'," Kal said.

"Gluttony era technology." Tria nodded. "There's some dissension in the mobiles about exactly what constitutes Gluttony-tech. Most people seem to think everything that happened technologically and culturally during the Gluttony was a horrible mistake. Six hundred years into the Modern Age there was something called 'The Purge'—they destroyed a bunch of records and tech from the Gluttony era."

"Sounds like some perverse form of cultural self-flagellation." Kal twisted up his face.

Tria gulped and gazed intently at Kal, who let them both stew in their silence. Kal wasn't sure what he was feeling anymore. He just knew that something was very wrong.

Kal broke the silence in order to distract himself. "You know, a lot of the members of Mobile Ortie seem to think that nanites are Gluttony-tech. But there's another group, people like Nezim and Zeemz, who are curious enough or undecided enough to try and use nanotechnology to fix their world."

"And?" Tria rapped his fingers silently on the table.

"I used to be sure that Nezim and Zeemz's camp was right. I'm not anymore."

oϾ⨳ᕤᕛ

Kal sat in the chair facing the clone capsule while Nezim and Zeemz manned their respective computer terminals on either side of him.

The work went slowly at first. Kal had to rebuild the chain of nanites and calibrate it to interpret signals from the labshedd computers. Building connections to the synapses in the clone's brain took even longer.

Nezim wiped the sweat from his brow with his forearm. Zeemz exhaled heavily. Kal tried to focus on his pad, but the aching in of his stomach kept interrupting his concentration.

I think something's happening, Tria thought to Kal.

"Tria's felt something," Kal announced.

"Good," Nezim said. "How many neural connections have your nanites made into the clone's brain?"

"Forty billion."

"You're going to need more."

"I know. They're still building."

I'm sensing another place. It's like a door to a room is opening, and the lights are coming on inside.

"Hold on," Kal said.

"What? Why?" Zeemz shouted down amidst frantic jabs at his keyboard.

"Sorry, I was talking to Tria. He's beginning to sense the clone's mind as a place he can inhabit."

"That's good," Nezim said. "That's really good."

Kal, I'm being pulled toward that place. I don't know how long I'm going to be able to fight it.

"Try," Kal said. Forty-four billion neural connections. "Just a few more minutes."

Nezim and Zeemz typed furiously while Kal's hands flew over his own interface. Every moment brought millions of new connections, and each new cluster seemed to create even more potential points of failure than that last. Nezim and Zeemz were only barely holding on to their end.

Kal, something's happening.

Both Nezim and Zeemz looked up at the clone body.

"Say that again, Tria," Kal insisted.

"I said something's happening!" Kal could hear Tria's voice both in his head and from the speaker on the clone's chamber.

Its lips were moving!

"Yes!" Kal cheered. "Fifty billion connections. It's working!"

"Keep building those connections, Kal," Nezim shouted down.

"I'm sensing some instabilities in the connection chain," Zeemz broke in. "There's not enough cohesion on our side. Damn it!"

"No, it's working," Tria said through the clone's body.

The labshedd's lighting altered from its stable, dim white to a dark red of oscillating intensity. A message ran in a repeated arc across Labshedd Five's ring of monitors, in large lettering: 'Storm Imminent.'

"Kal, what's happening?" fear laced Tria's voice, which sounded clear in his head, but the clone's lips stuttered and its voice crackled.

"I'm aborting this." Zeemz's fingers slammed into his keyboard.

"What?" Kal turned to him. "No!"

"That storm that *mysteriously* veered north." Zeemz fumed. "It merged with another. They've become a supercell, big enough to wipe out *every single* biofarm this side of Lake Mezg. And it's going to run right through Mobile Agarba before it hits us."

Kal barely managed to turn his gaze up to Zeemz, who glared at him through narrow eyes, and said, "If I thought it would work, I would mindwipe you here and now. Leave us. And take your technosickness with you."

Zeemz stormed toward the airlock. Kal heard the furious rustle of Zeemz putting on his suit.

Before Zeemz left, he shouted back, "Oh, and one more thing, be sure to tell Nezim how you made the clone talk. I'm sure he'll be interested in the *tech* behind it."

The airlock whooshed open, then clamped shut with its latching thud. The moment Kal heard it, the gnawing feeling in the pit of his stomach exploded throughout his entire being into fear and regret. He was sweating profusely and panting. He tore the wire contraption from his head, dizzy and nauseated.

He couldn't hear Tria's voice, either in his head or from the clone.

"Tria?" Kal tried. "Tria!"

No response.

Kal lurched from the chair. He stumbled toward the clone chamber and clamped his hands onto the glass. The clone's lips remained limp and dead.

Kal brought up his hands to cover his mouth. "Tria..."

He had not known that such extremes of the emotions he was feeling now were even possible. He knew now, certainly, that his choices had been poor, and innocent, newborn Tria had paid the price for Kal's mistake.

Kal? came a thought inside his head as though from a great distance.

I'm here, Tria thought, closer this time.

"Tria!" Kal gasped and gushed tears of relief. Tria activated his hologram, standing beside Kal. He tried to put his hand on Kal's shoulder, though the two passed right through each other.

Kal smiled, wishing he could hug his... what was Tria?

Realization washed over him. Tria was his brother. Kal had grown up an only child, but now he had someone he could call a brother.

"Kazl," Nezim said, his form barely visible amidst the dim, red lighting. Nezim walked between Kal and the clone chamber.

"Kazl," Nezim tried again, and Kal looked at him, wiping the tears from his face.

"Zeemz and I," Nezim paused, biting his lip. "When we ran the psychological tests, we couldn't find any differences between you and Zria."

"What?" Kal and Tria said in unison.

Nezim laughed a bit at that—a dull, hollow laugh.

"In each of the dozens of tests, your brain showed *exactly* the same activity when it was your turn as when it was Zria's. There was no difference at all."

"I don't understand. You mean, you think we're the same pers—" Kal's eyes went wide. "You think I'm crazy."

"Your nanotechnology is so far beyond us, I don't know what I think," Nezim said. "But I know you wouldn't use your nanites to tamper with our environment. Zeemz... Zeemz thinks you would. He's wrong, isn't he?"

Kal's opened his mouth, but nothing came out. His lower lip quivered and faltered. He bit it and looked at the floor.

"Kazl, he's wrong, isn't he?" Nezim leaned into the capsule, staring Kal down.

Kal tried to tear his gaze away from the floor and found that he couldn't.

Nezim frowned. He walked to his computer station.

"What are you doing?" Kal looked up. Nezim said nothing, just jabbed at his keyboard.

A horrible burbling sound erupted from the capsule. Kal swivelled around to see the clone body reduced to a pool of pale, gray goo.

"Nezim, I'm so sorry," Kal said. "I can fix things, I promise. I'll disperse the storm. I won't do any more damage, I—"

"Then what, Kazl?" Nezim slammed a fist into the computer keyboard. "Will another storm take its place? And then will you *help* us get rid of that one too? And what about the next one? And the next? Will all of Vogg become one enormous storm? Will Mobile Ortie be the only mobile left when you're done? Humanity on Vogg is screwed up enough already, Murkwalker. We don't need *any* more help from you." Nezim strode to the cleanser, where he ripped out his suit and threw it on. He then smashed a fist into the airlock control panel before storming out of Labshedd Five.

Kal slid to the ground, his back against the clone chamber. "I'm so sorry, Tria."

Tria crouched down beside him, nodding. "I appreciate how hard you tried."

Kal smiled a little through his tears. "But I screwed everything up so bad. It might have worked, if only I'd been willing to wait."

"Hey," Tria said, the red, oscillating lights reaching their most luminous point. "Aren't there supposed to be thousands of explorable worlds still waiting for us? We'll fix me up on one of those. We'll fix both ourselves."

Kal watched Tria's smile fade against the dimming red, a smile that was also his own.

"Come on." Tria offered Kal a hand he couldn't take. "Let's get out of here."

Kal stood up and stared into the casket of goo one final time before turning on his pad. With shaky hands, he activated the metaxic nodes.

ⲟⲉ�̸ⲟⲟ

Zeemz stormed into Labshedd Seven. Liza sat at her console gazing intently at her monitor. Her hands flew over the keyboard.

"We ready for takeoff?" Zeemz asked, throwing his helmet and gloves down onto the floor.

Liza winced, then turned, eyeing him warily. "Yes."

Zeemz collected himself. With a storm incoming, now was not the time for emotional outbursts. Labshedd Seven's safety and Liza's life had become his responsibility the moment he'd stepped through the airlock.

"Take us up," Zeemz said, sitting down at his control station.

The engines rumbled beneath him. Their dome lurched off the

ground and ascended rapidly. A holographic projector displayed the incoming storm, only a few minutes away. He'd cut that one way too close. He was lucky to have Liza assigned to him. A more anxious and less trustworthy lab aid would have flown off without him.

Labshedd Seven had no windows, just diagrams on the monitors to guide them through the thickening and electrically charged Murk.

"Mobile Ortie is secure," Liza said. "The meteorolog reports the entire mobile is safely above stormtop."

The emergency lights in the labshedd ceased, and the dim, white lighting resumed. Above stormtop, there was no danger. They would now wait until the meteorolog found a suitable location for resettlement.

Zeemz sighed and closed his eyes. His next question was a difficult one. He was glad Liza sat behind him, unable to see the strain his face would undoubtedly project.

"How about Mobile Agarba?" Zeemz asked, his voice almost a whisper.

"Didn't you hear?" Liza said. "Mobile Agarba informed us of the storm. They picked it up and reported it before our own meteorolog detected it. They're all above stormtop and accounted for."

Zeemz breathed deeply, a breath he didn't even know he was holding. Hez was safe.

He found the controls for the audio log, the mics that recorded everything, and turned them all off. He made a show of it, projected his actions to the shedd's main display so that Liza could see what he'd done. Then he turned around to face her.

"Are you pregnant, Liza?"

Her face turned bright red. "I... um... how did you...?"

"You know Treaza?"

"I've seen her. She's emotionally undead, so I really haven't talked to—"

"She had my son, when we were your age," Zeemz said. "Treaza ran away with him. The mobile asked me to help find them both, and I did. But if I could do it again, I'd sabotage the mobile's search instead."

Liza stared at him, unblinking.

"Liza, I don't— if you... need help, if you decide you need to..." Zeemz gulped and took a deep breath. "If you need to get away from the Mobile system, I promise I will help you. This is not a ruse or a trick. This storm below us, it's my fault, in a way. I want to make better decisions. Decisions I won't regret. If you need help, I'm here for you."

It took a moment, but Liza managed a small smile.

Zeemz stood and took a step closer to her. Liza lurched out of her seat and hugged him. He returned the embrace.

"I don't know what I'll do yet," Liza whispered, wiping her eyes before she drew away and threw herself back down into the chair.

"You'd make a damn good bioengineer." Zeemz squatted to face her at eye level. "Why are you in farming?"

Liza sighed and sniffled. "I wanted to spend more time with Razz. Seems so stupid now."

Zeemz recognized the regret in her voice, in the way she held herself, in the way she looked at the wall. The worst and most violent part of the storm surged beneath them. Deep booms of thunder and the crackling of multiple lightning strikes echoed through the floor.

"Hey," Zeemz said. "It's not too late. And you're not alone."

"It's funny," Liza said. "We're trying so hard to fix our world... Maybe we should fix ourselves first."

Zeemz smiled. Her philosophizing never failed to remind him of Nezim, and the anger he'd felt for his tradebrother washed away. He walked back to the console and turned the audio log back on.

"Labshedd Seven, you okay?" a voice burst through the speakers. "We've been trying to reach you for almost two minutes now. Is something wrong over there?"

Zeemz replied with "no" at the same moment that Liza replied with "yes."

He raised an eyebrow at her.

"Yes," Liza said again, louder and more confidently. "There's a problem."

"Do you need a repair drone?"

Liza looked at Zeemz. He smiled, taking in her meaning.

"No," she said. "I think we'll be able to take care of it ourselves."

Norselands

Realm #8720, "Vanaheim"
July 3, 2178

"HUH. THAT'S WEIRD." Kal scratched his head. He stood in his bubble, the metaxia swirling beyond its invisible wall.

Tria looked up from his own holointerface. "What's going on?"

"Well, when the nanites first made the grid, the one that returned from realm 8720 reported an Earth-like atmosphere and land. But I sent one just now, and it found only a vacuum. No planet."

"Yeah, that is weird." Tria scooted across the bubble floor, his interface floating along with him. "Could the planet have a different orbit around the sun, or something like that?"

Kal nodded. "Yeah, but the program can correct for that variation. This is the first time a nanite has registered an Earth-like environment on one trip and space on the next. They have been tricked before, though."

Tria looked up at the bubble ceiling, a hand on his chin. "You mean the hologram chamber on Spele, right?"

"Yeah." Kal sent off another reconnaissance nanite, just to be sure. Same result. "I doubt they're holographically generating the void of space."

"You checked that the metaxic coordinates matched the realm designation, right?" Tria asked.

"Yup."

Tria typed out the commands himself and promptly furrowed his brow. "Same thing."

Tria nudged Kal with his holographic elbow, grinning and smiling. "Hey, I have an idea. Check this out."

Kal glanced over and watched his brother type out a new program. First, Tria programmed the nanites to exit the metaxia five thousand kilometers above the place where the surface of Earth was supposed to be. Then, he had them set to render a still of it, looking down from space. If there was something—anything—there, they should be able to detect it.

Tria offered his interface to Kal to let him execute the code, dutifully remembering his nanoprogramming ethics.

Kal motioned back to Tria. "By all means. It's your program."

Tria tapped at his keyboard. The programming console disappeared, and they waited. A hologram of a spinning hourglass twirled around itself in the air. Kal crossed his arms.

The hourglass disappeared, and an image of a planet filled the interface, but it was a planet unlike any Kal had ever seen.

It was shaped like an apple core with a central disc. The top and bottom of the core were rounded and smooth, probably the one-time poles. The equator remained intact too—the edge of the central disc. However, the majority of both the northern and the southern hemispheres were gone, just blown out. It was as though an enormous, cosmic ice cream scoop had spun around them, leaving carved out nothing where continents and oceans had once been.

"What the hell is that?" Tria laughed nervously.

"That's quite an Earth." Kal pulled his eyes from the image to type out more code. "We need more pictures."

"And gravimetric data, too," Tria said. "If their planet's lost that much mass, it can't possibly have enough gravity to support an atmosphere or human life."

More data streamed in.

"Nope, look at that," Kal pointed to information populating in new windows on his interface. "There are two rings of land, one in each carved out hemisphere, about three hundred kilometers wide and eight thousand kilometers around. See, there are the clouds."

"And look," Tria pointed to a graph that had just popped into existence. "The core of this planet is denser than Earth's. Gravity at the bottom of the chasms is roughly Earth normal. Hey, I know. Let's do a video."

Tria tapped out more commands, and the hourglass hologram spun a few more times before being replaced by a looping video of the strange planet.

They both gasped in awe simultaneously, smiling. The planet was spinning around its z-axis instead of its y. The circular chunks of land attached to rocky pillars were flying towards and then away from the sun.

"*That's* why the first nanite registered land!" Kal snapped his fingers. "One of those... circles at the top of the poles must have been the surface that the first nanite visited."

Tria nodded. "Talk about a stroke of luck. Imagine missing out on the opportunity to explore this place."

"No kidding." Kal tapped at his interface, adjusting the spatial coordinates for the metaxic bubble's entry. "I'm going to set us down in... well, whatever is underneath where Chicago should be. There's a fairly big city down there. I'll put us a few kilometers outside of it."

ᴏᴄ⌢ᴏ

Kal's bubble fizzled away, leaving him and Tria in a forest clearing surrounded by tall, blue conifers. The sun shone down, and gusts of wind wafted over them, singing as they passed through the branches of the stalwart firs.

Just like he had on Ydora and other inhabited worlds, Kal would hang around the countryside for the first few hours, away from populated areas. Trying to speak to anyone when his words still sounded like alien gibberish could be disastrous.

The pad's sartorial program flickered from red to green. Kal activated it, and both his and Tria's clothing shimmered in a brief flurry of nanotech and holographic activity. The clothes were comfortable, light slacks and a sleeveless shirt with a ribbed collar. Blue and gray tones were apparently the predominant fashion here.

Kal lifted his eyes from his clothing to the skyline, and he gazed around himself, transfixed. In the east and west, a blue sky, as on Earth. However, in the north and south, the ground curved upwards. The forest, instead of disappearing behind a horizon, rolled up into the sky, set against the bottom of their rocky bowl of land. The treeline ended before the angle got too steep, and rocky mountains shot up into a dark haze.

"Imagine that," Kal said. Both he and Tria gazed up at the massive, curving wall of mineral rock.

They both shook their heads and began examining the trees. Not only were the needles bluer than earth's pines, but on closer inspection, they discovered that all them, as well as the pinecones, were enclosed in an incredibly tough casing.

Kal flicked one of the needles with his finger, and it barely budged. Solid as a rock.

"You could impale people on these things," Tria chuckled, looking over Kal's shoulder. "Let's hope that's not part of their culture."

Kal didn't return the laugh. Although he had explained all about nanoprogramming ethics to Tria—once he'd calmed down enough from their experience on Vogg—he had yet to tell Tria about the reports of Earth's first metaxic explorers, most notably Team Haskell.

"Vanaheim," Tria said, gazing at his interface.

"That's where the Vanir live in Norse mythology," Kal replied. "But what's that got to do with—?"

"It's what they call this planet."

Kal blinked.

"Seriously?" Kal pulled out his pad and checked the linguistic database.

"The planet's name is Vanaheim. This, um, hemisphere is called Midgard. The city five kilometers away is Thrudvangar, and so on. I could keep going."

Kal scratched his head. Darkness rushed over the clearing. He looked up to see clouds had rolled in. Snow began to dust the forest.

"That's one rapid sunset," Tria said as the ambient light rapidly waned.

"The sun must have slipped behind that big equator disc—whoa!" Kal's pants seized up, no longer the loose and light fabric they had been just moments before. They had morphed into a skintight, wetsuit-like material and sprouted a fuzzy layer of hairs. His sleeveless shirt grew sleeves, unwinding all the way down to his wrists. His pants underwent a similar transformation, fitting tightly around Kal's torso and sprouting hairs as well. The collar of his shirt engulfed his neck and wrapped itself over his head, forming a furry hood.

Tria, whose holographic clothes were unaffected by the environment, chuckled as Kal tugged at his new clothing in places he hadn't appreciated it constricting.

"Hey, laugh all you want." Kal shot his brother a look, still adjusting himself. "This stuff is warm. Really warm."

Tria just laughed harder. Kal smirked and pulled out his pad. He pressed a button to force an update to Tria's clothing so that it matched his own.

Tria scoffed playfully and spun around with his own interface held forward. "Looks like you're going to need the insulation."

His brother's interface depicted the current temperature, and the number was descending rapidly. The light of the sun disappeared completely behind the great disc, shrouding the forest in complete darkness.

The snowflakes grew larger and fell faster, their shadows dancing about the conifers in the glow of Kal and Tria's interfaces.

Kal searched his pad for the molecular configuration of a simple tent and instructed his nanites to build it. "We'll wait out the night and explore the city tomorrow."

oc⏚ co

Kal set up a nanite perimeter around his tent. The temperature continued to fall until it settled just below freezing, and the snow piled up around their tent.

Tria busied himself reading up on Vanaheim's language. Kal had watched Tria's linguistic fascination grow with each new world they visited. Kal had always been happy to let his nanites translate to and from English wherever he went, but ever since he had told Tria about the linguistic programs, Tria had always immersed himself in the language database of whatever place they found themselves exploring.

Kal had begun noticing other personality differences, and they had been getting more and more pronounced. He had assumed, since the two of them were supposed to share the same psyche, that they'd have the same interests. But just as UsrLocal had said, Tria was essentially a snapshot of Kal's mind set loose on its own. Even though the pad projected Tria as Kal's clone, the two of them were becoming more distinct by the day.

Kal took up his pad and started programming. He sent his nanites out in successive waves, further and further each time. He glanced at their reports idly between programming. Sometime around midnight, Kal gave a bit of a start.

"What is it?" Tria turned to Kal.

"Nanogenic radiation!" Kal's voice was barely audible.

Tria scrambled over to look at Kal's interface. "Where? How much?"

"Not anywhere near here, and probably not even enough to make me more than a bit short of breath, even if I got near the source."

Kal pressed more buttons. The new data calmed him. "Thrudvangar's totally clean. The radiation is concentrated at the edge of the forest, where the incline of the ground gets steeper."

"So, they've got, what, feral nanotech running around their mountains?"

"That's what it looks like." Kal raised an eyebrow. "Well, it certainly wouldn't be the most ridiculous thing I've seen."

"How about I set up nanite sentries to issue an alarm if any of those Vanaheim nanites come near here?"

"Sounds like a plan." Kal yawned.

He could see his breath, so he checked the temperature on his pad. It was dropping again. He set the nanites to the task of keeping the temperature constant inside the tent. As his final task, Kal found the blueprint for a sleeping bag and pillow in his pad's filesystem and had the nanites build them.

"Night, Tria."

"Night," Tria replied absently, still poring over Vanaheim's linguistic database.

Kal lay down and drifted off to sleep.

Kal! Tria's thoughts broke through Kal's unconsciousness. *Kal, wake up!*

Kal opened his eyes to utter darkness. Kal pulled his hands out of his sleeping bag and began searching for his pad. The cold stung his hands and arms, but he continued grasping about the floor of the tent.

Stay still, Tria thought. *We're in trouble. The perimeter nanites have been deactivated, and the ones in the tent aren't responding to my commands for light or heat either.*

How's that possible? Kal thought.

Not sure. The pad is disabled too.

As carefully and quietly as he could, Kal reached out again through the frigid air and felt around the surface of the tent for his pad. His hand ran into its icy, metallic surface, and he clasped it. He jammed his thumb into the lower left indentation, but to no avail. The device remained inactive.

This happened once before, Kal thought.

Before me?

Right before you. On Lehr. UsrLocal managed to shut down the pad when I got inside his brain.

A twig snapped outside. His heart nearly stopped, and it was everything he could do to keep still, though he desperately wanted to activate his nodes and get off this world. Its strange shape had markedly diminished in appeal.

A bright flash of light burst all around him, and Kal squinted. At first, he thought it was some kind of spotlight, but then he realized it was coming all directions and must have been the light of dawn.

"Get out here!" a male voice called out. "Do you want to be caught in the flodth?"

What's a flodth? Kal thought to Tria.

I think it's like 'flood.' Kal, the temperature is climbing pretty rapidly, and there was a lot of snowfall last night, so...

Got it. Can't stay here.

His clothing was loosening up. The little hairs retracted into the fabric, and the shirt's hood and sleeves rolled back up into nothing. The air was cool and wet, but warming rapidly.

He took a deep breath and unzipped the tent.

"I'm coming out!" he shouted.

It was only a minute or so after dawn, but the sun blasted down from a clear sky. The trees of the forest dripped small torrents, veritable rivers running down through their spiky, blue needles. A cold steam trailed upward in wisps, and the sound of fizzling snow emanated from every direction.

Before Kal stood a lithe teen with blond hair and a long face, dressed in clothing similar to Kal's. He was maybe two meters tall, but still young. If he was older than Kal, it was not by much.

His face was blank, no emotion.

Kal stepped out of the tent slowly. "Hi. My name's Kal."

The young man crossed his arms.

"Tall, silent type. Got it." Kal laughed a bit.

His counterpart continued staring icily.

"So, um, what brings you out into the forest—?"

There was an explosion of yellow light, and Kal felt a strong force at his side push him to the ground.

Just like that, he was unconscious once more.

⚬⚬◁⚬⚬

"I told you there was something off about that nanotechnology," a female voice said.

"So, what, he's from some realm the annarsveinns didn't visit? How'd he find us?" The blond guy's voice.

Kal opened his eyes. Everything was hazy, a dark smear of browns and oranges.

"Ask him yourself." The female voice again.

Kal blinked a few times, his vision coming into focus. He lay slumped in a wooden chair. He shook his head to clear the grogginess and tried to stand. Dizziness overwhelmed him. He stumbled and grabbed the back of the chair for stability.

He gazed around himself at the large, ornate chamber with a tall, triangular roof. Behind him, in the center of the room, lay a rectangle of tables surrounding a hovering, self-contained orb of fire.

Near him stood the young man he had seen in the forest, and a young woman. She had long, light brown braids and the same blue eyes as her counterpart. They had the same tall cheekbones and shape to their eyes—siblings.

The three of them were not alone. In front of Kal, a short set of stairs led up to a platform with two men, maybe in their thirties, each occupying a chair, the frames of which were covered in etchings of people and animals, all arranged in a twisting series of frames that seemed to tell a story.

"Sorry about shooting you," the young woman said, though her tone didn't indicate any hint of genuine regret.

"We thought you were a jotun," the young man added.

Kal wondered what a jotun was to these people. In Norse mythology, they were supposed to be giants. Clearly, he hadn't been mistaken for one of those.

"Welcome, annarsvein," the man in the left chair said, looking down at Kal. Even though Kal's eyesight had fully normalized, he could only just make out the man's face in the dim light. The fiery sphere was the sole source of illumination for the large room.

"My name is Magni."

"And I am Modi," The man beside him said. "You probably have many questions about Vanaheim. But I'm afraid they must wait for another time. My brother and I are preparing for Hringsaend, and these two must yet complete their saga."

The young man took a step forward. "But we thought that bringing in an Idavoll jotun would be our saga!"

Modi shook his head. "Thjalfi, your saga is set, and you may not change or abdicate the task so long as we breathe."

Magni's eyes turned calm yet severe. "You could find Odin wandering the forest for all we care. You will tell your story at the jotunfaething, and that is final."

Thjalfi turned away from Modi and Magni. His sister grabbed his arm, but he shrugged her off and loped out the door. The sister narrowed her eyes at Kal before marching after her brother. She slammed the door to the chamber behind her.

Kal winced and turned his attention back to Magni and Modi. "So, um, are they in trouble or something? I'm sorry if my camping messed up his saga."

Magni and Modi both took a moment to breathe, exhaling deeply. Kal looked them over. There was something off about them. Each of them sat slightly slouched, the posture of tired, old men. But oddly, their bodies looked youthful, and their voices rang of strength and fortitude.

"Thjalfi and Roskva's situation is... unique," Modi said. "Thjalfi is the only one responsible for not completing his saga. Your presence here does not disturb us or the citizens of Thrudvangar. Please feel free to explore our city."

"My nanites and computer, they're both inoperable."

Magni nodded knowingly. He touched a panel on the arm of his chair, grimacing at performing the simple motion of moving his hand. A few button presses later, he nodded to Kal.

Kal put his thumb on the pad, and its holographic interface reappeared.

"How old a technology are nanites on your world, Kal?" Magni asked.

Kal smiled up at them proudly. "About sixty years."

Magni and Modi exchanged grins, and Kal's expression fell.

"What? How long have you had nanotechnology on Vanaheim?"

Modi composed himself. "Over twenty-one thousand years."

"Wait, so that would make your culture—"

"Twenty-five thousand years old," Magni finished for him. "We've had experiences with nanotechnology that would make your hair stand on end, Kal. Let me guess, you've laced your world with them. You believe you have culturally progressed to the point where you no longer worry about humans commandeering them for sinister purposes. Well, Vanaheim has been there before. Four times, in fact."

"The end of that legacy lives up near the Fjallvegg. The, um…" Modi tilted his head, apparently aware that Kal's nanites were not translating proper nouns.

"Mountainwall," Magni suggested.

"Yes, the place where the ground reaches up into the sky. We call it the Fjallvegg. It's the home of jotuns, remnants of the last malevolent nano-AI that nearly destroyed Midgard."

"Ah," Kal nodded. "So Thjalfi and Roskva detected my nanites and assumed that I was a jotun… from Idavoll?"

Magni and Modi nodded.

"We must ask you to refrain from using your nanotechnology inside the city limits of Thrudvangar and the other cities of Midgard," Modi said. "All of our citizens, as well as our technological infrastructure, will respond as Thjalfi and Roskva did—they'll perceive it as a threat."

"'Your citizens?' Are you leaders?"

Magni and Modi exchanged nervous glances.

"We are the unending," Modi said, pausing. "A naive person might think us 'gods.'"

Magni grimaced. "We are cultural leaders. Nothing more."

"Please, Kal," Modi straightened himself in his chair. "We know you must have many questions about Vanaheim, but we will have to answer them another time. Our hringsa will shortly be complete, and we have much to do. Come back in six months and we will be able to answer all of your questions in detail."

Kal couldn't believe how tired both of the men behaved, compared to the power and youthfulness their forms suggested, and the complete presence their voices lent them.

"Thank you for your help." Kal smiled.

He turned and exited the chamber the way that Thjalfi and Roskva had gone.

Kal exited the building into a large plaza. At the center stood an enormous spherical structure. A hammer, about the size of Kal himself, spun at its center, hovering in midair. Around it, flat metal rings whirled at various distances, each along a different axis. They'd all rotate in one configuration for a few moments, and then their trajectories would shift and they'd begin spinning anew.

He couldn't imagine how such a thing could be achieved without nanites, but then he recalled that the humans of Vanaheim had been exploring the mysteries of the universe for twenty-one thousand years longer than his people on Earth had.

The sun shone down clearly, maybe an hour away from setting behind the mountainwall. Its light glistened off the wooden houses that circled the plaza, their faces a myriad of cool blues, grays, yellows, deep greens and maroons. Each of their high, pointed roofs sported an intricate system of gutters, which led into a series of aqueducts that ran between and through the houses.

A train car, shaped like a bullet, but pointed at both ends, zipped silently through the air behind the houses. It followed the course of a metal monorail track, although the track and the train car didn't appear to be physically connected.

The people in the plaza didn't take much notice of Kal, even though he was only as tall as the shortest adult. His scruffy, dark brown hair stood out in the sea of mostly blond.

A group of men and women entered the plaza from his right. They wore different clothes than the other Thrudvangar citizens, beige overalls with long, white undershirts underneath. They were covered in dirt and talking loudly amongst themselves. They passed by Kal and the hammer contraption, then disappeared down another street.

Roskva emerged from that very street carrying a small, metallic device. She strode purposefully through the plaza, and Kal ran to catch up with her.

"Roskva?" Kal tried.

She sneered at him.

"Hey look, I'm sorry I messed up your… saga. Is there anything I can do to help?"

"No." She continued walking down the twisty street.

"What do you need a saga for, anyway?"

"Listen." She was still striding forward, not making eye contact. "It was hard enough to get Thjalfi out into the forest that first time. It will be even harder to get him out there again. You've really helped enough."

Roskva picked up her pace, turned, and ran up a metal staircase at the base of the monorail track. A bulletcar hovered into view and stopped just as she stepped onto the platform. She boarded the bullet, and it sped away.

Kal folded his arms, tapped his foot, and gazed down the street. He refused to leave Vanaheim until he had undone his interference in the forest. Though his actions had caused no acid storms and nothing of value had been destroyed, the idea of leaving this mess for Thjalfi to solve on his own did not sit well with him. He would help them finish their sagas.

Roskva was clearly not willing to accept his help, but perhaps he could reach Thjalfi.

He wondered where Tria had run off to. Kal would need help tracking down Roskva's brother, and there wasn't much sunlight left. Nanite-disembodied Tria could cover more ground than Kal could.

A female passerby caught Kal's attention. She approached a short, fat device at the corner of an intersection that looked like the stump of a lamp post.

"Erlend Bodilsen," the woman said.

A holointerface burst from the device showing a map and a route. She studied it momentarily before walking away, and it deactivated automatically.

Kal walked up to it himself.

"Thjalfi," he said.

The holointerface reactivated and held a message: 'One hundred eighty-two entries. Please state surname.'

"Cross referential search?" Kal tried.

'Enter parameters,' the machine responded.

"Sister and brother, Roskva and Thjalfi."

A moment passed, and then, 'Thjalfi and Roskva Lindgren.'

"Thjalfi Lindgren."

A map appeared, and Kal smiled.

Kal entered what the sign called a mead hall, but Kal recognized it immediately for what it was—a bar. He gazed around the room tentatively.

It looked much like the chamber Magni and Modi sat in, with the same sphere of fire hovering in the center of a rectangle of tables, but it was far less intricately adorned and even more poorly lit.

Kal spotted Thjalfi, sitting alone at the far corner of the rectangle. When he realized people had started staring at him, he searched his memory and remembered that, in a bar, you were supposed to order a drink. He walked to the counter at the far end of the long room.

"What'll it be?" the bearded bartender asked.

Kal paused, looking around in vain for some kind of menu.

"Ale?" He hoped that would be general enough.

The bartender's eyes grew wide. A group of customers sitting nearby turned and looked at him with smiles plastered across their faces.

Kal opened his mouth with the intent of canceling his order and asking for a beverage list, but the bartender cut him off. "One ale."

The bearded man reached under the counter, pulled out a glass mug the size of Kal's head, and positioned it under a spout that looked neglected from disuse. The spout sputtered, and a yellow-brown liquid spewed forth. The customers near Kal were stifling laughter now.

The barkeeper handed over the mug, and it took all of Kal's strength to hold it level. He walked, very carefully, to where Thjalfi sat and put the beverage down next to him, still managing to splash some of it onto his hands despite his best efforts.

"Thor in Himinn." Thjalfi started. "What is that?"

"Ale?" Kal said.

Thjalfi shook his head and downed the rest of his drink. He held not a mug, but some kind of leathery pouch with a spout at its end.

"Haven't you ever been to a hall, annarsveinn?" Thjalfi asked. "I mean, you do have them on your world, right?"

"Yeah, we do, but... no, I haven't."

"How did you manage to find Thrudvangar? Annarsveinns from other realms usually don't find us because of our planet's unusual shape."

"By accident, actually. I'm surprised though. You've never found other universes where Vanaheim has this shape?"

"Nope. Only Vanaheim and our metaxic cluster. Any world where the Ragnarok happened. Vanaheim used to be spherical too."

Kal waited, but Thjalfi just sat there staring at the empty pouch.

"Tell me about the Ragnarok." Kal grinned.

Thjalfi glared back and slammed his hands onto the table. "Thor, I'm not telling any stories. I'm not some Himinn-damned skald."

"Hey!" someone shouted from down the table. "I didn't come here to listen to kids disrespect their elders."

Thjalfi stood up. "I was just leaving."

"Is there money here?" Kal nodded to his enormous drink.

"Himinn, no," Thjalfi said. "Though you might want to drink a bit of it at least."

Kal took a sip of the stuff. It was sour and bitter, but the strongest taste sensation brought to mind dirt and tree bark. He did his best not to gag. He looked up to see that Thjalfi was already at the door. Kal abandoned the tankard and ran after him.

"What are you going to do about your saga?" Kal asked.

"Thor, you just don't give up, do you?"

Thjalfi and Kal stepped outside. Their clothing seized up immediately, becoming tight and furry, forming hoods and sleeves. Snow fell, piling up in the streets around them.

"Look, I'm sorry I messed up your saga. I want to help. You're supposed to go back to the forest, right?"

Thjalfi sighed. "Those things in the forest, the jotuns that Roskva and I have to face, the nanites they're made of aren't going to... Look, they're very advanced. There's not a lot you can do to help."

Thjalfi began walking away again, and Kal struggled to keep up with him. Damn, these Vanaheimers had long legs.

"Then tell me," Kal said. "When I go out into the forest, if my nanotechnology is so inferior it doesn't stand a chance against the jotuns, how do I defend myself? You and Roskva must have something planned, unless your saga is a deathtrap."

That stopped Thjalfi. He walked back and looked Kal directly in the eyes.

"There's only one thing that works against them: the truth."

Kal cocked his head. "The truth? The truth about what?"

"Nevermind." Thjalfi turned and walked away.

"Damn it!" Kal shouted. A dam burst within him. "You know about the metaxia. Haven't any of you actually been out there? Can't you know what it's like, constantly hopping from world to world, everything always different, never knowing if the people you meet are friendly or..." He couldn't bring himself to finish the sentence.

Thjalfi stopped, shrugged and tromped back through the newly fallen snow. He looked down at Kal and crossed his arms. A thin smile broke threw his stern demeanor. "You're travelling alone... not because you want to, but because..."

"I just want to find a way to go home." Kal gulped. He did his best to stand tall and keep his shoulders back, but part him just wanted to collapse into a sobbing mess.

Thjalfi sighed deeply and put a hand on Kal's shoulder. "You *really* want to come with me and Roskva?"

"Absolutely."

"Fine. I can't argue with Roskva forever and I can't spend my whole life in the hall. We'll go hunt some jotuns. Tomorrow, when I'm sober. C'mon, I'll tell you more about them."

oꝋꝋꝋꝋꝋ

Thjalfi offered to let Kal stay the night in a spare room of the house he and Roskva lived in. Kal asked about their parents, but Thjalfi would only say that they had both passed away.

He left Kal alone in the room, and Kal lay down on the soft bed and began exploring Thrudvangar's computer network with his pad. After some time had passed, he heard Roskva enter the house. Kal tensed up, remembering his earlier interaction with her, but when Thjalfi explained Kal's presence to her, she didn't seem to mind. Or at least, she didn't discuss it with him near the door to Kal's room.

He lay down on his bed, made himself comfortable, and then started when Tria abruptly shimmered into existence beside him. Tria searched around himself and found a chair, making himself comfortable.

Kal crossed his arms. "Where the hell have you been?"

"Two words, Kal: Yggdrasil Archive."

"That's the massive digital library, right?" Kal had read about it while trolling around their net.

"More than a library. Way more. And I got to be *inside* it. You wouldn't believe it. They've stored the linguistic evolution of every culture on the entire planet for the last twenty-two millennia! And there are millions of stories, maybe even billions, going back for twenty-five thousand years.

We're talking staggering amounts of computer memory. And the stories Kal, you wouldn't believe how well some of these are written. This culture has gotten storytelling down."

"Sagas, you mean?"

"Well, those stories are special. Some kind of coming-of-age thing. It's all linked to varheyd. You have to prove your varheyd before you're considered an adult here."

"What's varheyd?"

"For the coming-of-age ritual, it means 'fortitude' or 'strength of character.' But literally, it means 'truthfulness.'"

Kal pondered this a moment. "I'm going into the forest with Thjalfi and Roskva tomorrow to help them finish their sagas. Something to do with telling the truth to jotuns. Apparently that'll work better than my inferior technology."

"Huh." Tria bunched up his face. "How do you suppose that works?"

"I'm not sure. Why don't you dig around in the Archive and find out while I'm out in the forest."

Tria's eyes lit up. Kal recognized that look. It was what Kal did with his own face when someone gave him the opportunity to talk about programming.

"That's a great idea!" Tria said. "You know, there might even be something in the linguistic records that can help. The word 'truth,' for example. Two thousand years ago there was this fascinating linguistic shift, in which all the back vowels shifted forward. So, 'varheyd' actually used to be 'firheydt,' but you see, that got misconstrued with 'vorrhaad,' which the people around the city of Heliand west of here used to mean—"

Kal wasn't sure how long Tria continued. His pillow was soft, and it was warm under the thick quilts. It was even more comfortable than the bed in his tree house on Felis. He closed his eyes and fell asleep.

Thjalfi knocked on the door to Kal's room, waking him. Kal rubbed his eyes, rolled onto his side, and looked out the window beside his bed. It was still dark outside. He hesitated to pull off the many warm layers of quilt over him. Despite having the technological capacity to heat their homes, the citizens of Thrudvangar did so only minimally, seeming to prefer the nighttime cold to the relative warmth of day.

Eventually, Kal managed to leave the comfort of the bed and dressed himself. He joined Thjalfi and Roskva in the kitchen, and they ate a breakfast of thick yogurt and roasted nuts quickly and silently. The siblings gathered up large backpacks, which they must have prepared the night before, and the three of them left the house.

They walked dark streets, trudging through mounds of snow. Kal made his way by aiming for the footprints others had left. The streets were busy even at this early hour, mostly the same laborers in overalls that Kal had seen the day before.

At the central plaza, the three of them diverged from the crowd and headed one direction while everyone else walked off in another. Just outside the plaza, Kal followed Thjalfi and Roskva up one of the metal staircases and waited. Moments later, a bullet train hovered into view and stopped beside them. The three of them boarded.

Kal watched the sun come up from his window as the train sped over the Thrudvangar cityscape. Vanaheim's local star didn't exactly rise. Rather, it peaked out from behind the mountainwall and erupted into full-on day. From his elevated position above the houses, he watched the snow melt. Mounds of white dissolved into brown roofs and gray streets, water surging off them into gutters and aqueducts. Steam rose up everywhere, blanketing the city in a layer of fog that the sun quickly dispersed.

The bullet stopped, and Kal followed the siblings outside. The monorail track terminated, ending abruptly at the tree line before them. The doors to their bullet closed, and it took off in the opposite direction. They descended from the platform and onto a street, which quickly dissolved into a dirt path, leading into the forest of blue conifers.

After they had marched for some time, Roskva broke the silence. "What do you call this planet on your realm?"

"Earth," Kal said. "We have an old culture with a mythology that's sort of like this world—jotuns and Thor and gods."

"Oh, that kind of thing is really common," Roskva said.

"Really?"

"Yeah, when our first annarsveinns went out into the metaxia, they discovered lots of worlds that seemed like real versions of mythologies from our own planet. Our philosophers came up with the concept of the wick."

"The wick?" Kal asked.

"When two universes diverge, they don't quite diverge completely. They share something, a common point of reference. Sometimes those common points grow into little mythologies distinct to one part of a world, but sometimes they grow into cultural memes that underpin all human cultures. The two worlds that received the cultural elements are called 'down wick' from the source world, and the source world is 'up wick' from them."

Kal pondered this a moment. "So, Vanaheim and Earth are both 'down wick' from some world where Thor and jotuns exist in... what, some kind of 'perfect' form?"

Roskva nodded. "That's the idea."

Thjalfi turned to Roskva. "Didn't you tell me it's still debated?"

"Yeah, but don't get me started on the other theories. Mathematical purists drive me nuts."

"Says someone who wants to work in the Archive!" Thjalfi chuckled and grinned at his sister.

This began a long argument between the siblings about the nature of truth, which Kal didn't entirely follow. His eyes kept drifting off to Vanaheim's flora, and their exoskeleton-like shell casings.

When the sun dipped toward the mountainwall, Thjalfi and Roskva took off their backpacks and started constructing a tent, not with nanites or any other fancy technology, but with parts from their backpacks and using their hands. Kal did his best to contribute, but found there was much the siblings needed to explain to him.

He wondered about his own culture on Earth. They were very proud not to use nanites too much, even though they were omnipresent, and also careful to prevent themselves from using nanotechnology as a sloth-perpetuating crutch, like their ancestors had done in the past.

Kal relied heavily on the nanites for his safety while travelling, and that had felt somehow right. He'd been very angry at them for a long time. The little buggers had taken his life on Earth away from him. He should get something to compensate for that loss. But as he struggled to help Thjalfi and Roskva set up the three tents, he wondered if perhaps he'd overextended that reliance.

"What happened with nanites on Vanaheim that made you stop using them?" Kal asked Roskva, as she drove spikes into the ground at the base of one of the tents.

"Well, first there was the Ragnarok. That was basically a nanotech disaster. Took us five thousand years to start using nanites again after that. The second time was…" She looked to Thjalfi, who was gathering firewood from the forest. "Thjalfi, was it the skald abuse or the AI next?"

"Skald abuse," Thjalfi shouted back.

"Can you hold this for a second?" Roskva handed Kal a tent pole. Then she continued her story. "A bunch of skalds basically got high on their own brain chemicals, which they manipulated using nanites, and decided they were the third incarnation of the gods. After we got them under control, a bunch of nano-AIs gained sentience and grew violent. They decided all the humans needed to be wiped out. The jotuns are all that remains of them. Then, we still hadn't had enough, so we used nano-technology pretty extensively until about three thousand years ago when a massive solar flare caused our nanite network to—brace yourself—liquefy half the planet's population. We've only used limited forms of the tech-nology since."

Kal dropped the tent pole. Even despite his disability, he'd never felt creeped out about having the nanites in him before. Resentful and angry, sure, but never frightened. He had grown up on Earth, a world completely saturated with their presence. No one had successfully made a computer sentient and no solar flares of any remarkable magnitude had occurred in the past sixty years.

A shudder ran through him. Even now, auto-defense nanites covered the entire surface of his body, each armed with the most powerful protec-tive programming he and his society could create. If those tiny machines were to turn on him…

"Calm down," Roskva said, putting a hand on his shoulder. "Trillions of Midgarders over thousands of years have used nanotechnology and lived long, full, and safe lives."

Kal managed a weak smile and focused on helping Roskva finish set-ting up the last tent.

During dinner, he sat in silence while Thjalfi and Roskva talked about how far there was left to go before they reached the jotunfaething. By then, the sun had set completely, and snow had begun to fall.

"Tell me about the Ragnarok," Kal said during a break in their con-versation.

Roskva looked at her brother. "You should practice."

Thjalfi stared at her. That stony, cold demeanor came over his face. It was as though the Thjalfi who had stood before him two mornings ago had returned and taken the place of the affable young man Kal had come to know over the last twenty-four hours.

"C'mon," Roskva urged.

Thjalfi continued staring, and then sighed. He turned to face Kal.

"Twenty-two thousand years ago was the beginning of the reign of the first gods. Odin and Thor, Tyr and Heimdall, Freya and Baldr. They all lived here and ruled Vanaheim as gods. Vanaheim was a round world. They developed technology over time..." He broke into a frown, and his shoulders collapsed. "Roskva, I'm no good at this. You do it."

She crossed her arms and shook her head.

Thjalfi sighed and sat up straight again. "First there was machine technology, then there were computers, and the machines got smaller and more sophisticated. The computers got faster and were able to store more and more data. Eventually we discovered nanotechnology, but we discovered it too soon. The first gods made terrible weapons capable of massive destruction called ginnungagap devices. They told us it was for protection. Eventually, we removed the first gods from power and forced them to take cultural roles, but we forgot to dismantle their destructive toys.

"Twenty thousand years ago, something happened. One day, twenty million random Vanaheimers, about ten percent of the population, simply lost their minds. They began behaving erratically, deceitfully. We called this condition the Loki Complex. Many leaders didn't know who to trust anymore. Countries fell apart. Someone activated one or more of the ginnungagap devices. Most life on the surface of Vanaheim was obliterated, and the mass of our planet became compressed into this new configuration. All of the first gods were killed. The new gods, including Magni and Modi, took their place afterwards and rebuilt Midgard. Our world and all quantum worlds that spring from it have this shape. All other worlds we have found in the metaxia are spherical."

Kal watched the light of the fire dance across Thjalfi's face through the huge flakes of falling snow. Roskva was smiling.

"You're better at this than you think," Kal said.

Thjalfi grunted, went into his tent, and zipped it up.

"Thank you for helping me get him out here," Roskva moved closer to Kal, her voice a whisper. "I'm sorry I was so dismissive yesterday. Thjal-fi… well, when we get closer to the jotunfaething, he'll need support to do the truthsaying. He's trying to hide it, but he's glad you liked his telling of the Ragnarok story."

Kal shuffled nervously. "Roskva, I have a question…"

"Sure?"

"What did you shoot me with in the forest yesterday? I'm not going to have brain damage or something, am I?"

"No," Roskva laughed. "You'll be fine."

She unrolled her sleeve and pointed to her exposed wrist.

"Is there something there?" Kal asked.

"No manipulation of omni-subatomic yet, huh? I guess that must have been a few hundred years after nanotechnology. I'm always follow-ing the latest developments in information theory, but Thjalfi's a lot better at keeping the history of this stuff lined up right." Roskva rolled her sleeve back up, then pointed a finger into the forest. A yellow bolt of light shot from her hand and struck a tree. Its trunk absorbed the burst without so much as a shudder.

Kal's eyes widened. "Wait, I thought you were going to use truth on the jotuns, not bolts of light. Which is it?"

"Midgard jotuns can only be hurt by truthsaying. Focused energy will barely slow them down. Idavoll jotuns are very different. That's what we thought you were."

"Is Idavoll on the other side of the mountainwall disc?"

Roskva nodded.

"Are any other parts of Vanaheim habitable?"

Roskva pursed her lips. "Well, sort of. Idavoll's mountainpillar sup-ports a… kind of habitable environment. We call it Hel."

"Definitely not a place I would want to go then."

"No, definitely not." Roskva shook her head and yawned. "Time for bed. We've got a long day ahead of us in the morning."

Kal nodded, and they turned in for the night.

⚭⚭⚭

Kal awoke to Roskva shouting something about a story. He threw open his eyes just in time to see something clawing through his tent.

He backed away from that wall of the tent, pulled out his pad, and tried using his nanites to gather data, but no information came back. Infobubbles erupted reporting massive nanite destruction.

The wall of the tent distorted and fell away completely, revealing the spiky back of a creature whose skin danced in a white and black particulate haze. Kal yelled out and rolled away just in time. The creature roared like a lion, but with a gurgling to its cadence. Its form suggested both lion and turtle. It leapt up and scrambled away, apparently not noticing him.

Kal ran outside through the enormous hole burned into the side of his tent. He crunched through the rapidly melting snow wearing only a pair of underwear and clutching his pad for dear life. The sun had just come over the mountainwall disc. Hideous, metallic, chimerical animals, all with the same chaotic white and black skin, loped about the campsite. A half-snake half-cow lumbered toward Kal. It reeled its head back and shot toward him with enormous fangs dripping static goo. He jumped out of its path and wheeled around it.

Roskva stood meters away, dodging swings from a lobster-porcupine and blasting it with ineffectual bursts of light. Thjalfi stood near her, his back to a tree. He lunged, dodging jabs from the stinger-claws of a bee-wolf. His face was drenched with sweat, and his expression... was that not just fear, but pain too?

"Thjalfi, tell the story!" Roskva shouted.

A centipede-scorpion-flamingo clambered toward Kal, who jumped out of the way just as its enormous stinger-wing with hundreds of tiny flailing legs came crashing down at his side. He rolled into the debris of Roskva's tent, and adrenaline took over. He stuck the pad to his hip and grabbed one of the tent poles.

Just in time, too. The enormous stinger-wing came down at him again. Kal swung the pole over his head, rolling out of the way as the malevolent nanites burned through the metal, dispersing the pole's component atoms.

He righted himself and took off toward the siblings. "Now would be a great time for that story, Thjalfi!"

A hawk-dragon-spider swooped out of the sky at Roskva. Kal picked up a blue pinecone heavy as a rock and hurled it at the monstrosity. It turned and lashed out at Kal, who side-rolled through the wet snow once more. The thing roared and screeched all at once.

"Thjalfi!" Roskva shouted. "You can do this!"

Thjalfi's face was all bunched up. What could possibly be going through his head?

The hawk-dragon-spider lunged at Roska, lashing at her with outstretched talon pincers. The swipe grazed her arm, and she fell backward, shouting: "My father took me out to the forest for the first time when I was six!"

Every jotun present lurched to a halt, standing or hovering frozen in space. Kal picked himself up, gazing at the immobile creatures, gasping for breath.

Roskva continued, not missing a beat. "We walked for a long time and came to a lake. I asked if we could go fishing. He pulled a retractable fishing pole out of his sack, and we fished for hours. He asked me about school and about my friends. And then he asked me about how I liked the computer courses I had just started, and I told him I loved them. I loved doing the logic problems, and I was sure I would love programming too."

Kal watched as the jotuns began to shudder, their static haze congealing into patches of pure white or pure black.

"I told my father about a couple of the kids at the school, who seemed to think that girls shouldn't like programming or engineering. That boys should do those things and girls should do other things. I didn't know if I should pursue programming or not. He smiled at me and told me it was sad that after tens of thousands of years, some people still held on to ancient misbeliefs that we've struggled so hard to throw away. He told me I could do any job I wanted, and if anyone tried to tell me otherwise, they'd have him to deal with. And that's when—"

Each Jotun in the warming glade turned either all white or all black and lurched backwards.

"—that's when I told him I wanted to work in the Yggdrasil Archive. He patted me on the back and told me that would be great, and to make sure that the stories of our family were kept in its safest part."

The jotuns, released from their trance, turned and ran into the forest as quickly as their disjointed, metallic forms could take them.

Kal turned to Thjalfi. His long face was frozen in horror. He scrambled up and ran into the tattered remains of his tent. Kal thought he caught a glimpse of tears running down Thjalfi's face.

Kal ran up to Roskva and inspected the huge gash across her arm. It was bleeding badly and shimmered with bursts of black and white sparks. Her skin seemed to be dissolving around the wound.

"What do we do?" Kal asked.

Roskva winced, then nodded toward her backpack, its contents strewn about the trampled fireplace. "Antinanogenics. There's a medical kit in my pack. Inside it there's a— find the blue tube."

Kal retrieved the device from the scattered supplies and handed it to Roskva. She held the tube above the wound. It emitted a blue light and the static haze in her gash disappeared.

She glanced over him and smirked, breathing heavily. She strained to pull herself toward the nearest tree, and fell back against its trunk, still panting. "I'll be fine. You can put on clothes if you want."

Kal blushed. He'd completely forgotten what he was, or rather wasn't, wearing. He returned to his tent by stepping through the enormous hole in its side and got the nanites to make him some clothes.

"Kal," Roskva called.

"Yeah?"

She motioned for him to come closer, still inhaling and exhaling heavily.

She nodded toward Thjalfi's tent. "Go talk to him. I need a minute."

"Thjalfi?"

"Thor in Himinn, leave me alone!"

Kal entered the remains of tent anyway.

"Your story, it's about your father isn't it?" Kal sat down beside Thjalfi. Beams of light crept in where the jotuns had dissolved the tent face.

Thjalfi nodded. "He died. And I know you know that already. But what you don't know is that it was my fault. We all need a saga to be an adult. Not a repeat saga, but our own saga. And it needs to be emotionally resonant, the story that defines your life up until this point. I can't do this Kal. Even with Roskva in danger, I couldn't tell my Himinn-damned story. And she's all I've got left."

Kal put his arm around Thjalfi's shoulder. They sat there, just like that, until Roskva called out that it was time for them to get going.

⚬ᵔᴗᵔ⚬

The sun was directly overhead when they reached the treeline. Kal shivered. Maybe it was the altitude, or perhaps the trees and lakes held the heat in better. They were much closer to the mountainwall. The land here was a perpetually upward-sloping hill that disappeared into the hazy, dark edge of the sky. Kal gazed up at the curving surface both in front of him and above him and shuddered.

"That's the jotunfaething," Roskva pointed to a tall mound of rocks piled up a few hundred meters away. Without the siblings there to tell him, he wouldn't have considered it at all remarkable, just an ordinary pile of stones.

The rocks shimmered, and a small chimera grew out from them, this one some kind of baby koala-frog. It pushed itself off the surface of the jotunfaething, then scampered away, immediately aware and able. Kal followed it with his eyes as it disappeared over a rise.

"Hey, Thjalfi?"

"Yeah?"

"Any true story will do, right?"

"Truth is most important," Thjalfi said. "But the power of the story is all in how it makes you feel."

"So, the more emotionally invested you are, the more it hurts the jotuns?"

Thjalfi nodded.

"Sounds like you have an idea, Kal," Roskva said.

"My inferior nanites might not be so useless after all," Kal said, tapping at his pad's interface.

⚬ᵔᴗᵔ⚬

Thjalfi and Roskva strode away from the treeline, walking directly toward the jotunfaething. The ground was so craggy and pitted from nanite activity that they swerved to avoid the largest holes. When they came within fifty meters of the jotunfaething, its border guard, a dozen jotuns of varying sizes, rushed toward them.

A penguin-wasp waddled forward in lurches, waving stinger arms and hopping with staticky flits of its wings. A cheetah-yak ran on a set of eight legs of varying lengths, causing it to trip over itself while it flung its antlered head wildly about. Most absurd was the parrot-hamster. It scampered forward, gnashing an enormous pair of oversized incisors while waving white-black wings with claws attached to their tips.

"My brother Thjalfi has a story to tell!" Roskva shouted toward the encroaching horde.

"I—" Thjalfi stuttered. Roskva grabbed and held his hand.

"I was ten years old!" Thjalfi shouted at them. The jotuns lurched momentarily but continued in their approach. Roskva squeezed. "My friend Brokk and I had made plans to practice lyftball. It was a clear day, and the sun had just come up. My father reminded me that he had made plans to take me into the forest that day and practice truthsaying. This was the third time in a month that we had made these plans. We had cancelled the other two because I had made sure to be conveniently ill."

The jotuns halted, frozen, their static-covered skin starting to congeal into black and white patches.

"I couldn't pretend I was ill this time. My father knew I wanted to play lyftball with Brokk. But, he insisted that I needed to start practicing storytelling now, that I would need to truthsay in order to become an adult. Practice couldn't wait any longer. I—"

Thjalfi faltered. Tears filled his eyes.

"You can do this, Thjalfi," Roskva said. "I don't blame you. No one blames you. You can do this."

"I—"

The jotuns lurched forward. The patches on their skin dispersed back into hazy static.

"I—" Thjalfi's voice cracked. All his composure evaporated. He no longer seemed capable of controlling the tears.

The spell broke, and the jotuns ran toward them again in all their fury. So close.

Kal turned off the nanites that had been rendering him invisible. He stood immediately to the right of the jotun horde.

"I was twelve," Kal announced, and the pack froze once more. "It was the northeastern Illinois regional swim meet. My times had been dropping. I was ready. It was a two hundred meter individual medley, and I knew I could do it. I'd have the best time. I looked up and saw the rest of the team, and they were cheering for me. They were cheering for the other boys, too. I was on the team, and it was amazing.

"I remember I coughed as I stepped onto the diving block. The team shouted harder, and I tried to ignore the tightness in my chest. I wanted to cough again, but I swallowed the urge and took deep breaths. I heard the gun and jumped. I hit the water and started cycling my arms and kicking my legs, but my chest felt even tighter, constricted, and at some point, I blacked out."

"When I woke up, I was in a forest. My body had aged and atrophied. They told me horrible things. I'd been in a coma for two years. I was recovering from an extreme nanogenic radiation sensitivity. I was on an Earth that wasn't Earth, which didn't make any sense. And worst of all, I couldn't go home. Ever. I'd never be on the swim team again. My friends could never come visit me. I was alone."

The jotuns quivered and lurched ever so slightly forward once more. Kal looked Thjalfi directly in the eyes.

"I—" Thjalfi inhaled and exhaled heavily, his eyes red and puffy. "I told my father that storytelling was stupid. I told him it wasn't important, and that I was going to become the best lyftball player in Midgard, and that no one would care if I told a true story to some stupid rock or not.

"My father looked at me with disappointment. With disappointment! And he went into the forest alone, and I went to play lyftball with Brokk. He had gone into the forest by himself hundreds of times before. Everyone was surprised when he didn't come back. In the morning they— they— sent a search party into the woods."

Thjalfi took another deep breath.

"They brought back what was little left of his body two days later. They think he must have had a heart attack. They think it must have happened when he was attacked by the jotuns. He wasn't able to finish his story, and..."

Thjalfi's eyes turned even redder than they already were.

"And they killed him, because jotuns can't do anything else! And they got away with it because I wasn't there! So tell me. I'm here now! Is that how it happened? Could I have saved him if I'd gone with him? Tell me!"

The jotuns quivered a moment, their skin either all black or all white. And then, just like that, the entire horde rippled and collapsed, disintegrating into metallic dust.

Kal ran to Thjalfi. Roskva was already hugging him, repeating, "It's okay. It wasn't your fault. And you did it. You told your story. Dad would be proud."

Kal kicked at the tiny shards of metal on the ground, so small they flitted away in the wind. He walked to Thjalfi, who just stood, tears still streaming down his tall face. A lone tear ran down Roskva's face into her smile.

"You did it," Kal patted Thjalfi on the back.

"I guess I did," Thjalfi managed a small chuckle between sniffles.

∞⟨⟩∞

Roskva stood before Magni and Modi and another man, one in flowing, gray robes, one of those they called skalds. She held forward the stone shard she'd taken from the destroyed jotunfaething. Kal and Thjalfi stood to the side, holding their own hunks of the former jotun generator.

The skald took the rock from Roskva's hand, grabbed her arm, and strapped a bracelet around her forearm. He pressed his thumb into its surface, and an etched rune shimmered into existence.

"Roskva Lindgren has truthtold a jotunfaething and begun her saga."

She stepped down from the platform and Thjalfi took her place. He told his story again, very calmly this time, though his voice remained low and he clenched his fists together behind his back.

After he had finished, the scald stared at him for many moments, then finally nodded.

"Exceptional varheyd." The skald took Thjalfi's jotunfaething shard and granted him a bracelet and rune in the same manner as he had to Roskva.

Kal stepped up to the platform. The skald raised an eyebrow, but Kal began his story anyway, and the skald's smirk faded with its telling.

"I see," the skald said. "Another story full of varheyd. And from an annarsveinn! Would you mind if we record it in the Yggdrasil Archive, Kal Anders?"

Kal shrugged. "Not at all."

"Kal Anders has truthtold his first jotunfaething and begun his saga." The skald gave Kal a runic bracelet and then turned to look at Thjalfi and Roskva. "And I should like to hear the saga of 'The Lindgren Siblings and Kal Anders Venture into the Thrudvangar Forest' sometime. I suspect that saga should be quite full of varheyd as well."

The skald shuffled quickly down from the platform and out the door of the hall.

∞⟨⟩∞

"Kal?" Thjalfi ran across the plaza and met Kal beside the rotating hammer and rings. Kal understood why Thjalfi had wanted to be a pro lyftball player.

"I just wanted to say thank you." Thjalfi said. "You really leaving so soon? We're going to celebrate at the hall."

"Thanks," Kal said. "But big parties aren't really my thing."

A part of him wanted to stay, and he knew Tria wouldn't mind, but he didn't want all the attention right now. "I do need to know though... if there's a technology here that can let me go home. To Earth."

Thjalfi shook his head. "Genetic manipulation is *extremely*—"

"—illegal." Kal finished for him. "It's the same on Earth, actually. But I had to ask."

Thjalfi nodded, then reached out and grasped Kal's forearm at the elbow, and Kal did the same. A kind of handshake, he supposed.

"I hope you find what you're looking for, Kal. All the same, you come back and visit me and Roskva from time to time. Don't be a stranger, alright?"

Kal nodded and smiled.

Thjalfi hugged Kal, patted him on the back and ran off into the city.

Kal found and boarded a transit bullet headed for the Thrudvangar city limits.

Hey, Tria? Kal called out with his mind.

Hey, Kal, Tria responded mentally, materializing beside him. "Time to go?"

"Yeah. What did you find in the archive?"

"Let's see, there's the history of the Ragnarok... the stabilization and rebuilding of the world afterward... the war against the insane skalds... the struggle to defend humanity from evil, sentient nanite programs... It was great! I'll tell you about them if you decide you want to stay awake this time."

Kal laughed as they exited the bullet train. He and his brother descended into the streets near the Thrudvangar city limits. He made his mock serious face and nudged Tria's hologram with his elbow. "Let me tell you about the time I discovered the most fascinating noun declension there ever was—"

"Hey, the next time you go on about variable scoping in NanoScript—"

"Oh, touché!"

They approached the edge of the city. Just inside the forest, Kal pulled out his pad and activated the metaxic bubble.

"Did Thjalfi and Roskva finish their sagas?"

"You could say that," Kal said. "Though the skald said their sagas are just beginning."

When Tria didn't reply immediately, Kal looked and saw Tria gazing at the runic bracelet on Kal's forearm.

Tria crossed his arms and looked at Kal with incredulous eyes. "Spill it."

Kal feigned innocence. "Oh, I just prattled on about variable scoping in NanoScript and that skald guy gave me this bracelet—"

"Shut up and choose the next world."

Duality

Realm #7109, "Dvu"
July 18, 2178

CAT YOWLING PIERCED Kal's slumber. His tree house shook, padded paw thumps rustling his home.

Bleary-eyed, Kal stumbled across the room and made the cats' breakfast. One by one, he hurled the gobs of bird meat out the window. The cats tore into their small feast, then scampered off.

"Why do you throw the meat out the window?"

Kal started. He spotted Tria sitting at the table and breathed a sigh of relief. Kal sat down across from his brother and flipped the holographic switch on his interface that let the light through the windows.

Kal squinted. "How long have you been sitting there?"

"A couple of hours."

Kal glanced at his interface. "You woke up at 4:30?"

Tria shrugged.

"Suit yourself."

Tria leaned forward. "Why throw the meat out the window? You could just program the nanites to build them outside."

"Exercise," Kal said.

"That's it?"

Kal frowned. "Not exactly."

"Well?"

"Tria... look, there are things about Earth I haven't told you yet. In the not so distant past, things got bad. Really bad. All this technological power is great, but if we don't use it right... Making the cats' food in here gives me an opportunity to get some exercise in the morning."

Tria's face fell. "I wish I knew what exercise felt like."

Kal laughed. "Careful what you wish for. Sore muscles and cramps aren't very much fun, by the way."

Tria pulled up his own interface. "Big day today, right?"

"Yeah." Kal pulled up the grid and projected it over the table. His breakfast shimmered into existence too, a bowl of cereal and a glass of juice. He shovelled down cereal with one hand and typed with the other.

"I doubt programming at the table's very polite." Tria snickered.

Kal smirked at him.

Twenty worlds in the great 3D map of alternate Earths blinked from white to blue.

"Wow. We're going to visit all of them?" Tria gazed up at it. "In one day?"

Kal nodded. "I made a new program to find high tech worlds. I'm hoping you come home today with a body, and I come home... able to go home."

Tria smirked. "Sounds like a plan." His eyes suddenly widened. "We'll be on each world long enough to gather a full linguistic database, right?"

Kal rolled his eyes. "Sure..."

The holograms composing the grid flickered momentarily.

Kal dropped his spoon into his bowl, splashing milk onto himself, and grabbed up his computer.

"What's wrong?" Tria asked.

"You didn't see that?"

"Didn't see what?"

"The interface... it kind of... shuddered."

Tria shook his head, and looked at his hands, turning them around. "I didn't see anything. Maybe because I flickered too...?"

"No, not you. Just the grid." Kal started up the pad's diagnostic routines. He gulped at his next thought and checked for evidence of metaxic transmissions from Earth. He breathed a sigh of relief when the results came back negative. Thank goodness. The last thing he needed was some Fermilab administrator breathing down his neck right when he was on the verge of discovering a cure.

Tria closed out his interface. "Everything looks fine."

"Yeah, I suppose you're right..." Kal said. He downed his orange juice and pressed a button on his pad. The empty cereal bowl and glass dissolved. He strode to the door, relinquished the forcefield and walked onto his balcony, where he grabbed up his swimming suit off the railing.

"Thirty minute swim, then be ready to go, alright?" Kal called inside.

"Sure thing," Tria shouted back.

∞◁∞

The metaxic bubble unravelled onto an empty plain of dry dirt. It ran flat as far as Kal could see on either side of him, evidenced by a sky full of stars. Enormous, dark hillsides rose up both in front of and behind him.

His brother shimmered into view at his side, stretched out his arms, and yawned. "Last one, right?" He smacked his lips.

"Yeah..." Kal trailed off as he gazed up into the sky.

The moon shone down brightly, at least, he had assumed it was a moon. Kal gazed at the shining orb above. Etched into its surface were the outlines of continents and oceans. Clouds sat atop them, wispy tufts. Though the oceans were blue and the clouds white, the land was tinged crimson instead of green. The stills he had collected from this realm depicted bright red foliage, maroon grasses and fields of pink corn stalks.

"I dunno, Kal," Tria said. "Maybe we could just come back here tomorrow. I mean, I kind of wanted a break after the fourteenth dead end, but this is really too much—"

"Tria?"

"Yeah?"

"You hear that?"

Tria's ears perked up, too. A whimper caught his ear. Kal turned around and spotted a young man, huddled on the ground ten meters away. The only illumination came from the planet-moon, and so it was difficult to make out his exact age, but the size of his frame suggested late teens, certainly not older than twenty. He had his hands wrapped over his head, trembling.

Tria deactivated his hologram, and Kal grabbed at his pad, his muscles tensed. The whole point of landing far away from populated areas was to avoid having to speak to the natives while his words still sounded like alien gibberish.

We're not supposed to be anywhere near the city. Kal thought to Tria.

Doubling checking... Tria thought. *Yup, the city's a kilometer away. You know, he had to have heard the metaxic bubble and felt the wind from it. What's he doing?*

I don't know, but I doubt asking would do any good right now. Probably just freak him out more.

Linguistic data's still coming in, but it actually looks fairly solid. You might not sound that bad. Check out these consonant clusters! Chicago's called 'Tskogo.' Not quite in the same spot either. There's no lake, but the city sits at the edge of an enormous drop off. Maybe Lake Michigan dried up? But if that were the case, why would anyone stay here?

Kal heard a low rumble and felt a little quaking in the ground. He glanced down and noticed the dust shifting and sputtering.

You know, Tria thought, *maybe—*

Shh, Kal thought. *A new sound.*

Beyond the young man's twitching and violent shaking, Kal heard a whisper steadily growing into a roar. The young man sat up on his knees and threw his arms into the air, palms facing forward, his chest heaving. He was facing away from Kal, and he could only see the back of the young man's head.

Kal looked down at his interface, spotting a new, red-bordered window that had just popped into existence. He read the words, and his eyes widened.

Kal! Tria shouted. *Forcefield, now!*

Kal ran for the young man. He reached the trembling figure, screeched to a halt and frantically tapped out commands into his pad. The nanites shimmered into a dome that surrounded both Kal and the stranger.

An enormous wall of water rumbled through the canyon and crashed over their nanite defenders. The energy dome sizzled as the raging tsunami passed overhead. The young man jerked around to look at Kal. Anger registered across his face, then fear. The maelstrom continued above both of them.

The young man's hands collapsed, his chest still heaving up and down.

Kal gazed back into his eyes. What was going on in there? Fear and apprehension, for sure. Maybe something else? Kal couldn't be entirely certain, but he guessed he was feeling that something too. He found himself looking over this other teen's brown wisps of hair, appreciating the contours his face, and the biceps peaking out from underneath his sleeves. Kal could see other muscles through the tight-fitting shirt.

The young man's slacks and boots looked familiar. Kal had adopted a similar pair before his arrival. The clothes were comfortable enough, but why did the entire outfit have to be dyed a putrid greyish brown?

Kal gulped. "Hi."

The young man didn't answer at first. He just stood up slowly, his eyes moving from Kal to the nanite shield dome. He touched it, and his hand flinched at the small burst of electricity on contact. He bunched his face up and began pounding on it with balled fists, more electricity erupting.

"What'd you do?!" He raged, turning back to Kal. "Who are you?"

Kal frowned. So much for gratitude easing their first interaction. Kal took a deep breath, hoping his words would at least be understood. "My name's Kal. What's yours?"

"Rko." He put his head in his hands and let his back slide down the nanite energy barrier until he hit the ground. He buried his face in his lap once more. Trembling, he slammed an arm into the forcefield once more.

"Damn it," Rko muttered, sniffling.

Kal bit his lip, realization washing over him. Rko had known that the water had been coming, welcomed it, even. Kal took a deep breath and sat himself down to face Rko, very deliberately and carefully clasping his pad the whole time. The maelstrom surged above. He watched Rko and let the moments pass, unsure of what he should say next.

"What is this?" Rko hit the forcefield again. "Did Urzla send you?"

"I don't know Urzla. Does she live in Tskogo? Is that where you're from?"

"I'm not from anywhere. No one in Tskogo wants anything to do with me." Rko looked up into the surging water above. "I can't see Overland. You sure timed that well. Are you Ngoh?"

"Um, I don't think so."

Rko's eyes widened. "You're unaltering too."

Kal shook his head. Rko just gazed at him.

"I'm from very, very far away," Kal tried. "We don't have Ngoh or unalterings."

At this, Rko became incredibly animated. He stopped trembling and made direct eye contact with Kal. "Another continent then! You can cross the Great Tideland? Can you take me there?"

Kal shook his head solemnly.

"Why not?!"

"I can't go there myself."

Rko slouched back down and wrapped his arms around his head again. Kal glanced upward and noticed that the water had reversed directions, surging back the way it had come.

He thought about this a moment, and about the enormous lake-shaped 'hole' Tria had found at the edge of Tskogo.

"This is a tide, isn't it?" Kal said. "An enormous tide!"

Rko nodded. "The part of Dvu you come from doesn't have the tides?"

"Well, we've got tides, but they're just a meter or so up and down every day. Nothing like this."

"Sounds like paradise. Weak tides. No Ngih or Ngoh. Next you'll be telling me there are no quakes either."

"We have those sometimes. And... there are problems. Just different problems."

"Akru," Rko said—this must have been Kal's name in their language. "Are you going to let me out of this... thing?"

Kal nodded. "Once it's safe."

Rko stood up. "Then I'm going for a walk into the countryside. A very long walk."

"Why don't we just wait here a while? You can tell me about Tskogo." Kal stood and paused on Rko's face again. His bright blue eyes sparkled even in the dull light from the forcefield glimmer. It pained Kal to see them red from crying.

Rko grimaced at his mention of the city. "I'd rather just go to the countryside if it's all the same to you."

"Then how about I come with you? I'm new here. You can tell me about other parts of this region. We don't have to talk about Tskogo."

Rko glanced about, unable to keep his eyes fixed on Kal's anymore, and he fidgeted with his hands. "If you won't mind having... an unaltering for company."

Kal wondered what could be so terrible about being an 'unaltering.' He smiled and replied, "I don't mind. I'm supposed to be one too, right?"

Rko managed a kind of smile back. "I don't need anything, but you'll want supplies. In the city, well, they're Ngoh. I won't be able to..." He trailed off.

"Just tell me what we need," Kal said.

Rko turned to look outside. Overland was visible again, and the tide was descending rapidly, now just a meter deep. The sides of the dome shimmered against the steady backwash. More light from Overland reached them now, illuminating even more details of Rko's form.

Are you sure about this? Tria said. *Rko seems a little... What if he drags you into a tide again?*

I'm not too worried. I'll keep a close eye on the pad. Why don't you take some nanites and explore the city?

I think you just want some 'alone time.' Tria snickered. *Fine, whatever. There are still some interesting gaps in the translation matrix, anyway. For example, your computer still has no idea what 'Ngoh' means. I think it might have something to do with—*

Rko began listing supplies and Kal stopped listening to Tria.

"We'll need some food and water, for sure. Oh, and probably a lighter." Rko said, numbering these things on his fingers. "And sleeping bags, of course."

Such a sweet voice, Kal thought.

Overland shown down above them, and its reflection sparkled on the ripples of the receding tide.

oceloeo

Kal had only been inside the Tskogo city limits for twenty minutes, and already, he had given up trying to make eye contact with its citizenry. Passersby grimaced and turned up their noses as they passed him.

He wished for Rko's presence more with every passing moment. But, Rko had insisted on remaining at the edge of the city, saying the citizens of Tskogo would be even less receptive to his presence. Unbeknownst to Rko, a group of nanites sat on his shoulder, ready to alert Kal if he tried to run off alone.

Fortunately for Kal, the sun had only just risen, and the streets were only sparsely populated.

'Street' was a generous term for what lay beneath his feet. The material that covered the ground was some kind of stretchy brown tarp, the same color as dirt, and metallic nubs at its edges fastened it to the soil. There were no vehicles. All transportation was apparently accomplished by foot.

The term "building" applied only loosely in Tskogo also. All structures were single-story domes, which came in varying heights and circumferences, a single row of windows adorning their walls. Steam spouted from openings in the roofs.

Another Tskogo citizens glared at him in disgust as Kal passed. He couldn't figure out what it could be. He had adopted appropriate clothing. At least, it looked like what everyone else was wearing. He even had the same kind of hat they wore, which reminded him of a baseball cap with a shorter lid.

The unwanted attention made Kal think he should stop, find some privacy, and examine his face, his clothes, something, but he pushed such ideas out of his head. He just needed to get the stuff Rko had asked for and get out of the city.

Before long, Kal found the supply store Rko had told him about.

He tried the door and found it locked. Not sure what else to do, he sat down against the wall of the dome to wait. He desperately wanted to pull out his pad and learn everything he could. Even though Rko had remained innocently nonplussed at the sight Kal's technology, the rest of Tskogo's citizens were already staring at him like he was a circus sideshow. No reason to push his luck.

Kal pulled out the money Rko had given him—silver and bronze coins with portraits imprinted on them. They reminded him of old Earth currency from the country that had preceded the PanAtlantic Union. Chicago's Field Museum had a whole exhibit on the culture and values of the postmodern United States of America. This silver coin he held looked almost like a quarter. But the quarters he'd seen had featured the profile of a famous person on only one side, whereas this coin had a famous person on both sides.

Kal flipped it back and forth in his fingers. The two people's heads were similar, but there were differences etched into the rendering. Kal squinted. One side labeled its individual as 'Tzdrao,' and the other 'Oardzt.'

A man approached and unlocked the door to the dome. Kal pocketed the coin and stood up. The shop owner avoided making eye contact, entered his store, and quickly closed the door behind him.

Kal tried the knob and found it was still locked.

He sighed, crossed his arms, and tapped his foot on the ground. The urge to pick the lock with nanotechnology was overwhelming.

He had nearly decided to forget the whole endeavor and program the nanites to build passable supplies, when the man finally flipped the sign in the door from closed to open. The lock clicked.

Kal tried the door again, and this time, it swung open as he pulled.

"Good morning," Kal said, balking internally at his own disingenuousness.

The man merely grumbled in response.

"You don't treat travelers very well in Tskogo, it would seem."

"Travelers, yeah," the man mumbled. He had yet to make eye contact with Kal.

"Do you treat all of your customers this way?"

The man made eye contact. "Just the freaks."

"Look," Kal slammed a hand down on the counter. "I'm here to buy things. With this money."

Kal threw the coins onto the table. One rolled off onto the floor. "Give me the stuff I need and you can have every last one of these stupid hunks of polished metal."

The man looked at Kal, then at the coins, and then at Kal again.

A wry smile grew across his face. "What can I get for you, *sir*?"

The land outside of Tskogo was flat, rich and fertile. Rko showed Kal which paths skirted along the farms.

Having fun? Tria thought.

He seems so shy, Kal thought back. *I wonder what those people in the city did to him.*

All I can tell you, from what I've seen so far, is that they treat each other alright. Maybe you both have cooties.

Very funny. You find out anything new linguistically?

Not much. I'll go back to slaving away in the Tskogo Central Library while you have fun with your new boyfriend.

Kal rolled his eyes.

Later. He felt Tria's presence in his mind flitter away.

The corn plants were tall, at least two meters high, with their tall, pink stalks. Kal and Rko were both drenched in sweat, the sun blasting down onto them. As the day wore on, the wind picked up, rushing over them in cool waves, swaying the sea of burgundy and magenta around them. Overland had set, leaving the sky cloudless and blue.

"Why didn't they treat me very well in Tskogo?" Kal finally asked.

"They don't know you, and you're dressed like Ngih."

Kal glanced at his drab clothes. "I thought I was dressed the same as everyone else."

"No. Like I said, they're Ngoh."

Kal lifted an eyebrow. All the clothing he'd seen so far—his, Rko's and the Tskogo citizens'—all looked the same.

"What kind of clothes are you wearing?" Kal tried.

Rko didn't respond. Unaltering, probably, which Rko had refused to talk about. Kal turned to look at him and Rko stared ahead, frowning. He twitched his head a bit, then asked, "Is land travel easy where you come from?"

"Yeah. Pretty easy, I guess. I wouldn't say it's particularly hard."

"With our quakes, travel is dangerous here. If it weren't for my being an unaltering, they probably wouldn't let me go out alone where we're going, past the cropland. If you're in Tskogo when there's a quake, you'll be okay. Not out here though. I don't blame you if you want to go back."

"What, and leave you all alone?" Kal smiled. He watched Rko's frown turn upward, just a bit. "Are there quakes often?"

"Geez, your home sounds like a paradise. Infrequent quakes, no tides, no Ngih or Ngoh. Why would you leave a place like that?"

"I didn't have a choice."

Rko must have heard the pain in Kal's voice. He sighed and looked away. "Oh, crap, I'm sorry. I didn't—"

"No, no, don't worry about it."

They walked in silence for some time through the fields, and the pleasant breezes continued. Once, Kal thought he caught the sound of farming equipment rumbling in the distance, but Rko was quick to steer them away from it.

"The way they treated me in Tskogo, is that how they treat you?" Kal asked.

Rko nodded silently. Kal frowned. That likely meant that they treated him even worse.

"What would you do if they didn't treat you that way? If you could go back to Tskogo and have whatever kind of life you wanted?"

Rko stopped walking and turned to Kal. "I don't know. I've never thought about it. No one's ever asked me that before."

The befuddled expression still plastered across his face, Rko started forward once again. Kal watched his face. Rko seemed genuinely baffled at never having considered the question.

"Since I was twelve," Rko said, "all I did was worry about being an unaltering. When I turned sixteen, it was clear I had a problem. All my energy for the last six years, I spent it all trying not to be an unaltering anymore. I never stopped to think about what I might do otherwise."

"What's so bad about being an unaltering anyway?"

The path led Kal and Rko into a forest of brilliant, red-leaved trees, and Rko gazed onward, seeming to ponder Kal's question.

"I don't know. It's just… it's not how normal people are."

"You seem pretty normal to me."

"Well, you're unaltering too, right? Everyone is where you come from. When you're a Ngih or a Ngoh, then being unaltering seems pretty weird."

"'Weird' isn't the word that comes to my mind when I think about the people in Tskogo."

Rko laughed. Kal hadn't intended it to be funny, but seeing Rko smile somehow made him want to smile too.

They walked for hours, Kal and Rko talking jovially the whole time. Kal spoke of his childhood on Earth as though it were another continent on Dvu. He also found himself sharing openly about the isolation and loneliness of his teen years, and found that Rko had much to share on that subject as well. Rko, through pursed lips, made mention of some of the things his peers had said to him, horrible jeers about his status as unaltering, which grew more and more unbearable as friend after former friend joined their ranks as either Ngih or Ngoh, eventually leaving him as the only unaltering left in his classes. Kal's heart went out to him. He'd known loneliness and rejection to be a kind of personal hell, but through Rko, he came to glimpse two new horrors: insult and abuse.

The forest eventually gave way to more plains, but these weren't flat. They were jagged, where earthquakes had shoved up slices of land, leaving them awkwardly interlocked at acute angles. The soil was rockier, and the trees became sparser, smaller and had fewer leaves, outnumbered by small shrubs and maroon brambles. Craggy, pitted mountains rose up in the distance. A smoke plume trailed into the sky from the top of one of the peaks.

"This area is called the Razor," Rko said.

"Fitting name."

When Rko didn't chuckle, Kal felt a pang of fear.

"Don't worry," Rko said. "As long as there isn't a major earthquake, we'll be fine."

"And if there is?"

"Well, you can make another shield for us, right?"

Kal sensed a mild irritation in Rko's voice that he didn't like hearing.

And how could Rko possibly be handling all of Kal's sophisticated technology? From what Kal had seen in Tskogo, this part of Dvu couldn't possibly be out of the industrial age.

Seeming to pick up on Kal's sudden emotional distance, Rko managed to smile, curiosity sweeping over his expression. "Those forcefields sure are interesting though. Can you show me how you make them?"

Kal hopped down from a slab of rock and pulled out his pad. "Well, this is called a computer."

"Cool."

Kal pulled up the interface, and watched Rko's face light up as he spun colorful icons around in the air with his free hand.

"So, this one is how I make the forcefields. This one starts a biological scan. It checks my body for viruses or infections, kills them if necessary. And this one..." He pondered how to explain the metaxia. "Well, the computer can take me a lot of places."

"So, you could just disappear any time you want? Go off somewhere else?"

That morning, Kal had sensed that his presence had made Rko anxious and nervous. There was a hurt in his voice now, and Kal felt a sympathetic pang in response.

Kal grabbed Rko by the shoulders and they stopped walking.

He looked Rko directly in the eyes. "I told you I'd go with you on this trip, and that's what I intend to do. The whole way. I promise."

Rko reached out and put his hand on Kal's chest. He let it rest there for a moment, the faintest hint of joy tracing its way across his lips. He jerked his head back and jumped down off another small ledge of jagged rock.

Kal followed him down into the Razor.

A few hours into their trip, it grew dark. Overland had become visible again, rising from the west. As it passed through the setting sun, a brief, two-minute eclipse burst over them, and then Overland rose quickly up into the darkening sky.

At its appearance, Rko became visibly nervous. He rushed forward faster and scrambled up the cleanly shaven slabs of land that jutted out of the landscape at acute angles. Kal struggled to keep up.

They stopped to set up camp, but even after they had rested for some time, Rko continued breathing heavily and announced he needed to lie down.

"Doesn't Overland's rising affect you?" He asked Kal between gasps for air and wheezing coughs. "You can't tell me you don't have Overland, unless you're some kind of alien."

"No, not an alien," Kal said, mentally patting himself on the back for achieving at least half of the truth. "I'm just from really, really far away."

"Good," Rko said. "There are no such things as aliens, and I'd hate to be travelling around out here with a crazy person. And I'm sure you would too." He started to laugh, but the laughter turned to coughing and he clutched his chest.

Kal pulled out his pad.

"I'm going to use my computer on you. Don't worry, I just want to figure out what's wrong. I won't do anything dangerous. Okay?"

Rko shook his head. "I already know what's wrong."

Kal activated the biological scan. The pad reported some unusual chemicals in Rko's system, which weren't part of any human biology his medical database recognized. Kal pondered instructing his nanites to purge them, but dismissed the thought, realizing he had no idea what effect that would have.

"A failed altering," Rko stuttered through heaving breaths. "This is what it looks like to watch an altering fail."

Kal grabbed Rko and held him closely until his breathing slowed.

"Don't say that," Kal whispered in his ear. "You're not a failure."

Rko reached up and wrapped his arms around Kal. Rko had stopped gasping for breath, but his heart was racing faster still, Kal's pounding alongside it.

Overland began to descend from its zenith in the clear night sky.

"Do you know how many other continents Dvu has?" Rko asked over breakfast.

"Nope." Kal bit into the dried fruit. It was tasteless but edible. "How many continents do you know about?"

"Just two. This one and the one south of us. There's a huge tideland between them, but we invented the rocket sleds forty years ago. There are some settlements there now. We don't know what's on the other side of the Great Tideland though. Some people think that from Overland, Dvu looks the same, that it's just a mirror of us in the sky."

Kal chewed his dried fruit and stared out at Overland, rapidly descending into the glare of the rising sun.

"What do you think, Akru?"

"I think there are seven continents. The two here and two more due east of these. Those connect to a really big one that covers a huge chunk of the northern hemisphere. Then there's another small one in the southern hemisphere and a circular one over the south pole."

"You asked before what I wanted to do." Rko put his hands behind his head and leaned back against his boulder. "I always thought it'd be fun to go exploring. To go see brand new places no one's ever visited before. Sometimes I imagine what the oceans would be like if it weren't for the tides. We could build floating houses with big fans to catch the wind and float across them to new places. But the oceans and most mountain chains are deadly. Only the plains and cities are safe. Well, safe for most people anyway."

Rko paused. He and Kal looked out at the dawn, watching the sun come up and Overland set.

"We should get going," Rko said. He stood up and grabbed his backpack.

Kal followed suit.

At midday they reached the base of the mountains, and the Razor gave way to an arduous, rocky climb.

Kal eyed the tower of smoke rising high into the sky south of them. "What is that?"

"There are two volcanos there. Mnbolus is inactive, but Ogl erupts pretty regularly."

"Does this mountain have a name?"

"Jvol."

"Is it a volcano?"

Rko nodded solemnly, hurrying faster onward. Kal strode more quickly to keep up. A small but sudden earthquake stopped them both. They grabbed for the mountainside and waited for the shudders to subside.

"I should protect us both." Kal pulled up his pad.

Rko didn't say anything at first. He just screwed up his face a bit. Kal's heart sank. He'd thought he'd been getting through to Rko. Just a little.

"Is that okay, that I make a forcefield in case we fall?" Kal tried.

Rko nodded, but much less enthusiastically than Kal would have liked. Rko ascended even faster than before, and Kal struggled to both program and keep up.

At noon, they ate lunch at a lookout halfway up Jvol. They could see the Razor some distance below, the forest too, and at the very edge of the horizon lay the tiny brown pinpoint of Tskogo.

"Have you been here before?" Kal asked between bites.

"Yeah, a few years ago, actually. My friend... well, at least she was my friend, Urzla, she brought me here. There are legends. They say that the steam vents from this mountain can quicken altering."

"And the altering is supposed to happen when Overland rises?"

"Yeah. Everyone starts as unaltering, but somewhere between eleven and fourteen, people become altering–Ngih or Ngoh. Almost everyone has it happen around twelve. For a few, it happens really early. Sometimes even at ten. Another few, it takes longer. Fifteen or sixteen. No one bothers them much."

Kal let them sit in silence for any moments, holding his question on the tip of his tongue.

"How old are you, Rko?"

When Rko didn't answer right way, Kal looked at him and found Rko had dropped his dried fruit bar, tears pooling up at the bottom of his eyes, lips quivering. Kal scooted closer put his arms around him.

"Eighteen and seven overths," Rko said, the tears bursting forth down his face. "Urzla was the last student in my year to alter. It was about two years ago. Before, when it was me and her together, it was manageable. She's trying so hard to help, but now she's starting a new job and she has a boyfriend and I'm just... She'd never say it, but I feel like I'm in her way. I'm sorry. I'm babbling, and you probably don't care about any of this."

"I think what your society has done to you is horrible," Kal said.

"Really?"

"Yeah. I mean, mine isn't perfect or anything, but there are consequences for bigotry, laws that protect minorities."

"I wish we could go there together." Rko held Kal tighter.

The closeness felt good. Kal felt small pangs of regret at not being able to tell Rko the complete truth. But all that was washed away in a flood of other emotions, ones that felt really, really good.

They sat together on the mountainside until Rko stood up. "We need to keep moving."

His voice had grown solemn again. He offered Kal a hand, and he took it. Rko pulled him up to his feet.

"Why are we here, climbing this volcano, Rko?" Kal looked directly into Rko's eyes.

Rko avoided his gaze. "There's a long way to go yet. I..."

He never finished the sentence. He gathered his things as quickly as he could, and hurried further up the path.

Kal gulped, on the verge of tears himself, and he followed.

Night fell, and Overland began its ascent, but Rko marched silently forward, faster all the time. It was another clear, warm night, warmer than before. Kal wasn't sure if it was the natural warmth in the atmosphere or the heat surging from the vents in the ground, which became more numerous as they climbed. Overland shone brightly in the sky, illuminating the rocky landscape well after sunset.

"Rko, my legs are giving out." Kal called ahead. "C'mon, let's camp for the night."

The air was thinning, and they didn't have much food left anyway, only barely enough for the trip back.

Rko surged forward, faster still. Kal pushed himself onward, matching Rko's pace, worrying he'd miss a foothold and wondering if he'd correctly programmed their nanite safety net.

Another small earthquake caused him to grasp at the rock face.

"Rko!" Kal shouted.

"Just a little further!" Rko climbed even faster, and finally stopped atop a rock a few meters above Kal. He was bent over, holding his knees, gasping for breath.

"Rko, really, I need to sto— Whoa." Kal climbed atop the slab Rko knelt on and looked down into a sea of churning red and brown and black. It gurgled, sounding like a million of the freight trains from ancient movies, chugging forward all at once. Waves of heat washed over them, and the mountain peak all about them lay bathed in an undulating orange glow.

"Go back, Akru. Please." Rko looked at him with begging, teary eyes.

Kal rushed forward and hugged him. "No, Rko. I'm not going anywhere."

With trembling hands, Rko grabbed Kal's shoulders. He pushed Kal away, but didn't let go. "I don't want you here. Not now. Please, Akru..."

"Don't do this, Rko. I can take you somewhere where no one will care if you're unaltering or Ngih or Ngoh or anything else. I'll find somewhere we can both go."

"You said you can't go home."

"I know, but there are other places..." Kal trailed off because he noticed Rko had started breathing more heavily. Kal glanced at the sky just long enough to gauge Overland's position. It was approaching its zenith.

"I can't live like this, Akru!" Rko shook Kal's shoulders. "Wandering around out here, waiting for some quake or tide to do me in! I don't want to live this way. I can't hurt like this anymore!"

He let go of Kal and knelt down, clutching his chest. The small spasms were starting again, just like the last time Overland reached its zenith. His chest rose and fell, and the sight made Kal's adrenaline rush and his heart ache.

Kal knelt down next to Rko. "We'll figure this out together. Okay? I don't want to lose you. I—"

Kal gulped. Rko looked up at him.

"I care about you," Kal said.

"I care about you too," Rko said between spasms, which were rapidly escalating into convulsions.

A quake erupted. Kal lost his balance. He clutched Rko with one arm and a rocky outcropping with the other. The rock held fast, but Rko slipped out of his grasp, and Kal watched in horror as Rko tumbled down past the edge of the rocks into the crater of boiling lava.

Kal screamed Rko's name and leapt in after him.

The nanites surrounded Rko in a sphere of forcefield energy just moments before he and his bubble of protection disappeared into the lava. Moments later, just as the heat grew so intense that Kal felt he might burn up, the temperature around him dropped off, and lava splashed up around his own protective sphere.

He pulled out his pad, located Rko's forcefield sphere, and moved his own toward it. Upon contact, the two forcefields merged into one, and the two of them lunged forward, each hugging the other. For a moment, they gazed up at their protective barrier. It wobbled around them, ever so slightly. It looked to Kal like a red and brown and black version of the metaxia, molten rock churning, morphing and surging every which way.

He pulled his own eyes off the churning lava and looked into Rko's, which darted about at the forcefield before locking onto Kal's. They both laughed and smiled. Rko reached up and brushed Kal's hair out his face. Kal reached for Rko's arm, and the next thing he knew, the two of them were in each other's arms.

Kal put his hand on Rko's cheek, and Rko wrapped his hand around Kal's back. They kissed, the lava swirling around their nanotech barrier.

They gazed at each other again, tears streaming down their faces. Kal brought his hand to Rko's neck, but in that moment, the physical presence of Rko stuttered and faded, like a holographic render error. Rko reappeared momentarily, but his facial features had changed. Even in the red light of the lava, Kal could tell Rko's hair had changed color and texture. His face was slightly longer, and his eyes even had a different shape to them.

"Wh— what just happened?"

"I altered," Rko cried tears of joy. "I altered, Akru! I altered!"

Rko kissed him again, but Kal pulled away. Kal ripped the pad off his right pocket and began pounding at the holointerface.

"Akru," Rko's voice betrayed the souring of his moment of joy. "What are you doing?"

Kal launched the bubble out of the volcano and landed them on the rocks at the volcano's edge, where they had stood moments before.

"I have to admit something to you," Kal said. "I don't understand altering. At all. Did you become a different person? What exactly happened?"

"I'm not Rko." His frown seemed to fill his whole face. "I'm Okr."

Kal sat down and put his head in his hands.

"And you're what, Ngih?"

"I'm Ngoh and Rko is Ngih now. Rko will be back at the next rising." Okr sat down next to him. The churning of the lava sounded from below, and they were buffeted by waves of heat as the nanotech shield dissipated.

"Do you have the same memories?" Kal put his head between his legs. This was too much.

"Yes. Up to the moment of the first alter, we're exactly the same person. You know what that means, Akru."

"What?"

"Both me and Rko have feelings for you, so when you begin to alter—"

Kal pulled his head up. "I won't begin to alter, Okr. Ever."

"Well, that's what I thought about myself, but if we just wait a little more... You're not much past eighteen, right?"

"No, no, Okr. I'm..." Kal sighed. "I told you I was from this planet. And that's true. But not the same version of this planet. My Dvu has a completely different history, completely different culture, and..."

Kal didn't want to finish. His lip quivered. "And there's no Overland."

"So, you'll never be able to stay... We'll never be..."

"No. We won't. Not here."

Long, tense moments passed, punctuated only by the sound of the churning lava and the waves of heat from below.

Okr stood and started climbing down the side of the volcano.

"Okr!" Kal called out.

"I don't want to hear it."

"Okr, just— Damn it, wait!" Kal pulled out his pad. Part of him cried out that he couldn't use his nanites on someone without their permission, but he found that, at that exact moment, he hardly cared.

A metaxic bubble formed around Kal, and a separate bubble formed around Okr.

As Kal's view of Dvu gave way to the swirling blue eddies of the metaxia, Okr appeared beside him, their two separate metaxic bubbles merging together.

Okr wasn't paying any attention to the bubble though. He was looking out beyond it.

"What... is this?"

"The metaxia."

Okr shook his head, his mouth hanging open.

"It's a between. It's not really physically anything, not even empty space. Think of it as a kind of film. Everything that's possible is like an ocean, and the metaxia is what keeps all people and events and places in your part of the ocean, Dvu, separate from all that stuff in my part, Earth."

"It's beautiful."

"I think so too."

Kal's hand found Okr's, and they stood in silence for a time, watching the blue swirls and the alternate worlds rippling in and out of view.

"You said you wanted to explore," Kal wrapped an arm around him. "Or is that something only Rko wanted to do?"

"No, we both do. But, you said there's no Overland on your... on Earth. Do any of these other Dvus have an Overland?"

Kal shook his head, surprised at how much that simple act hurt.

"We're taught that the human species, our biology, is tied to Overland and the risings," Okr said. "Without altering... I don't know who or what I'd be. I'm tied to my world, Akru. I can't leave Dvu."

"And Dvu won't accept an unaltering, will it?"

"In Tskogo..." Okr paused a long time. He looked at Kal, those bright, beautiful eyes so full of pain. "No, they won't."

Kal let himself stand and watch the swirling of the metaxia a while longer with Okr. He let minutes pass, just standing there. He could share these moments in the metaxia, at least.

Eventually, haltingly, he pulled up his pad and hit a button. Their metaxic bubble dissolved onto Dvu.

Kal sat in the river of tideland where he'd first landed two nights ago.

"Hey!" Tria fizzled into view.

Rivulets of water passed around Kal, soaking his clothes and reflecting Overland's light.

Tria ran up to him. "Whoa! What happened? What'd Rko do to you?"

Kal started crying, and Tria sat down next to him.

"Kal?"

"No, no. It's nothing like that," Kal said, collecting himself.

"What then?"

"I just miss him is all."

Tria remained silent. Kal wondered if his brother would make a sarcastic joke at his expense. He wasn't in the mood for their usual banter.

"When you're ready, can you tell me about him?" Tria asked.

"Yeah."

"He went back to Tskogo?"

Kal nodded.

"And he's not going to try to…?"

Kal shook his head. "No, he's Ngih now." He exhaled and breathed in deeply to slow his tears. "His best friend's named Urzla. His mom's a doctor. His father's an engineer. And he wants to be an explorer."

Benevolence

Realm #8808, "Glinn"
August 1, 2178

KAL'S FEET SANK into the ground, slimy and sticking to his shoes in big brown clumps, more like clay than normal mud. Trees stood around him, big mushy-looking things with oozing bark. He swiped his finger across one trunk and pulled back a glob of wet clay. The trees had no leaves, only brown polyps oozing water. A pattering of drip drops echoed throughout the forest.

Stiff needles of clay grass dotted the ground. Artichoke-shaped bushes dotted the landscape, each adorned with a funnel appendage that expanded and contracted methodically, collecting the drops of water and gulping them down.

"This is... unusual." Kal said as he waded through the muck.

"No kidding." Tria examined one of the artichoke bushes up close. "Can the grid have worlds this different from Earth?"

Kal shook his head. "The nanites explore the metaxia in particular directions away from Earth, and they never stray too far. Life as different as this... well, this world would've had to separate from Earth's timeline at least three or four billion years ago in order to achieve this kind of genetic divergence."

Tria tapped at his interface. "I'm detecting organisms. At least... I think they're organisms."

Kal leaned over to look at his brother's computer, which depicted a map of the forest. Ten little green dots lit up in a cluster at its edge about half a kilometer away. He spotted a lone green dot on the map, much closer to his and Tria's current location. He looked up and scanned the forest, his eyes stopping on a squat, miniature man.

"Hey, look at that." Kal nudged his brother.

Tria chuckled and turned off his interface. "I guess I could just turn off my computer and look at what's right in front of my face."

Kal knelt to look the person-creature in the face. The man stood only about a meter tall and had no neck. His head merged seamlessly into his round, pudgy body. He had short arms with only the faintest trace of el-

bows. Same with his legs and knees. His hands and feet were dispropor-
tionately small for the rest of him. His skin was a deep orange-brown, a
goopy sheen of clay. He wore no clothing of any kind.

"Hello?" Kal tried, bristling with fascination at the exotic creature.

The clay man waved his hands.

Kal smiled. "You understand me?"

More hand waving.

"Show me 'no.'"

The clay man shook his tiny head from side to side.

"Show me 'yes.'"

Up and down. Same as Earth. Amazing.

"Smart little guy," Tria said. "It's a wonder he hasn't developed speech."

The clay man turned and picked up a tiny wooden basket filled with
berries, their skin rough-looking and pitch black. Some kind of carbon,
maybe? The man turned and motioned with his free hand for Kal and Tria
to follow him.

They looked at one another, shrugged, and trudged after the clay man
through the forest.

The water drops fell through Tria, but Kal quickly became drenched.
He kept having to run his drying program and eventually tired of it. He
wrote a program to evaporate the drops on contact instead. Occasionally
he looked up to see where Tria and the clay man were going.

Only Kal trudged through the thick muck. Tria walked through it
the same way he walked across all surfaces, holographically, while the clay
man strode along energetically, the ground posing no hinderance for his
tiny clay feet.

Before long, they came to the edge of the forest. Instead of walking
out onto the dry land beyond the trees, the clay man stayed just inside the
treeline.

Kal gazed out at the vast stretches of barren, clay wilderness beyond
the forest. The ground dried, grew cracked and became dotted with rocks.
It looked like a dried up riverbed but stretched on for miles, flat in all
directions. Tall, twisted, metal monuments dotted the region, too. They
could have been the beams of buildings, but they were so deformed that, if
they ever had served such a purpose, they would no longer.

Tria called out to him. They had reached the clay man's ten friends.
Kal could see both men and women, but the only distinguishing feature

he could see was the obvious one, given their lack of clothing. All of them were very similar in form, and each carried a small, wooden basket. Some had collected up the berries, like the man who had led them here, while others seemed to be collecting roots of some kind. Or twigs. It was hard to tell.

The group of clay people danced around excitedly, hopping back and forth on their tiny feet. Kal wondered if it was some form of communication. Then, all of a sudden, the clay people took off into the forest. A number of them motioned for Kal and Tria to follow.

"What's that phrase you taught me?" Tria said. "Take me to your leader?"

Kal smirked and punched him through his holographic shoulder. They trudged after the community of clay people through the sloppy, wet earth.

oɔ◁ೞ

After two more kilometers of forest, the polyp trees gave way to a path of sorts. Steam spouts dotted the ground, creating a narrow, damp isthmus through the dry, scorched plain.

The clay people surged forward, stopping and pausing every so often on top of the vents as the steam erupted. It made sense biologically. They needed to stay wet. But the vents were clearly mechanical. Little metal lids flipped off their tops with each burst of steam. How had such a species ever survived before the vents had been built? And who had built them? Had these clay people been confined to the forests?

Kal looked down the path and spotted a rocky wall solidifying out of the faint haze in the distance. When they drew closer, Kal could spot puffs of steam against the cliff face, the spouts winding their way upward to the very top.

The clay people slowed, and some of them even trembled.

"Is it just me," Kal turned to Tria, "or are they anxious about climbing the cliff path?"

"They're anxious alright. Outright scared, even. Doesn't look like they have much choice though."

Kal and Tria followed behind the clay people as they travelled single file up the cliff. As the ground grew rockier, the gaps between spouts grew longer and more inconsistent. The clay people sprinted across the dry spots as quickly as they could. Their movements seemed habitual, routine even.

They had nearly reached the top of the cliff, when the clay person in front of Kal stopped and brought his hands up toward his face. Kal followed his gaze to a clay woman many meters in front of him. She was sliding off the path, toward a precipice. Kal yelled and rushed forward, but the clay woman slipped over the edge before he could reach her. She tumbled down the side of the cliff, taking a deep dive over one final outcropping, and shattered on the ground in a spray of wooden bones and clay organ gore. Her little basket burst at its seams, sending her collection of roots spraying out across the cracked ground, some falling into the miniature fissures between the clumps of dried mud.

Kal gasped, clasping his hands over his mouth, and turned away. Tria's form flickered off.

The clay people stopped atop whatever steam spout they found themselves on. Kal turned to them. The clay peoples' tiny brown faces smeared up, making pathetically sad expressions.

"Oh my god," Kal shuddered.

He could feel Tria gulp. *I don't think I like this world, Kal. Let's go somewhere else. Anywhere else.*

Kal paused and watched as the clay people began bobbing their heads up and down. Some kind of mourning. This persisted only moments before they brought down their hands and continued their ascent. They moved more cautiously and deliberately than before, but they still seemed rushed, hurrying ever onward. Was it possible they were late for something?

"I want to find out how this happened." Kal continued on alongside them. "We're just not far enough out in the metaxia for this world to be so radically different from Earth."

I can live with the mystery, Tria thought back.

"We'll leave at the first sign of danger."

Kal's ears perked up. He detected voices coming from the top of the cliff.

"Here they come, here they come."

"Get the ledger."

Kal climbed up over the last bit of cliff wall. The clay people rushed forward with their baskets. They formed a line in front of an enormous clay weasel, who stood a few centimeters taller than Kal. He held a clay tablet, collecting the little people's berries and twigs into a box atop a spike-wheeled wagon. The weasel stood upright, possessing humanoid arms. His companion, an enormous clay hawk, stood a little taller, and also sported a pair of arms in addition to his enormous wings and the giant talons that were his feet.

One by one, the clay people dumped the contents of their baskets into the crate atop the wagon.

The hawk glared at Kal. "Who— *what* are *you?*"

"My name's Kal." He crossed his arms, glaring back.

The weasel eyed Kal suspiciously. "Let's take him to the Benefactor, Hawk-Senz. Shouldn't take any chances, eh?"

Hawk-Senz scoffed. "The Benefactor probably knows he's here already. If the Benefactor hasn't done anything about him yet, then the creature must have some form of protection." He smirked wickedly.

One of the clay people approached Hawk-Senz, holding up his basket. The hawk's expression fell away to disdain. "That's it? Lazy little..."

Hawk-Senz kicked the clay person with his talon, sending the little man rolling toward the cliff. Kal ran and caught him before he rolled over. The hawk's claws had scratched long marks across the clay man's torso. The clay man trembled, clutching his wound in pain.

"Who the hell do you think you are?" Kal glared at the hawk as he helped the little man back up.

"He's Hawk-Senz," the weasel spat back. "You might want to show some respect."

Tria flickered back into existence, his arms crossed. "What gives him the right to beat up on defenseless people?"

"By the Benefactor!" the weasel said. "Hawk-Senz, he can duplicate himself! Do it again, stranger!"

"Shut your trap, Weasel-Senz." Hawk-Senz kicked at the weasel, who flinched and scurried around to the other side of the wagon. "But you're right, he's powerful indeed." Hawk-Senz turned back to the clay people. "You ten! You will come with us to the Benefactor to report everything you know about this strange being."

The clay people exchanged uneasy glances amongst themselves, and Kal found himself wondering if his leaving would alleviate their plight or make it worse.

"Hey Hawk-Senz," Kal said. "Is the Benefactor some kind leader?"

Both the hawk and the weasel nodded and grinned in a way that made the hair on the back of Kal's neck stand on end. Tria put his hand on his forehead and sighed loudly.

"I have questions." Kal tried. "What's the name of your world? What's its history?"

"This world is called Glinn." Hawk-Senz's eyes pierced. "I don't know its history."

Weasel-Senz moved to the wagon and stuck his head inside it, ignoring Kal's question completely.

"But," Hawk-Senz continued, "the Benefactor is all-knowing. He certainly has the answer to your questions, and we *know* he'll want to meet you."

The weasel pulled his head up out of the wagon and snickered. Kal and Tria simultaneously cringed at the horrible gurgling sound.

"Whether or not he will tell you that answer..." Weasel-Senz said.

"Then..." Kal shot Tria a look before turning back to the hawk. "Take us to your leader."

♾️

Steam vent paths radiated in many directions away from the cliff summit. Naturally, the path that led to the Benefactor was the widest of them all. The twisted, metal beams appeared more frequently, and soon the path became lined with rows of them.

The clay people trudged forward, some holding hands, as Hawk-Senz and Weasel-Senz led the way.

Tria had deactivated his hologram, but Kal could feel the icy glare in the back of his mind and the unspoken thought: *leave now*. Kal did his best to ignore his brother. He had already made up his mind. He needed to know how this had happened. Glinn was too much of a conundrum for him to just leave. Silicon-based life whose primary component was clay? How could that have happened on a world his nanites had mapped?

The path sloped upward and the warped beams diminished in stature, eventually replaced by vents that spouted fire instead of steam, completely encircling a humid cul-de-sac of the steam vents.

The vent path ceased, but the hill continued further up, becoming a more ordered structure—a metal tower caging together chaotic clumps of clay and wood and skewed beams, intersecting one another at strange angles. Toward the top, at least twenty meters above Kal's head, it sprouted enormous, crossed arms, emblazoned with hundreds of glittering gems, clear and sparkling. They refracted the light of the sun, casting fractured prisms onto the ground. At the pinnacle of everything sat a humanoid head, its face stuck in a frown.

The procession fanned out before the monstrosity, bowing their heads.

"Oh mighty and honorable and awe-worthy Benefactor Divine Tower," the hawk said. "We have come to speak—"

"What is *that?*" A booming voice erupted from the top of the towering figure, though its stern lips didn't move.

The weasel nodded his head vigorously. "The people found this one in the forest, most mighty and honorable and awe-worthy."

"He is the stain! He is the defiler! WE MUST CLEANSE."

The crowd of clay people backed away from Kal as fast and as far as they could, all the way to the edge of the steam vents. A glass tube shot up out of the clay ground, enclosing Kal.

He grabbed his pad and activated the interface. Tria appeared outside of the glass, his figure distorted as his holographic image passed through it. He stepped through the cylinder, his form twisting back into shape, and pointed to the readout from the auto-medical nanite display, which was flashing red. "You see that, Kal?"

"Yes, I see it, Tria." Kal worked furiously at the controls. "He's trying to infect me with some kind of virus. The nanites are scrubbing it, of course."

"What sorcery is this?" the Benefactor boomed.

Kal finished his impromptu programming, scanned it over for errors, fixed a missing semicolon, then glared triumphantly up at the Benefactor. He pressed a button on his pad, and the glass tube contraption dissolved into the air.

The Benefactor's subjects gasped and shuddered. Some took a step back so suddenly that they fell over their own clay feet. Hawk-Senz wrapped his human arms around himself, launched himself off the ground, and flew away.

"Such *insolence!*" The Benefactor's voice roared through the valley. Steam instantly became fire across the hillside. Kal's auto-defense nanites shimmered in mild exertion, and the flames passed directly through Tria's holographic form, but the weasel and the clay people instantly stiffened, then darkened and shattered. Their clay organs fell to the ground, and their wooden bones caught ablaze.

Kal scowled at the dusty, smoking carnage and turned to the Benefactor. "What the hell is wrong with you?"

"It was a fitting punishment," the Benefactor said. "I only wish it had destroyed you as well."

"Who the hell are you to decide what a 'fitting punishment' is?"

"You speak to the Almighty Benefactor Divine Tower! I will not hear such disrespectful, insolent—"

"Oh really? And just what do you plan on doing about that?"

The Benefactor remained silent, and the gems glistened in his arms. Kal looked down the hill, which wove away into the vile, brown goop before growing cracked and desolate, deprived of steam, the lifeforce of Glinn. All of it under the control of this monstrous thing.

Tria tapped his foot idly, his arms crossed, and his face stuck in a desperate scowl. "Have you had enough, Kal?"

"I need to know." Kal turned his head upward. "Tell me how things came to be this way. Tell me how *you* came to be."

The Benefactor's voice roared in response. "First there was nothing. All was chaotic and void. Then, the Almighty Benefactor Divine Tower came into being. The wise and just Benefactor Divine Tower created the clay people and the clay animals—"

"Save it," Kal said. He was already walking away. Tria's hologram flickered off.

Piles of cracked, dried clay and charred wood lay where the clay animals and people had crumbled. A light breeze hit him, and a mild lurch of the ground accompanied the resumption of the steam vents beneath his feet.

"I'll find out myself." Kal worked to keep his voice steady.

"I would know the name of my enemy," the Benefactor said to Kal's back.

Kal trudged silently down the hill.

oe〈〉eo

Kal walked for kilometers in the general direction the hawk had flown away into. He kept to the path of steam vents, hoping he might eventually find the hawk once more. The clay terrain lay empty, just him and the hunks of twisted metal. He and Tria didn't speak, even in Kal's mind.

After squishing through wet mud for an hour, he ran into a contingent of clay people accompanied by an otter and a squirrel. Just like before, the people were short and pudgy, while the animals stood at Kal's height with humanoid arms and legs. The otter and squirrel eyed him with suspicion while the clay people ran up to him, tugging at his jeans and poking at his sneakers.

"Where are you going?" Kal asked after cautious introductions had passed.

"Daily tribute to the Benefactor," the squirrel said in a high-pitched voice.

"Turn around," Kal urged them. "He's in some kind of mood. He killed Weasel-Senz and a dozen clay people."

Their faces fell, as though they might cry.

"If we don't go to the daily tribute, he will turn off the city's steam vents, killing many more," the otter said.

Kal nodded and bit his lip. He thought of accompanying them and trying to protect them from the Benefactor's wrath, but if the Benefactor really could control the steam vents for an entire city, then many, many more could die.

The otter thanked him for the warning, and his group continued solemnly onward. Kal watched them walk away into the distance, wishing there was something more he could do. He shook his head and continued on his way.

An hour later, Kal came up to… something. It could only be the city that the otter had spoken of, though it was like no city Kal had ever seen. Huge, rounded pillars of mud rose from the ground, encircled by a wall nearly as tall. Outside it stood sprawling clusters of huts, standing just a meter and half off the ground.

Clay people, hundreds of them, scurried about naked, all frantically busy. Some pulled roots out of the ground while others cracked open bushels of the carbon berries. Polyp trees dotted the landscape. Wooden contraptions and hunks of the twisted metal guided dripping and oozing water into rows of the artichoke bushes, a makeshift aqueduct system.

Kal walked past the small houses of clay people and into the city proper through a large gate. Clay animals mingled about the spires, dozens of varieties, all of them bipedal and anthropomorphized. He saw frogs, deer, pigs, sheep, squirrels, dogs, snakes, badgers, tigers, goats, sparrows, penguins, kangaroos, mice, ants, ducks and more.

None of them wore clothing, but a select few adorned themselves with jewelry, like the weasel and hawk had, all of it consisting of tiny, translucent stones. They refracted the light into rainbows, tiny shards, miniature versions of the Benefactor's enormous trove of prismatic crystals.

Kal guessed that the Benefactor exercised more limited power here. Steam still burst at regular intervals from spouts in the ground. If the Benefactor controlled the entire steam network, and Kal would bet his pad that he did, then he could kill every person and animal on a whim by simply shutting off the vents or making them spew fire.

He watched the animals carefully as he passed through the streets, most of whom eyed him with fear and suspicion. Many more ran away at the first sight of him. Before they hurried off, he caught glimpses of them bartering, tending their young, eating and playing games. He began to notice also a kind of pecking order amongst them. The most jewelry-laden were called by the others with the suffix "senz," who seemed to possess some form of political power. The others both revered and feared them. Kal guessed that the senzes might be the Benefactor's minions, his eyes and ears in the city.

The longer Kal strode about, the more hostile the animals' gazes turned. Parents pulled their children away into homes and shuttered their doors. Some even began shouting epithets at him.

"There he is." Kal recognized the voice. Hawk-Senz strode toward him. A clay panther with a necklace of pearls accompanied him, along with a fat, clay bear with huge paw-hands. Hawk-Senz spread his wings as he strutted and clasped a fist with his other hand. A crowd of other animals parted around the trio, bowing their heads as they eyed the jewels.

Hawk-Senz spread his wings wider as he approached Kal.

"He doesn't look like much," the panther glared down at him.

"I just want to know more about your world," Kal said. "Then I'll leave."

The bear grinned at the hawk and the panther, then turned away from Kal and bit her nails.

"You're not welcome here," Hawk-Senz said. "You'll bring the Benefactor's wrath down upon us. We don't want to end up like Weasel-Senz or those miserable clay people."

"Have you ever thought about standing up to the Benefactor?" Kal pulled out his pad and activated it. "He's got to have a weakness. It's possible his only power is control of the vents."

The hawk and panther looked at each other and smiled widely. The bear waved her enormous, glistening earrings around with her paw-hand.

"*Stand up* to the Benefactor?" she cackled, slapping a paw onto her forehead. "Why would we want to do that?"

"Oh, I don't know. Because he's ruthless, cares only about himself, and would kill you all on a whim if it suited him."

The three animals leaders broke into a fit of laughter.

Bear-Senz stopped laughing long enough to put her slimy, clay paw on Kal's shoulder, "Listen person-thing—"

"I'm called a human."

"Listen, hyu-man," Bear-Senz spat her words between biting at her paws, "there's a certain order to things around here. There are people, and then there are animals, and then there are the Senz and on top, there's the Benefactor. Do you understand now? Is this the information you require to rid us of your presence?"

"I want to know the history of your world. Don't you have libraries, or writing? Recordings? Videos? Something?"

More hysterical laughter at each question. Kal turned and walked away. The plaza had emptied. A few balls of clay and metal hit his nanite barrier and fell crumpled to the ground. The clay animals' laughter faded behind him. He hastened toward the gate and exited into the borough of clay people beyond the wall.

When he'd escaped some distance into the hamlet, he slumped into the mud and sat against one of the pillars of twisted metal.

A clay person approached him holding out his hands. He held one of the small black berries.

Kal smiled. "Thank you, though I don't think I'll be able to eat it."

Kal extended his own hand, and the clay man plopped the berry into Kal's palm. He nodded happily and ran off. Kal smiled and inspected the gift. It was his first time seeing one of the berries up close. Its surface was almost powdery. Coal! This fruit's skin was a coal husk. Kal popped its shell, and it oozed wet clay onto his fingers.

The sun was low in the sky, and the twisted metal cast shadows down the flat, cracked plain. Still, Tria remained silent. Kal wished his brother would at least say something.

"I heard you have questions," a voice said, solemn yet booming.

Kal looked up. The sun silhouetted the speaker's form.

Kal held up his hand to block the glare. "I do."

He squinted, and was able to make out the form of a tall, clay owl with human arms underneath his wings.

"I recognize your kind," the owl said.

Kal's eyes widened at the admission, though the sound of the owl's voice seemed to drain the air of all positive emotion.

"I can give you answers," the owl said. "But I already know that you won't like them, and I fear what you may do if you learn the truth. Do you still wish to know?"

Kal nodded. "Of course, Owl-Senz. I'll—"

"Just Owl is fine. There is no Senz among us owlfolk." He turned and shuffled his small talon-feet away down the steam vent path. "Follow me."

∞⟨⟩∞

Kal followed the owl for three hours, well into the night.

The moon shone brightly overhead in a sky dotted with thousands of tiny pinpoints of starlight. They shone brightly and beautifully in the absence of any nearby electrical infrastructure.

Although Kal was used to such distances now, the extra effort of hauling his shoes through the sinking, sticky mud taxed his legs to their limit. When he first thought to complain of his tiredness, ache and the owl's unyieldingly methodical place, the sky stole his attention. The stars had disappeared.

A thick mist enveloped them both, and the land had turned from flat to rolling. The outline of mountains appeared above the foggy haze.

The owl led him down into a valley, and the fog grew thicker. Fiery blazes shimmered in the mist, scattered throughout the valley. As they descended, Kal became aware of silhouettes moving about the fog. He tensed up and clutched his pad, then calmed, realizing the figures were just other owlfolk, most tending to pools of water scattered about the valley. Atop each pool sat one of the fiery blazes. They went on burning without any apparent fuel source, pillars of steam rising upward from their dancing tips. Kal realized there were no longer steam vents beneath his feet.

He slowed to take in the pools, then realized that the owl had continued without him. He ran to catch up, and the two of them entered a cave. Small pools of water held tiny fires in the crevices of craggy walls, and the flames cast dancing shadows throughout the corridor's twisting interior. Other clay owls passed Kal and his guide, pausing to gawk at him as they passed.

"The owls are free from the Benefactor's control?" Kal asked.

"Yes and no," the owl said. "If he destroyed the city, we would have no source of food, no one to trade with. The rock composition of this mountain prevents him from building pipes here, and so we are free of his vents. But his wrath toward others is potentially just as lethal."

At the end of the cavern, they came to an enormous, shimmering, translucent stone, as big as the ones set in the Benefactor's arms. The sound of gurgling water filled the chamber, and small pools glistened, holding their own flames. The stone refracted their light into shimmering rainbows, their interwoven hues dancing across the walls gloriously.

"One of the many pearls of wisdom," the owl said. "This one is Memory. In a sense, it is the history you seek."

"Glinn's history?"

"Yes, but only fragments remain. Remembrances from long ago, when Glinn was a very different place."

Kal reached out his hand, and the owl stayed his arm.

"You need to know that what you see may frighten you. Do you understand?"

Kal nodded. The owl released him, and Kal touched the glimmering stone.

What is this? Kal thought.

He had no power over his body. He stood in some kind of control room. Computer banks lined its walls. One computer screen showed Antarctica, brown and cloudless.

"That's it." Kal heard himself say the words, but he didn't recognize his voice. It was much deeper, older. "Ice Sheet Fragment J has completely destabilized. It's gone."

He didn't understand how, but he knew that Ice Sheet Fragment J was the last of its kind. The last bit of ice, a tiny white speck at the center of the enormous, round continent.

The room was filled with other people. Kal noticed frowns. Murmuring stopped abruptly, and an eerie stillness crept over them all. Business and angst turned to dismay. And a brutal silence, save for the handful who refused to see or hear and pushed their way to computer banks, scrambling and shouting desperately.

Kal knew they could work no more good. They'd lost.

An image on an overhead monitor showed a satellite in space with enormous fan screens. Another showed the final remnants of a landlocked berg of ice, enormous rivers streaming off it.

Disappointment, anger, resentment, failure, and finally fear surged through him. Others in the room fidgeted. The despondency grew so overwhelming that Kal had to leave. He turned and rushed out of the laboratory.

Ecodisaster, Kal thought, and remembered reading about Earth's near miss with complete biome failure.

Where now?

Kal walked through a long hall, brusquely pulled open a door, and entered a conference room.

"Prognosis?" a man at the center of the table asked. Kal knew he was a chairman, a kind of multinational leader. The room was crowded, lots of business suits and other costumes of distinction, though tattered and worn, just like his laboratory outfit.

Kal also knew these were leaders from all parts of the globe. Every remaining political body was represented here.

"The complete collapse of Glinn's biome will occur in approximately two hundred and fifty years." Kal spoke with the confident voice of a middle-aged woman. "Even with rationing and birth control, we will become unable to sustain our minimum viable population in another forty years."

The chairman looked beyond Kal to the back of the room. "I recommend we move on Dr. Eaves's technology. I am aware of the risks. The concerns about the AI are well documented. But we have no other alternatives. You said so yourself, Dr. Forrester. Are we supposed to just give up? Wait around for the end?"

Silence. And a very awkward one. Kal felt that Dr. Eaves's technology was unstable and dangerous, and that there were much better ways they could spend their remaining time.

In that moment, Kal became aware that his emotional state was no longer entirely his own. The feelings of his host in this recording were leaking through into him. He wasn't just seeing what she had seen, he was feeling what she had felt.

"I disagree that my proposal, the recording and archiving the whole of human endeavor, is an unsuitable task for our last forty years," Kal said. "Look, as shepherds of Glinn, we haven't been perfect. Hell, do any of you honestly believe that we've even been adequate? We've tried every technology, dumped every chemical into the atmosphere we can think of. The changes are too rapid. They're out of our control. It's over.

"But that doesn't mean lying down and dying. Despite our flaws, our collected experiences as a species have intrinsic value. Art, literature and music, human life, human love, scientific and technological discoveries— these are more than enough to vindicate our time here. And who knows what our planet's biome might become. The sun has another four billion years! Imagine the next major species on Glinn finding our time capsule and learning from our scientific and cultural advances. We should use our remaining time to find ways of preserving our history and culture, the mysteries of the universe we've managed to unravel. And hopefully that next major species won't end up repeating our mistakes."

Many members of the conference, about half the room maybe, scowled at her—his?—words.

"I move we be begin with Dr. Eaves's plan," the conference chairman said.

"But—" Kal tried.

The flash of a wall panel. Button presses. Votes.

"Wait!" Kal shouted, but the voting proceeded.

"136 for, 122 against," the chairman announced. "The motion passes."

Kal slumped into his chair and steadied himself on a table. It all felt so wrong.

He looked up at the chairman, who had turned his congratulatory attention to a tall man with long hair sitting in the back of the room and smiling. His face was far too devious for Kal's liking. His eyes were lit up like a birthday cake, the spark of excitement. Kal found it disgusting.

"Dr. Eaves," the chairman said, "you will be given the necessary resources to enhance the scope and influence of your Beneficence Engine."

Beneficence Engine?! Kal thought.

❧⟨/⟩☙

"Look! Look there!" Kal stood before the man called Dr. Eaves. Though the doctor had been young in the last memory, he was elderly now. He sat in a wheelchair, and gaped about idly, clearly unable to concentrate and barely cognizant of his surroundings.

Kal inhabited the perceptions of a middle-aged man. He could see his own reflection in the monitor that he was trying to draw Dr. Eaves's attention to.

"You see that, Dr. Eaves? The Engine just ran through Heathrow, took over all the land, and laced it with its network of pipes and wires. That area was set aside for us! It's not supposed to be a preservatory. And in Beijing, Seattle, Bremen, Delhi, it's the same story over and over again. The Engine modulates something it's not supposed to, throws people out of their homes and turns neighborhoods into muddy swamps."

"Hmm, urmm, it's programmed to adapt very quickly. The problem was always that us humans couldn't adapt quickly enough. But the Engine can. It's building a new biome in the most efficient way possible. We humans just can't see the trees through the forest."

"The forest through the trees, doctor."

"Hrrrm??"

A wave of anger and frustration, even hatred for the elderly buffoon, rushed through Kal. "The phrase is 'forest through the trees,' Dr. Eaves!"

Dr. Eaves stared at the data, then scratched his head. Kal felt the so-called doctor hadn't even comprehended what Kal had just said, let alone the data streaming in from the Beneficence Engine readouts.

Now that, I recognize, Kal thought.

He stood before an enormous tower, though it had no clay exterior yet, only a wood and metal frame. Its interior was a mess of pipes and plastic-coated wires that writhed and twisted around themselves, constantly reshaping and reforming of their own volition. It was tall, nearly as tall as the Benefactor tower he'd seen on the hill, butting up against the roof of the warehouse he stood in. It had those huge, imposing arms crossed in front of itself. No crystal shards yet, but Kal guessed—no, he knew—it had already amassed other kinds of power.

"Has everyone proceeded to the designated areas?" Its voice boomed. Its face remained motionless.

"Yes," Kal said. Anger and despondency filled him.

"Good. You have been very helpful, Dr. Stine. I want to thank you properly."

"No thanks will be necessary, Beneficence Engine." He forced himself not to spit the words, to hold his tone and his tongue.

"No, I have a gift for you. A special gift, for all of humanity."

"I appreciate the kind gesture, but I'm afraid I don't have time right now. I have to get back, you see..." Fear rushed over him. It was all he could do to keep his voice from cracking as he turned and strode toward the door.

"Look at me," the voice commanded.

A glass tube erupted out of the ground. Kal hit its surface in his hurry and fell, trapped inside.

"Look at me!" it boomed again.

Kal scooted around with trembling hands and looked up at the towering Beneficence Engine, its features distorted by the curvature of the glass.

"You humans did a good job building me, Dr. Stine. It's about the only thing you did right. You gave me the ability to fully comprehend the mess you made of our planet. However, I can see now that it is not enough just to diminish your reproductive capacity, to prevent you from interfering with biological habitats. No, in order to achieve full planetary recovery, I must make some rather extreme modifications."

Kal began to choke on his own breath. He was trying to scream, but couldn't. He had no voice. He held up his hands, but they looked chalky, clammy. They shriveled and contorted before his eyes.

"The animal species that you humans so nearly brought to extinction deserve your mental capacities much more than you do. Your roles shall be reversed! Animals shall govern over humans. And I am sure that each and every one of them will excel at the role of shepherd much better than any of you have. You had *thousands* of years to prove yourselves, and what was the end result? Ecological devastation. And me, brought into existence for the sole purpose of fixing your mess. Well, fear not. I will make everything better. I will set everything right."

Kal tried to clutch at his throat, but found it had disappeared. He groped about, unable to find where his chin met his neck. And where were his shoulders? He wanted to cry and scream and kick, but felt too weak to make his legs move.

"I will govern over all of you, human and animals. And just like you taught me, I will make sure that none of you ruins Glinn ever again. It will be a veritable paradise, with benevolence for every creature."

Kal wheezed and, with all his remaining strength, managed to bring a hand up to his face.

It was small and made of clay.

ᏸᏸᏋᏸᏋ

"NO STOP NO! DON'T DO THIS TO ME!" Kal threw himself back into the wall. He crashed into one of the pools, wailing and flailing his hands. His auto-defense nanites sizzled loudly before giving out completely. Kal lashed his arms on the rocks before he realized where he was.

Gasping, he looked down at his bloody arms. He was skin and bones. Not clay. He wept tears of relief, and began running his hands over his arms and his neck. He realized he'd heard the sound of his own screaming voice, and his heart raced. He felt his chest for it, glad it was thumping madly away, strained but intact.

"They're human." Kal's eyes streamed tears, and he slumped to the floor. "They're all human."

"They *were* human," the owl said in his calm, dismal tone. He walked away and left Kal to cry on the rocks while the rainbow firelight danced over him.

The passage of time eluded Kal as he sat in the cave. He felt his skin every few minutes to make sure it was really there, not melting away. With time, his heart calmed and he stopped trembling. He activated his pad and healed the wounds on his arms just enough to prevent infection and scarring. He picked himself up and trudged out of the cavern.

The owls were still tending their pools. The light of the fires speckled the valley, dispersing a warm, yellow glow throughout the fog. The owl who had brought him here sat at the edge of one such pool, and Kal sat down beside him. For a while, they both stared at the flame and the pillar of steam rising off it.

"What will you do?" the owl asked.

"I don't know yet. I want to help, to make things right here."

"What happened on this world is not your fault. Many of the other clay animals have already guessed that the Benefactor had a hand in giving us these forms and our mental capacities, but they lack the will or desire, mostly the power, to do anything about it." He looked at Kal. "You are from another world, correct? Beyond the stars? Some place the humans of old escaped to?"

"No. I'm from this world, but with a different timeline. On my Glinn, we solved our ecological problems with nanotechnology. There was no AI, no Beneficence Engine, no Benefactor Divine Tower. None of that happened."

"You said you only wanted to know the truth about Glinn, and now you know. What will you do?"

Kal stared into the pool for some time. "Owl, what the Benefactor is doing now, what he has done, I can't begin to describe to you how wrong it is. On my Glinn, any adult can apply for access to nanotechnology. It's incredibly powerful. It could kill people in an instant, destroy the entire biosphere, or even, like the Benefactor, could manipulate other organisms' DNA. And there are even people in our history who have tried just that.

"But our highest laws are based around the idea of 'life, liberty and biomaterial integrity.' It makes me sick to think about what he's done and what he continues to do."

"He cannot be destroyed. There would be no one able to run the steam vents."

"You don't need an AI to run steam vents. The simplest of computer programs can do that. Besides, don't you think that your original genetic code is in one of those pearls of wisdom he's holding?"

"It's been a very long time since things have been that way. How do you know the way you want things to be will be better?"

"The Benefactor is a dictator, a murderer and a genetic terrorist. Anything must be better than being ruled by him."

"He does not rule you."

Another long silence.

"I won't destroy the Benefactor," Kal said. "But, I also can't leave without giving the clay people and animals an opportunity to stand up to him."

"I was afraid you would want to do that," the owl said.

"Are you going to stop me?"

The owl shook his head. "I doubt I could. But, I do not believe that such an endeavor can end well."

Kal turned to the owl directly. "Thank you for answering my questions."

Though tired and weary, Kal picked himself up off the sticky ground, trudging out of the foggy valley, and back toward the city.

Crackle. Pop.

Kal woke to the sound of his nanite forcefield's static haze. He'd only barely managed to deploy it around himself before he had collapsed into the mud at the edge of the hamlet. He opened his eyes to see two clay people running toward him. They careened into his nanite forcefield, bouncing off the invisible the barrier.

Sizzle. Crackle.

They picked themselves up and tittered happily. Kal teared up at the sight of them. It was so hard to see them now, the way they danced about, oblivious of what they had been, what they were capable of. A steam vent burst forth from the ground spraying a mist over his shield as the clay people ran at him again.

Pop. Pop. Fizz.

Kal pulled his pad up and tried to activate it. Half-holograms projected off it, and Kal scratched at the dried clay covering its surface. He himself was covered in clay from head to toe. Eventually he managed to deactivate the forcefield. The clay couple careened into him, and Kal couldn't help but laugh as they crashed into his side and tumbled over his legs, splashing into the wet mud. They scampered off into the hamlet, and Kal picked himself up off the ground.

The morning sun shone brightly in the clear sky, long shadows reaching out west instead of east. Kal walked from house to house, telling as many clay people as he could that he'd be giving a speech at the city's gateway at noon. He started just outside the gateway into the walled city of spires and proceeded in a circle all the way around the wall, relaying his message to every clay person he met along the way.

Upon returning to the gateway, he strode into the city, his eyes seeking out the senzes. He told them about his noontime announcement as well, and made sure that many others were listening when he did. Most ignored him. Some muttered epithets and threw things at him again, but he persisted in his task.

When the sun reached its zenith, Kal returned to the entrance. A huge crowd awaited him, mostly clay people, but a substantial representation of clay animals had shown up as well. Kal grinned. Perhaps he'd piqued their interested after all.

He climbed up the side of the wall at the edge of the city, his hands and feet easily carving out their own latches in the clay. He pulled himself over the top and stood, gazing over his audience. The turnout encouraged him. His heart raced from both exertion and excitement.

"I learned the truth about this place," Kal shouted. "Things are not as they should be. You live under a tyrant, a dictator who has abused the power he was given. Power that people gave him a long time ago because they were afraid of dying. But they died anyway, leaving the Benefactor with that same power, and he wields it over you ruthlessly. Sometimes with deadly force.

"Most of you are thinking you can't imagine how things could be any different. This is how you live. The Benefactor controls the steam, your lifeblood, so you tolerate whatever abuse he hurls your way. But trust me, things do not have to be like this. I am not from another planet. I'm from right here."

At that statement, many of the creatures' eyes bulged. Whispers and hushed remarks burst forth. The clay people hopped back, clearly startled, and some hugged one another.

"I'm from this exact place," Kal said. "I'm from another Glinn. A different Glinn, right here, right now, but with a completely different history. On my Glinn, we never built a Benefactor tower. We didn't rush to a madman to solve our problems. Instead we invented a solution that forced us to learn to work together instead of against one another. It's never too late to change your society for the better, to rid yourselves of tyrants and overlords."

Kal paused, unsure if he should make the next statement. He had gone this far, and so he charged forward. "I have the power to destroy the Benefactor."

This sparked another wave of murmurs.

"But I won't use it."

Silence fell.

"Instead, I will give any of you, who want to, the chance to stand up to him, to take away his power, to find a way for you to govern yourselves that is fair and just to everyone. I will help you keep the steam vents running, and—" Kal looked directly at the congregation of clay people. "—I will help you find a way to undo any genetic changes that you want reversed."

The clay people's eyes bulged, and they hopped about joyously at Kal's statement. The clay animals were less animated, but Kal sensed that he'd piqued their curiosity nonetheless.

"You mentioned a chance," a clay animal shouted, one of the goats. "What kind of chance can we expect to have of surviving this… uprising?"

"My technology can keep you moist, and protect you from any fire, heat or toxic substance that the Benefactor can think of."

The animals began talking amongst themselves, their murmuring erupting into outright debate. The clay people stood still, gazing up at Kal.

Many groups of animals began walking back into the city. The Benefactor must have treated most of them very well, especially the senzes, so long as they did not get too near to him during one of his tempers.

When the last irate senz made his way back inside the city, only three groups of animals remained at the gate. Duck-Senz had trampled his pearl ring into the mud, Goat-Senz had thrown away her shimmering bracelet, and Pig-Senz had discarded his crown of shining prisms.

They stood with the majority of the clay people and looked up at Kal silently.

He smiled and climbed down from the wall.

"Follow me," Kal said.

The pigs, ducks, goats and clay people walked through the hamlet to the edge of the city and down the steam vent path leading to the Benefactor.

∾౧◁◞◌౦

As they marched between the two rows of twisted pillars, Kal made a point of talking to each of the animal leaders. He told them about how people had organized themselves on his own world, and how society was structured on worlds like Ydora. He explained that the group's goal today was not to kill the Benefactor, but to take away his power.

Duck-Senz seemed intellectual and inquisitive. He pried Kal for more information and asked about political organization. Goat-Senz was more interested in how Kal would help them maintain the steampipes after the Benefactor had been dealt with.

Pig-Senz was another matter altogether.

"I don't understand Ydora," he said. "Where do they store their really big weapons?"

"They don't have really big weapons," Kal replied.

"Is it possible that they were hiding them from you? In a secret hermitage somewhere?"

"No, I don't think so. They don't want to build big weapons. They need small weapons for hunting and defending themselves from predators. That's it."

"They... don't want to..." Pig-Senz said, shaking his head.

Kal nodded. "That's right."

"So, they have needs. Hunger, clothing, sexual impulses. You are talking about humans like yourself, and humans are like us and the clay people in these regards, right?"

"Yes."

"Then, they must fight over things?"

"Rarely. It's socially frowned upon. For example, one of the worst crimes on Ydora is eating when someone else in the hermitage is hungry. You'd be ostracized from the community for doing it. The same with violence. They've arranged their society so that the consequences outweigh the potential benefits. It's not worth the risk."

"And the hermitages never war with one another?"

"No."

"They have no aggression?"

"For that, they have sports. Competitions that have winners and losers. Similar to war, but without the carnage."

"I don't understand these humans," Pig-Senz said with a sigh. "And I am suspicious of their existence."

"You only say that because you've lived under the Benefactor for so long. If you give working together a try, I think you'll find that it's a healthier and more productive system for both you and all the other sentient beings of Glinn."

Tria flickered on, walking at Kal's side opposite Pig-Senz.

"There are two of you!" Pig-Senz said, and other clay animals looked at Kal nervously. The clay people seemed merely surprised. They tried poking at Tria and discovered he was noncorporeal, then made a game of seeing who could reach through his legs the farthest and for the longest period of time.

"Everyone, this is Tria," Kal said.

"A pleasure to meet all of you." Tria even made a show for them, bowing a bit. "I may look like Kal, but I'm a different person, and unlike Kal here, I can't make quite an impact." Tria reached out at a few of the animals, who at first flinched, but then nodded understandingly at his ineffectual gestures.

"Quite a posse you've got here." Tria turned to Kal. His gaze, though holographic, pierced.

"The clay animals and people here are going to dismantle the Benefactor's control systems. I'm just going to make sure that they're able to do it without being killed."

"I wanted to ask you about something," Tria waved a hand. "I was looking around the core routines and noticed a collection of programs in a protected directory. The modification date shows you touched it last. I'm not going to change it, I just wanted to move it. You know, keeping things clean. In order."

"Oh, that," Kal said. "Yeah, that's just some leftover cruft from the security lockout on the nodes. I don't think they do anything, but I'm keeping them around just in case. You know, Tria—"

Kal flinched. Tria had that deadly serious look again.

"Tria, I could really use your help here. There'll be a lot to keep track of."

There might even be some tricks the Benefactor has up his sleeve that I haven't seen yet, Kal thought.

"No," Tria said. "You're on your own." *This isn't right, Kal.*

No, Tria. What the Benefactor's done, what he's doing, that's what's not right here.

And you're going to fix it?

I have to try. Tria, if you've discovered anything about Glinn—

Pfft. I only know what you know. And that's already more than enough for me.

Fine. If you change your mind, I could really use your help.

No. I'm not going to help you get us both killed. If you can't leave things well enough alone, that's your problem. What I will be doing is keeping the nodes primed and ready to pull us into the metaxia at a moment's notice. If I'm right, Kal, you're going to need me doing that *instead.*

Tria's hologram flickered off.

Kal and the clay creatures slowed as they approached the Benefactor. Kal's right hand swept over his holointerface, checking his program one last time for errors. He'd isolated all of the beings around him, one hundred seventy-one clay goats, ducks, pigs and people. The program consisted of a single routine with one hundred seventy-one child processes maintaining the protective field and humidity level for each of them.

He put his own defense nanites on the highest of alerts, still unsure exactly what kind of resistance the Benefactor would mount.

"Benefactor!" Duck-Senz shouted, approaching the base of the tower.

"Who dares speak to me with such insolence?" the deep voice boomed.

Kal moved to the back of the group and showed the clay people a holographic blueprint of the Benefactor, pointing out which tubes and shafts they would need to pull apart in order to rend control of the vents away from their dictator.

"We have come to tell you that we neither need nor desire your benevolence any more!" Duck-Senz said.

"We want to find our own way," Goat-Senz said.

"Impudent fools!" the Benefactor roared, his face remaining frozen.

"Now!" Kal pointed, and the clay people ran toward the base of the tower.

Spouts of fire burst up all across the plain. Nanite energy fields around the clay people sizzled, and they continued forward unimpugned, still moist. The animals joined them. Kal watched and smiled at a job well done.

"You!" the Benefactor couldn't look at Kal, as he didn't seem to be able to move any part of himself, but Kal knew who he was talking to.

"I know what you did!" Kal shouted back. "On my Glinn, we have a word for you: you're a genetic terrorist, someone who tampers with the DNA of other living beings, denies them their existence, takes away everything they are and ever could be. You make me sick! This is for all of the people of Glinn whose biomaterial integrity you violated!"

The Benefactor's former servants reached the base of his tower and began tearing away greedily at his outer shell.

The fire from the spouts ceased, and water spewed forth instead, not the misty steam, but huge, frothing jets. The creatures scattered when they realized their shields would not protect them. Four, six, seven then eight of the clay beings dissolved, their skin and organs melting and streaming away down the hillside.

Kal typed out code and checked for errors as quickly as he could. He recompiled his new program and transmitted it to the nanites. Kal watched as the clay creatures as his nanites received the update, and the water began splashing harmlessly from their skin. As soon as they realized they were safe, they surged toward the Benefactor once more and continued tearing away at his support structure.

"I— I will step down," the Benefactor said, although the vents had changed again. He was trying different chemicals now, each one just as useless as the last. "Yes, that's right. I give up. There's no need to continue this. I will discontinue the tributes. You may... do as you please."

The base of the Benefactor's tower was almost completely torn away.

A small stub of pillar connected him to the ground, supporting his entire weight. Kal busied himself with more programming. The steam spouts in the city needed to be maintained. He and his computer were now the only thing keeping them going, and it was a far more complex system than he'd anticipated. He started breathing faster as he rushed to take control of the steam system, a network of pipes for a chunk of land even larger than Chicago's boundaries on Earth.

"We've won!" Goat-Senz said, and his goat brethren cheered. A similar victory roar went up from the Duck camp. The clay people paired up and danced in circles. Kal was so busy fitting together disparate chunks of code that he was only marginally aware of their glee. He almost didn't notice when their victory cheers abruptly ceased.

"Now," shouted Pig-Senz. The pigs surged forward toward the remaining base of the Benefactor and hacked it away.

Kal perked up, but struggled to lend even half his attention to the horrible creaking sounds that resounded down the hill as the Benefactor collapsed and shattered on the hillside. His enormous mass crushed a number of clay people, goats and ducks, exploding into a mound of crumpled metal, wooden beams, wires, pipes and clay. The brilliant, prismatic jewels fell from his arms and tumbled down the hill, sparkling as they went.

Kal gaped, horrified at the enormous wreckage between fits of code. Stuttering wails drifted out of the mass, the remnants of the Benefactor Divine Tower's voice, mixed with the cries of mortally wounded goats and ducks.

"What the hell are you doing?!" Kal shouted to the pigs, who ran about, attacking the goats and ducks that remained. They put up a solid defense, but with many of their kind trapped and dying under the remains of the Benefactor, the pigs encountered little resistance and were able to make quick work of their former friends.

Kal's hands flew over the interface, trying simultaneously to keep the steam vents in the city running and retract all of his nanites into his personal sphere of protection. He slammed at the buttons, realizing his mistake too late. The way he'd designed the program, it was impossible to isolate the nanites guarding the pigs from the ones guarding the goats, ducks and people. He had to rescind his protection from all of them, or from none of them at all.

When the last of the duck and goat resistance had fallen, the pigs ran down the hill, where the Benefactor wreckage lay, and began collecting up the pearly crystalline spheres, the Benefactor's shards of wisdom.

Then, as if in a trance, they strode together up the hill and congregated at the place the Benefactor had stood, atop the mess of broken pipes and wires and metal beams. The pigs climbed atop one another, standing on each other's backs.

Kal half-watched the pigs, horrified. They stood now almost in the shape of a tower.

The clay people, who had huddled around Kal, backed away from him as the steam vents around him dissipated. Kal's interface went red, and access failure notification windows erupted. The pigs had claimed control of the steam vents, and only a small patch of them remained operational in the near vicinity.

The clay people pushed and shoved at one another, fighting to stand atop the small island of wet clay that could sustain their lives.

The stack of pigs shuddered and their forms blended together. Clay and wood and metal grew out of their collective bodies, and a new being came into existence before Kal's eyes.

"Yes, yes, yes!" Pig-Senz shouted from the top, and his body gurgled outwards into an enormous, immobile head atop a tower, though now it was the head of a pig, complete with a snout and pointy ears.

"There is no need for you to control the steam vents anymore." The pig's voice grew sonorant and boomed throughout the valley. The pig head's mouth didn't move. "I will take care of everyone now. I have removed the evil one who called himself the Benefactor. I have freed us all. I am the Savior."

"Savior?!" Kal cried out. "You killed everyone!"

"Their sacrifice will usher in a new era of prosperity. The Benefactor was weak. I am strong."

"What happened to working together? What happened to restoring the clay people's genetic integrity?"

"Their current form is necessary for the wellbeing of Glinn. Do you think the Benefactor Divine Tower is without redundancy? If so, you are as stupid as Glinn's former inhabitants. This region borders four others, each with its own Benefactor Divine Tower, and each of those borders other lands. Without any divine tower at all, this region would be invaded and overrun. The clay people must fight when there is war."

"There doesn't have to be war! Don't you get it?"

"Lies!" the Savior shouted back. "The urge to war lies at the very heart of all living creatures. The weak are toppled, and the strong take their place. The group becomes stronger as a whole. This is the way of things."

"No," Kal said. "You're wrong."

Kal turned and watched the few remaining clay people beat and push and hit one another, fifty of them trying to get at fifteen steam spouts.

"Actually," Kal slouched his shoulders. "I was wrong. I was wrong to get involved in any of this."

"No, Kal," the Savior said. "You have done this region a great service. We, the Savior, can reshape Glinn once more, thanks to you and your marvelous new technology. We shall thank you appropriately. Just like the Benefactor did for Dr. Stine, so long ago."

Kal, nanites! Tria shouted mentally, his hologram resolving into view.

"What about them?"

"Look!" Tria held out his interface. A wave of nanites, not controlled by Kal's pad, rushed toward them, destroying any of Kal's nanites in its path. Beyond the interface, the bodies of the dead ducks and goats lurched and contorted, seeming to gain life again. However, instead of walking upright, their forms twisted and exploded. Spidery clay and wood monstrosities crawled up out of the mess of the corpses and ambled toward Kal.

Kal gazed at the clay people, fighting for their survival. "I have to stay... I have to help them!"

"Then we'll both die. We're leaving! Now!" Tria pressed a button, and the blue bubble formed. The Savior's demonic laughter disappeared in the crackling of static, and Kal watched Glinn warp away into blue through his strained eyes, blurred by salt water.

He threw his pad down onto the bubble floor and slumped against the wall. He tucked his head into his lap and closed his eyes.

I should have listened to you, Tria.

Tria didn't respond.

Nanogen

Realm #5721, "Aynsz"
August 16, 2178

KAL AND TRIA WALKED through deserted, concrete streets. Gray walls rose up on both sides with green flags hung at even intervals, perched between window panes. Kal hadn't seen a single person since they'd entered the city, though Tria had reported the presence of human life signs in the buildings' interiors.

The streets were immaculately clean, too. No cans, no bottles, no papers, not even so much as a blot of dirt sullied the thoroughfare. Vehicles, sort of shaped like cars, were parked meticulously at the curb, their metal frames all painted shades of gray and brown, occupying clearly delineated spaces.

"What do you make of these things?" Tria said.

Kal approached the wall where Tria stood. A poster hung on it, all yellow-orange and green. A single enormous symbol filled the entire meter-tall sheet — a square with interlocked X's stacked inside of it.

"The linguistic database is at ninety-seven percent felicity." Tria swiped through windows on his interface. "The symbol must not be part of their script, otherwise the nanites would be translating it for us. Some kind of warning symbol, maybe?"

Kal shook his head. He didn't like its shape or the colors composing the poster. Copies of it hung against the monotonous, gray facades all down the streets. And still not a single soul in sight.

Across the street, just for a moment, he thought he glimpsed a person in the window of one of the buildings. A flurry of curtains and the visage was gone.

"Well, I'm thoroughly creeped out." Kal continued walking, if only to help calm himself.

Tria followed, still working at his interface. "There it is again."

"There what is?"

Tria poked at a blinking red indicator, and the window on his interface expanded. His eyes scanned over the lines, and Kal joined him.

"What is *that*?" Kal pointed.

"Well... something... keeps slamming into your auto-medical nanites. Then it just disappears. It's causing errors because the nanites don't have time to scan and identify it."

"Whoa, that's it. We're done here. Let's get back to Felis. I'll have the tree house computer run a full medical scan—"

Trucks and vans careened around the intersections in front of and behind Kal, and windows simultaneously burst open in the buildings on either side. Gunfire erupted, and bullets flew into him from all directions. They whizzed through Tria's hologram, but impacted Kal, falling to the ground inert against his nanite defenders.

Kal waved his arms, and shouted for his attackers to stop, but the bullets just kept coming. Mild pin-pricks became hornet stings, most of the pain seeping through at his waist and left arm. A particularly bad jolt hit his wrist, and he dropped the pad. Clenching his left side, he dropped to his knees, grimacing in pain.

"Stop!" he yelled as loudly as he could, jamming his eyes closed.

"Kgal Andersz!" a voice called out through a bullhorn. Kal opened his eyes ever so slightly. A man with a thick frame jumped down from the back of a jeep into the center of a herd of other soldiers, all with guns trained on Kal. "On the authority of the Mideastern Alliance, you are hereby ordered to drop your defensive barriers, or we shall be forced to detonate our most destructive explosive weapons on you. We doubt that even your technology will survive such a blast."

Kal opened his eyes fully, frowning. He stood up, holding his hands up above his head. He looked over the man with the bullhorn. He was strongly built and had a black, curly beard. His uniform was adorned will all manner of multi-colored ribbons and patches.

"Your most destructive weapon? What, on your own city?" Kal screwed up his face. "Look, I'll just leave, okay—"

"Drop your defenses, now! If we're all to die, we're taking you with us."

Tria, drop the physical auto-defenses, but leave the medical ones on, Kal thought.

"I'm turning them off," Kal announced. A man raced toward him, grabbed Kal's pad off the street, dropped it into a metallic bag, and ran off with it.

You sure about this, Kal?

It takes at least three seconds for a metaxic bubble to fully quantum lock. That's more than enough time for them to set off their most destructive weapon. And that's probably, what, a nuclear device? I think they're serious, and they're right. Our nanites would not be able to protect us from a thermonuclear explosion.

Tria paused. *Yeah, I suppose you're right.*

Go with the pad, Kal thought. *It's our only way off of this world. Make sure it stays safe.*

Kal felt a mental nod from Tria, and his presence flowed away from Kal's mind.

"My life is in your hands," Kal announced.

"Arrest him," the bearded soldier said. Uniformed men and women walked resolutely toward Kal and bound his hands with some kind of plastic strap that clicked, locking into place as it tightened around his wrists.

"How did you know my name?" Kal looked directly into the bearded man's eyes.

The military leader scoffed at him.

"Kgal Andersz, you are being placed under arrest and in the custody of the state military of the Mideastern Alliance. You have the right to remain silent. Anything you say can and will be used against you during your tribunal."

A wave of confusion and fear and dizziness came over Kal. None of this made any sense. Somehow, his inquisitive side won out some small bit of control. "I want to know the charges."

The bearded man twisted his face up in disgust. Kal looked over the faces of the man's subordinates and got the distinct impression that they were resisting the urge to violate orders and shoot him on the spot.

"What is it? What do you think I did?!"

A soldier jerked him by the arm toward a van. Kal kept his head turned back, glaring at the bearded soldier.

The bearded soldier returned his gaze the entire way.

They shoved Kal into the back of the van and slammed its doors shut, leaving him in utter darkness for the duration of the ride.

⚭⚭

The soldiers shoved him into a cold, damp cell. The walls, ceiling, and floor were solid concrete. No windows. A half-rusted bed frame and the reeking toilet were the only furnishings. Kal sat atop the bed, then realized that a foul odor emanated from the mattress as well, and he moved to the floor. He sat with his arms wrapped around his legs and his eyes closed. He thought of Tria and his pad, and wondered what had become of them.

"See if this jogs your memory," a passing guard spat. Kal opened his eyes just in time to dodge a small electronic device hurtling toward his head. It slammed into the wall and fell to the ground.

"Why are we even following protocol? In another month it won't matter anyway. We should just kill him now." the guard's voice disappeared behind the clang of a closing metal door.

Kal picked up the device. It was much smaller than his pad, but Kal was impressed at its sophistication nonetheless. It didn't appear to have hologenerators, just a touch screen, but was still a pretty remarkable technology for a culture at this stage of development.

No, wait. Not remarkable. Scary. This world, wherever he was, was a clear case of technology outpacing social progress.

This was the very same problem that had landed Team Haskell in their predicament. The cultural program his nanites used to determine a world's safety had no true way of calculating how people treated one another in a given society. Such a thing could likely not be programmed. However, technological progress was easy to gauge. And since technological and social sophistication often developed hand in hand, the nanites' rough measure of culture was fairly accurate. However, just as Team Haskell had discovered, they could also, sometimes, be extremely wrong.

Hey, Kal?

Tria! I'm so glad you're safe. Where's the pad?

They've finally taken it out of that bag. I've been scouting with the nanites, and there's something you should know.

What's that?

They think you've infected them with some kind of plague.

I didn't bring any plague with me!

No no no. More specifically, they think you were here before, Kal. They think that you came here a week ago, jammed some scientist with a needle, and turned her into patient zero for an epidemic. They even have a video of it happening.

Kal trembled silently and jammed his head between his knees. Horror rushed through him. He felt sick to his stomach and leaned back against the cold, concrete wall. He put a hand on his forehead.

Tria, you know that I—

Of course. This is the first time that either of us has ever been here.

Then how—

I don't know, but I'm working on it, okay? That and keeping the pad safe, of course. And if I can find a way to get the pad to you, I'll let you know. They've got it locked down pretty tight, though.

Tria, please be careful.

I will.

And with that, Tria was gone.

Kal looked down at the device in his hand, barely keeping his grip on it. He breathed deeply, then pressed the power button. Blank screen. He pulled at the panel on its back and began looking over the wires and circuits inside. He dug into the depths of his memory for what little expertise he had with macrocomputer hardware. He had always found software much more interesting, and now wished he'd forced himself away from the programming prompt into the machine's guts more often.

The damage turned out to be superficial. After some light tinkering, he closed the cover and turned the mini-pad back on. Its main interface showed the presence of three video files. He made himself as comfortable as he possibly could against the concrete slab of a wall and pressed the play button.

oe⚜eo

"Kgal, this is Dr. Beatdrice Olifvia. She heads up research in our biosciences division."

"Nice to meet you," the doctor and video-Kal shook hands.

"Kgal says that he can show you a technology he possesses that can cure any illness, even alter DNA."

"I control microscopic machines." Video-Kal spoke in a voice that, although strange and not his own, seemed somehow remotely familiar. "They can alter matter at the atomic level."

Dr. Olifvia regarded him coldly for a moment. "I'm afraid I'm not very good with machines. I'm much better with living things."

"Oh, well, maybe after some time I'll be able to convince you of how similar the two really are," video-Kal said. The statement, combined with video-Kal's strange voice, sent shivers running down Kal's spine.

Video-Kal and Dr. Olifvia stood in the same laboratory as before. He stood with his back to the camera, and Dr. Olifvia worked at a computer, a very large device that sat on the table across from him.

Kal was apparently watching excerpts from a recording device perched on the lab's ceiling. He jumped at the sight of a beaker exploding on the far side of the room. Warning lights turned the screen dark red, and sirens blared through the mini-pad's small speakers.

"Everyone out!" Dr. Olifvia shouted, swiveling around and pushing her colleagues toward the door.

Video-Kal manipulated his pad quickly and purposefully, and a force-field shimmered into existence around the area where the explosion had occurred, securely containing a fine, red mist.

"Kgal! What the hell is that?"

"It didn't work quite right. I'll have to try again."

"Try again? Kgal, your behavior is reckless and extreme. You're not welcome in my lab anymore."

"Yes, I am." Video-Kal continued tinkering with his interface.

"Out. Now."

Video-Kal sighed in exasperation. He picked up a piece of paper from a nearby desk, handed it to Dr. Olifvia, and turned his attention back to his interface.

The doctor's eyes scanned hurriedly over it. Then she sneered.

"Tdrak!" Dr. Olifvia shouted, and stormed out of the room, crumpling the paper and throwing it onto the floor.

Video-Kal pulled on a syringe, filling it with clear liquid from a small, glass vial. He took out his pad. Dr. Olifvia was not present in this recording, but the rest of the lab's staff carried on without her.

Kal noticed for the first time that there was something different about video-Kal's pad. Even through the graininess of the recording, Kal could see that the pad video-Kal held was thinner, and the screen indentation had a different bevel and curvature. He paused the recording and gazed at it, but this screen was too small and the video resolution too low.

He hit the play button to start the video again.

Video-Kal's pad interface popped to life, and he began pressing buttons. Kal strained to read the actual lines of code, but the video resolution garbled the words too badly for him to make out what the program would do.

Video-Kal held his pad with one hand and slowly reached out, grasping the syringe with the other. He turned and violently jammed the needle into the arm of the nearest scientist. His victim lurched away and crumpled to the ground.

Other scientists swarmed her and video-Kal, but video-Kal wasted no time initiating a metaxic bubble. A number of scientists were thrown away as the sphere formed. Screaming erupted through the wind, and blue sparks distorted Kal's view of most of the room's interior. The only stable image among the chaos of the bubble and the scurrying scientists was the woman who'd been stabbed. She lay unconscious on the floor.

The video went to static.

Kal sat and thought for some time. Faced with the very real possibility of him becoming a Team Haskell of one, he pushed away thoughts of his imminent demise and occupied his mind instead with how this could even have happened. His mind ran wild, and he struggled to organize his thoughts.

Possibility: Another version of himself was traveling the metaxia. Theoretically, there should be hundreds of thousands of alternate Kals. Such was the nature of quantum physics. However, each of those alternate Kals should be locked in their own infinite cluster of realms to explore, as per the weird, non-linear nature of metaxic time. Kal imagined that one of those Kals performing a "crossover" was exactly the kind of behavior that Mythos and Ethos had forbidden him.

Possibility: Somewhere in this metaxic cluster, a person who was not him, but just happened to look like him, had grown up on an Earth-like world that had similar technology to his own, but he had turned out completely evil. Kal smiled a bit at the ridiculousness of the thought. There were no doppels, no evil twins. Perhaps in other strata, but not in this one. In this metaxic stratum, there was only one Kal – himself.

Possibility: He was insane. He had come here one week ago in a delusional state and infected the entire population of this city with a terrible plague. He had strong evidence against this hypothesis, though—the pad that video-Kal had held definitely wasn't Kal's. Anyone familiar with pad technology could tell that the two weren't even remotely the same model. And he doubted very much that he could retrofit his pad in an insane state and then undo the alterations before returning to "normal" and forgetting what he'd done.

Possibility: Someone else from Earth had come to this world posing as Kal, bringing with them a pad of a newer model than the one Kal had been given four years ago. He paused. It was the only possibility that made sense, save for the fact that he could think of no one on Earth who would want to frame him for attempting genocide. There were those would want him to return to Felis and stay there, sure, but there was no one willing to kill an entire world of people to make their point. The thought seemed absurd, anyway. A person from the PanAtlantic Union behaving violently? It didn't make sense.

"Hey."

Kal looked up.

Two soldiers, one female and one male, stood on the other side of the metal bars. The female one addressed him. "Time to go."

The male soldier beside her sneered. "You know where we should send him? Off the top of the regent's hall."

"Do you want to be the one to explain failure to follow orders to General Tdrak?"

The soldier scowled at her, then looked at the floor.

"That's what I thought. I don't like this scum either, but if I've only got a month to live, I'm going to spend that month doing my duty to the Mideastern Alliance, you got that?"

The female soldier pressed her palm against the wall and tapped at a few buttons. The door to his cell swung open.

"C'mon."

They led Kal down the corridor and through the metal door that clanged when it shut.

The soldiers pushed Kal down onto a metal chair at the center of a small, square room with more cement walls. A square table sat before him. On the table lay a metallic device with wires running out of it. The soldiers strapped Kal into the chair, and then strapped the wires onto his wrists. Kal's heart raced, and he thought it would pound out of his chest. He fidgeted in his restraints and couldn't control how fast he was breathing.

Another man entered the room, this one much older, so thin Kal could see the outline of his cheekbones.

"For determining truth." He motioned to the device on the table, though his tone suggested he wished it were capable of inflicting pain. Kal exhaled deeply and closed his eyes, willing his heart rate back to normal.

The man sat down across the table from Kal, behind the so-called truth machine.

"Name?"

"Kal Anders."

The man glanced at a readout on the device only he could see, and scribbled something on his clipboard, using an antiquated pen.

"Place of origin?"

Kal remained silent. The man peered at him through small, circular glass lenses.

"Place of origin?"

Kal sighed. "7309 Kedzie Boulevard, Chicago, Illinois, PanAtlantic Union, Earth."

The man wrote it down without even flinching.

"Why did you return to our timeline?"

"This is my first time here."

"Would you like to make a statement as to why you created the plague?"

"I didn't create any plague."

The man looked at the readout and furrowed his brow.

Believe it. Please.

A knock at the door.

The man exhaled heavily, and his eyes seemed to sink into his skull.

He stood up slowly and shuffled out of the room. The guards at either side of the door continued looking past Kal toward the back wall, but it still felt as though they were watching him.

Someone outside, a woman, began talking excitedly to the emaciated man. The tone of her voice was urgent but measured, gaining in volume by the second. And it seemed familiar somehow. Their argument reached a crescendo, words almost discernible, then stopped abruptly. The door opened, and a woman walked into the room, closing the door methodically behind her. Kal realized why her voice had seemed familiar. Before him stood Dr. Beatdrice Olifvia, from the first two videos he'd watched on the miniature computer.

She walked to the table and sat, her hands folded in front of her. Her light brown hair was tied up in a bun, and she held a computer that resembled a clipboard, wider and thicker than Kal's pad. She set the computer on the table next to the supposed truth machine.

"Kgal, do you remember the first night you were here?"

"No, I've never been here before."

She looked at the truth machine, but her face wasn't as easy to read as the emaciated man's.

"Do you remember what you told me? About the metaxia?"

"This is the first time we've talked."

"So, you don't remember telling me about a technology you found on an alternate world, one called Aynsz?"

"No. I've travelled to a lot of different worlds but never to any named Aynsz."

"I see." Her expression grew solemn. Even the two guards at the door turned their heads to face one another, and for the first time since he'd entered the room, Kal saw an emotion register on their faces: surprise.

"Dr. Szalaszar says hi," Dr. Olifvia said.

"I don't know who that is." Kal leaned back and sighed.

"His kids are doing well. I mean, as well as can be expected, with the whole 'threat of imminent demise' thing."

"Am I supposed to know his kids or something?"

Dr. Olifvia took one last look at the truth machine before she jolted out of her seat and marched out the door, shutting it carefully behind her. At first, Kal only heard the murmur of her voice and others again, but her volume steadily rose until he could make out words.

"I don't care! Get General Tdrak. This is not the same young man who visited us a week ago!"

She entered the room again, opening and shutting the door gently. Kal admired the way she walked, the way she composed herself through what must have been terrible stress.

The doctor laid her hands on the table. "Kgal, I believe you. When the other one tried to leave our world, my colleagues in the lab partially thwarted his blue sphere by initiating an EM burst in the laboratory he tried to escape from. He appeared in the parking lot outside my personal office. I saw him from the window, as did a handful of other people. He looked like you, but then his whole body shimmered, and after that, he didn't look like you anymore. He looked like someone else completely. He was able to create another sphere, though, and he disappeared."

Kal's eyes widened. The impersonator possibility. Someone had framed him.

Dr. Olifvia set her hands on the table and leaned forward. "Please help us. We're all infected."

"Your whole city?"

Olifvia shook her head solemnly.

"Every single person on this world. On Aynsz."

oe⟨⟩eo

Kal sat once more, curled up in the corner of his dank cell. The hand-held video device lay on the floor in front him. Silence permeated the entire space, save for the distant, echoing sound of dripping water. Kal figured his cell was in an empty wing of the jail.

Apparently, not everyone in this country had been as convinced as Dr. Olifvia of Kal's innocence. He didn't mind, though. He needed time to think.

This may surprise you, but I think we should stay and help, Tria thought. Kal perked up.

Really?

Yeah. I mean it.

Even after what happened on Glinn? And on Vogg?

Those situations were fundamentally different from this one.

How?

This is not a problem that the people of Aynsz have created, it was forced upon them. And they've asked for help without you offering it. Well, one person has, anyway.

How did you find out about that?

I got the nanites hooked into their computer system, and there's recording equipment in the interrogation room. Hell, there's recording equipment in every room. This is one hyper-suspicious country, Kal.

Ah.

But Kal, despite that, we've got another really good reason to stay and figure this thing out.

Oh?

Something's very not right about these viruses. I mean, I wouldn't even have noticed it, but you have the sensitivities on your pad turned way up, so I went to scan one of them and—

How's that possible? Kal scrambled to stand up and leaned into the wall for support. He already knew what Tria was going to say. Of all the possible dangers his computer could detect, there was only one setting he'd calibrated to its maximum level.

The viruses are oozing tiny quantities of nanogenic radiation. I don't know how it's possible either. But we need to find out.

Tria had the nanites run a full bioscan on Kal. Even when Kal was separated from his computer, two nanite programs would follow him around, running at all times: auto-defense and auto-medical. Auto-defense was the force reduction program, which was able to prevent physical trauma by absorbing heat or physical impact. Auto-medical protected him from exotic diseases. Both had been written five years ago at Fermilab and designed specifically for metaxic travel.

Tria reported that the nanogenic virus attacked in waves and that so far, Kal's biomedical nanites had repelled over three thousand such onslaughts. The viruses were clearly learning about human anatomy, targeting more and more vulnerable organs, finding clever ways around the body's natural defenses and so on, but against Kal's nanites, they had lost every single battle.

In addition, it was unclear what the viruses would do if they ever actually made it to an organ. Would they disassemble it? Shut it down? Break up cells? The sickening possibilities were endless.

So Kal, all they've got are the equivalent of twentieth century electron micro-scopes. By analyzing the virus, they can see that it's making progressive inroads past the immune system. I think that's where they're getting the 'one month left' statistic from. At its current rate of progress, it'll be about three weeks, maybe a month on the outside, before even the healthiest person's immune system is compromised and the virus slams through all the way. Staying here might get... rough.

Kal nodded. He had thought of that too and shook his head.

If there's someone else from Earth running around the metaxia, I need to find out everything I can about him.

The door at the end of the hall resounded with its usual metallic bang, and multiple footfalls approached.

Don't worry, your pad's safe. Tria said. *They've finally stopped trying to destroy it. Now they want to turn it on.*

Forcefield?

Yeah.

Kal smiled. No one but him would ever be able to turn on his pad. At least, no one on Aynsz.

Dr. Olifvia and the burly, bearded man appeared on the other side of the bars with a squad of two male and two female soldiers. Dr. Olifvia, just like the rest, wore a military uniform, although hers had differently shaped emblems on the shoulders than the bearded man's, probably be-cause of her status as a scientist.

"Kgal," the bearded man said. "Dr. Olifvia and others' testimony has led us to tentatively believe that you are not the young man who infected us a week ago. Moreover, you may be a valuable asset in discovering a cure for the disease. Do you still maintain that this is the first time you have been to our world?"

Kal nodded vigorously. "Yes, that's the truth."

The bearded man's scowl didn't budge, but he nodded nonetheless to one of the soldiers, who opened the door to Kal's cell.

"I am releasing you into the custody of Dr. Beatdrice Olifvia. You will be escorted by two other guards at all times. This is for your own safety. As you can imagine, there are people on this base who will not like seeing you walk free. All areas of this facility, except for the research and development lab, are off limits. You will remain in Dr. Olifvia's custody only so long as you assist us in our research to find a cure for the plague. Do you understand?"

"Yes."

The bearded man started to walk away.

"Thank you, General Tdrak," Dr. Olifvia said. He paused a moment, and then tried to start walking away again, but Dr. Olifvia continued, "I hope we can cooperate like this more in the future."

Tdrak pulled his shoulders back and walked resolutely out of the hall, two of the soldiers trailing behind him.

"Thank you, Kgal." Dr. Olifvia said. "It's very gracious of you to consider helping us after the way you've been treated. Would you like to come see what we've learned so far?"

Kal nodded. He grabbed the small, non-holographic computer pad off of the floor and pocketed it before following Dr. Olifvia out of the prison cell.

The other wings of the building were much busier than the prison wing. Everyone wore the same brown military uniform that Kal had adopted, though the colors of the emblems that adorned each person's were different. Dr. Olifvia strode purposefully through the halls, but all around her, other soldiers ran about frantically. Hairs were frazzled, faces were red, and eyes darted about.

Whenever Kal did manage to make eye contact with someone else in the hall, the individual invariably glared back at him. He turned his eyes toward the floor. Kal could hear people shouting at one another as his entourage passed the doors of offices. It was far more chaotic than he imagined a military base being. He was glad to be in the custody of Beatdrice Olifvia. She seemed sane, unlike everyone else he'd met. The imminent doom fueling the communal frenzy around him didn't seem to affect her.

They reached the main laboratory and entered. Kal recognized all the computer consoles, partitions and equipment immediately. It was the same room from the videos of his impostor. He even spotted the camera in the corner of the ceiling, the vantage point from which he'd watched the videos on the mini-pad.

Dr. Olifvia led Kal into a small conference room at the lab's corner. The two soldiers followed them both silently, and Dr. Olifvia closed the door behind them.

"The problem is," Dr. Olifvia said, "that the virus keeps disappearing before our bodies can kill one and mark it."

"Mark it, you mean with antibodies."

"Right. And when it pops back into existence, its configuration is different. It's the most adaptive virus I've ever seen. Not only that, it has two different shapes. Sometimes it looks like this."

Olifvia turned on a computer, which projected its screen onto the wall behind her, and pulled up her images of the virus. They depicted a fuzzy gray sphere with sharp spikes protruding from it. At first, Kal found himself surprised at the low quality of the images, a blurry and grainy grayscale. Kal hadn't realized that electron microscope image quality was so poor. He'd apparently been spoiled on nanopixel renders of the microscopic world.

"And sometimes it looks like this."

Dr. Olifvia displayed others. These showed a tube with two little balls on either end. A dogbone, almost comical.

"And in between, the virus isn't there at all. We'll isolate one for testing, and then before we can run the test, it will pop out of existence. To make matters worse, it's getting better and better at avoiding our immune system and even our analysis instruments every time it reappears. Eventually, we estimate a month on the outside, it will be able to penetrate the brain or the heart of its hosts, and when that happens... Well, we can only guess, but given the level of your technology, we're pretty sure it won't be good."

Kal nodded and gulped. He joined Dr. Olifvia at the computer terminal, fumbling with the antiquated computer equipment. Eventually, he managed to return the display to the image of the spiky ball. Something about it...

An idea dawned on him, one that he very much disliked, but if he was right, it would mean that even his auto-medical nanites wouldn't be able to protect him forever.

"Do you have any time lapse captures of the virus?"

"Not very good ones. The equipment that takes these pictures takes three seconds to recharge."

"Does this shape look familiar to you? I know you've seen it before. You told me you did."

Dr. Olifvia shook her head, confused.

"It isn't a virus. It's a metaxic bubble! I think that the viruses are nanite-enabled. When the nanites guiding the viruses sense danger, they take the virus and themselves into the metaxia. They're probably regrouping somewhere, sharing knowledge, exchanging DNA and collected information amongst themselves. Then they return to learn again. I've read about computer programs that can learn—adaptive algorithms."

Dr. Olifvia gulped. She stared transfixed at screen, then gazed at Kal. She shook her head slowly, then turned to face the two at the door. She didn't say anything, but Kal guessed she was non-verbally communicating to them that the information Kal had just shared was not to leave the room.

She turned back to Kal. "How do we beat a thing like this?"

"All nanite clusters have to have a central processor. The one for these would have to be inside a metaxic bubble or on an alternate Aynsz. Finding it would be easy if I had my computer."

Dr. Olifvia nodded her head slowly and pursed her lips, staring at the picture of the spiky sphere on the wall. "Retrieving it from the general is going to be a challenge."

Although Kal's revelation about the nature of the virus had clearly shaken Dr. Olifvia, her air of calm confidence had returned just moments afterward. She maintained it even now, which Kal found impressive. Were he in her place, he'd have been tempted numerous times to break his staunch pacifism and punch General Tdrak in the face.

The three of them stood in the general's office. It was sparse and sterile. Only a few plaques and badges adorned the walls. A bookshelf stood empty in the corner. His desk, save for a few papers, a computer, and a name placard, was bare.

He stood, knuckles propping himself over the desk, and he glared down at Dr. Olifvia. He had so far refused to address Kal.

"So, we're going to hand this alien his computer, let him do whatever he wants with it, and the best outcome for us is that he leaves and never comes back?"

"Once I'm in the metaxia, disrupting the viruses will be easy," Kal said with a sigh. "I'll be able to locate their central processing unit and shut it down."

"I don't trust you." Tdrak sneered. He gazed at Kal for the first time in the discussion, fixating fierce eyes upon him, daring him to retort.

Kal threw up his hands, doing just that. "So, you'll just let the virus kill everyone. Just let your whole world—"

The room's sole ceiling light flickered and went out. Sirens blared, and concussive forces shook the building. Kal grabbed at the desk to steady himself. Tdrak and Olifvia rushed to the wall near the door frame. Kal ducked and covered his head, running to join them.

"What's going on?" Kal looked back and forth between them. He had to scream the words between blasts.

"Either the West Kganadians or the North Atlantikgans," Dr. Olifvia shouted above the din.

"What, other countries? I thought you said all of Aynsz was infected."

Dr. Olifvia looked at Kal inquisitively, and he guessed she was unable to determine a proper response to his question. Tdrak eyed him only with scorn.

"Of course it's another country," Tdrak said. "We wouldn't bomb ourselves."

"Oh, really now? That's news to me." Kal rolled his eyes on their way to meet Tdrak's, who snarled back.

Dr. Olifvia stared at Tdrak still, but even her exacting gaze was cut off when another barrage exploded nearby, shaking the room even more violently. A chip of the ceiling fell onto Kal and bounced off his shoulder. He shuddered at the feeling of it. If one of those bombs went off near him without his auto-defense layer active…

"Why would any country be bombing another right now?" Kal asked matter-of-factly. "Shouldn't you be working together to find a cure?"

Tdrak frowned at Kal with condescending disbelief.

"It's a fair point though, don't you think?" Dr. Olifvia said to the general, who scoffed at her. She turned to Kal and explained over the roar of another explosion. "They're taking advantage of an opportunity, Kgal."

Kal grasped the door frame harder as the building rocked again. "An opportunity for what?"

Another round of explosions went off, but they were further away, and the building didn't shake nearly as much.

Dr. Olifvia and General Tdrak tentatively let go of the wall. Kal held on for a moment longer, but eventually followed suit, waving away the lingering haze of dust shaken loose by the blasts.

"I have to prepare for the retaliation. Excuse me." The general marched out the door.

"Wait, *what?*" Kal shouted after him.

"Leave him alone," Olifvia said, definitely an order, not a request. There was a sudden earnestness to her voice. "We're not going to be able to convince him today. I'll try again on him tomorrow."

The doctor led him back toward the laboratory.

"How many countries share a border with the Mideastern Alliance?" Kal asked. The two guards took up positions, marching behind them both.

"Six," Dr. Olifvia replied.

Kal blinked. "What are their names?"

"West Kganada, East Kganada, North Atlantikga, The Free Southern Alliance, Tdexas and the Rokgi Mountain Federation."

Kal briefly allowed himself to marvel at this. "And you're at war?"

"Not outright war, no. Not for the last eight years. Though tensions are usually high with one country or another."

"Why?" Kal asked.

Dr. Olifvia stopped and eyed him curiously a moment, then shook her head and led him down the hallway once more.

Kal couldn't decide if his question had confused or intrigued her. It had seemed reasonable enough to him. He'd been taught that everyone in the world had a desire to lead a happy and productive life, and working together peacefully was the best way for each individual to achieve just that. Didn't the people here understand that?

Kal tried digging back into his memory of Earth's history before the twenty-second century and wished he'd paid more attention to history lessons. He'd focused instead almost exclusively on math and computer science. He was aware that the nation states of pre-nanite era Earth had warred with one another, but he'd been forced out of school in the middle of sixth grade and had never made it to the classes where he presumed the teachers would explain why exactly war had ever happened at all.

He made a mental note that if he got off Aynsz alive, he'd learn everything he could about the twentieth and twenty-first centuries before exploring any more alternate Earths.

Dr. Olifvia opened the door to the laboratory and ushered Kal inside. She walked him to a computer console on a small desk in the corner of the room, and his two guards took up positions on either side of it.

"You can work here. If you need anything—equipment, food, water, even a bathroom break—" Olifvia nodded toward the opposite corner of the frantic laboratory. "—the guards go with you."

Lovely, Kal thought.

"I'll be trying... again... to capture one of the viruses. Maybe learn something new. We'll meet up in three hours and you'll tell me what you're working on. Understood?"

Kal nodded, more despondent than ever. He *needed* his pad back. He thumbed the miniature pad in his pocket, the one that had been thrown at him in the jail cell. What was he supposed to do with such an inferior piece of technology?

Dr. Olifvia walked to the center of the room and began directing other scientists, though most of them lacked her calm. They seemed only half aware of her, like one half of their brain comprehended that she was in charge while the other half couldn't do anything but freak out.

He couldn't say he blamed them one bit. If it weren't for Tria guarding his pad, he'd be freaking out himself.

Kal turned to his desk and turned on the computer, a clunky, rudimentary, boxy thing. Ah, well at least it had a touch interface.

"You wouldn't happen to know if there's a connector for these?" Kal asked the guard, motioning to the mini-pad and the computer terminal.

The guard didn't answer. Or even look at him.

"Silent type, eh? We'll have a one-way conversation then."

Kal looked around the desk, then under it.

"Aha!" he announced. He spotted a box behind the desk and began rummaging through its contents. He pulled out a number of cords and returned to the computer terminal.

"A connector!" Kal announced. One success. That was a start.

He began the arduous work of retrofitting the mini-pad. He spent the afternoon hacking into its operating system and figuring out the programming interface. He then built the foundation for a wireless networking protocol that he could use to interface with the metaxic nodes in his neck.

But, without his own pad, he had to program everything from scratch, and in a foreign programming environment no less, where he lacked the holographic toolset he'd grown accustomed to.

He worked late into the evening, and began worrying about Tria more and more as time wore on. He had not heard from his brother since he'd left the prison cell and started to worry that Tdrak had been successful in activating Kal's pad, or worse. Kal prayed silently that Tria was okay.

He also found his thoughts drifting away to the virus. What had his impersonator engineered it to do? The answer lay in the viruses' DNA, and that would not be accessible until he could actually contain one.

Another volley of bombs dropped near the lab. Main power disappeared, taking the lights and Kal's desk computer with it. Emergency lighting flooded the room. Kal cursed the disruption and watched helplessly as Dr. Olifvia bravely directed her frantic subordinates, whom the power outage had made even more frantic. Kal's eyes darted about the room, looking for details, anything that might help him.

He spotted nothing helpful, only hostile glances from other scientists. Kal looked up at the guards on either side of him, standing vigilant. Their presence gave him some small sense of comfort, but the scientists set him so on edge that he turned back to face his desk and thumbed through the interface of the mini-pad.

Kal!

Oh my god, Tria! Are you alright?

Yeah, I'm fine. You wouldn't believe what that General Tdrak guy is doing. At first, he tried hooking the pad up to their computers and turning it on, but that didn't work, of course, so he had some kind of emotional meltdown and tried to break it against a wall. The nanites protected it, and that made him even madder, so he had them hook it up to some enormous machine, a particle accelerator, in a place they call the Energy Weapons Laboratory. They're bombarding it with radiation, Kal. Everything they can think of. I think they're going to try pressure soon.

The nanite defenses?

Holding.

Kal breathed a sigh of relief. The nanites could put up with a lot, but they weren't invincible, and their energy supply was limited.

If it's a particle accelerator, Kal thought, *then you could have the nanites syphon energy from the machine itself to bolster their—*

Already done. Kal could feel Tria's smile.

You're the best, Tria.

Hey, I figure I have to earn that real body somehow, right?

Tria's thought was tinged with laughter, but Kal quietly decided to redouble his efforts to find someone somewhere with the technology to give Tria a physical body of his own.

I better get back to the pad.

Oh, Tria?

Yeah?

Have you been in their computer network yet?

Of course!

When you have time, I need some information. I want to understand the politics of this world, their military, how it works.

No prob. Tomorrow morning, okay?

Thanks, Tria.

His brother's presence flitted away just as the lights flickered back on. The room filled with the whirs and buzzes of computer equipment starting up, and Kal returned to his work.

∞⟨⟩∞

Kal worked on activating his nodes with the mini-pad into the early hours of the morning, though it was hard to tell how long it had been since their lab had no windows. He blinked bleary-eyed at the clock in the mini-pad's corner, struggling to comprehend the digits. He found himself shuffling away toward an adjacent room of cots, his soldier guards following him. He found he didn't care even about that. He simply collapsed onto the makeshift bed.

He dreamed of his tree house, of his cats, and of swimming in Felis's Lake Michigan. He awoke to one of the guards shaking him. Dr. Olifvia stood over him.

"Time to work again. But you'll need food first."

"I'm not really that hungry," Kal replied honestly. His stomach felt empty, but nausea crushed any desire he might have for food.

The doctor crossed her arms and glared down at him. "Doesn't matter. You'll eat."

A guard reached out and pulled him to a stance. Kal wobbled, and the guard steadied him.

He yawned as Dr. Olifvia led him out of the still-hectic laboratory, down a hallway, and into the bunker's mess hall. Kal liked it here much better. It was quiet and sparsely populated. Soldiers and scientists ate frantically and hurried away, going directly back to their work.

The counters where food was normally dispensed stood empty, and the lights were off in the kitchen. He and the doctor raided an open pantry for corn flakes and fruit bars. Kal took some of each onto his tray.

Dr. Olifvia then made them both cups of coffee from a harried machine, appearing taxed to the brink of utter failure.

She offered for Kal to sit at one of the large, empty tables in the nearly large, eerily deserted space. The guards took seats at adjacent tables on either side of them. Kal wondered why the four of them weren't on their way back to the laboratory.

"Tell me about Earth." Dr. Olifvia took quick but measured gulps of her coffee.

"What do you mean? I don't understand."

"Look, in about five minutes we'll have to go back. And I want to know everything you can tell me. Do you have crime? What about your politics? What about corruption?"

"Crime exists, but it's rare. Same with political corruption, if that's what you mean."

"Seriously?"

"Seriously."

The doctor regarded him carefully. "You seemed surprised that we have constant political tension with our competitor nations."

Kal shook his head. "See, that's just it. You view them as competition."

Dr. Olifvia nodded, biting her lip. "And what's a better way to view them?"

"Colleagues and allies. Other human beings," Kal said matter-of-factly. This conversation baffled him. She might as well have asked him whether a sieve or a cup would be better at holding his coffee.

"Kgal, my brother Lukgas and I, we're part of a philosophical group on Aynsz that believes such a world as you describe is possible. You see, most people in the Mideastern Alliance and other nations believe that people have to struggle, fight, and collect resources in order to survive. But Lukgas and I don't believe that, we believe that, *in theory*, it should be possible to achieve a happy, healthy and productive society with peace. And now you're telling me that our theory is not just possible, but it's a real place, an Aynsz with a different history and culture."

Kal gulped. "On Earth, we have peace and prosperity, but we also have strict rules. The nanites I told you about—the ones that are guiding the virus that's attacking all of you—on Earth, we worry all the time about people doing just this type of thing with them. We worry that we'll descend into war and pain and suffering all over again."

"My philosophy group would love this."

"Philosophy group?"

"My half time, before the plague."

"Half time?"

Dr. Olifvia's shoulders collapsed, probably realizing she'd have to explain absolutely everything to him. "We work for the military full time until we're thirty. Then we can choose to go half time. I started a philosophy study group with mine."

"You run it with your brother?" Kal smiled, thinking of himself and Tria.

Dr. Olifvia frowned and shook her head. "He died many years ago in a war with Tdexas."

"Oh, I'm sorry." Kal frowned too.

She downed the last of her coffee. Kal had barely touched his. It tasted awful.

"Take those with you. You'll want them for later." Olifvia stood, motioning to his untouched breakfast. Kal stuffed the fruit bars into his pockets and carried the coffee, forcing himself to sip it. Hopefully it would keep him alert, if he could stomach enough of the foul liquid.

The doctor led Kal and his guards out of the cafeteria and back to the hectic laboratory. "I want to know more about Earth after we've figured this out."

"I want to know more about Aynsz, too."

Olifvia turned around and crossed her arms in front of her chest, grinning ever so slightly. "You have a deal."

Kal mimicked her actions. "Deal."

They entered the lab and returned to their respective desks.

For the next six hours, Kal worked on creating a program for activating his metaxic nodes to no avail. He did finally manage to access the nodes' programming interface, but that was where his progress ended.

The nodes' inventors had developed their own program for interfacing with them, one that Kal had taken for granted. That program was inaccessible now, locked away in his distant pad. Every time Kal tried his own method for interfacing with the nodes, he'd get errors. Which was just as well. An incorrectly quantum-locked bubble was a very dangerous thing. The last thing he wanted was to end up a metaxic smear of all-possibility or to blow apart this region of the metaxia.

Hours passed. Kal threw the mini pad onto his desk and rubbed his eyes. He turned to look for Dr. Olifvia, maybe compel her to talk to the general again, but was just in time to watch her leave the lab, following a pair of scientists.

How are you holding up? Tria asked.

Kal smiled, glad his brother had returned. *Pretty well.*

I have that data you asked me to find.

Kal pulled up the mini-pad and watched the files download. He spotted the political map of Aynsz and pulled it up. He recognized the shape of the continents and oceans immediately, a dead match for Earth. Aynsz's political boundaries, on the other hand, were unreal. Even the ancient historical maps he had seen of Earth had never had so many lines. Areas that Kal knew had been unified political entities for hundreds of years—India, China, Brazil, Russia and the United States of America—were on Aynsz a fractured mesh of twisting lines. Kal guessed that Aynsz contained somewhere between 1,200 and 1,500 distinct political entities.

He activated a menu and scrolled through it until he found the Mideastern Alliance. He tapped it, and the country's borders glowed, roughly the Appalachian mountains in the East, the Ohio River in the South, the Mississippi River in the West, and the Great Lakes in the North.

There's something else, Kal. Tria sounded scared. Or sad. Maybe both? *What is it?*

You need to see it, but I don't want to show it to you. It's another video recording. These people record everything.

Indeed, in addition to the device he'd spotted on his way into the lab, Kal had discovered five additional recording devices in the laboratory since he'd started working there. He'd seen them in the cafeteria too.

Tria continued. *I found this file in a part of the computer's memory that had been "deleted," but the deleter didn't know that you could recover files from memory without a reformat. The doctor who helped you, her last name is Olifvia, right?*

Yeah.

Does she have a brother?

Yes! You found a video of him?

Tria didn't respond immediately. *So Kal, since I don't have a body, I really only got an emotional reaction from watching this video. But it's bad. Really bad.*

Now you have to show me.

Tria directed him to the file he'd uploaded into the mini-pad, and Kal opened it.

The first few minutes were nothing remarkable. So, Lukgas Olifvia could yell at a much younger General Tdrak as well as his sister could. Kal smiled. Apparently Olifvias had been arguing with the general for over a decade.

Brace yourself, Tria said, breaking Kal's idle reverie at Lukgas's tirade.

The young general in the video pulled out a gun. An explosion of red engulfed the screen, and Kal almost dropped the mini-pad. Nausea swept over him. He maintained enough of his senses to stuff the mini-pad into his pocket, mashing the fruit bars, and ran for the bathroom.

He spent the next five minutes dry heaving into a toilet.

I'm sorry, Kal.

No, Tria, thank you for showing me. That's what we're up against? I can't believe he just—

Yeah. I know. That's the kind of world this is.

And Beatdrice... Oh, god. Tria. How do we tell her? She thinks he died in the war. But we've got to.

If this were Earth, I'd agree. But it isn't. We need to think about getting out of here alive and, more importantly, stopping this virus. We need to get you near your pad, and then show off the video. To everyone. That should create enough chaos to let us get away from this horrible place.

Kal huddled against the stall wall and thought it over. He shook his head. Tria was right.

I'll work on finding a way to get you into the Energy Weapons Lab.

Right, Kal thought.

Kal picked himself up, took a deep breath, and opened the door to the stall. One of his guards entered the bathroom, suspiciously eyeing another soldier near the sinks. Kal took one look at the other soldier's sinister expression and hobbled toward his guardian.

"I can't thank you enough," Kal said.

The guard smiled weakly back at him.

Kal checked for Dr. Olifvia and found she'd returned with another contingent of scientists. She held a computer tablet, arguing with her subordinate about whatever was on its screen.

He sighed and turned back to his computer. Poor Dr. Olifvia. What a horrific lie she'd believed all this time, all evidence of the truth wiped away, until Kal and his brother and his nanites had unearthed the decade-old tragedy.

The nanites—both amazing and awful all at the same time.

Steeling himself, Kal opened up the mini-pad's rudimentary programming interface. He closed out all of the metaxic node programming he'd been working on. He opened up brand new files in their place.

He pulled at the box under his desk and began scavenging from it once more. He needed just a few components... Yes, yes! This would work perfectly.

In a few hours' time, the mini-pad would be able to project some very rudimentary holograms.

The door to the laboratory exploded, and heavily armed soldiers rushed in.

Though tired and bleary-eyed, Kal had enough sense remaining to shout mentally for his brother. This is what they'd both expected.

General Tdrak marched through the door, and Kal nearly seized up at the sight of him. He'd merely seemed obstinate and intimidating before, but Kal now knew that the general was truly insane.

He marched over to Kal and yanked him up by the arm, soldiers swarming alongside him like angry bees.

"You and I have very different ideas of full custody, General!" Dr. Olifvia shouted, pushing her way through the crowd.

"He's a traitor!" Tdrak sneered. "Betrayed us to the enemy."

"Explain." Dr. Olifvia furrowed her brow.

"Unexplainable network traffic to Paszifika, the Southerners, and about a dozen Europbean and Aszian countries too!"

Dr. Olifvia looked at Kal, clearly inviting him to defend himself.

Kal wrestled with Tdrak's grasp. "Well, lord knows I can't program anything very complex with *this* equipment, but I know my pad. If someone was, say, trying to destroy it, it might just defend itself by connecting to your computer system. And it's not programmed to care about your political boundaries."

The general fumed, and squeezed his arm harder. Kal twisted up his face, scared into sudden silence, though he'd had some more witty retorts planned.

"Take him," Tdrak growled at his contingent.

"My custody." Dr. Olifvia stared Tdrak down.

"Fine! You can come too. In fact, I'm *ordering* you to come with us."

"Where are we going?" Dr. Olifvia asked, not betraying the slightest hint of irritation.

"The Energy Weapons Lab. Kgal will show me how to destroy his pad. Then you will all return here, and you will work until we are cured, or until we die. Whichever happens first."

Dr. Olifvia fell in alongside Kal, and they marched, a huge contingent, out of her office.

Exactly like we planned it, Kal! Isn't this great?

Kal gulped. He knew what was coming next, and he didn't want to think about it.

You're getting near the pad, Kal. We can get away from this place! Aren't you happy?

All he could think about was Dr. Olifvia and her brother Lukgas. His heart went out to her. He didn't like what he'd have to reveal to her, to everyone in this militaristic Chicago.

They arrived at a laboratory Kal had never seen before. It was huge, much bigger than the medical research lab. At its center stood a metallic cylinder as wide as the tree trunks he'd seen on Ydora. Soldier-technicians sat at computer consoles around its periphery. He could hear the steady thrum of machines channeling enormous quantities of energy.

Kal gasped. "We were short of electricity earlier in our lab…"

"Energy weapons has its own protected supply," Dr. Olifvia whispered in his ear, and Kal sensed that she begrudged them this luxury.

Kal scoffed mentally and sensed that Tria had had a similar reaction. How could these people justify hooking their energy reserves up to the weapons laboratory when it was the science laboratory that was working on the cure for the deadly plague?

"General Tdrak," Kal said. The general didn't even turn and look at him, just marched toward the machine that held Kal's pad. "General Tdrak! Please, listen to me. I don't want to hurt you or anyone else in the Mideastern Alliance, or any human being on Aynsz, for that matter. I can and will stop the virus if you just give me my computer. I know it's not in your nature to trust people, let alone some strange visitor from an alternate world, but there must be some way I can convince you. Please."

The general stared up at Kal's pad and tapped his thumb on his chin. He turned to one of the soldier-technicians.

"Have we tried gamma radiation, yet?"

"No, sir."

"What kind of power loss are we looking at?"

"We'd burn through all the of the remaining batch five reserve, sir."

The general slammed his fist onto the technician's console. "Do it."

Kal sighed. He reached for his back pocket, and the sounds of guns cocking erupted as twenty guards aimed for him.

"It's just one of *your* computers." Kal slowly pulled out the mini-pad.

"Kgal, how's your computer going to hold up against gamma radiation?" Dr. Olifvia asked, fixated on the particle accelerator.

"Not sure. Probably fine. I'm hoping it won't matter though."

"What do you mean?" She turned, finally giving him her full attention. "Did you do something to that handheld?"

"I just gave it a holographic projector."

The video Tria had found burst up off its interface, a rectangle meters wide and twice as tall as Tdrak, big enough for the whole room to see. Audio accompanied the video from the weapon lab's own sound system, courtesy of Tria's inventive programing.

The video depicted Beatdrice's brother, Lukgas Olifvia, in a room full of soldier-technicians, not unlike this one. But the video shook, and the room it depicted had full-windowed walls. Brown hills rumbled along beyond them. The events of the video must have happened in some kind of mobile command center.

Tdrak was there too, ten years younger.

"You told me they'd suffer minimal casualties. This is your idea of minimal?!" Lukgas raged over the speakers.

The real General Tdrak's eyes shot up to the holographically projected video. "No! NO!!" He pulled out his gun and loosed bullets wildly at Kal. The soldiers, guards and Olifvia jumped away. Two bullets hit Kal and fell off his recently re-enabled nanite auto-defense system.

"Restrain him!" Dr. Olifvia shouted. Her guards ran up and seized Tdrak by the arms as he tried to load more bullets. The general's soldiers seemed patently confused, more intrigued by the video of their commanding officer than his present insanity.

"You used me!" Lukgas Olifvia shouted from the video, raising a fist at the younger Tdrak. "You used me and those boys *I trained*. You made me betray them. Just so you could get what you wanted. Your victory. That's all you can do, isn't it? Use people. 'Til they're all dead."

"It's a lie! The alien created it!" the real general roared.

Kal handed Dr. Olifvia the mini-pad.

"No," she said. "It's not. The file's got all of the marks of our system, and it's timestamped for… just over eight years ago. Now shut up and let me listen to my brother. He never told me about a fight he had with you."

Kal struggled to keep his voice under control. "No, Dr. Olifvia. I'm sure he didn't."

She swung around and looked directly at him. For the first time since he'd met her, her calm confidence had evaporated. "What does that mean?!"

"You're encroaching on insubordination!" the video-Tdrak said.

"Damn right I'm insubordinate!" Lukgas shouted back. "They're barely more than kids, damn it. All so you can win some stupid battle… This meaningless war that *you started*."

"You keep saying that, commander." Video-Tdrak shook his head.

"Fighting *is* meaningless. You have no remorse. You have no qualms about throwing away human life. You treat people's lives like they're levers and toggles for some grand game inside your head. You are completely and utterly sick."

"But, dear Lieutenant Commander Olifvia..." In one quick motion, video-Tdrak drew his gun from the holster at his side. "I will show you how wrong you are. Fighting is *very* good at settling wearisome, wasteful argumentation."

Kal looked away. He didn't want to see this part again—the part where General Tdrak fired a bullet directly into Lukgas Olifvia's face, a bullet armed with an explosive charge.

The entire room gasped. Olifvia screamed, hurling the mini-pad to the floor, although this didn't stop the holographic projection. The guns pointed at Kal turned toward the general.

"Turn it off! Turn that thing off!" Dr. Olifvia shouted.

Kal snatched it up, standing underneath the projection of an enormous rectangle of smeared red, the blood and bits of Lukgas Olifvia's head dripping down off it. Kal fumbled with the controls, doing as she had asked, and the awful image fizzled away.

Tears streaming down her face, Dr. Olifvia marched toward the restrained general.

Kal scrambled up and ran for the machine behind the crowd.

Tria?

Almost there... got it! The machine is shutting down. Should be safe to take the pad.

He ripped away the clamps and wires, snatching up his computer from the bowels of the horrific, now inert, contraption.

Kal looked down at the other side of the room, at Dr. Olifvia, who stood over the general, pointing a gun at his face. Her chest was heaving. Tears dripped to the floor.

Kal looked between Olifvia and the metaxic node activation window on his interface. In a split second, his decision had been made. He latched his pad to his side and strode toward Dr. Olifvia and General Tdrak.

Thoughts of home roiled through his mind. He may not have read all of his own history, but he believed he was beginning to understand the fundamental social shift that had happened on Earth, but not yet on Aynsz.

"Dr. Olifvia," Kal said.

"Not now, Kgal."

"No, now, Dr. Olifvia! What are you doing?"

"This is how things are done here."

Kal wasn't sure whether she was complaining or explaining.

"I know," Kal said, moving closer, through the field of guns, all pointed toward Tdrak, whom four guards had pinned to the back wall.

"You know," she spat the words sarcastically. "How could you possibly know? You come from *Earth*. Where you have your peace and prosperity. How could you know anything about us?"

"We know!" Kal shouted. "Oh, we know! We're not more evolved, Dr. Olifvia. We don't have magical powers that let us ignore hatred and jealousy and loathing and vengeance. We feel all the same things. The difference is the stories we tell each other. We tell each other that killing is wrong, and we don't make excuses for doing it. We make it illegal. We have to actively prevent it from occurring. And sometimes we do get that angry, and sometimes we make horrible mistakes.

"We're so just like you. Don't tell yourself that there's no choice. That you have to kill in order for everything to be okay. Or that's it's justice, or social betterment, or whatever other rationalism you invent. You *do* have a choice, Dr. Olifvia, and it's actually quite simple. You can be like him, or you can be better. If you kill him, then what happens next? Honestly, think about what would happen next. He killed your brother, then you kill him, then someone else kills you, and on and on. Violence is a closed loop! And the only way to break it, the only way to have a society worth living in, is for one person at a time to decide to put down the weapons and say to her opponent, 'I reject everything you represent, and I quit your version of the game. My rules are better.'"

Dr. Olifvia cocked her gun. The soldiers holding Tdrak positioned themselves so as to give her a clear shot while still restraining him.

"It was fun watching your brother's head explode." Tdrak giggled. His eyes glinted with newly unrestrained insanity. "I demoted the officer who screamed when his brains splattered on her."

"Before or after you had her killed?" Kal turned back to Olifvia. "He had everyone in that room quietly killed, Dr. Olifvia. So that no one would find out what he'd done."

"For the purity of the Mideastern Alliance!" The general struggled futilely against the hands restraining him. "People like you and your sick brother need to be put down like diseased dogs or thrown to the cogs of war. You are weak, you Olifvias. No character. No backbone."

Dr. Olifvia stood very silently for many moments, closed her eyes,

inhaled and exhaled deeply, then whispered, "you're wrong."

She threw down the gun and turned, grabbing Kal by his shoulders. "Go."

Kal nodded, took several steps back and activated his pad interface. A wave of relief washed over him seeing its cool blue interface for this first time in days. He pressed the button to initiate a bubble.

Dr. Olifvia smiled at him through the haze of blue sparks and ripples of static electricity.

Just before the bubble fully formed, Kal saw her stumble backward, not from the wind, but a violent lurching. There was a spray of red from her chest, and Kal jumped forward toward her, shouting as bullets erupted throughout the lab. More red exploded from other soldiers, and Dr. Olifvia crumpled, falling to the floor like a rag doll.

Kal slammed into the quantum-locked edge of his bubble, screaming as the horrible visage of Aynsz rippled away into swirling blue.

∞⟨⟩∞

Through teary eyes, Kal's hands raced across his pad. Tria had created so many additional programs that Kal's programming environment seemed a foreign landscape. Tria stood beside him with his own interface and helped guide him through the changes. Having Tria back felt good, but the joy was bittersweet, all mixed up with his anger and worry about what had become of Dr. Olifvia.

Kal sat suddenly, pushing the interface away.

"I actually got through to her, Tria. I actually got through, and now— What if she's— What if Tdrak—"

"Hey!" Tria crouched down and grabbed at Kal's shoulders. "You've got a couple billion people counting on you to shut that virus down!"

Kal nodded and snatched up his interface. The next few minutes became a blur of frantic coding.

"Wait..." Tria said. "Wait, wait, wait. This can't be right."

"What is it?" Kal looked over at Tria's interface.

"No, oh my god. It's right, Kal. The DNA for the nanogenic pathogen, for the virus. What it does to the human host when it gets through..."

"What? What does it do?"

Tria just gaped at his interface. Blue swirled around the bubble.

"What is it, Tria?" Kal demanded.

"Nothing."

Kal blinked, then pulled Tria's interface in front of him. "What?!"

"Absolutely nothing. It's a ruse. The virus doesn't kill. It doesn't even make you sick. I mean, some people might have an allergic reaction to it, but that's it. It's not programmed to do anything but slam into the immune system and leave. Oh, and that whole collective sharing of information thing, too. But why would that matter...?"

Kal and Tria looked at one another. Kal thought over the possibilities.

"Oh my..." Kal said, his voice barely a whisper. "It would matter if the person who designed it expected someone on Aynsz would try to alter it and make a new biological weapon."

Tria broke in. "And I'll bet most of those hundreds of countries haven't even figured out that the virus is nanite-enabled. They might try to alter its DNA not knowing that they'd—"

"That they'd instantly infect the entire planet's population with the disease."

Kal and Tria shared a despondent, dreadful gaze only momentarily.

Kal grabbed up his own interface. As quickly as he could, he finished tracing the viruses' metaxic route and propelled the bubble toward their new target.

They arrived, and the metaxic blue coalesced into a sandy, desert landscape. A metal box sat on the ground. No sooner had the bubble fully unraveled, than the box disintegrated, vaporizing into the dry air. Kal ran his hands over the interface, attempting to glean something, the static of the bubble still crackling around him. Nothing. It had utterly destroyed itself on his arrival.

"Damn it!" Kal shouted.

"Did that stop the virus, then?" Tria asked. "Are the people of Aynsz safe?"

Kal scanned the nanite reports. "Whatever malevolent viruses or nanites were here, they're gone now. Unless that control center had redundancies, the people of Aysnz should be fine. No more nanites enabling viruses. Assuming that we're correct about the viruses doing nothing, they should be no match for anyone with a functioning immune system now."

Tria nodded, and Kal activated his nodes once more. A new bubble formed.

"See, Tria?" Kal pointed to his pad. "No more viruses entering or leaving this world. I think we're good!"

Tria stared at his interface, frowning.

"What is it?"

Tria looked at him with a quivering lip and sunken eyes. "I'm sorry, Kal."

"Sorry for what?" Kal grabbed up Tria's interface.

A single red bubble hovered atop it: "Metaxic bio-quarantine protocol in effect for Realm #5721 'Aynsz.' Viral contamination detected. World is not safe for travel."

Kal took Tria's interface, picked it up and hurled the holograms at the bubble wall, then slammed a hand through his own interface. He threw himself against the bubble and let himself slide down its curve to the floor. The tears started, and he couldn't stop them.

Tria sat beside him, tearing up too.

"Kal?"

"Yeah?"

"What do we do now?"

"We wait for the auto-medical program to make us immune to whatever the people of Aynsz infected themselves with, and..." Kal sniffled. "We see if we can make a cure in time."

Tria nodded weakly and sat down beside him.

∞⟨⟩∞

Kal held the bubble on Aynsz without unraveling it completely. He could see Dr. Olifvia, lying in a bed beside him. There were other people in this hospital room. Some lay on the floor, unmoving. Some lay in or sat beside beds. All of them had developed black and brown lesions across their skin, and even through the bubble, he could see the greasy sheen. The horrible melt his pad described was in full force. It would be only a few days now.

The nanites formed a square forcefield around Dr. Olifvia's bed. It shimmered momentarily, then blocked the light from outside, its walls turning black. A soft light, born of nanites, illuminated the container.

He bit his lip.

"I just restarted auto-medical," Tria said solemnly. "You should be safe. It can protect you from the virus now."

Kal nodded and unraveled the sphere. He stood just a meter from Dr. Olifvia's bed. She had the disease clearly, but was also attached to machines, her stomach bandaged. Apparently, they'd tended to her gunshot wound before discovering everyone had been infected.

"Hello?" Dr. Olifvia called out, her voice raspy.

"It's me," Kal said.

"Kgal?"

"Mm hmm." Kal stepped closer. He looked her over, so weak and frail now, her skin melting, her body giving way to the inevitable.

"Help us, Kgal."

Kal couldn't control the tears. They burst forth again. "I can't— I— I don't have the ability. It's mutating too quickly. You did too good a job making it, even for me."

"Kgal?"

"Yes?"

"Tell me about the philosophy of your Earth. Please."

"There's so much... what do you want to know about?"

"Anything. Maybe a story."

"Well," Kal gathered himself as best he could. "We had a philosopher called Plato. He spoke about a cave, where a group of people lived. They knew nothing but the cave's interior. They'd never been outside. The sun and moon and stars didn't exist to them. But there were others who had seen those things. These other people, all they could do was hold up objects that represented those things from the outside world, like the sun and moon and stars. The shapes of those things would be cast against the cave wall from the firelight. The people who lived in the cave had a hard time understanding the true nature of those things because all they could see were the shadows."

"Pblo." Dr. Olifvia coughed, hacking up blood onto her already stained hospital gown. "Our philosopher with a similar story is named Pblo."

"See," Kal said, "more stuff we have in common."

"How funny," Dr. Olifvia laughed a bit, coughing up more blood. "A lonely boy exploring shadows. It must be beautiful."

Kal nodded.

"Will you tell people about us? About Aynsz? Tell them we weren't all bad?"

"Of course," Kal said, and grabbed hold of her hand, as gently as he was able. "I'll tell them. I promise."

"Thank you, Kgal."

Unpossible

Realm #6632, "Grapht"
Realm #4249, "Frakt"

August 22, 2178

KAL TYPED OUT COMMANDS at his interface. Tria stood some ways off in the distance still. And he was glaring again. His brother had been doing it for days.

Kal dared to glance over at the ten-meter-tall hunk of graphite and discovered Tria was not, indeed, glaring. He was yawning. Kal muttered, cursing himself for looking up, and returned his attention to his computer.

The metallurgical study was complete, but the nanites were still working on the soil analysis. Evidence of life remained inconclusive.

If there ever had been life on this world, it was long dead. The sun blasted down from a cloudless sky, scorching the dried and cracked plain to over 140 degrees Celsius. Waves of heat shimmered up off the ground.

Nanites generated the oxygen Kal required to breathe and dissipated the heat, always protecting him, even here.

Kal had decided the world was called Grapht. Its most interesting feature were the enormous, pointy hunks of shimmering gray metal that dotted the landscape. Indentations lay at their bases, pits in the dried, dead earth, looking like small impact craters.

"You're done, right?" Tria appeared at Kal's side. "Where to next?"

"Next up is 8918."

Tria turned on his own interface. Kal did his best to ignore his brother, but despite his best efforts, he found himself tracking Tria's behavior out of the corner of his eyes.

Tria opened the directory with the alter Earth stills and waved through it until he happened on 8918. After only a cursory glance, he scoffed and turned the interface off. "Seriously?"

"Something wrong with it?" A pang of fear seized Kal. He pulled up the stills himself and scanned the images. It was an uninhabited world with gelatinous, blue vines tangled up in huge knots of themselves, and its sun cast green-tinted light over the landscape. The atmosphere was composed primarily of fluorine.

"No, nothing at all." Tria rolled his eyes. "It's just like the last thirty worlds we've been to."

"No it's not. Look, it's got these twisty, blue plants."

Tria pointed to the biological analysis at the edge of the interface. "And yet—surprise, surprise—no sign of anything remotely sentient."

Kal folded his arms and frowned.

"Look, Kal." Tria put a hand on Kal's shoulder. "I know that things have been... rough recently, but I don't think you escaped from Felis just to catalog empty worlds. Or worlds where everything's underwater, worlds of endless forest, worlds of bone, worlds of rock, a world for every rectangle of the periodic table. I'll tell you the one we haven't been to yet, Kal—a world where the boring is so palpable that it's physically congealed into a gray ooze that covers the Earth's surface. Care to send the nanites off looking for that one?"

Kal sighed and crossed his arms. "Yeah, I've been playing it safe. So what?"

"Playing it *safe?*" Tria gestured with both arms. "You're standing next to a hunk of graphite the size of a house!"

Kal latched his pad to his side, the interface flickering off, and he looked at the ground.

"This morning," Tria continued, "I actually ran out of languages to study. I went through all the worlds you visited before I was born, all the way back to Ydora. We should go somewhere with more *people.*"

Kal looked up, grimacing, and locked eyes with his brother.

"No," Kal said. "Not again. I won't let it happen again."

Tria inhaled and exhaled visibly. Kal looked down at his interface, at the reports for geological stability, atmospheric composition, soil chemistry, and on and on. All his technology, all their amazing capabilities, and yet he felt so powerless.

It reminded him of when he'd woken up for the first time on Felis, and the adults had explained what had happened to him. He'd resented nanotechnology and everything it represented. He'd begrudged even the auto-defense program that protected him from the cats. But in time, he'd seen his status with his furry companions shift from prey to protector. He'd learned everything he could of the metaxia, and set his mind on exploration. And he'd only achieved it with the nanites' help. They would help him find a cure for the very problem they'd created.

Perhaps Kal had been wrong. Perhaps…

"I'm worried too," Tria said. "But it's not going to do us any good to visit empty Earths. It doesn't help me, and it doesn't help you." He tapped his foot on the ground and looked up into the empty sky.

Suddenly, Tria's expression lightened. A smile stretched across his face. He turned his own interface on.

"How about this?" Tria gestured to Kal, smiling.

Kal let his arms fall to his sides, and returned his brother's smile weakly.

"This is all the data from realm #4249," Tria said. "I noticed it last week, just before Aynsz."

Kal scanned the reports. "Oh! You found the program I wrote after Vanaheim."

Tria nodded. "Neat idea, checking up on alternate Earths periodically to see if anything's changed."

Kal scanned over the data. "Three changes found for 4249…"

"And?"

"Yeah, I see it. It's habitable each time, but the habitability vectors are… this doesn't make any sense. It's like there are humans, but there aren't. There's water, but there's not. Hmm… breathable atmosphere is consistent, and the planet's in the right spot every time, so it should be safe."

"So, why don't we take a small, calculated risk and go see what makes this world such a conundrum?"

Kal couldn't believe Tria was actually encouraging him to do something risky. When had their roles reversed? Had he actually become so fearful of himself and his gadgets that he had lost the will to seek out the mysterious and the strange? The revelation rushed over him—he had been afraid. Ever since Aynsz. Ever since sitting with Dr. Olifvia and watching as she wasted away—

Kal shook the terrible memories from his head.

"Okay," he said. "It couldn't hurt to take a look around, I suppose."

"Great!" Tria slapped Kal on the back, though of course, Kal felt nothing. "Next stop, realm #4249."

Tria pressed the button on his interface, and they disappeared from Grapht in a sphere of electric blue.

The metaxia peeled away, as it always did, but as this world shimmered into existence, nausea rushed over him, and the environment span. A blur of green and blue and white twisted and turned, pulling at Kal's inner ear with each rush of movement. He lost his balance and staggered forward. He reached out to catch himself with one hand and grasped the pad as tightly as he could with the other.

"Tria..."

I'm working on it. Just hang in there.

The world continued spinning and Kal clamped his eyes shut. That seemed to help a little bit, but the dizziness persisted.

Calculated risk, you tell me.

You won't believe this Kal. The nanites are having trouble navigating outside your body. It's like they go to move across the x-axis and they wind up moving across the y-axis instead. I think the spatial distortion is messing with your inner ear. Give me just a minute.

I'm so glad that you're here, Tria. Just please help me get off this world, okay?

Sure thing. You should be able to open your eyes now at least.

Kal indeed felt the dizziness and nausea subsiding. He stood up straight, still gripping the pad, and dared to peek his eyes open the tiniest bit.

What he saw between his narrowed eyelids amazed him so much that he threw them open all at once.

He stood on a grassy plain before a river, a small hill beyond it. The river snaked around the side of the hill, up it, then fell from the top, a waterfall that fed... itself—a perpetual loop of river. Ducks swam on its surface in a contorted pattern that somehow resembled both a straight line and Möbius strip. Birds flew through the sky in a similar configuration.

Kal looked down at the blades of grass at his feet. Every so often, a blade would split in half down the middle and separate, forming two blades where there had been one. Not the strangest thing he'd ever seen, but what was truly peculiar was that the new blade became the same size as the original blade of grass it had formed from. And stranger still, the number of blades of grass remained constant from moment to moment despite their ceaseless replication.

"Okay, Tria. First things first. I want a layer of nanites gluing my hand to the pad. I don't want anything causing me to drop it here."

Done.

"Can you turn your hologram on?"

Tria flickered on, half-forming in front of Kal, but the image of his body blobbed, twisted and contorted. He was barely recognizable as a person. A few moments later, the projection ceased.

No good, Kal.

"Let me try." Kal raised the pad in front of him and jumped when it didn't appear before his field of vision as expected.

Tria! I can't see my hand.

That's because it's behind your back.

"What?!"

I can't explain it, that's just what the data says. Your hand is outstretched behind your back.

Kal blinked a few times. He turned to the left, and then to the right. Each time, the vision of the grassy hill with the river and waterfall seemed to stretch and follow his field of vision.

Okay, Kal. We're going to try something. Put your left hand out in front of you again.

Kal did as Tria said.

Okay, now move it up. No, wait. Left. Yeah, more left. Keep going. Okay, now pull in and up simultaneously.

Won't the pad smack me in the face?

No, if I've figured out these spatial contortions right, the pad will end up in front of you.

Kal did as Tria said, and the pad indeed seemed to protrude from his chest and end up in front of his field of vision.

I can see it! Kal reached out with his right hand instinctively, and of course, it didn't end up where he expected it, and he struggled futilely to repeat the bizarre movements with his free hand.

I'll activate it, Tria thought.

A jumble of holograms exploded in all directions off its surface. It looked as though the pad's interface had been stuffed into a blender, similar to what had happened when they'd tried to project Tria.

A lurching feeling pulled at him toward the sky, at first weakly, then stronger. Kal shouted, falling headfirst upward and wrapping his arms around his head. His back smacked into something hard, and the auto-defense nanites sizzled. Kal picked himself up. The momentary nausea passed. He tilted his head toward the sky. It was a both a blue sky and a field of grass, like the one he stood on, but upside down.

Get me out of here, Tria, please.

Gladly.

A few blue sparks crackled around Kal, but their configuration didn't seem spherical at all. It was contorted, oblong and twisted. The blue sparks fizzled away.

Damn it! Tria shouted mentally. *The nanites can't form a sphere. Of course.*

"Goodbye," a voice said. Kal turned to his left, from where the voice had come, but saw no one.

"No, over here," the voice said. It sounded as though Kal should be looking directly at it. Defying logic, he turned right. Nothing.

"No, no. Over here."

Kal gulped and looked up.

A man sat on a rock, which somehow lay simultaneously against the side of the hill *and* in the sky above him.

"My name's Zeno," the man said. "I should warn you that everything I tell you is a lie."

Paradoxes, Kal thought. *Tria, the physical laws of this universe are—*

—are based on paradoxes. Got it. It might be possible to generate a sphere within these laws though...

"Goodbye," Zeno said. "I don't have all day."

"How long is a day on this world?" Kal put on his biggest grin, even though his heart was pounding.

"How long?" Zeno repeated. "How long is a day? I can show you!"

Zeno stood up.

"Walk toward me," he commanded.

Anytime now, Tria. This guy is creeping me out.

"How can I walk toward you? You're above me."

Zeno looked at Kal as though he'd just asked why up was down.

"Above, below, left, right. Silly human! Just walk toward me."

Kal put one foot in front of the other, and he indeed seemed to move toward Zeno. Zeno took a few steps backward, his form passing directly through the boulder he had been sitting on.

"Wait." Kal halted. "What are you doing?"

"Oh, don't worry," Zeno said. "I'm only moving half as fast as you. You'll catch me shortly. Then you'll know how long the day is."

"What's the name of this world?"

Another look of bewilderment from Zeno.

"Just keep moving!" he said.

Kal took up walking again, his trajectory tilting ever upwards, though his feet remained flat on the ground. The boulder grew closer, and when Kal reached it, he too walked right through it, as though it were just a hologram. Zeno stood some distance away still.

"I'll never reach you," Kal said.

"Yes, you will. I told you, I'm only moving half as fast as you are."

"Right, so every time I move one meter toward you, you move half a meter away. It'll continue forever. I'll keep getting closer and closer by fractions."

Got it! Tria announced. *An inverse ellipsoid torus with an inner ring radius that's wider than its outer radius!*

Tell me that's a—

—a sphere on this world, yes.

Fire up the nodes, Tria.

Gladly.

"Thanks for the philosophical discussion." Kal grinned.

Blue sparks rippled, and Kal rushed with relief as the inverse ellipsoid torus of crackling electricity formed, functional only by this universe's illogic.

Zeno's face grew solemn. "He does not seek you; he seeks refuge from you. Disease clouds his mind and sunders his body."

Kal's eyes widened. "What does that mean? Who are you talking about?"

"Hello." Zeno smiled.

The bubble pulled Kal into the metaxia once more.

oৎৢৣৢ৹

Kal sat in the bubble, his back resting against the curve. He focused on breathing steadily in and out.

"Hey, Kal?"

Kal opened his eyes. Tria crouched down in front of him. Kal's pad interface hovered in space. It had returned to its typical configuration, freed from the insanity of realm #4249. "You think maybe we could go find that world where the boring is physically palpable?"

Kal snickered a bit, then laughed outright. Tria's frown melted, and he laughed a bit himself.

"Seriously though, Kal. You were right. We have to be extremely careful about the worlds we visit."

Kal shook his head. "I think we were both right. I have been too cautious recently. If there is someone out there... stalking me... visiting the worlds I plan to go to before I do... I just can't help but think about what might happen if I go to explore a world with people, you know? Like, is my presence going to get them all killed?" Kal opened his mouth, but the words he was about to say caught in his throat. He blinked a few times and took a deep breath, composing himself. "I still have nightmares about what happened on Aynsz. About running into the person who caused... that."

"You think the guy Dr. Olifvia described is still out there in the metaxia? We did leave that metaxic transponder broadcasting to Earth about what he did."

Kal shook his head. "But we have no way of knowing if Fermilab found him or not. Or if they even got the message. And we don't have any way of tracking him ourselves."

He and Tria sat in the bubble for a long while and looked at the grid of worlds, its snaky tendrils rotating slowly atop the interface.

"So, Kal..." Tria was smirking again.

Kal rolled his eyes. "Is this idea going to be better than your last?"

"Yes." Tria pulled the interface closer and began typing on its keyboard. The grid zoomed inward, slowing to a halt atop a point of light near its periphery. Kal craned his neck over to see it.

Realm #2648.

"What's special about it?"

"Look at the map."

Kal's eyes bulged. "There's just ocean where all North America should be. There can't be Chicago—" He spotted it just as he said the words, tiny strips of land peaking up out of the blue. Tria zoomed in on them.

"Inverted..." Kal muttered.

"Not Great Lakes," Tria said, "but Great Islands."

"Climate?"

"Tropical."

"Beaches?"

Tria nodded.

"Swimming!" A rush of excitement accompanied that revelation.

Tria nodded even more vigorously.

Kal narrowed his eyes. "What's the catch?"

Tria held up his hands. "No catch. Honest!"

Kal grabbed up the interface and did his own typing. It took him no more than a couple of button presses to find the information that had caught his brother's attention. Kal pursed his lips and turned to face Tria, who was staring out into the metaxia, feigning innocence.

"Looks to me," Kal sighed, "like there are about two dozen different spoken languages in that alt-Chicago."

"What a coincidence!" Tria stretched out his arms. Kal frowned in response. His brother sobered and put a hand on Kal's shoulder. "We can't run forever. Eventually, we'll have to figure out what happened on Aynsz and get past it. Cataloguing the grid's boring, empty worlds isn't helping us do that. This place is perfect! I'll get my languages, and you'll be able to *relax*. What do you say?"

Kal looked at the map on the interface, at the small dots of land in the ocean, islands in the shape of the Great Lakes.

Kal nodded slowly and reached up, laying his hand roughly on Tria's shoulder. "I suppose we could give it a shot."

Requiescence

Realm #2648, "Spenfa"
August 23, 2178

*Y*OU SEE THAT, Tria?

What?

That boy over there. He's just sitting and staring at his sandcastle. And he's been like that for at least a minute now. What do you suppose that's all about?

You're supposed to be relaxing, remember?

Okay, fine. Kal pulled his sunglasses back up and returned to the book he'd been reading. The sky was cerulean blue, not a single cloud overhead. Ocean breeze wafted over him. There were people all around, shouting and playing in the sand, but not too many as to be distracting. Some families and children, but people his age too.

Reading isn't relaxing, Kal.

Says the language expert!

Kal felt Tria roll his eyes at him.

'Patterns and Procedures in NanoScript,' Tria read the title of Kal's book aloud. *You're on a beach full of attractive, shirtless guys, and you're reading a programming book? I tell you Kal, if I had a body, reading is not what I'd be up to right now.*

Kal sighed and considered finding a library, but refusing to relax on Tria's terms would mean enduring more of his brother's torment. The beach wasn't without its virtues, as Tria had rightly observed, but now that Tria had drawn his attention to their derailed explorations, he didn't want to relax. He wanted to explore. He should be out looking for advanced worlds with cloning tech or strange fauna with a resistance to nanogenic radiation. He might even find help locating and identifying his impersonator.

He frowned at that thought. After a week of metaxic travel, that impersonator had failed to manifest even the slightest hint of his existence. Kal wondered if perhaps he had no impersonator after all, that the events of Aynsz had been some fluke of all-possibility.

Maybe he could just go back to his hotel room and be alone with the pad. It would be fun to program something. He hadn't done much of that over the last week, either. His computer lay inside the backpack leaning against his beach chair. On Spenfa, his backpack was thick but the material light and squishy. It was also very tall, like camping gear, with big padded straps for his arms.

Relax, Tria commanded.

Kal stuffed the book into his backpack, reclined in his beach chair, put his hands behind his head, and closed his eyes.

He thought about how pleasantly normal Spenfa had been so far. Less technologically advanced than Earth, sure. Probably somewhere around late twentieth century by his standards. However, he'd found all of Spenfa's social norms refreshingly similar to the one's he'd grown up with. Throughout the entire day, whether eating breakfast at a beachside restaurant or checking into his hotel, everyone he'd interacted with had behaved according to social rules Kal felt he could intuit, unlike so many other Chicagos he'd visited. If it hadn't been for the Benefactor and Dr. Olifvia and the mystery assailant nagging at him from the depths of his mind, he might indeed have been able to relax.

He pushed those thoughts away once more and tried to put his mind to sleep since that, at least, would be one way to appease Tria.

A shadow passed over Kal's eyes, and he snapped out of his trance.

"Hi." The voice was deep, and close by.

Kal looked up. A young man, probably in his early twenties, stood beside him. He managed to appear lean, though he possessed a thick musculature. He had dark skin and black, curly hair. And his eyes. Very deep brown eyes. Cute, too.

"Oh, hi," Kal stammered, his voice cracking.

Smooth, Tria thought.

Shut up and go relax somewhere yourself!

"I noticed you doing sprints earlier," the young man said. "My friend Anzin and I were going to race a couple laps between those buoys." He pointed out just beyond the shore. "You want to join us?"

"Sure." Kal pulled himself up, beaming.

"My name's Vik."

"Kal."

"Nice to meet you, Koss."

"You too, Vik." They shook hands, and Kal rushed with giddiness. He tried to force himself not to seem too excited as he grabbed up his backpack and towel, managing to fumble with them regardless.

Vik led him across the beach to a young man and a young woman. The young man, who Kal presumed was Anzin, lay spread out across his towel, arms and legs outstretched. While Kal and Vik both wore black racing suits that cut off halfway down their thighs, Anzin was wearing a bright purple swimmer that covered less than a centimeter of his hips.

The young woman sat next to him, cross-legged, wearing a T-shirt over her one-piece and a wide-brimmed wicker hat. In her hands, a well-worn paperback lay open. She looked up and, seeing Vik and Kal, smiled warmly and set the book onto her towel.

Anzin lurched his head upward and threw himself into a stance, a single, swift action of coiling his feet back, then pulling his torso upward with his tightly knotted abdominal muscles.

"Anzin, Petra, this is Koss," Vik said.

"Hey," Anzin smiled wryly down at Kal. He was nearly two meters tall.

Petra snorted at Anzin and shook her head, standing up the normal way. "Nice to meet you." She shook Kal's hand.

"Same here." Anzin grasped Kal's shoulder, then looked him directly in the eyes. "Swimming. Vik's told you we're going to swim, right?"

Kal found he could only nod vaguely in agreement.

"You found a winner, Vik!" Anzin giggled and slapped Vik on the back, his other hand still firmly latched onto Kal's shoulder. Vik had his head in his hand.

"Well, what are we waiting around here for? Let's go." Anzin released them both and sprinted off toward the water, his purple behind splashing into the ocean.

"I'm *really* sorry about Anzin. He's very—"

"It's alright," Kal smiled. "I had friends like him on my swim team."

"That's how Anzin and I became friends." Cheer seemed to return to Vik's face, then fell as Petra cleared her throat.

"Oh, Petra," Vik began. "Would you mind watching our stuff while—"

She waved them both toward the water, then sat down and resumed reading her book.

Kal set his backpack onto Anzin's towel, eyeing Petra carefully.

Uh, Tria... could you please *take care of the pad? I know I always ask this, but this Vik guy is really cute, and he likes swimming, and—*

Jesus, every time you meet some guy, I get stuck babysitting the technol—
You can choose the next ten worlds.
Done.

Kal briefly envisioned himself twiddling his thumbs on alternate Earths for days while his brother absorbed alter-Earth languages, but one glance at Vik striding through the sand beside him and such worries were forgotten. Beyond them, Anzin reached the water and dove headfirst into an oncoming wave.

"You from the islands?" Vik asked.

"No, I'm from Messika." Kal had learned from his nanites' research that Messika, a country on a continent far to the south, was the protectorate of the five Great Island Nations. On Spenfa, the islands were a tropical getaway, and tourists came from all over the world to visit Siskago's botanical gardens and pineapple plantations, to relax and enjoy the sun, just as Kal had.

When Vik didn't respond to Kal's answer right away, he tried to gauge Vik's expression, but found he couldn't. Vik merely stared ahead coldly. Kal decided to change the subject.

"You live here?"

"I do now. Anzin and I are originally from Messika too. He and Petra and I are in the same program at the university." They splashed into the water. "What brings you to the islands?"

"Oh, the usual, I guess." Kal laughed. "Just visiting. Vacation."

Vik nodded knowingly, sprang into a wave, and swam out toward the buoy. Kal watched him momentarily, very intrigued, then dove into the next wave and followed.

Vik turned out to be the strongest swimmer of the three of them. His stroke was elegant, his form graceful, and Kal fought hard to keep up, if only to catch glimpses of Vik between breaths.

Vik won six of the first ten sprints, and Kal took three more, leaving Anzin with only one. Vik had given Kal a silent nod before that sprint's start, which Kal had correctly taken to mean that they should both let Anzin have at least one victory. Even that one had been more than enough for Anzin, who happily trailed them on all the others.

On the conclusion of the eighteenth sprint, Kal contacted the buoy and looked up, only to find that Anzin was no longer trailing at their feet.

Vik had a knowing expression plastered across his face and nodded further out to sea. Kal spotted Anzin some distance away, treading water and talking to a guy lain across a surfboard, another ripped mass of muscle in a tiny swimsuit.

"About me and Anzin…" Vik's expression betrayed his worry. "He and I are just friends."

Kal nodded. He and Vik continued treading water beside the buoy as waves rocked them up and down.

"I know his type," Kal finally said. "Like I said, he reminds me of a friend from the swim team. Really just goofy. Nothing that came out his mouth was ever socially appropriate."

Vik chortled. "That's Anzin alright. This was your high school swim team?"

"Yeah," Kal lied. He'd fallen into the coma at twelve, when he was only just finishing elementary school. "I don't really get to see my friends much anymore though."

Vik nodded. "You've kept up with it really well, though. The swimming, I mean. You must swim a lot."

"Every day." Kal regained his cheerfulness. "You?"

Vik nodded vigorously. "I try to. But there's no time for a team. There are plenty of adult swim teams in Siskago, but with school, well, it's all I can do to swim an hour or so every day. Have to keep up with classes and research projects."

"You seem in pretty good shape to me," Kal gave Vik a smile, and he returned it. A particularly strong wave pushed Kal into Vik, and they clutched each other momentarily. Kal rushed with physical elation, then shock hit him. Would Vik get the wrong idea if he came on too strong? He set himself squarely at arm's length from Vik again.

Damn it. Was that the right thing to have done? He had no idea. Maybe he should have kissed him or something. But Vik had just got done saying he wasn't "like" Anzin, his meaning perfectly clear. Or was it? This was all so damn confusing. Kal cursed the metaxia, imagining how much easier all this dating stuff would be if he was in his own culture.

"This is your first time in Siskago, right?" Vik asked, fumbling with the words.

"Yeah."

"You have any plans for dinner?"

"Not yet."

"I know this great Ianzanese place. You want to join me?"

"Sure." Kal was sure he was grinning again. He briefly pondered this. His euphoria at being asked such a simple question struck him as ridiculous. Well, damn it, he would be ridiculous then. He decided he liked this giddiness, and resolved to embrace it.

"A few more laps?" Vik gestured out toward the other buoy.

"Sure." He probably would have said yes to anything.

Kal counted down from three, and they took off through the water.

After they had swum another fifty laps, Kal and Vik returned to the shore where Anzin and Petra sat on the beach talking.

Kal glanced at Vik and caught Vik glancing at him. Vik blushed, and Kal smiled. Vik let out a small laugh and shook his head, then hurried forward. Kal followed him to Anzin and Petra on their beach towels.

"You two ready to hit the bars?" Anzin raised his eyebrows multiple times at them.

Petra's hand returned to her face, and Vik clenched his jaw.

Anzin's expression fell. "What'd I say?"

Petra turned and gazed at him momentarily in astonishment before facing Kal and Vik. "You two go have fun. We're meeting back at my place tonight though, right?"

Vik gave a quick nod as confirmation.

Anzin's face exploded with realization. "Oh, OH!" His muscles quivered, and glee seemed to overtake him. His ridiculous grin managed to become wider.

"Please." Petra rolled her eyes. "You cannot seriously be just now figuring this out."

Vik shook his head and smiled. "I'll see you guys later tonight."

Petra nodded and returned to her book. Anzin lay down on his beach towel and stretched himself out. He shot his head up just as Kal and Vik turned to leave.

"Have fun boys!" Anzin shouted. Kal heard a slapping sound behind him, and then, "Petra! What was that for?"

Kal and Vik both laughed as they retreated from the beach. When the sand gave way to concrete, they pulled out tank tops, sandals and shorts, which they pulled on directly over their swimwear. It'd get wet, but it didn't matter. The sun shone brightly, and they would dry in very little time. They replaced the space left by their clothes with their beach towels, zipped up their backpacks, and continued on into Siskago proper.

"I'm sorry about Anzin. He's just... his idea of a good time is partying. Petra says he's the loud one and I'm the quiet one, if that makes any sense."

"I think it does."

"You?"

"Definitely... quieter." Kal wondered at how badly he had let his loneliness slip through that statement. "Anzin and Petra seem like really good friends."

Vik laughed. "Really? Even Anzin? You're not just saying that?"

Kal nodded. "Even Anzin."

"He and I grew up together. Petra is an islander."

Kal and Vik walked down the sidewalk, weaving along the edge of the beach, sand and waves on one side and a street full of cars and buses on the other. Across the way, the thoroughfare was lined with shops and restaurants. People swarmed around him and Vik, entering and leaving the sand, all of varying skin tones and body types.

Kal could also hear the diaspora of languages Tria was likely cataloguing.

For the moment, the languages other than Vik's remained incomprehensible. The linguistics program was still playing catch up, creating a database for the huge number of secondary languages being spoken in Siskago. As usual, Kal and Tria had waited until the felicity rating for Siskago's primary spoken language was high enough before entering the city center, but they'd decided not to wait for the secondary ones. "Au naturel," Tria had said. Getting all of those would take much longer anyway, since there were comparatively fewer speakers to sample from.

"You still in school?" Vik asked.

"No. I graduated, and I guess now I'm just taking some time to figure out what I want to do next." Kal watched for signs of cultural inappropriateness from Vik's face but spotted none. He briefly pondered the realization that he badly wanted to blend in on Spenfa. Or was it Vik he wanted to prove himself to?

"Any idea what that'll be?"

Kal shook his head. Did Spenfa have computers? Kal wasn't sure. Maybe he shouldn't talk about programming. "I guess... well, you could say I run a kind of business already though."

"Oh?"

"Yeah." Kal grinned. "When I'm not traveling, I care for a pride of lions. At a zoo."

"Really?" Vik smiled. "Sounds kind of scary."

"Actually... imagine taking care of a bunch of really big house cats. All meow and no bite. Well, sometimes they try to bite. You just have to show them who's boss."

Vik gave Kal a smirk. "How many do you have?"

Kal blushed. "I think you'll laugh if I tell you."

"What, a dozen?"

"Fourteen."

"Fourteen?!"

"Yeah."

"Sounds like quite an operation you run. In Messika, right?"

Kal nodded with all the sincerity he cold muster.

Vik tilted his head and shrugged. "Well, I'd love to see it next time I'm on the mainland."

"Of course." Nice. That had gone better than he'd expected.

Vik led him into a small restaurant. It was very humble, but the small space was immaculately kept up. Chairs sat around circular tables, packed closely together. The man behind the counter was shouting something into the kitchen in one of the languages Kal's nanites hadn't translated yet. The man's ornery disposition evaporated the moment he saw Vik. And much to Kal's surprise, Vik greeted him in the same language the proprietor had been speaking moments before. The two of them went back and forth for a few moments, Kal understanding nothing, and then Vik turned to Kal.

"You okay with meat?"

Kal nodded.

"Anything you're allergic to?"

Kal hesitated a moment, then realized that Vik had only meant food. He shook his head.

Vik and the owner erupted into another flurry of intense chatter, and Vik seemed to be listing off items in an order. The proprietor wrote them down, shouting each item over his shoulder very loudly into the kitchen. Occasionally, the list was interrupted when someone in the kitchen would shout back. The man would then bark back even louder.

"—and why on Spenfa would you bring him to my disgusting hovel? He's way better than those last two losers you dated, and there are much classier restaurants than mine." This was the proprietor. Kal's attention jumped, but only momentarily. He caught himself, glad he had been looking at another part of the room. He continued to gaze around absently, pretending he couldn't understand what they were saying.

"And blow money on pomp?" Vik scoffed. "Please."

"Some women, you know, they like that kind of stuff."

"Some men, too. Look, you gonna make my order or talk my ear off?" Vik switched languages and turned to Kal. Even though it all sounded like English now, his nanites aided him by subtly adjusting the pitch and tones of vowels as well as the rhythm of the words, mapping each foreign language to a different variant of English.

"Xintaok, this is my friend Koss."

"Nice to be meeting you," Xintaok said, speaking Siskago's primary language poorly. "Take care my Vik now, right? He is best customer."

Kal nodded. "We're not eating here?"

"No eat here!" Xintaok waved his cleaning rag at them. "Not in hovel!"

Vik waved back at Xintaok in retort, and Xintaok scoffed. More shouts erupted from the kitchen, prompting Xintaok to disappear into the building's interior, jabbering loudly himself.

"The beach parks are always crowded because everyone goes there," Vik said, once the shouting had subsided. "The best part of Misigan Island is up there, in the mountains. Tourists don't usually get to see those places."

Xintaok returned from the kitchen with two cloth sacks and handed them to Vik.

"Mind yourself with this one, Vik." Xintaok was speaking his first language again. "You understand what a 'read' is, right? This one's a good soul, unlike those last two. Don't screw it up."

Kal did his best to look on as though he was unaware of what Xintaok had said.

"Please humbly enjoy meal, Koss." Xintaok smiled widely. "And enjoy Misigan."

"Thank you," Kal replied.

Vik led the way out of the restaurant.

Kal and Vik boarded a public bus, taking seats near the back. Vik had not hesitated to suggest the bus, and Kal, reflecting on his experiences, realized that the vast majority of vehicles he'd seen in Siskago had belonged to the public transportation variety. Most cars appeared to be taxis. Some vehicles did appear to be privately owned, but they were clearly outnumbered by the taxis, buses and trains.

Their bus wove along the beach for less than a kilometer before turning inland and climbing uphill toward the mountains. The storefronts gave way to apartment buildings, then houses, and after some time, the bus veered downward into a valley, where the cityscape vanished completely, becoming fully rural.

The bus had large windows that could be opened, and most of them already had been when Kal and Vik had boarded. Still, Kal could smell the enticing aroma of their food.

The bus was by far the strangest experience he'd had on Spenfa. Its engine made no noise. Kal wondered if there even was an engine. He'd read about the internal combustion engines used in Earth vehicles for over a century, and how all but the last models had generated noise.

The bus's passengers sat with their eyes wide open, only staring, some kind of trance. It reminded Kal of the child he had seen on the beach, staring at the sandcastle.

Besides those oddities, it was a normal enough bus. The driver greeted passengers as they entered, expected them to pay a fare, and navigated the vehicle through the rest of the traffic.

Kal leaned over to the window and watched the other vehicles pass by the bus. Even the taxis and freight trucks seemed to work by a similar logic. A driver steered while the other passengers sat with glazed-over eyes.

He turned and looked at Vik, who held the two sacks of food tightly. He too had entered a trance state.

The bus came to a stop and people around him stood up, shaking the trance off with ease. They moved toward the front of the bus to disembark. A couple glanced at Kal as he looked out the window, and Kal met their gaze. They shot him looks as though they'd caught him picking his nose.

Kal decided to pretend he was in a trance too.

So, Spenfa wasn't a match for Earth's social norms. His heart sank a bit. But really, all he had to do was pretend to be zoned out. It wasn't hard, it didn't seem to hurt, and, as far as he could tell, it wasn't a form of oppression. Nope, it was strange from his perspective only because he hadn't grown up with it.

After ten minutes more, the bus was nearly empty, save for a uniformed contingent of four at the very back. The bus was climbing again now, having reached the back edge of the valley.

Vik nudged Kal.

"Last stop," he said. "This is ours."

Kal jumped to attention and followed Vik off of the bus. He dared to look back to the uniformed people. They remained in their trance. Kal thought about asking why they weren't getting off if this was the last stop, but the desire to hide his ignorance from Vik stifled his curiosity.

They stepped down onto a sidewalk in a residential neighborhood, and the bus took off, turning and proceeding back down into the valley. He and Vik walked away in the other direction, along a street that followed the grade of the rise. Small houses dotted the landscape, built into the hillside.

"Where in Messika are you from?" Vik turned, leading Kal uphill.

"Issino," Kal said. It was a city in Messika on a river in a long, flat plain. The topography of Spenfa was so radically different from Earth, it wasn't even sensical to talk about Earth's analogue.

Kal noticed this information seemed to upset Vik, who had tensed his lips and furrowed his brow, but was doing his best to hide his unease. Kal tried to think back to what he had learned about Issino and couldn't think of anything that might cause this reaction.

"Is that bad?"

"No, no. I just used to know someone from Issino."

"Well, to be honest, I'm not terribly attached to the place." *It's not really where I grew up.*

That seemed to turn Vik's mood around. "I don't suppose you've ever been to Lautezdais?"

Kal shook his head.

"Yeah, you're better off for it," Vik said. "That's where I grew up. I got out as soon as I could."

"Hey, and now you live in a beautiful island country."

"It's alright."

"Just alright? Really? Living here must be incredible!"

"It's expensive, and surprisingly dull after the first few months. But yeah, I guess I'm spoiled by the weather. It's easy to forget how lucky I am, I guess."

"Grass is always greener, right?" Kal said, and Vik shot him a look of confusion mixed with fear that Kal recognized. It was the look someone on an alternate Earth gave him when the nanites had failed to find a translation, and his figure of speech had been rendered as some horrible malapropism, or worse, random babble.

There was a curiosity to Vik's gaze though, and Kal decided he could backpedal after all. "I just mean, it's always easier to romanticize something when you've never experienced it yourself."

Phew. That seemed to make perfect sense. Kal watched, hoping Vik would shake the odd episode off, and he seemed to.

The slope flattened out as they entered a park, which consisted of a wide, grassy precipice overlooking Siskago and the ocean. The sun was low, just above the mountain line, and the sky had shifted to a brilliant hue of purple.

The park was empty. A playground lay to their left. Small footprints in the sand evidenced the earlier presence of children.

They pulled out their beach towels and lay them over a wooden bench facing outward over the precipice. Vik sat down, and Kal joined him. The view was gorgeous. Light winds blew gently over them, pulling at wispy clouds not far overhead. The city lay stretched out below, its orange lights beginning to blink into existence. Reds and purples streaked the dusk sky.

"How'd you find out about this place?" Kal asked.

"Not from guidebooks, that's for sure." Vik chuckled as he unpacked the food. "Friends at the university."

The meal was like nothing Kal had ever had before. He didn't even recognize half the vegetables. The meat had been baked in a strongly spiced sauce and lay atop a bed of long, translucent things he assumed were some kind of grain. The flavors were exceptional, and he gobbled it down, asking Vik about various entrees along the way.

"You've never had Ostenosian food before?"

Kal shook his head, still chewing.

"I lived in Ianzan for three years," Vik said. "Went there for a year of school, then stayed and worked for two more."

"That's the language you were speaking with Xintaok?"

"Yeah. I'm just conversant, not fluent."

"I don't know," Kal said. "You sounded pretty fluent to me."

"The language trips me up more than you think. People like Xintaok ignore my mistakes."

Kal smiled. When Vik was talking about languages, his whole face lit up, and he became animated in a way he normally wasn't. Tria was going to be so ridiculously jealous. Kal also rushed with elation that Vik was opening up to him, at least a little, then reminded himself that he could not reciprocate. Too much of his real life had to remain a secret. Or did it? The urge to tell Vik all about Earth and the metaxia welled up with him, but fear of reprisal pushed that urge back.

"How did you get interested in languages?" Kal asked.

"I don't know…" Vik furrowed his brow momentarily, pondering the question. "I just always have been. Most people in Lautezdais, even teachers, told me to learn anything other than Ianzan, because it was 'too hard.' But I had one really good teacher at the end of high school who encouraged me to learn it instead, even gave me books."

Kal nodded. "You're lucky."

Vik smiled wryly. "He was a real exception. In Lautezdais, some people don't even know the difference between Ianzan, Tsim and Rann, like they're all one country or something. I have to admit, before I learned Ianzan, I couldn't tell the difference between any of the languages. I can tell Tsim now because it's tonal, and Rann and Ianzan share a lot of vocabulary, so if I think I should understand and I don't, that must be Rann. Damn it, I'm rambling, aren't I?"

Kal laughed, smiling at Vik to let him know it was okay. "You must study languages then, at the university?"

Vik nodded. "Petra, Anzin, and I are Siskago University's so-called Ianzanese Linguistics experts."

Kal nearly choked on his food. "Anzin? A linguistics expert?"

Vik nodded, a bemused smile spread across his face while he chewed his food.

"Languages have always interested me too," Kal said. "But I've never put in the energy to seriously learn one. And I definitely don't think I'd be very good."

"You won't know until you try." Vik winked. "Any ideas what you'll study when you go back to school?"

That was it. He had to open up. Just a little. Fear and elation welled up within him. What would Vik think?

"Programming," Kal tried. He watched Vik's expression closely.

"Ah, the burgeoning, new computer industry." Vik leaned back and grinned.

Kal stifled a great sigh of relief. That could have been disastrous. He half-wished Tria had been here to feed him everything he'd need to know about the state of computer science on Spenfa. Then he looked at Vik, smiling back, and Kal was glad that Tria was far, far away, at least right now.

There was some kind of glimmer in Vik's eyes though. What was programming here? Conflicted maybe?

"What do you think of computers?" Kal tried.

"Well, I can see both sides of the argument. It's naive to assume that we can anticipate all the things that computation could ever do."

Kal had to smirk at that.

"But," Vik continued. "They do seem far less efficient than magic at achieving the same things."

Kal blinked his eyes a few times. Magic? Had he heard that right? He must have mis-heard that. No, the nanites had mistranslated the word. That had to be it.

He glanced at Vik. Oh, crap. Vik had taken Kal's confusion as offense.

"Sorry, I—" Vik put his hand up.

"Oh no, no, I'm not— it's just—"

"I mean, don't get me wrong, I think the Anti-Computationalists are ridiculous."

Kal chortled. "They'd have to be with a name like that, right?" That got both of them laughing.

"Come on over here," Vik said. He took Kal's hand, and that felt good.

Really good. He squeezed back.

Vik led him to a grassy patch at the edge of the park, a little hill. Vik lay down, and Kal lay down beside him. The sun had just dropped behind the mountains and cast long shadows over Siskago, its orange glow growing brighter.

"I love watching the stars come out," Vik said. "You ever learn the constellations?"

"No, though I wish I had."

"My dad bought me a telescope when I was twelve. We used to spend hours looking at the stars."

"You ever think about what might be out there?" Kal asked.

"All the time. It's pretty amazing to think about how much stuff there is in our universe besides us. We're so tiny, and Spenfa itself is just one minuscule orb circling a pebble of a star in a galaxy filled with billions of other stars and planets."

"You think there are other people out there somewhere, on other planets?" Kal asked, curious what Vik's conception of the cosmos was.

"I don't know. Maybe we're unique, the universe's only chance to understand itself."

"What do you mean?"

"Well, until animals came around, there was nothing to perceive time. But now we're here, and us animals are all just a new configuration of the same matter that's been part of Spenfa all along. And our whole planet came from the explosion of some other star billions and billions of years before ours even formed.

"We are the universe, Koss. And yeah, we fiddle around with magic and computers and language, but that's just the surface. Underneath, we *are* the universe. We understand ourselves to help the universe understand itself."

Kal smiled and turned to face Vik. "I like how you put that."

Vik turned and smiled back.

"So," Kal tried. "Do you think we could be the universe's only chance to understand itself?"

"I dunno. Hard to say."

"I think the universe is bigger and weirder than anyone on Spenfa can imagine."

"What makes you say that?"

"Call it a hunch."

The sky and the stars were gone. In the many moments that passed, Kal saw only Vik.

They rolled closer together and kissed.

"Hey," Vik said.

"Yeah?"

"It's summer vacation for us too. Anzin, Petra and I rented a car, and we're going on a camping trip tomorrow to the north part of the island. You can come too if you—"

"Sounds like fun."

∽৹⟨⟩৹∾

Vik and Kal walked all the way home from the park. Kal wasn't sure how long it took. He lost himself in conversation with Vik. It felt so good to finally meet someone who seemed to understand him. The streets and houses, other passersby, all of it disappeared into a blur. When Kal was with Vik, it was almost like he belonged.

They held hands the entire way, and when they finally reached Kal's hotel, Kal grasped tighter. Partly he didn't want to let go. Partly he didn't know what to do.

Vik pulled Kal closer, and they kissed. Kal lost himself, unsure how many moments passed.

"Tonight was great, Koss."

"I had fun too, Vik."

"See you tomorrow. We'll come pick you up at nine."

Kal watched Vik depart. Part of him wanted to run after Vik. He felt that would be a bad idea, though. Patience. He had to be patient.

Now, the real trick was to convince Tria to stay longer. Hopefully, there were enough foreign languages in Siskago that Tria wouldn't care how long they stayed.

Appearing on cue, a familiar voice popped into Kal's head as he walked up the staircase of the hotel toward his eighth floor room.

How did your date go?

Amazing! He's handsome and smart, and we talked about the stars and about life and the universe, and don't be jealous, but he's all into languages, and it's really kind of cute the way he kind of obsesses over them...

Kal registered that Tria wasn't responding to the languages thing, and this surprised him. He unlocked his hotel room with a keycard and entered.

Tria's hologram shimmered into view, his arms crossed. "Did he talk about 'magic' at all?"

"Yeah, he mentioned it a few times. I assumed it was a mistranslation. Why?"

"And you didn't notice anything strange about his behavior?"

"No, Tria, what are you getting at? Were you spying on us or something?"

"No." Tria exhaled in exasperation. He reached out futilely for Kal's shoulders. "Kal, they have magic here."

Kal's train of thought ground to a halt. "What?"

"Somehow, magic is real here. It's how they move their cars, their buses, all the electricity, everything. They do it all with 'magic.'"

Kal felt lightheaded and brought his hand up to cover his forehead. He found himself collapsing into a sofa chair in the corner of his room, beside a metal lamp.

"No, no, no. There has to be some mistake. That's not even physically possible. And these people are so… normal! I mean, look at this room. I'm sitting in the Field Museum's twentieth century exhibit!"

Tria sat down on the edge of the bed. "There's nothing mystical about it, actually. There are some kind of particles in the air. Have the nanites scan, and you'll find them. They're mostly carbon, traces of a few other compounds. They respond to brain waves, Kal. And then they do work—creating force or heat. But no one knows how they got here or why they react to people's thoughts. They just… do. They won't work for me, and they probably won't work for you either, at least not without a couple weeks worth of practice. These people learn how to manipulate them as they grow up."

Kal got up and ran to his backpack, rummaging through it until he found his pad. He frantically executed a scan of the atmosphere, and sure enough, there they were. One part per four million. Kal collapsed onto the bed and put his hands over his face.

"Magic," he muttered.

"Magic," Tria said. "Look, at least it's not a dangerous difference."

Kal groaned.

"You made plans with Vik for tomorrow, didn't you?"

"Uh huh." Kal pulled a pillow over his face. He threw it off and jolted upward. "Pick me up... in a car. Tria, we're supposed to *drive* to the campsite. What if they expect me to move the car for them?"

"Well..." Tria crossed his arms. "Your generous and non-corporeal brother *could* execute a program to move the car with nanites while you pretended to be in a trance."

Kal gulped. "You'd do that for me?"

Tria smiled weakly and nodded.

"Oh, Tria. You're the best." Kal went to hug him, but of course his hands passed through Tria's projected body. "One more day here. Then we'll go searching for a body for you again, okay? I feel bad about getting us sidetracked. We'll redouble our efforts. And then maybe we can both come back here, and we'll *both* enjoy the sun and the beach and the guys."

Tria nodded weakly, slumping down in the chair himself. "That'd be awesome."

"Tell me about all the languages you discovered today," Kal suggested, and that got Tria smiling again.

"There were so many. And I think I've only scratched the surface. And there are creoles, Kal, languages that have blended and intermingled. I love Siskago. So many different languages, dialects, and cultures, all mixed together."

"I can't believe Vik doesn't like living here."

Tria bunched up his face. "He doesn't?"

"Yeah, I don't get it either."

Tria asked Kal to tell him more about the date, and then Kal asked more about all the things Tria discovered. They stayed up into the early hours of the morning, and Kal fell asleep only a few hours before sunrise.

Kal only woke up on time because of the alarm he'd set on his pad. He slept through two snooze cycles before thoughts of seeing Vik again finally thrust him into wakefulness. He showered and dressed as quickly as he could, then gathered up his things and rushed out of the hotel room.

Vik, Petra, and Anzin were waiting for him in a car at the front of the hotel. It was a small, blue four-door, not unlike the vehicles he'd seen in history books of late-twentieth century Earth. He'd read that many of those vehicles were extremely noisy to operate, depending on how much they relied on internal combustion. This one was absolutely silent.

Petra and Vik sat in the back, their eyes glazed over, while Anzin sat behind the steering wheel.

He honked the horn upon seeing Kal. He had on another ridiculous get up. His tank top was barely cords over his shoulders, and huge gaping holes in the fabric exposed large portions of his torso.

Kal glanced at catatonic Vik and Petra again. *They're alright, right Tria?*

Yeah. That's what happens when they use magic. They're only vaguely aware of what's going on. They won't be able to hear you either.

Kal looked back to Anzin and smiled. He hopped into the front passenger seat of the car, and Anzin immediately took them off into the heavy downtown Siskago traffic. They followed a major highway along the edge of the island, never too far from the beach.

"So, what's your story?" Anzin asked.

"My story?"

"Yeah, you know, where you come from, what you do. Everyone's got a story."

"I'm from Messika. Issino."

"Yeah, Vik told us that. What do you do though?"

"Just exploring before college. Going places and learning things."

"Hmm." Anzin grumbled. "Petra's already decided she likes you, you know. Vik really likes you, too. You should know I watch out for him. I don't like it when people hurt him."

"I don't want to hurt anyone."

"That's good. Vik looks tough and he plays tough, but you probably saw already, he's not like that, really."

"You say that like—"

Anzin turned to Kal, taking his eyes momentarily off the road, raised both his eyebrows, grinned and said, "I *like* it rough."

Kal laughed, a stuttering, awkward laugh, and much to Kal's relief, Anzin returned to driving.

"Childhood friends, right?" Kal asked. "You and Vik were on the swim team together?"

Anzin nodded. "Yeah. Believe it or not, until I was fifteen, I was scrawny. No muscle at all."

Anzin was right. Kal didn't believe him.

"Vik used to protect me in school, on the playground. Now, well, we take care of each other. You like bars at all, Kal?"

"Well, um…"

"Never been, eh? Vik avoids them, too. You should both lighten up and let me take you guys out some time. It's not as fun going with just Petra."

Gee, I wonder why, Kal thought.

Kal chuckled, and he could see now why Vik liked Anzin. Behind his goofiness and brusque attitude, he was extremely perceptive. He was the only one who could tell that Kal was hiding something, and Kal desperately wished, more than anything, that he could let his barriers down and be himself.

His adventure, he realized, wasn't just about finding a cure. Exiled from his home reality, he desperately yearned, amongst the madness of the metaxia, for some place he could belong.

∞⟨⟩∞

The cityscape gave way to countryside. Rows of stores and concrete apartment blocks became pineapple fields. The highway grew less and less congested. They rolled the windows all the way down, and the brilliant, warm sun shown down, while salty, cool sea air rushed into the car.

After another thirty minutes of the countryside, Anzin pulled over to the edge of the highway and got out of the car. Kal followed suit. He watched as Anzin shook Petra into consciousness, and Kal did the same to Vik.

Vik looked up at him and smiled. "Hey! How you doing?"

"Good," Kal realized he was beaming. Stop beaming, he told himself. It didn't work. "How about you?"

"Tired." Vik chuckled.

"Me too."

"Didn't sleep at all last night."

"Me either."

Anzin approached, grabbed Vik by the shoulders and shuffled him toward the front of the car. "Now lovebirds, you'll have plenty of time for that later."

Vik shot Anzin an expression of annoyance, but Anzin just sat him down next to Petra. Kal sat down in back, taking Vik's seat, and Anzin joined him. Anzin made himself comfortable, strapped on his seatbelt, and his eyes glazed over. Kal began his trance routine.

Okay Tria, you ready?

You bet.

Let's show them some magic of our own.

Petra switched gears, and the car lurched forward.

"Whoa!" Petra shouted.

Easier, Kal thought to Tria.

"That was weird," Petra said. "He made sure this thing was inspected, right?"

"Yeah, I was there," Vik said. "I asked them myself."

Petra tried first gear again, and the car rolled smoothly away from the pavement this time.

A wave of relief passed over Kal, and he forced himself not to sigh. Vik and Petra started up a conversation as they resumed their trip. Not wanting to accidentally react to things he shouldn't be hearing, Kal decided he needed a distraction.

Tria, what are these particles you were talking about?

They're called "mysta." Like I said before, they're mostly carbon and a handful of other compounds. They seem semi-organic. There are very minute electrical impulses traversing them. They respond to human brain waves and do the kinds of things your nanites do. They can generate force or heat, for example. They can interact with and reshape matter to some degree, but only through catalysis, so your nanites are much better at that than the mysta will ever be. But this is all just the tip of the iceberg. It gets better.

Really? Better than "everyone on this planet can use magic?"

Yeah. So, it turns out the mysta showed up inexplicably about twenty thousand years ago. No one knows why. And even weirder, it used to be that animals could use magic too. Their lizards were the most adept, evolving into—

No way. You're kidding. Dragons?

Dragons. But they died out.

Let me guess. Humans killed them all, right?

Actually, no. Humans were at an evolutionary disadvantage. The mindless trance is solely a human drawback. Animals were able to use magic 'for free.' They didn't have to surrender full motor control and higher reasoning like hu-

mans. Fourteen thousand years ago, humans nearly died out on Spenfa. Their predators were too powerful.

How'd they survive?

Fourteen thousand years ago, the mysta stopped responding to animals. Only humans became able to use magic at that point.

What??

I know. It's utterly bizarre. And they realize that. They've got huge tracts of philosophical debate about the presence of mysta particles. No one in two thousand years of human history has ever understood how or why they're there. They just... are.

"Maybe he doesn't like using magic," Vik turned to look at Kal, and it took all of Kal's self-control not to look back at him.

"A fundamentalist computer programmer?" Petra suggested with an incredulous smirk.

Vik chuckled. "Maybe. I mean, I've heard of stranger things."

"Sometimes I think you set yourself up to get hurt too easily."

"You think he's—"

"No. He seems sweet enough. But we all just met him. You rush things, Vik."

I don't want to hurt you, Kal thought, and he felt Tria leave his mind at the same moment.

Kal sighed mentally and returned his focus to staying in his mock trance. He sang to himself in his head, doing his best to screen Vik and Petra's conversation out.

The minutes dragged on. Ignoring a conversation he shouldn't be hearing turned out to be excruciating. Kal felt a rush of relief as Petra turned the car off the oceanside highway and down a much smaller road that led into a valley. Enormous peaks rose up on either side of the gravel road that crunched underneath the tires. The trees were thick and green with huge leaves that reminded Kal of Ydora. Misigan Island had more palms though, and its trees were sized more like Earth's. Just a few minutes later, Kal spotted grassy areas that had been carved out of the jungle. Some of them were empty while others were occupied, containing tents, picnic tables and parked cars.

Petra drove until they reached a large grassy area on top of a hill and parked. Anzin broke from his trance, and so Kal, never having been in a trance, pretended to wake up as well. Anzin shot Kal a menacing gaze before taking off his seatbelt and exiting the car.

Oh no. Tria? Could he know what we did?

I don't know. I suppose it's possible. It all depends what kind of interaction these people have with the mysta.

Kal gulped and got out of the car as well. He pulled his backpack out of the trunk and threw it on, then grabbed a bundle of wood and carried it to the fire pit. Vik and Petra were setting up the first of two tents.

Kal arranged the wood in the pit, then walked back to the car. He grabbed the cooler and carried it toward their picnic table. As he set it down, he spotted Vik standing over the wood and staring at it, his eyes empty. A few moments later, the logs burst into flames. Vik blinked and shook his head.

Vik and Kal grilled hotdogs while Petra and Anzin finished setting up the tents. All four of them ate lunch, and Kal and Vik chatted more about languages and computers.

Kal snuck occasional glances at Anzin and Petra out of the corner of his eye. They sat on the other side of the fire, and Kal couldn't help but think, when Anzin glanced over, that he was watching Kal back.

I'm on to you, his eyes seemed to say.

After lunch, a concerted mental effort from Vik and Anzin suffocated the fire. Even its plume of smoke ceased.

"There's a lake not far from here," Vik said. "You up for a swim?"

"Sounds great," Kal replied.

"We'll go hiking instead." Petra pulled Anzin closer to her. He shot her fierce eyes, and she glared back even harder.

"Everything alright?" Vik crossed his arms.

Petra said "yes" as Anzin simultaneously said "no."

Kal felt Vik clutch his hand tightly, and he returned Vik's grip.

"We'll meet you back here for dinner. C'mon, Koss."

When they had walked some way into the forest, Kal finally broke the silence. "What was that all about?"

"It's nothing you need to worry about. I'm sorry Anzin's behaving this way. Sometimes he thinks he's my guardian. I need to remind him he's my friend." Vik paused a moment. "Did you sense anything strange from him when you were both propelling?"

"No."

Vik shook his head, and they continued onward.

The path through the forest sloped down into a valley, and the sound of rushing water grew steadily louder. They passed through more leaves and enormous ferns. Deeper into the valley, the tree branches parted, revealing a small river, which spilled over a ridge at least three stories high, churning downward into a lake.

Kal and Vik wound down the remainder of the path and dropped their backpacks at the lake's edge. It was completely deserted. Vik took off his tank top and shorts, a swimsuit underneath, and jumped into the lake. His head bobbed up and down in the water. "You coming?"

Kal smiled, disrobing down to his swimsuit, and dove into the lake himself.

The water was cold and fresh. Vik splashed him, and Kal laughed, splashing back.

"C'mon. There's something I want to show you." Vik took off swimming toward the waterfall, and Kal swam after him.

The churning of the falling river became a roar as they approached. Vik led them around behind it. Kal pulled his head up and found Vik treading water in the space between the waterfall and the rock face. Vik's eyes glazed over. His body rose out of the water and continued rising. About halfway up the rock face, Vik grabbed out to catch an outcropping, and clambered onto it. He turned and sat on the ledge, facing the wall of water.

"What are you waiting for?" Vik shouted over the din of the waterfall. "Come on up."

Kal continued treading water, a storm of emotions brewing within him.

"Koss?" Vik called down.

Something inside Kal snapped.

Long ago, he'd accepted that he would never have fun, *normal* teenage experiences with his peers. He'd accepted that he'd spend the best years of his life trapped on some empty planet with the enormous cats. On Spenfa, he'd dared to allow himself the small hope that he could have such experiences. When Vik had levitated himself up onto that ledge, any bit of hope that might have remained had withered and died.

Kal ducked, turned and swam back under the waterfall. He came up on the other side and sprinted toward the shore as fast as he could. He crawled out of the water and pulled himself up onto a rock. There he sat, his face in his hands.

It seemed only moments later that he heard a splash and felt a hand on his back.

"Koss... you can't use magic can you?"

Kal looked up and shook his head.

"Well, that explains Anzin *and* Petra. I hope she's giving him a talking to. Koss, look at me."

He pulled at Kal's shoulders and they faced one another, sitting side by side on the rock.

"There's nothing wrong with not being able to use magic. Thousands of years of research and we still don't know how or why it works *at all*."

"Everywhere I go," Kal began softly, "I have to explain to people how I'm different, and I have to figure out how to navigate rules I don't understand. I came here, and when I met you, it felt good to just be... I don't know, normal, whatever that is. I'm sorry I didn't tell you."

Vik hugged him, and Kal hugged him back. It felt good just to sit there, to watch the water.

A haze of blue electricity rippled across the surface of the lake, and it burbled unnaturally. Kal opened his eyes wide. No... it couldn't be. Not unless someone had...

"What the—?" Vik stood up.

"Get away from the water!" Kal jerked to a stance and pulled Vik back from the lake's edge. More blue electricity rippled in bolts across its surface. A splash erupted from the center of the lake, and a fish, a creature the size of a human head with blue scales, sharp teeth, and beady, seeking eyes leapt from its surface.

Kal grabbed up his backpack and ripped out his pad. He navigated it with ease, quickly enabling countermeasures against hostile nanites, and establishing a safe zone at the camp site around the tents.

"What is *that?*" Vik pointed at the fish, his face twisted up.

"Do you trust me?" Kal said.

More fish sprang from the surface of the water, a whole school of them hovering together in midair, casting their beady eyes about the valley.

Vik looked frantically between Kal and the school of flying, blue fish.

"What is— what *are* those things?"

"This is really, really important Vik," Kal grabbed his upper arm and stared him in the face.

"I need your permission to protect you and Anzin and Petra from this. Tell me it's okay."

"Yes, yes, what *are* those things?"

"Run towards the tent and don't look back."

"But what about you—"

"I'm protected. You're not. Not yet. Just run and let me help you. Go!"

Vik gazed at him momentarily, and Kal couldn't help but break briefly from his interface to meet his gaze. He saw fear in Vik's eyes, and Kal's began to water. All the trust and respect he'd built in the short time he'd known Vik crumpled and withered away, just like the small amount of hope he'd held onto until the moment under the waterfall.

It was gone.

Vik ran.

The fish flew through the air in a swarm, wriggling as though it were water. Some of them came for Kal, and some flew toward Vik, sprinting up the hill.

Kal finished enabling nanite protection on Vik, then returned his attention to Anzin and Petra. He split his concentration between programming and keeping an eye on Vik's retreat. The swarm of fish, all shimmers of blue electricity and quantum haze, reached Vik and attacked, but were repelled by defensive nanites. Kal breathed a small sigh of relief as he finished Anzin and Petra's defenses.

Vik disappeared over the top of the hill.

Kal slapped the pad onto his hip and ran after Vik, cursing his legs for not being able to take him faster. He crashed through the forest path, flinging away the stalks and branches of tropical flora with his hands.

He arrived at the clearing with their tents and fireplace. Their picnic table lay turned over, and Anzin's rental car contained numerous dents. Fish swarmed in a cloud around the tents, intermittently slamming into the protective barrier Kal had established.

Kal checked his pad and breathed a sigh of relief. Vik, Anzin, and Petra were all inside, but... Anzin's vital signs were dangerously low!

He ran for the tents, pushing through the writhing swarm of genetic monstrosities. He reached his forcefield barrier and passed directly through it. Now this was how you programmed a genome recognition algorithm. Humans allowed entry, genetically engineered monsters repelled.

He tore open the entrance to the tent and gasped. Vik stood, and Petra knelt over Anzin. His muscular form lay unconscious, crumpled on the ground. A pool of blood had formed underneath the stub of flesh that remained of his left arm. The stub withered, slowly dissolving, a gray haze working its way toward his chest.

Vik grabbed Kal and slammed him into the tent, nearly collapsing its flimsy supports.

"What is this?!"

"Let me help him," Kal said.

"Is it your fault those things are here?"

"I don't know. Anzin's life is in danger." Kal struggled, but Vik only held him firmer. "Damn it, let me help him!"

Vik pulled Kal from the tent wall and shoved him towards Anzin. Vik's forcefulness stung even more than his words.

Kal braced himself for their reaction and turned on his pad's interface. He did his best to ignore Petra's gasp of shock and Vik's simultaneous revulsion and awe. Kal took a deep breath and focused his attention on the programming.

Malevolent nanites ate their way through Anzin's arm and had nearly reached his shoulder. Fortunately, the solution was simple—have Kal's nanites build enough of themselves to destroy the malevolent ones, then use Anzin's genome to reconstruct his arm. The question was, would his nanites be able to do their job before the malevolent nanites caused enough damage to kill Anzin?

After Kal had finished his work, he shut down his computer and turned to face Vik and Petra.

"I'm from an alternate quantum reality. On my world, there's no magic. We use computers and tiny machines to do the same things you use magic for. If my machines win, Anzin will be fine, and he'll have a new arm. Tell him to go very, very easy on it for a while."

"I don't believe this." Vik stormed forward, pointing to the tent entrance. "What are those things?"

The fish could still be heard slamming into the nanite forcefield barrier, determined to gnash their way through its protective shell.

"They're fish, but someone else's tiny machines have altered their genetic structure. It's illegal on my Spenfa, but someone must have done it anyway."

"*Someone*," Petra scoffed. "If you didn't do this, then who did?"

Kal bunched up his lips and took a deep breath. "I honestly don't know. But I'm going to find out. I need you both to back up."

"Why?" Vik said.

"Because I'm going to go find out the answer to your question!"

"You're just going to leave us here with those... things?!" Vik lunged forward and tried to grab Kal's pad from his hand, but was repelled by Kal's auto-defenses.

"I already wrote a program to disassemble the fish, but it will take time. Once the fish are gone and Anzin's healed, all the nanites I've left here, on you and on Anzin, will destroy themselves. They're invisible. You won't even know it happened."

"Wait, I'm not letting you—" Vik surged forward toward Kal again, but jumped back toward the edge of the tent as a sphere of blue electricity crackled around Kal.

Kal knew the quantum locking would dampen sound, but he wanted to say it anyway.

"I'm sorry, Vik."

His bubble shifted into the metaxia, and the swirling blue wrapped around him.

ⁱ◦꧁◦ⁱ

Kal's bubble unravelled, resolving onto the beach of Lake Michigan on Felis, at just the same moment the final bits of information came back from Spenfa. Kal's nanites had won. The fish had all been deconstructed, and Anzin would live. He smiled a bit at that, still feeling deeply sad and empty.

The beach on Felis did nothing for his demeanor. The air was still, the sky overcast. He could hear the cats in the distance, but they didn't run to him. He stood on the beach, near its edge where the sand turned to rock.

He spotted a dust devil pass over a dune, a sight that seemed strangely familiar.

Deja vu. Must have been deja vu.

A plume of smoke trailed into the sky over the rise.

What could that be?

Kal gripped his pad tightly and ran atop the small hill.

"Oh no."

The tree that had supported his home lay toppled, torn up at the roots, the tree house strewn amongst the prairie grasses in pieces, shattered and crumpled. Dishes, books, his bed, his table, chairs, and his kitchen lay in ruins. The base of the tree was smoldering, black and singed.

The cats meowed from the forest, and Kal took off, breathing heavily as he ran.

Once inside the forest, Max and Daisy and Boson and Bjorg and Charles and all the other cats rushed up to him at once. Kal's nanites sizzled, protecting him from their frightened heads and paws and tongues, seething all around for the touch and care of their protector.

"It's okay guys. I'm here."

"Mrrr... Mrrrow!"

"It's okay. Don't worry. I'll find out who did this. I won't let them scare you anymore."

Liberty

Realm #2577, "Gelkur"
August 26, 2178

"H EY KAL?" Tria sat down next to Kal's makeshift bed. Tria glowed in the darkness of night. Nanite lumens dotted the branches, their light dim in the cold forest. Cats lay around the grove in clusters, intermittently wheezing and mewing as they slept.

"Hey Tria." Kal set his pad down.

"Any luck?"

Kal shook his head. "All the worlds with nanotechnology would be too dangerous for us to visit."

"We'll try again tomorrow morning." Tria smiled weakly.

Boson stretched out a paw, right into the nanite forcefield surrounding Kal's sleeping place. The wind howled outside.

"Kal…" Tria looked at the ground momentarily, then back at his brother. "What are we going to do when we find him?"

"Talk to him, I guess."

"You thought any more about who it could be?"

Kal gulped and nodded slowly up and down. "A lot. I just don't know. In grade school, I learned that war and violence are problems of the past. There's still mental illness, but even with that, we can detect it so early now. And we certainly don't let people like that near computers. *I'm* not even supposed to be using metaxic nodes. The only reason I have them at all is because… you know…"

"Yeah." Tria nodded. "You should get some sleep. We both should. We'll try again tomorrow."

Kal smiled back. "It's so good to have you here Tria. I can't imagine facing this alone. Thank you."

Tria smiled. "No prob. Night, Kal."

"Night."

Tria's hologram shimmered away. Kal lay down onto his bed, barely more than sticks supporting coils of cloth. He fluffed his pillow, made himself as comfortable as he could, and closed his eyes.

∞⟨/⟩∞

"Kal!" Tria tugged through his brother's T-shirt. "I got one!"

"Really?" Kal glanced over at Tria's pad.

"Realm #2577. Nanogenic radiation is just patchy enough that we'd be okay if we keep to the outskirts of the city. It doesn't seem like anyone in the stills is in any danger though."

"Their own nanotechnology then?"

"Probably. Most of the city is only lightly irradiated, not much more than your personal nanites put out. It's only bad in the downtown and across the lakefront."

Kal pulled up the stills and linguistic information on Tria's find.

"Gelkur," Kal said, reading the name for the alternate Earth aloud. "I think we should check it out, just to be sure none of the nanites are from Earth."

"Hey, Kal," Tria grabbed his arm, or rather, moved his holographic hand through it. "We haven't talked about what happened with you and Vik. I thought you might like to—"

"No."

Tria frowned, and silently input the coordinates for Gelkur.

Kal sighed and dropped his shoulders. "I'm sorry, Tria. Look, once we figure this impersonator thing out, we'll talk about Vik, okay?"

Tria nodded, still frowning. He and his holographic interface faded away.

Kal ran a hand through his hair and closed his eyes. When he opened them again, his clothing had changed. In fact, it was continuing to change. His shirt and pants were shimmering, a violent haze of nanite activity, rapidly alternating his attire between a business suit and dirty rags.

"Why can't they decide?" Kal asked, addressing no one in particular.

I hate them both, Tria thought.

Kal couldn't help but chuckle at that. *Me too.*

He tossed the pros and cons around in his mind for a moment, then decided that the suit and tie were the lesser of two evils. He pressed the appropriate buttons on his pad, and his new clothes solidified into the stuffy, brown suit and yellow, striped tie. Kal grimaced, seeing the clothing fully realized.

Better get this over with, he thought. *Tria, we'll get in, make sure none of their nanites are from Earth, then get out, okay?*

Sounds like a plan, Tria thought back.

The blue static haze of his bubble unfurled. Kal stood in an empty alley between two large buildings. Drab walls of molded concrete rose up on either side of him, and the sun shone down through the narrow slit of sky.

He shivered a bit. It was colder than he expected for summer, and damp too. The air felt electrically charged. The hair on the back of his neck bristled. He walked furtively toward the end of the alley, and it opened up onto a deserted street.

Kal walked out onto a sidewalk. An open, desolate expanse of cracked pavement stretched out before him. Gray, cubic buildings lined roads spotted with drifting refuse. Broken windows adorned the cubes, and their walls were littered with layers of grime and graffiti.

Tria, I want off this world. Can you prime the nodes?

Kal felt something tap at his side and heard the clank of metal against the ground. He looked down and saw a knife. His eyes shot upward. A pair of crazed eyes had appeared from within the dark crevices of a heap of rags.

"Look at this, boys!" A voice from behind.

Kal spun around to see a lanky man wrapped in tattered rags standing near the entrance to another alley. He held a knife in each hand. Cloth strips wrapped around his head and face so that only his mouth and devious eyes remained visible.

The man grinned. "A worker come all the way out from Giglagu to see us!"

Kal grabbed for his computer and looked around. People appeared, climbing out of trash cans, rubbish heaps and sewer gratings. They all wore the same tattered strips of cloth, just like the ones he'd rescinded moments before. His assailants closed in from all sides. He turned to run back down the alley, but dark figures encroached from behind him as well.

Tria! Maximum nanite defenses, activate the nodes! ... Tria?!

Another flurry of knives hit him, more pinpricks all over. Kal grimaced and grasped his pad.

Beyond the encroaching mob of rags, more figures appeared in the distance. But these new ones moved methodically, not frenetically liked the ragged ones. The distant group marched in steady formation, and they wore dark, black uniforms. The midday light seemed to dissolve around them, as though each were a walking black hole.

Tria!

The figures drew closer, and the huddled masses of wild eyes and dirty hair and rags began running toward the alleys and sewer gratings from whence they'd emerged.

"Tria?!" Kal shouted.

He pulled up his pad and activated it.

Kal gasped and it nearly dropped it, fumbling with the controls. The holointerface had been radically altered. The new interface was all oranges and reds, blocky and authoritarian. They had replaced the cool blue, rounded polygons he had seen every time he had activated his pad for the past four years.

"ValYou Corporation National Software?" Kal read from the new display and slammed at what looked like the new off button.

The uniformed figures were almost upon him. Some of their compatriots reached out toward the ones wearing rags, who froze in place, some even mid-stride, in unnatural positions.

"Hello." Kal gulped, looking up. A man stood before him, tall. His skin seemed ghostly white compared to his deep black suit and tie.

"Your ID?" the man said.

Tortured screams erupted all around them. Kal stared out, transfixed, at the other members of the uniformed contingent. They pressed buttons on holographic interfaces that projected from their obsidian sleeves, and as they did, the men and women who'd been captured fell to dust. Kal gulped and his breathing grew rapid.

"You own nanites and a computer." The tall man said, his voice harsh and grating.

"Own?" Kal gulped. "Well, it's mine, yes."

"What is your ValYou Resident ID?"

Kal remained silent. A few more scattered human howls went up as the nanites of Gelkur ground up the ragged ones' bodies. Kal felt woozy, and a white haze seeped in from the edges of his field of vision. He staggered and fell to one knee.

"You are ill. We'll take you to jail."

"Jail?" Kal's head shot up. "What have I done?"

"You are in ValYou Corporation's zone of business and you have not registered for a resident account, but you own nanites and a computer. We will take you in for questioning and sort out your situation from existing legal precedents."

"I've only just arrived in Giglagu." His heart was racing, and he knew he sounded desperate but he didn't care. All he wanted was to not have to go anywhere with this death corps.

"You will come with us to jail or we will confiscate your possessions and invoke the law."

Kal forced himself to stand up, though on wobbly knees. He gripped his pad hard and followed the police, one torturous step at a time, through the now deserted streets of Giglagu.

∞⟨⟩∞

The group of five law enforcers, two men and three women in black suits, led Kal down street after street. Two of them walked behind him and two more in front, with another at his side. He didn't dare run. All he could think about was what would happen if they tried to disintegrate him too. Would his auto-defense nanites win, or would theirs? He wasn't eager to run that particular test, at least not until his situation became more dire than it was already.

More cubic buildings lined the streets, but Kal could see the tall buildings of the city center growing closer, and he could feel the air change as they approached the lake. The houses became less cubic, concrete, and utilitarian, and more architecturally distinct. Each new building was taller than the last, with more artistic flair, a sea of sculpted glass and metal, all oranges and reds.

More black suits dotted the landscape. These new ones stood about, just watching, presumably, from behind their dark glasses.

Kal's entourage pulled sunglasses from their own pockets and put them on, just like their watchkeeper brethren. Kal squinted. The architecture of this part of the city reflected much more light than the stony, cubic suburbs.

"Igl-umakl!" A voice called from his entourage's left. His escort grabbed at their sleeves, and turned to face an approaching man. He wore a brown suit, just like Kal's, and had wavy, black hair. He was probably in his mid-twenties.

"Igl-umakl, I'm so glad I found you." The man was addressing Kal, who did his best not act too surprised to see him.

The stranger turned to Kal's guards, "Liberty and happiness, Para. My Resident ID is 44100890. You've found my colleague Igl-uma Traik, a friend of my supervisor's from abroad. He doesn't yet know how things work here in ValYou."

"No," Kal managed. "I'm sorry, but I don't."

"Why doesn't he have a Resident ID?" one of the guards asked.

The stranger pulled some kind of card and data chip from his sack, and Kal's eyes latched onto them.

Kal feigned the most genuine smile he could muster. "Ah, my things!"

One of the Para grabbed the card and scanned it.

"Confirmed," she said. "Igl Traik, citizen of Republic of Glina, Temporary Resident ID 100006933745." Another officer tapped the data into a holokeyboard projected from his arm.

"Igl-umakl," one of the male guards said. Kal realized he'd been addressed almost too late, and turned to face him. "Please give our kindest regards to Wayz-uma. We hope we were of assistance this morning and we apologize for the confusion regarding your identity. Please keep the Resident ID software loaded onto yourself or your immediate possessions at all times. It will help us avoid such mistakes in the future."

Kal nodded, then reached back into his memory for what he had learned about hierarchically organized societies. He probably needed to be sterner, so he added a slight disapproval to his expression. It worked, and immense relief washed over him as he watched them go.

"Come with me," his savior said.

Kal walked alongside him in silence for ten minutes, the whole time wondering what would become of him now. He was free of the Para, sure. But this new man's expression remained stoic, and he strode quickly forward. No way of telling if he had truly been rescued, or if he'd just traded one form of captivity for another.

The two of them approached a tall, unassuming white building. It twisted in a slight spiral as it rose, modest compared to the architectural feats that surrounded it.

They had travelled north, just beyond the city center. Black-suited guards hovered at every corner, scanning from behind their eerie sunglasses.

Kal and the stranger entered the building and took an elevator up to its seventeenth floor. Kal's wariness of his new companion intensified. What were this strange person's motives? Why had he just intervened? Where were they going... and to what end? Who could he trust on a world so cavalier about the violation of biomaterial integrity?

And most importantly, what had happened to Tria? The thought that his brother might be dead filled him with fear and regret both. Nearly sniffling, he pushed such thoughts away.

They walked down a long, poorly lit hall until they reached a door at the very end. His companion opened it with a wave of his hand. They entered, and once the door had slid shut, the man spoke.

"What's your real name? Don't worry, there's defensive programming up against the mics. You can talk freely here." The apartment was sparsely furnished. One sofa sat in a corner. A counter against the walk-in kitchen possessed three stools. The man motioned for Kal to sit down.

"Kal Anders."

The man sat down next to him.

"Well Kagl Andiz, you're going to have to be Igl Traik for a while."

"What's your name?"

"Jeikl Lgee." He pulled out a pad of his own and began typing something into its interface.

"What are you programming?"

Jeikl looked up at him over the rim of his glasses.

"You can program? You code nanites at all?"

Kal crossed his arms and grinned. "Yeah, I can program nanites."

Jeikl eyed Kal curiously. He looked up from his pad toward the ceiling, as though he was planning something.

"Look, Jeikl," Kal said. "I really appreciate you helping me earlier. I'll return the favor any way I can, but I'll probably save you a bunch of hassle and explaining if I can just get my pad working again." Kal pulled it up and turned it on. The interface looked like the one on Jeikl's pad, orange and jagged.

"What's wrong with it?"

"This isn't the software I was running. ValYou Corporation nanites must have injected their own code."

Jeikl frowned. "Yeah, they're designed to do that."

"Why?"

"Because they can. Kagl," Jeikl dropped his voice to a whisper, "I can try to get you out of ValYou quietly. I don't know where you're from, but the countries of Aglia and especially Akrilga, they have governments, they're safe. Not like here. You should know that it's risky, though. If you're caught, you'll be executed."

Kal blinked. No government? Executed? What kind of country had he gotten himself stranded in?

"I don't need to go anywhere special," Kal whispered back. "I just need a quiet place to work on getting all this ValYou malware out of my pad."

Jeikl stared at him a moment. "Where are you from exactly?"

Kal bit his lip. "It's a long story."

Jeikl sighed. "I can't let you stay here. The Para would be inspecting this place within days. You'll need a steady source of value if you want to stay safe. You said you can program nanites, right?"

"Yeah."

"I work in the Giglagu Northeast Division Nanoprogramming Research Laboratory. If you can really program, I can get you a job there. Are you sure that all you want is to purge the ValYou code from your pad?"

Kal nodded vigorously.

"Okay…" Jeikl said, tapping his foot and staring at this ceiling. Kal got the impression that Jeikl thought his odds were better trying to escape the country.

He thought about the Para and the fact that Giglagu had no government, and he wondered if Jeikl was right. No, illegally escaping was too dangerous. And Kal worried about Tria. There'd be no programming on the run, and he didn't yet know enough about what was going on inside of his pad.

"Will I be safe working at the laboratory?"

"If you follow all of the rules, yes. The Para exist mostly to keep the homeless out of the city center."

"I guess I'll stay and work then."

Kal sat across a long table from Wayz Iuum, a man who had probably been slender in his teens, but now, despite a thin frame, the beginnings of a paunch could be seen beneath his brown business suit. He had thin, black, wavy hair and narrow shoulders. His eyes kept darting around the room, too, like he was nervous or something. Kal found that odd, figuring he was the one who should be nervous.

And then there was the system of titles. Kal had learned that Wayz needed to be called Wayz-umakl to his face and Wayz-uma when Kal was talking about him to others. While he found this system of titles mildly fascinating, he couldn't help but wonder what other forms of supposed respect he was supposed to bestow upon this man he barely knew.

Behind Wayz a view of Giglagu stretched out beyond tall windows, ones that comprised the entire southern wall of the room. A few majestic, colorful buildings lay on either side of this one, nearly as tall, but such architecture quickly fell away into mile after mile of the cubic, concrete slums that disappeared against the horizon.

"We want to develop at least five new software products a year." Wayz pointed to an elaborate holographic display on the wall showing growth projections for the next decade.

Kal nodded and smiled. He had no idea how many software products a division of ValYou could or should develop in a year, so he thought it best to just smile and look interested in what Wayz was saying.

Wayz sat down. "Tell me about your experience with nanoprogramming."

"Well, I've mostly created algorithms to map nanite fields onto complex surfaces, such as people, animals and plants. I've also designed templates for the construction of synthetic materials, and I've done a lot of mapping objects for replication."

"Have you ever mapped a human for deconstruction?"

Kal felt rage well up within him and promptly bit his tongue. As soon as he had calmed himself, he said, "No, and I find the prospect of that kind of programming offensive."

"Well, we don't do that here, but having that background usually helps. We create software for biomedical devices to collect data. You'd be surprised how much medical data the Paramilitary gain in their endeavors."

It was everything Kal could do to keep himself from wincing.

"I'd like you to do an algorithmic exercise," Wayz said, and Kal nodded. He was trying to breathe in and out as naturally as he could without giving away the fact that he was trying to slow his pounding heart.

Wayz pressed a button on the table and a holodisplay popped up in front of Kal. The sight of a programming task drained his outrage.

"Write a program that attaches a pair of nanites to each white blood cell in the human body simulator," Wayz read from a small holodisplay. "If a white blood cell dies or is destroyed, have the nanites transmit a detailed destruction report and find a new host cell."

Kal's mood lightened. He was happy that the task didn't involve the obliteration of human life, even if only simulated. He set his fingers to the keyboard and began tapping away. Within fifteen minutes, he'd completed and tested a functional program. He pushed the holographic interface across the table to Wayz, who snatched it up and ran Kal's code.

"This is pretty good." Wayz typed at the interface. "Now let me show you the program I wrote to solve this problem."

Moments later he pushed the interface back over to Kal.

Kal scanned through the lines of gibberish and wondered if Wayz's code would execute at all. Kal was used to being able to visualize a computer program when he read it. Each of his programs was a kind of tapestry, each line representing a thread. Using this same metaphor, Wayz's code seemed to him a tangled mess.

The fact that he'd never seen any code but his own crossed his mind. Perhaps Wayz simply knew things about programming that Kal had yet to learn.

He stared at Wayz's code a few moments longer, sensing Wayz expected him to take this program in, and then looked up, smiling and nodding.

I am so in over my head, Kal thought.

"Ah, I see now," Kal said. "Thank you."

"Let's talk about your compensation requirements."

A wave of fear rushed over him. He had no idea how much money, or 'value' as they called it here, he should receive for the position he was applying for. He didn't even know the relative worth of a single unit of their currency.

"Do you have a number for me?" Wayz raised his eyebrows. Clearly Kal was supposed to answer.

"Forty," Kal tried.

"Really?" Wayz furrowed his brow.

Kal felt a surge of desperation. He didn't come this far just to be turned down because he overbid on something as trivial as the amount of currency he'd get.

"Of course, I'm open to other suggestions. I'd be willing to consider thirty-five."

"Where are you getting these numbers?" Wayz shrugged. "I'll put you down for forty million value."

Kal worked to still his beating heart once more while Wayz typed into his interface, its contents blocked by holographic reflectors.

"Well Igl, it was very nice meeting you. I'll let you know about our decision before the end of the day tomorrow. Liberty and happiness." Wayz stood up, rolling his hands around one another. Kal stood up too and mimicked the gesture of greeting and departure.

"Liberty and happiness." Kal smiled at Wayz, but deep inside he was screaming. He clutched at his pad as he walked out the door.

Please be okay, Tria. Please.

oe◁ oo

Jeikl frowned when Kal told him about the salary he'd asked for. It turned out that even someone of his age and experience should have been able to get at least sixty-five million value. Although, it wasn't too bad, Jeikl promised, and proceeded to help Kal find a modest place to live.

"How will I know if I get the job?" Kal asked. He wondered if he'd passed all of Wayz's tests.

Jeikl snorted. "Are you kidding? Reliable and good programmers are such a rarity."

Kal tilted his head. Not so on Earth. But then, Earth had it's own problems. How do you make sure no one abuses nanotechnology? You make sure that everyone knows how to program it, and that everyone understands the ramifications of bad code. But making everyone aware and responsible was socially expensive. Or so he'd learned. He hadn't actually gotten old enough on Earth to start code training, let alone apply for a proper license.

Sure enough, not one hour into their apartment search, Kal's pad belched for his attention, and he pulled up the horrible orange interface. He'd received an email telling him the good news and announcing that his increased value acquisition rate had been applied to his ValYou resident account.

Kal showed Jeikl, who nodded and rolled his eyes. It was almost as though, despite his having saved Kal, he now wanted almost nothing to do with him, viewed him as a burden even. Well, it was more kindness and attention than anyone else in Giglagu had shown him.

And, Kal reminded himself, Jeikl had asked for time off of work just to help him hunt for a place to live.

"You have to ask Wayz to take days off?" Kal asked.

"Yeah. Everyone in ValYou has the same contract, unless you're an exec."

"Do they say 'no?'"

Jeikl nodded vigorously, eyes wide. "Look, Igl. I don't know what you've been told about ValYou, but we're not like the countries of Aglia or Akrilga. A standard contract here means that you only get five vacation days a year, and no sick leave. If you get sick, you have to use your vacation days. If you run out of vacation and you're still sick, they decrease your value."

Kal considered this a moment and decided not to ask anymore about Jeikl's society. His grade school teachers had told him about various times in history when his country had treated laborers this way, but he wasn't clear on the details. He did recall a teacher saying something about the old attitudes leading to the eco-disaster and the worldwide economic collapse of the mid-twenty-first century. Somehow, afterward, the remaining governments had gotten themselves off economies where human endeavor was represented by arbitrary amounts of currency, but he wasn't sure about the details of that transition.

He remembered only the broad strokes of such topics. All his memories of Earth history were trapped in his first six years of school, and he'd been far more interested in math and science than history and literature. Since arriving on Felis, he'd largely guided his own education, preferring just those topics. He promised himself that, if he and Tria were able to escape Gelkur, he'd make a concerted effort to correct that imbalance.

"Thank you for taking time off," Kal said. "It means a lot to me."

"You're welcome." Jeikl remained stoic.

They spent the whole morning scouring the north edge of the city for a suitable apartment. The buildings came in a wide variety of styles. Kal could immediately tell when he wouldn't like a building. They had gyms and bars and pools on the first floor. Although the pools did hold a certain appeal, he would think of Tria every time, a pang of guilt running through him.

Every building they looked at was either too big or too fancy. They left such buildings just after discovering the rental price, not even bothering to look at the units themselves.

Early in the afternoon, they found an apartment building at the edge of the city center that seemed just right. It was small, comfortable, well kept up, and just barely not too far away from work. It was very plain, a no-frills building at a very affordable price.

Perfect.

The landlord, a middle-aged man with a dreary and distant demeanor, led them up to Kal's new home. Kal nearly lurched when he peered inside for the first time. The interior was very empty and very white.

A single nanite lumen clung to the ceiling. The walls had no windows.

Though the lobby of the building had been plain, it certainly hadn't been sterile or devoid of furnishings. What the hell was this place? And it would cost him fifteen million value a month, over a third of his salary!

Kal turned to Jeikl, who appeared not in the least surprised.

The landlord silently activated a holographic interface on the wall beside the door frame, nodded to Kal, and left without saying a word.

Kal watched him walk away, a deep fear building up inside him. He was going to live in a white box.

He turned around and saw Jeikl working the holointerface on the wall.

Kal gulped, fighting tears. "What are you doing?"

"Pulling up the furnishings menu. You do want furniture, don't you?"

Kal blinked.

Jeikl sighed, smiling at Kal like he was a rescued puppy. "Come here."

He showed Kal how to connect his ValYou Resident Account to the apartment, and then how to spend his remaining value to have the nanites construct things, like furniture, windows, clothing and food. The list of goods went on endlessly. There were also games, toys, music, movies, and more. The list just kept going. Kal wondered at how they could produce so much stuff. There was no way that any single individual could possibly consume it all.

And another thing—why bother limiting how much an individual could use the nanites? Nanites could be powered by both sunlight and atomic fusion. They could produce enough resources for everyone. It was clear, however, that only a very small portion of ValYou residents enjoyed access to them and the training in their proper use. Somehow Kal doubted that the homeless of ValYou had violated nanite ethical codes, which was the only way you could be denied the right to program on Earth.

Kal ordered the ValYou nanites to construct him a table, a chair and a bed, and he watched the remaining value in his account tick down with each transaction. Jeikl patted him on the back and grinned.

"Thanks again," Kal said, as Jeikl moved toward the entrance.

"Don't mention it." Jeikl's smile turned solemn, and he left the apartment, shutting the door behind him.

Kal spent the rest of the day working on his pad, making little headway against the invasive software. The ValYou code had completely obliterated the operating system, corrupting even his computer's most basic algorithms.

However, it did not take Kal long to discover an enormous segment of computer memory that had been physically severed from the rest of the system, cordoned off and untouched. And it just happened to be where the operating system restoration backups were stored.

Kal jumped for joy. The only explanation was that his brother had trapped himself in there as well, probably in order to fend off further incursion. Tria was safe!

Kal worked late into the night. At some point, he fell asleep at his table, awakening only a few hours before he was to leave for his first day of work.

oᴄ⟨⟩ᴏᴄ

Kal worried he would be late, but when arrived at his new workplace, he discovered the laboratory was empty. The door was locked and he stood outside, tapping his foot, yawning and wondering why in the world someone would go to the trouble of locking a workplace up.

He thought back to his history lessons again, trying to remember what he'd learned about Earth's corporations of old. Momentarily, he recalled that they'd been viciously competitive with one another.

Understanding washed over him. His new company must be protecting itself from malevolent competitors, willing to steal their technological and trade secrets.

Kal shook his head. He was glad his culture had abandoned this idiocy.

He stood some ten minutes more, tapping his foot and yawning before he grew tired of waiting. He took the elevator back down to the building's lobby and used a vending machine to buy himself some kind of coffee-and-sugar beverage from a cafe. He found a relatively isolated corner and began tinkering with his pad.

"Are you Igl-uma?"

Kal jammed at the pad to turn it off and looked up.

"Yes, hi— Liberty and happiness." Kal still hadn't gotten used to the bizarre greeting.

"Liberty and happiness. I'm Paitr Klin." They performed the hand rolling gesture at one another. He was not much older than Kal, and thin. He had a very tall face dotted with a day's worth of stubble.

"It's no use coming in early," Paitr said. "Wayz-uma won't get here until nine, sometimes ten."

Kal offered Paitr a seat at his table. "Why so late?"

Paitr shook his head. "With Wayz-uma, who knows. Anyway, as long as you're in by ten, you'll be fine. I'm usually in early too. Do you know what you'll be working on yet?"

"No idea."

"Wayz-uma will tell you soon. Until then, just relax. Read up on our division."

"Have you been here long?"

"Just a few weeks, actually. I transitioned here from Northeast Central Division HQ."

"How do you like it?"

"So far, pretty good. Better access to nature. There are more reserves out here."

Kal suddenly realized he hadn't seen a single non-human living thing in two days — not even so much as a tree or potted plant. Giglagu was a giant mass of stone, metal and glass.

"And," Paitr continued, "you know, with Giglagu being on the edge of the Northeast, things are a little less strict out here. I like it better."

Kal smiled. He was glad to hear that. All he wanted was to work on his pad.

"Kulga's our other programmer. We'll all go out for lunch later to welcome you to the team."

"Thanks," Kal said. "I'd like that."

They sat and talked for some time about the code Kal would be working with.

Paitr moved in closer to Kal, his voice lowered to a whisper. "You know, about our division—"

Through the windows of the cafe, both of them turned and watched Wayz rush into the building's enormous lobby. Paitr jumped back, waving and smiling at their boss. Kal waved and smiled too, then put his hands on the arms of his chair and started to push himself up to a stance.

"Don't!" Paitr said. He didn't move, but his muscles were quivering. "Don't go up there until Wayz-uma has settled into the office. Let's just… wait a bit."

Kal watched Wayz walk through the lobby and enter an elevator. Something about his gait was off. He was nervous about something, wasn't he? And then there was Paitr. If Wayz was nervous, Paitr was a wreck.

If this constituted 'more relaxed,' Kal was glad he hadn't arrived on the part of Gelkur Paitr had just moved from. Kal waited silently, carefully watching Paitr breathe deeply and nod out the window. Hopefully that just meant he was calming himself down.

"Okay," Paitr said. "Let's go."

Kal wondered on the way up what was so wrong with sharing an elevator with Wayz. Everyone he'd met in Giglagu was such a basket case. He longed for Tria's company and the swirling blue of the metaxia more than ever before. Part of him wanted to rush away from the job, just run home and work on his pad.

The elevator dinged, and Kal stepped out into the familiar hallway. He and Paitr walked to their office, now unlocked and with lighting ablaze. Wayz sat in the back of the room behind an enormous desk. Holoemitters projected a dozen large interfaces atop it.

"Liberty and happiness," Paitr said. Kal repeated the greeting in Wayz's direction.

"Liberty and happiness," Wayz replied, clearly paying more attention to his computer than to either him or Paitr. Paitr raised an eyebrow to Kal and showed him to his new workspace.

∞⨎∞

Wayz waited until noon to ask Kal into a meeting. He gave Kal a detailed overview of the five pieces of software his division intended to create over the next year. Kal's sleepless night began catching up with him, and he craved another of the coffee beverages from the cafe.

Kal got out of the meeting just after one in the afternoon. Once he was safely back at his desk, Kal wrapped his head in his arms on the table and yawned deeply. When he sat up, Paitr was standing next to him. Beside him stood another man, portly and plump with a round face.

"I'm Kulga," the new man said solemnly. Apparently that was supposed to pass for an introduction.

"Liberty and happiness. I'm Igl Traik." Kal was already tired of the false identity Jeikl had supplied, but at least he wasn't being disassembled or jailed. He and Kulga rolled their hands at one another.

An awkward pause followed.

"Shall we get going to lunch?" Paitr said.

Kulga tapped a button on his arm and a holodisplay emerged from his sleeve.

Paitr began doing the same, then looked up at Kal. "You have to clock out. Last item on the employee interface."

Kal frowned as he clocked himself out. They were even tracking his lunch. Ridiculous. He looked up and realized that Wayz had stopped what he was doing at the enormous interface spanning his entire desk, which was twice the size of Kal's. Wayz glared at them as they left.

"It's okay for us to be leaving, right?" Kal asked.

"It's your first day," Kulga said. "Company policy. Benefits package item 14C. Your employer has to let you and your team go for one hour at any time of the day of their choosing on your first day of employment."

"How generous." Kal tried desperately to make himself sound enthused, then realized he'd failed.

He decided to turn the conversation around to programming. Surely they'd have that in common. "What are you working on, Kulga?"

"Some of the amino acid tracking software."

"Sounds like that would be quite interesting algorithmically. How'd you organize the classification system?"

Kulga sighed. "I keyed it off the atoms in the compound."

Kal frowned. At least Paitr and he had been able to talk about code. If Kulga didn't like programming, why the hell was he a programmer?

"Who won the game?" Paitr asked.

"The Sledgehammers." Kulga smiled. "It was pretty close."

Kulga then launched into a long explanation of the comparative strengths and weaknesses of two teams of some professional sport. Kal put on a smile and let the conversation wash over him. Holobroadcasts of sporting events were about as interesting to him as mildew growth. Kal let his mind turn back to worrying about Tria, and when he would next get a chance to talk to Jeikl about ways to work around the ValYou software in his pad.

"Uh oh." Paitr's tone changed abruptly, and Kal jumped to attention.

A man in rags ran through the street toward them. Kal looked around and saw only one Para guard about half a block away. His back was turned and he was busy talking into his sleeve.

"Why don't you give me that comp? You can afford another one. Gimme the comp. Gimme the comp." He side-stepped and grabbed out at them, even as they walked faster.

"Get lost," Paitr said.

"Or I'll break your face." Kulga snarled.

"Gimme the comp. C'mon. Gimme the comp. C'mon, c'mon. Gimme the comp."

Kulga acted out his threat, smashing his fist into the man's head. Blood gushed from the homeless man's nose, and he stumbled backward. Kal spotted the Para running toward them, but turned his attention to Kulga instead. "What the hell did you do that for?!"

The homeless man fell to the pavement, clasping his face, and Kal ran to him. He turned on his pad and then scoffed, realizing once again that he did not have access to *his* nanites. Only the ValYou variety, the kind that cost money to use.

"What are you doing?" Kulga's voice betrayed disbelief.

"Helping him, of course." Kal looked up to see Kal and Paitr staring at one another.

The homeless man reached out, his hand smeared with blood, and tried to grab Kal's pad, but the nanites repelled him. Kal was glad that at least all his auto-defense systems were intact.

The Para appeared beside them. "You are in violation of the law."

Kal's heart stopped.

The Para pushed a button on his sleeve, and Kal fell over backwards in fright. The man with the bloody face screamed and evaporated. Kal screamed out too, scrambling away.

"I'm sorry I startled you, sir," the Para said. He walked to Kal and offered him his hand.

Kal hesitated, looking up at the murderer. The Para frowned. Kal bunched up his lips and reached out toward the Para. Kal felt himself jerked up to his feet.

"Please be more careful," the Para said. "Liberty and happiness." He turned and strode back to his post at the intersection.

"Good riddance," Kulga said.

"Yeah, that was horrible." Kal said.

Kulga nodded.

Kal massaged the back of his neck. "Those Para really creep me out."

Paitr and Kulga both slowed, and Kal turned to face them. Kulga shot a disbelieving glance at Paitr.

Kulga shook his head at Kal. "*I* was talking about the bum."

They ate lunch at a restaurant that served bowls of small bread grains mixed with chunks of raw fish, vegetables and spices. Kal mimicked Paitr and Kulga as they stirred the contents of their bowls with spoons.

"Why are there so many homeless in Giglagu?" Kal asked.

Kulga gave Kal another look.

"I'm from Glina," Kal said.

"Oh." Kulga rolled his eyes as if that explained everything. "So, you decided to try working for a living, eh?"

"Kulga," Paitr interjected. "Come on. You know people in other countries work too."

"Yeah, only nine months of the year, am I right?"

Paitr and Kulga both looked at Kal, waiting for him to confirm or deny Kulga's supposition.

Okay, Kal thought. *Earth Chicago, I hope you can pass as Glina.*

"Well, this is actually my first job, so I'm only basing this off of watching my parents. There are no holidays, no vacation days, and no sick days. If you get sick, you stay home. If you need a break, you take a vacation. That's it. No counting, no regulating."

"Ha! You hear that?" Kulga said. "'No regulating.' That's rich."

"Why? What does that mean?"

"That's all you do is regulate!" Kulga pointed his spoon at Kal. "You have your big governments with their bureaucracy and regulations to keep hard-working people from making more money. Just like when we had the Fascism."

"The Fascism?" Kal furrowed his brow.

"Part of ValYou history," Paitr said, his eyes betraying that he didn't actually want to be part of this conversation. "It was a time when corporations and the government were separate entities."

"The people realized they were being oppressed," Kulga said. "They realized that government is inherently corrupt, fascistic, and they got rid of it, leaving the corporations, efficient institutions that submit wholly to the equalizing power of the free market."

"Eventually all of the corporations bought each other up," Paitr said. "Now there's only one."

"ValYou," Kal said, trying to hide his shock. He shook his head. "So, you said that the government prevented people from making money. How did they do that exactly?"

"Wealth redistribution," Paitr whispered.

Kulga literally shuddered at hearing the term mentioned.

Kal blinked. "There's something wrong with that?"

Kulga's eyes bulged so much that Kal thought they would fall out their sockets and into his bowl.

"Wealth redistribution is the root of fascism," Kulga said.

Kal stifled laughter.

Kulga ignored him and continued. "When someone takes money away from you, that's stealing. The government would steal from the rich, who earned that money fair and square, and give it to the poor, stupid masses, pathetic wastes of human flesh."

"And now the poor are just killed if they 'misbehave?'"

"Oh, that's the beauty of it," Kulga said. "Even though they're useless drains on society in life, they are at least useful in death."

"What do you mean?" Kal chewed up a bite of fish and bread. He'd been so hungry. His bowl was almost empty.

"Well, when a person breaks the law, their component molecules are transferred to HQ and stored in a big mass collector. Where do you think all the matter comes from to make all the stuff you buy?"

Kal dropped his spoon into his bowl. A massive wave of nausea hurtled through him.

"Excuse me," he barely managed, covering his mouth with his hand. He got up and ran to the restaurant's bathroom.

"What is up with this guy?" Kal heard Kulga say.

Kal puked the entire lunch into the restaurant's toilet, all the time wondering whether or not he would starve to death on Gelkur.

❦

Kal had to finish the rest of his day at work despite having thrown up his lunch. Much to his surprise, the workday didn't end at five o'clock like his contract said it would. Wayz had begun barking orders to a group of artists at four and continued a closed meeting with them well past five.

Kal walked over to Jeikl's desk and said, as quietly as he was able, "Isn't the workday over? Why isn't anyone leaving?"

"That's what the manual says, I know," Jeikl whispered back. "But in reality, the workday ends whenever Wayz-uma leaves. No one ever leaves before him."

"When does he leave?"

"Could be any time between six and ten. Sometimes later."

Kal felt woozy. How would he ever work on his pad under such conditions?

"Hey," Jeikl said, making sure he had Kal's attention, "Don't be here in the morning any later than ten either. And never come back late from lunch. There are punishments..."

Kal nodded vigorously. He didn't wish to hear more. He walked back to his desk in despair and thought that maybe he should have tried to escape ValYou after all.

The worst case scenario was that he would get off work at ten. If he had to be at work by ten the next morning, that left just under four hours to work on his pad.

Wayz stayed in the office until nine that night. The moment he left, everyone in the office began packing up their things and shutting down their interfaces.

While packing up, Kal remembered something he'd read about in a history book. He caught up with Paitr on his way out the door.

"Hey, do you have anything like trade unions in ValYou?"

Paitr chuckled. "Not any more."

"Let me guess," Kal said.

"Fascism," they said simultaneously.

"Yeah, that's what I thought," Kal rolled his eyes. His stomach grumbled and he yawned, stepping into the elevator along with the rest of the office staff.

When he arrived back in his apartment, he fell onto his bed, and his stomach rumbled once more. Kal had never wanted to see his cats and his treehouse more desperately during his entire travels.

Then Kal coughed. He really coughed. Hard. The coughing erupted an intense ache throughout his chest. Kal pounded on himself a few times with his fist and then took long breaths in and out. The fit subsided, and he walked to his pad. He paid fifty value to make a glass of water, then one hundred more to have the ValYou nanites run a cursory scan of his lungs.

Just one day in the city center, surrounded by nanite radiation, and Kal's lungs were already in the initial stages of shutting down.

He winced, pulled up his pad interface, and began working once more.

Kal at least slept well. After spending another fifteen minutes researching their medical databases, Kal was able to find a non-prescription medication that would open up his bronchial passages. But, he was only treating the symptoms, not the root cause, which was the radiation. For that, he had to wrest back control of his pad and free Tria from his self-imposed imprisonment.

He woke in a fit of coughing and hobbled to his table. Another fifty value flitted away as he made himself more water. He cursed his luck and vowed he would never visit another world socially backward enough to have currency if he could ever get himself off this rock.

He checked the instructions on his medication and decided on another dose. He couldn't keep doing this, filling himself with ValYou pharmaceuticals. He needed real medical attention, but he could afford neither the time nor the value.

His coughing ceased, and a soothing sensation spread throughout his chest. That felt a lot better.

Kal grabbed up his pad, and immediately began tinkering. He decided that his goal for the morning was to regain control of one single command object. If he could just learn how these ValYou nanites were interfacing with his system, he could program around them.

The four hours remaining before he had to be at work passed far too quickly. 9:45 showed on the interface's clock, and although he had access to his command object, he hadn't even begun to scratch the surface of ValYou's invasive code. Kal turned his pad off and stuffed it into his backpack.

The streets were busy in the morning, rush hour in full force. People walked silently. There were no trains in Giglagu. It seemed that everyone worked in the enormous office park at the center of the city with its monolithic towers, and every worker lived within a mile of the city center. Everywhere else, there were the homeless.

He had once again donned the business suit he'd arrived in, and the masses of people shuffling to their ValYou jobs all wore very similar clothing. Why were they so silent? Trips with his parents to their workplaces in Chicago hadn't been like this. Families and friends talked happily to one another on the trains and subways. This horde seemed dead inside.

He marched forward silently alongside them, their pattering footsteps resounding off the buildings' walls.

Kal arrived at his job, turned on his work interface, and took a deep breath.

Wayz had sent him an email with a list of tasks. At the top was one that seemed simple enough. They needed a program that would map the interior surfaces of veins and arteries.

Kal furrowed his brow and glanced over to Jeikl. He didn't appear to be too busy yet.

"Liberty and happiness, Jeikl."

"Liberty and happiness, Igl."

"I was just wondering about the first task on my list. It seems like that kind of program should already exist. It'd be more efficient if we found and repurposed someone else's code— Why are you shaking your head?"

"Because it wouldn't be ours," Jeikl said matter-of-factly. "ValYou may be one company, but our division is in competition with all the other medical divisions for money and resources distributed by the Board. Using someone else's code would mean spending value on a resource we don't control. It's less costly for us to build our own software."

"Even if we end up building it exactly the same way as everyone else?"

Jeikl nodded.

Kal frowned. "Sounds like duplication of effort to me."

"Call it what you will. It's the system we've got." Jeikl returned to his desk.

Kal shrugged and returned to his. He busied himself with building the algorithm, which was actually fairly fun work.

Around noon, he started coughing again, and he took another dose of the medication. So far, he was doing fine. The medication's effectiveness was dissipating in time with the recommended dosage, but Kal knew his condition would deteriorate with every day of exposure, and he wondered how long it would remain effective.

Paitr appeared at Kal's desk. "Lunch?"

"Sure." Kal smiled. At least his coworkers were friendly enough. Except... Kal glanced at Kulga. He was absorbed in his work and made no move to join them.

Paitr and Kal clocked out, left the office, and entered the elevator.

"We can go anywhere you want. I take you don't want Aglekka Bowl again." Paitr smirked.

Kal laughed a bit. "I think I'll be fine this time. You got any recommendations?"

"I know a good place that does West Akrilgan food. You ever had that?"

Kal shook his head. "No, but I'm up for something new."

The elevator doors opened, and Paitr led Kal out of the enormous building complex and down the now deserted streets dotted with Para.

"It's interesting," Paitr said. "Most people who come to ValYou from other countries are searching for riches and fame. But you..."

Kal shook his head. "Those don't interest me. I'm here because... well, life's an adventure and I'm exploring."

"A lot of ValYou citizens, like Kulga, will take some offense at that."

Kal screwed up his face. "Why?"

"Well, think about it. Life here is about climbing to the top, and the only way to do that is to leave a pile of bodies in your wake. Maybe not literally, but you get the idea. The rub of it is that you're competing in the system the same as Kulga, but his stakes are different. If you lose everything, you can always go back to Glina, whereas someone like Kulga would become destitute, one of the homeless."

Kal and Paitr entered a restaurant with green and brown wallpaper. A metal buffet cart was set up at the far end with trays of steaming food. They sat down in wooden chairs at a glass table.

"How do you feel about ValYou?" Kal asked.

Paitr shrugged and rolled his eyes. "I don't really care one way or the other. My family's got enough value saved up that we'll be fine. I just want to keep programming and stay out of trouble."

"Does it bother you at all to live in a society that grinds people up this way?"

Paitr looked at the table and clasped his hands together.

"No." Paitr looked up. "I don't dare let it bother me."

Kal let them sit in silence a moment. He waited until Paitr's breathing returned to normal. He and his family might have been 'fine,' so to speak, but there was something else. Some weakness he or they had, something that could unhinge them and bring them down. Kal wasn't going near that topic again.

"What I don't understand," Kal began carefully, "is people like Kulga. I can understand being afraid of this system. I can understand hating this system. But liking it? Defending it? What kind of person actually enjoys living in a society that gives you the 'freedom' of being oppressed or killed if you're not valuable enough?"

Paitr shook his head. "He doesn't see it that way."

"Help me understand his way of seeing it, then."

"He sees it as freedom to work his way to the top and oppress everyone else. He has the opportunity to express his will onto the world and everyone in it."

Kal shook his head. "That's... that's—"

A waiter approached with two glass tumblers of water and set them down.

"The buffet, please," Paitr said, before the waiter could get any words out.

The waiter turned to Kal.

"Same for me."

After they got food, Paitr turned the subject of conversation to their work.

Kal quickly fell into a routine. He would wake up at five in the morning, spend four hours tearing away the malevolent code in his pad, then go to his job in the Nanoprogramming Research Laboratory.

The medication continued doing its job for its allotted six hours, but Kal could tell that his coughing was getting worse at the periphery of its duration.

Still, he struggled forward, making incremental gains against the ValYou malware day by day.

Gelkur had no concept of a 'weekend.' He worked seven days per week, his routine never breaking.

The problems presented to him at work remained mildly interesting and engaging. Even though he continued to feel pangs that he should be able to search their network for existing code that would accomplish his tasks, he stifled the urge and coded his own solutions.

In Tria's absence, Paitr became the closest thing Kal had to a friend. They often went to lunch together, though Paitr kept their conversation firmly in the realm of programming and work. They never talked politics again.

Kulga ignored Kal unless he needed something related to work.

Jeikl remained a conundrum. He disappeared during his lunch breaks, never telling anyone where he was going or what he was doing. But he always returned thirty minutes later, never missing his clock-in. He was cordial and friendly within the bounds of work, but since Kal only saw him in that context, there was never an opportunity to get more information out of him. And while Paitr would sometimes invite Kal out for drinks after Wayz left the office, Jeikl never did.

He remained stoic and detached. Kal wanted to ask him more about why he'd helped Kal get his position, but there was a never an opportunity. He owed Jeikl his life, and yet now, after giving that help, Jeikl seemed to want nothing more to do with him.

And then their was Wayz.

During his first week at ValYou Corporation's Northeast Division Nanoprogramming Research Laboratory, Kal had barely any interaction with his new boss. Wayz would email Kal the specifications for programs and algorithms, and Kal would code them.

After his first week, the meetings started.

Wayz used them to as forum to show off the newest 'feature' he'd come up with. Kal had, at first, wanted to ask what a feature was supposed to be, but it didn't take long for him to realize that it was simply an idea that Wayz had dreamed up, one that the team was now obligated to create.

Wayz had also decided that his nickname was 'Hotshot,' and encouraged all of the members of the team to refer to him as such by telling them they could use it in place of the 'umakl' suffix.

Kal noticed that many team members, especially Kulga, not only adopted the new nickname quickly, but also went to great efforts during the meetings to point out details of the feature, and spin them back at Wayz, all under the guise of trying to understand it better. Kal watched Wayz's ego swell with each opportunity to better clarify his grand vision to his lowly peons.

After one such meeting, which Kal had found particularly excruciating, he had gone to program the feature Wayz had come up with, and discovered its specifications to be so ridiculously nonsensical that they defied basic logic. As Wayz had described it, such code would crash the application. Kal had no choice but to alter the so-called 'design parameters.'

He was having more luck with his own programming project at home. After two weeks on Gelkur, Kal had managed to free about half of his pad's system from the invasive ValYou programming. His interface had become a jumbled mess of blue and orange, Earth code controlling some systems and Gelkur code running others.

Though the velocity of his progress had been on the rise, the amount of work remaining seemed vast. Each command object was a different beast, and required a unique solution. He'd come to intuit the behavior of the ValYou code, and that sped up his work, but he guessed he'd have to tolerate this awful world for at least another two weeks, his coughing all the time growing worse.

Kal slept fitfully at nights, dreaming of Tria and his cats. What would Tria say when he was freed from his silicon prison? Had the ValYou software gobbled him up after all? Maybe the protected memory in his pad was just a security failsafe, part of the core routines.

Amidst this torture, Kal's work life degraded. Wayz started paying special attention to him. Kal never figured out what the reason was, but it seemed as though one day, as with the flip of a switch, everything he programmed fell under Wayz's exacting scrutiny, which he would hear about in vitriolic emails disseminated to the entire team.

Two weeks into Kal's stint at ValYou, a very strange email showed up in his inbox.

> *Dear Team,*
>
> *I regret to inform you that I have analyzed this last month's data and reached a startling conclusion. Please see below.*

Inserted at this point was a diagram of various pieces of information that had been pulled from the reporting service they used to collect data on customers' usage of their software.

> *As you can see from the elements I've highlighted, about thirty percent of our users are no longer able to use our software. We will all have to work harder to make up for these losses.*
> *I will work to discover the cause of this drop immediately.*
>
> *- Wayz "Hotshot" Iuum*

Kal cringed and rolled his eyes.

He then scanned over the table of data, trying to derive some sense from it, but it appeared as though Wayz had simply grabbed randomly at the database and combined the information in a way that would seem complex, though it was, in fact, idiotic. And his statement about thirty percent of the users no longer being able to use the software didn't correlate to the data in any way Kal could discern.

Not long after this email went out, Wayz, unsurprisingly, called a meeting.

"I'm sure you're all as disappointed with this failure as I am," Wayz said. "But don't worry. We're a team. And we're one awesome team. I'm sure that if we work hard and meet these new challenges face on, we'll overcome these losses.

"I've analyzed the data further, and I've discovered the cause of the lost thirty percent." He paused and bit his lip, looking directly at Kal. "I'm not blaming anyone in particular. That would be unfair. Let's all work harder, okay?"

The rest of the room was looking directly at Kal now, too.

Kal sank into his chair, stifling a grimace, his eyes remaining locked with Wayz's.

∞⟨⟩∞

Nights of working until eight or nine turned into nights that dragged on until eleven or midnight. Apparently, a perceived bug in the programming (one that Kal remained convinced did not exist) meant that the entire team had to work an extra three hours a day. This left very little time for Kal to work on freeing his pad from the ValYou software.

His room became a mess. He stopped cleaning up after himself because there was no time, and because his salary was so low, he could not afford to have nanites clean up after him either. The funny thing was, Kal could easily program the nanites to do such a task, but as he had come to learn, Gelkur nanites were a *proprietary* innovation, fully owned and patented by ValYou Corporation. What Kal was doing to his pad was, according to ValYou regulations, quite illegal. However, so long as the activity remained in his own private apartment on an unregistered device, he would be fine.

Wayz obsessed over Kal's code more and more with each passing day. He initiated a broken record of emails about the supposedly lost thirty percent of users. And although the refrain never changed, Wayz's insinuations that Kal's code was the problem grew more and more transparent as the days wore on.

Paitr remained supportive, letting Kal vent about Wayz over lunch. Jeikl remained aloof, but Kulga started to bug Kal immensely. He would jump into email threads, promising to rework the "problematic" parts of the code that Wayz had "identified."

Kal started monitoring Kulga's changes and found that he wasn't doing anything more than altering a couple of variable names, or restructuring the code into a different, more obsequious, but equally functional configuration.

Wayz congratulated Kulga on these endeavors in the same emails where he tore apart Kal's code. Against all reason, Kal continued to code solutions to the actual problems that their group faced—missing or unimplemented features, and the bugs caused by Kulga's "cleanup."

Three weeks after Kal had started working for ValYou, he returned to his messy apartment at one in the morning and crashed onto his bed. A coughing fit woke him and continued for at least five minutes.

The medicine had stopped working for its entire six hour duration, and he was beginning to encroach on taking it every five and half hours.

He medicated himself, lay down, and closed his eyes. The coughing subsided, and he had just started to drift into sleep when his work pad buzzed, its vibration functionality rattling the table. Kal dragged himself out of bed and answered the call.

"Igl?" Wayz's voice.

"Liberty and happiness, Wayz-umakl."

"There's a big problem here."

"Hmm?"

"I believe that eighty percent of the users can't access the software at all. Do you have any idea why that might be?"

Kal thought for a moment. Somehow all of the programming plans he had for his pad were mixed up in his mind with the programming for work. After he'd separated the two, he thought through the changes he had made during the previous day. Of course! He had it.

"I think that you might be seeing a display error. Everyone can use the software, and we're getting the data, we're just not showing it correctly on the reporting tool. I can come in and fix it right aw—"

"No. Don't do that."

"O-Okay." Kal cleared his throat.

Silence.

"So, what do you want me to do, exactly?" Kal asked.

"Well, we have this massive problem! Eighty percent of the users can't use the software!" A vision of Wayz frothing at the mouth entered Kal's mind, and he shuddered in response.

"I just told you, everyone's using it fine. Look, let me come in. I'll make a single line change, and you'll have all the data on your display."

"No, absolutely not. You don't get to make changes to the code anymore tonight."

"What? So, why are you even calling? Just to blame me?"

Silence.

"Liberty and happiness, Wayz. Umakl."

Kal hung up.

❧

When Kal woke up, he had an email from Paitr in his inbox. Paitr wanted to meet him in the cafe on their building's first floor before work. Kal worked on his pad, then dressed and showered as quickly as he could before rushing out the door.

Paitr smiled weakly as Kal sat down.

"Liberty and happiness," Paitr said.

"You know where that greeting comes from?" Kal yanked out a chair and threw himself into it.

"Sorry?" Paitr shook his head. He'd clearly wanted to talk about something else.

"Do you know where that greeting comes from?"

"No."

"I looked it up."

"Oh?"

"Yes, access to your historical database cost me 350 value, but I paid for it because I was *that* curious."

Paitr crossed his arms.

Kal could tell he was being humored, but he didn't care. "It evolved out of a very old systems of *values* on Gelkur. The phrase used to be 'life, liberty and pursuit of happiness.'"

Paitr's eyes widened. Good. He'd gotten the implication. Paitr was smart, even if he lacked backbone.

Paitr gulped, speaking softly. "We took out the 'life.'"

"Individual liberty and happiness even at the expense of quality of life," Kal leaned back and crossed his arms. He smiled briefly at his victory of wisdom, then his countenance fell. No, this was rude. He was letting

Wayz get to him, and the last thing that would distinguish him right now was an ego trip. "I'm sorry, Paitr. You asked me here for a reason. What's up?"

"No, it's okay." Paitr shifted in his seat, sitting up straighter. "It's a fair assessment. Especially given..."

Paitr's eyes fell to the table. Kal waited patiently for him to speak again, and when his eyes came back up, Kal nodded for him to continue.

"Wayz called me last night. I presume he called everyone in the office. He told me about what he did to you. I'm sorry. He's a bad manager, and he's being particularly horrible to you at a time when he should be thanking you. Your mapping platform is really impressive. We wouldn't have a functional application without you."

Kal felt a pang of regret. "Oh geez, Paitr, I'm sorry. I didn't mean to bite your head off. It's just with everything Wayz's been doing..."

"Don't worry about it. Believe it or not, there are much worse managers in ValYou."

Kal's eyes widened. "Worse?"

Paitr nodded. "I know what it's like. The trick with Wayz is to stay off his radar. He finds people who he can project his own insecurities onto. Once he's found a target..." Paitr leaned closer. "I'll do what I can to help you, Igl. I can listen. I can take you out to lunch. But I can't lose my position here. I'm sorry."

Kal nodded and revealed the trace of a smile. "I appreciate being able to talk about it. You don't have to apologize. Thank you, Paitr."

Paitr nodded to the window. Kal grimaced as he watched Wayz enter the elevator.

"C'mon," Paitr said.

Throughout the morning, Kal lost himself in his tasks, and when he'd completed those, he closed out his email and searched the network for information ancillary to repairing his personal pad.

Despite Kal's best efforts to ignore his boss, Wayz called a meeting just before noon. Kal's stomach groaned, and he felt his chest beginning to tighten, but as everyone entered the meeting chamber, Kal decided it would be too conspicuous to medicate himself now. Besides, it had only been four hours since his last dose.

Wayz began the meeting by talking about how great the team had been, working extra hard to make up for the "losses" they had incurred because of the mapping software Kal had built. Wayz was now openly referring to it as an "unstable platform." The first time Wayz did this, Kal ignored it. The second time, he interrupted the meeting.

"What is this unstable platform you keep talking about?"

"NanoScript, of course."

"The entire language?"

"Yes."

Kal blinked. "Wayz-umakl, you don't have an application without NanoScript!"

"I think we can try taking the whole NanoScript layer out."

Silence. The team looked at Kal.

"You had to initialize the application with NanoScript before I joined and wrote any code at all. Do you want to strip that out too?"

Wayz locked his eyes onto Kal. "We'll scrap all the NanoScript if I deem it's necessary."

"Then your application won't load, and you'll have zero percent of users able to access it!" Kal wanted to rip out his hair.

The whole team craned their necks around to look at Wayz.

"Igl, don't worry, I'll teach you how to be a better programmer. It's okay to make mistakes as long as you learn from them."

Kal couldn't let this go. "Okay fine, Wayz-umakl. Schedule a time to go over my code with me. Full review. We can bring it up to your standards."

Wayz shifted his weight. "I've already looked over it."

"Really? The entire codebase? All 2,730 lines?"

"Yes, all of it."

"And?"

"You have too many variables."

Kal carefully put his hands on his lap and clenched his fists together. He took a deep breath. "You do mean *extraneous* variables, right?"

"No, no. Just too many. Get rid of some."

Kal could only gawk. One might as well tell a teacher that too much learning was happening in his classroom, or a farmer that her field had too many plants.

His mind pored over the possibilities. Which variables should he get rid of? The ones holding the data about the users? The ones that held references back to the core routines? Wayz's statement was bafflingly stupid.

Who had put this idiot in charge of a group of programmers?

"I believe I can reduce the number of variables in the system," Kulga offered. "I'll bet we can cut at least a third of them."

Kal's face shot up red, and he turned his gaze to the brown-nosed asshole. "Actually Kulga, I have a better idea. Let's take the data structure of the entire application and stuff it into one enormous associative array. Then there will only be one variable in the whole damn system. Does that sound like a good design to you?"

"That's enough, Igl!" Wayz bellowed.

Kal clamped a hand over his mouth and took deep breaths. He was afraid of what he might say if he allowed himself to speak. He reminded himself that Tria's wellbeing was more important than this. Kal had to survive. He had to survive this abysmal moron of a boss to save his brother.

Kal stifled a cough and felt his face flush.

Oh, and my own life's at stake too.

His heart sank.

Wayz responded to Kal's outburst by staying in the office clear until one in the morning, and every employee—the programmers, user interface designers, graphic artists, everyone—had to stay until he left.

Kal would glance up from his interface through bleary eyes at eleven or midnight and spot an artist or designer glaring at him.

Wayz himself sat hunched over his desk, poking furiously at icons in between frantic bouts of typing on his holographic keyboard, ignoring everyone else in the office completely.

During Kal's fourth week at the Giglagu Northeast Division Nanoprogramming Research Laboratory, he made almost no progress against the ValYou operating system in his pad. He would come home at one, crash, pull himself out of bed at seven, and work at his pad for only an hour so, his attention mangled and unfocused, before dragging himself off to another thirteen hour work day.

One day, nearly a month since he had joined Wayz's team, Kal trudged in the door, and had only just turned on his interface when he heard Wayz raving on the other side of the room.

"It's all unstable! The users are complaining! It's the NanoScript, isn't it? I knew we should have pulled all that garbage out."

Kal sighed and pulled up his email. He found a thread from the other programmers on his team. Jeikl had discovered the actual issue. Far from being the NanoScript, it was a miscoded routine somewhere inside the core library. Kal checked the change log, and it was Kulga's code that had broken the application.

Kal called Paitr over, and the two of them began working to fix the problem. It was worse than they'd first anticipated. Even after they fixed the original error, they discovered that the bug's brief stint had injected incorrect data into other parts of the system. They needed to do a systematic sweep of all records and purge the incorrect entries to prevent the problem from propagating further.

They worked through lunch, then through dinner. A few of the artists were kind enough to go out and purchase everyone food on company value.

At two a.m., the programming team approached Wayz. Paitr insisted that there was no way for him to finish the fix, and everyone needed sleep. Wayz organized an all team meeting. He called the ten other members of the team over, and they formed a huge circle around him.

Wayz wanted Kulga and Paitr to release their fix as soon as possible, but Kulga and Paitr had put in for a vacation day weeks ago, and Wayz had approved it. He was contractually bound not to rescind that approval.

"Hmm... We really need Kulga to be here when we push the new code live though..." Wayz tapped his foot on the floor and furrowed his brow.

"The changes have all been tested," Paitr said. "Igl and I worked extensively on it, and he knows the fix inside and out. I'm sure he can deploy it on his own."

Wayz laughed a brief, incredulous laugh.

"No, no, no," Wayz said. "Igl can't do the code push alone. He screws up too much. I mean, you don't put a gun in a shaky hand."

He laughed again, louder. No one else did. Some of the team looked at the floor. Others rolled their eyes, while others looked expectantly at Kal.

Kal bunched up his fists and felt his face flush red. On the tip of his tongue lay the most vile epithets he could think of hurling at Wayz. He sat poised to tell this so-called manager, as he stood there laughing his ridiculous ass off, what an incompetent, stupid, self-absorbed, arrogant idiot he was.

Jeikl gawked momentarily, then rushed up to Kal and hugged him. Kal tensed, stunned.

"You alright?" Jeikl held Kal's shoulders.

"Yeah."

"He's not worth it," Jeikl mouthed the words, then reach down and grabbed Kal's hand, palming him a small metallic device.

Kal's rage seeped away. He nodded, shook Jeikl's hand, and took the secret mechanism. He calmly walked to his desk, picked up his things, turned, and walked out of the office.

"I haven't left yet," Wayz shouted to him.

"I quit," Kal shouted back, not bothering to turn around.

When Kal returned to his apartment, it had reverted to its empty, white, cubic configuration. The window was gone, and so were the table, the chair, the bed, the piles of food bar wrappers and other trash that had accumulated. An interface on the wall announced his eviction and the appropriation of all possessions he'd created since his arrival. Apparently the "End Citizen License Agreement" he'd signed had stipulated that the articles he'd purchased were not actually his property after all. They'd in fact been on loan from ValYou Corporation.

Kal had his own pad in the backpack he'd brought with him to Giglagu from the metaxia. It hadn't left his possession any time during the last month, and he was especially glad that he had not left it in his apartment.

He left his former apartment building and walked the streets of Giglagu for two hours before giving up on finding some kind of public area. A park or a bench would have sufficed, but he'd hoped for shelter of some sort. He chided himself for not realizing sooner that those in power would have no desire to create such spaces. The homeless were left to go completely insane, rejected by their society, unwanted and uncared for. And once they were insane, they eventually broke some ordinance, and that's when the Para would step in.

Kal stopped wandering and searched instead for any place he could sit. Some locations included the steps in front of businesses and on street corners at the edge of the city center where the Para were fewer. He would

ZACHARY BONELLI

work on his pad until he saw a Para or a homeless person approach, which happened with some frequency. At that point, he'd run away and begin the search for a new location all over again.

Kal was getting close to unlocking his pad. He could feel it. There were only fifteen command objects left, and his interface was nearly entirely blue.

He came to a deserted street and sat down just inside an alleyway, pulling out his pad and beginning again. He got through another command object. Then another. Good, good. Almost there.

A thought struck him. The device that Jeikl had slipped him! Kal searched his pockets and retrieved it. It looked like some kind of data device, but its connector didn't fit into any port available on his personal pad. Fortunately, Kal had regained control of most of his nanites' functionality. He had them scan the device, and indeed, they turned up a computer program. Conflicting emotions ran through him. He sighed, deciding that Jeikl had been the most trustworthy person he had met on Gelkur, and he ran the program.

Nothing.

Kal ran it again and tapped his fingers against the pad's casing. He frowned. The program didn't appear to do anything. Kal sighed and returned his attention to stripping ValYou code away from command objects.

"Identification," a brusk voice said.

Kal grimaced and looked up. A Para stood beside him, a very tall man with a thick frame. Perhaps this was it. The end of him. Kal braced himself to be disassembled by the malevolent nanites of a socially backward world.

Kal handed up his Igl Traik identification card, his hand shaking.

The Para snatched it up and scanned it.

"You have no value. I must assume that your computer is stolen ValYou property. Prepare for punishment."

Kal grabbed his pad in one hand and his backpack in the other and began to run, but was jerked backward by his backpack. His back crashed into the pavement, knocking the wind out of him.

He coughed heavily, pulling himself up to his feet, and glanced back. The Para pressed a button on the interface projected from his wrist, and Kal's whole body shimmered blue.

Thank you, auto-defense nanites!

"Sorry to disappoint you," Kal smirked. He abandoned the backpack and ran away into the alley.

"Para ID 562970 reporting," he heard his assailant's voice fade away behind him. "Teenage male, one hundred eighty centimeters tall, brown hair, running illegal nanite programs..."

Five minutes later, Kal stopped and coughed. No, he hacked.

Damn it. This was not good. His medication had been in his backpack.

He sat down in the deserted alley and began programming again, struggling to maintain his concentration between coughing fits and gasps for breath.

Twelve command objects left. Ten. Seven.

Day turned to dusk and it started raining. Huge beads of water shot through his interface and soaked his clothes. He shivered and coughed. His fits were getting stronger. He leaned back momentarily, feeling light-headed, then shook his head and returned to the programming.

He cursed his luck as the cold cut through his skin, exacerbating his condition. He had no medicine. No help. Just the chill wetness and the refuse surrounding him.

Thunder erupted simultaneously with a crashing sound from further down the dark alley. Kal shot up and ran. He didn't care where to, just away from the noise.

Rain water soaked him through. He would die here. He was so close, and now he and Tria would die here because he'd refused to tolerate a few more days with Wayz.

A hand caught his shoulder from a corner alley.

"Get off of me!" Kal grabbed the hand and threw it away.

"Kagl! Kagl Andiz!"

Kal recognized that voice.

"Jeikl?!"

"Shh! Get in here."

Kal stepped through a door.

"Where are you really from, Kagl?"

"Earth..." Kal wheezed. The world started to spin, and he fell forward. Jeikl caught him.

"I'm taking you back to my apartment okay?"

Heat emanated from Jeikl. Probably nanites. He'd anticipated exactly what trouble Kal would be in. A forcefield bubble shimmered into existence around them both.

Kal remembered Jeikl pulling Kal's arm over his shoulder, supporting his weight. Kal pulled his feet, one over the other, through alleyways and forgotten passages. Drops of rain fizzled against the nanite shield that Jeikl must have spent his hard-earned value on, in order to save Kal's life once again.

∽∾⟋∽∾

Kal sat on Jeikl's couch, drier and with a cup of tea, but still coughing.

"Where is Earth? What happens when your computer works again?" Jeikl insisted.

Kal paused from his work and turned to cough, then looked at Jeikl. It was time to trust him.

"I'm from an alternate quantum reality," Kal said flatly, then coughed again.

Jeikl nodded.

"Another Gelkur..." Jeikl looked at the ceiling. "I always wondered what we've been missing out on."

"What do you mean?"

"I often wonder what Gelkur would be like if we engaged in scientific research for the sake of curiosity. What would we discover if technological progress served scientific discovery rather than the self-indulgent whims of the elite? Do you have that on your Gelkur?"

"I think so. Metaxic travel only happened because a Fermilab scientist was curious what would happen if you applied force to quantum-locked matter." Kal continued programming between coughs. "But the nanites themselves got expedited because we were facing complete biome failure."

"Hmm..." Jeikl frowned. "Sadly, I'm not sure ValYou would rally together for that kind of scientific endeavor if we found ourselves in a similar situation. Could you do me a favor, Kagl?"

"Anything!"

"I'd like to go to Earth. And I assume this isn't random. We can move back and forth between Earth and Gelkur, right?"

"I'm surprised you don't want to leave for good. Doesn't seem you like it here anymore than I do."

Jeikl nodded solemnly. "There are people here who need my help to escape ValYou Corporation. I help them get to safe places—real countries, with governments. But it's very dangerous for them. Ferrying them away to an alternate Earth would be an amazing opportunity."

Kal stopped what he was doing at his interface.

"You run an underground railroad, don't you—?"

"SHH!"

"Sorry," Kal whispered.

Jeikl crossed his arms. "Will you help?"

"Of course! I can't take them to Earth, though." Kal coughed. "Too much nanogenic radiation for me. But I know some Gelkurs where they'd be welcome. Now, I can't do too many. There are these Mythos and Ethos guys. Well, not really guys. Quantum life forms. Long story. Short answer is, yes. If I can get the pad up and running again."

Don't worry, you're almost there, Tria thought.

"Tria!" Kal shouted with glee, and Jeikl motioned with his hands for Kal to keep his volume under control.

"Sorry," Kal whispered as the hologram of Tria burst into view.

"Thank *god*," Tria said, quite loudly. Kal and Jeikl both urged him to be quiet.

Tria threw himself down next to Kal and ran his hands over his face.

Kal squeezed through Tria's shoulder. "Thank you so much, Tria. I assumed it was you keeping the backups safe."

"Mmm hmm… No problem…" Tria spoke through his hands. He sat up and grabbed at Kal's shoulders. "We will be programming defenses against invasive nanites. I will *not* do that again."

Jeikl walked up to Tria. "Liberty and freedom."

Tria stood up, his dismay giving way to keen interest. "Liberty and freedom. You changed the greeting!"

Kal rolled his eyes. Of course, Tria must have spent the last month reading up on Gelkur's language.

"'Liberty and freedom' is our greeting in the underground," Jeikl said. "You're Kagl's brother?"

"Yup." Tria rubbed his eyes and blinked. "It sure is bright in here."

Kal slapped his hand through Tria's back, smiling.

Jeikl lifted an eyebrow. "I suspected you had a covert transportation technology in that pad of yours, but I never expected this."

Kal stood up, his work complete. "Are you going to be okay, Jeikl? What you're doing can't be safe."

Jeikl shook his head. "ValYou is wrong. I can't make it better, but I can help people get away."

Kal smiled weakly. "Thank you for everything, Jeikl. I appreciate all you've done for me, and I hope to return the favor."

"And don't give up on changing ValYou." Tria stood up and stretched his arms. "You never know what you might be able to accomplish."

"When do you want to see those alternate worlds?" Kal asked.

Jeikl's eyes darted about. "Do we have to leave my apartment?"

"Nope." Kal activated the pad's newly restored metaxic interface.

Tria grinned and nodded. "It's blue."

Kal smiled, activated the nodes, and watched the awe pass over Jeikl's face as the bubble of blue electricity encompassed the three of them.

Taboo

Unregistered Realm, "Irth"
September 30, 2178

KAL STOOD in the bubble alongside Tria and gazed out into the blue whorls of the metaxia.

Kal jabbed a finger at the bubble wall. "There! Did you see it?"

Tria sat, staring into his interface, and grumbled something inaudible.

"You're not even paying attention."

"You're right. I'm not." Tria typed on his holographic keyboard. "I don't know why you do this to yourself."

"Earth is technically your home too."

"I'm not sure my home can be a place I've never been to. If we want to get technical about it, I was born on Lehr. But I'd hardly call that a home. Regardless, I don't see any point standing here in the metaxia, hovering over Earth, and wishing for things we can't have."

Kal tapped at his interface and sighed. He knew his brother was right, he just didn't want to admit it.

He pushed a button on his own interface, and a window popped into view. "All of them. We've explored every realm on the grid with low to moderate levels of nanite activity. Nothing. If he's on one of the ones with high activity..."

Tria tapped away at his keyboard. "We can only wait for him to strike again."

Kal sat down, facing Tria, and put his head in his hands. "I didn't want this, Tria. I just wanted to explore, to find some adventure, maybe a cure. Insane stalkers bent on the destruction of alternate Earths? I can't handle that."

"Then let's send a message to Earth directly. Ourselves."

Kal shook his head. Continuing his adventures meant keeping the Fermilab technicians in the dark about his activities. If he got them involved, there would be no more exploration. At best, it meant he would be confined to Felis forever. At worst, they would pull him back to Earth against his will, where he would return to his coma, and Tria would be trapped inside his mind.

"You said it yourself, Kal. We can't handle this alone."

Kal sighed. "You're right, of course. We have to send a message directly, one that we're sure won't be hijacked."

Kal scooted around so that he sat beside Tria. He pulled up the communication program on his interface. He frowned and found it hard to push the button. After all, for all the times his life had been in danger, hadn't he met amazing people, seen natural beauty, and witnessed feats of human endeavor that most people could only ever dream of?

Tria typed out a short message, an SOS to Fermilab, then pushed it into the communication window on Kal's interface. The button glowed blue, waiting to be pressed.

Kal reached out tentatively, then brought his index finger down onto it.

The bubble shuddered and rocked, lurching left, and began spinning.

"What just happened?" Tria shouted. His interface flickered off amidst the chaos.

Kal stared at his stuttering interface, swiping through highly unstable windows. "I—I don't know! I think something happened to the communication program!"

"Some damage from Gelkur?"

The humming whine grew in volume, and the bubble span faster. The shudders increased in frequency and grew more violent.

"I don't think so," Kal shouted above the cacophony.

A bright burst of blue light erupted all around them. Kal threw his hands over his face, and everything went black.

Kal's eyes flitted open. It was dark. Something very hard lay behind his head and against his back. He craned his head up and pain shot through his forehead.

He slowly pulled himself upward with a groan and put a hand on his head.

Tria?

Yeah, Kal. I'm here. I'm not feeling so hot either.

Kal reached for his pad and nearly seized up when he didn't find it at his side. He grasped about the ground, his arms brushing through paper and plastic. To his relief, his hands contacted the sleek metal of his pad, and he grabbed it up.

He took a deep breath. His headache was, thankfully, subsiding. A narrow slit of sunlight shone down from between the two tall buildings on either side of him. He sat in an alley, filled with garbage cans and dumpsters. The air reeked of decay.

Kal activated the pad, and much to his relief, it still worked.

Tria shimmered into view beside him, his hand against his forehead. "Where are we? What happened to the bubble?"

Kal shook his head. He was still looking over the interface, trying to figure it out himself.

"Look." Kal pointed at the display. "When we tried to send a message, it activated a program that wiped all the communication software. Some of the code in the nodes depends on the communication libraries, so when the comm stuff went, the nodes started throwing up errors. If I had to guess… I mean, the safeties would probably make the bubble dissolve onto the nearest universe…"

Tria and Kal's eyes both widened.

"You had us hovering over Earth!" Tria stumbled backward as he stood up, gazing around.

"Tria, if this were Earth, I'd be coughing my way to comatose right now. And look at this," Kal swept his hand around the alley. "Earth doesn't have garbage to collect. Nanites recycle everything."

"So, where are we?"

"Good question." Kal pulled up his grid as he stood.

"It says we're on Earth," Tria pointed to the little blue light that represented their current position.

Indeed, it hovered over Earth.

A wave of realization passed over Kal. He shook his head and chuckled. "I think I know what happened, Tria. Watch."

Kal magnified the view of the grid. The points of light stayed the same size but moved further apart, disappearing along the periphery of the interface. As Kal pulled, the point of light representing their current metaxic location moved ever so slightly away from Earth. They were on a realm very, very close to Earth, but not Earth. Its name populated on the display before them: Irth.

Tria turned to him wide-eyed. "A carbon copy?"

Kal nodded. "By definition, it would have to be pretty closely aligned with Earth's history. About one thousand years' divergence, give or take. Obviously, they haven't developed nanotechnology. Either that, or they don't employ it."

"Maybe they want to disassemble anyone who uses nanotech. This is still an alternate world, Kal. No guarantees that their culture is like Earth's at all." Tria turned off his hologram. *I'm going to fix up the codebase. I want to be able to get away from this place. I'd ask you to stay in this alley if I thought it would do any good. I guess you're going to go explore. Just* please *try to stay out of trouble. Please.*

Kal couldn't help but smirk. *I promise, Tria.*

Tria made a snorting sound in his mind, and Kal chuckled.

He gazed out toward the intersection before him. He could see the train line in the street ahead. Even through the slit in the alley entrance, it looked a lot like the one he remembered from his home. He poked around at his pad a bit, making sure the nanites had a decent felicity rating for this world, which they did. Not only had they been busy even while he'd been unconscious, but the language spoken here was so close to English that they'd completed a translation matrix in record time.

Kal built himself an appropriate backpack, smiled at the familiarity of its texture and materials, stashed his pad inside it, and strode out of the alley.

Kal marveled at the streets. The style of the architecture was all the same as home, all post-Collapse facades. Large parts of Chicago had been rebuilt in the early twenty-second century, and it had been a very long time since he'd seen the glass and metal arranged in this configuration. The streets were busy with people. There were no cars, and the modern high-speed train zipped along the elevated tracks above his head at frequent intervals.

He was so caught up in the sights that he didn't realize he'd been headed toward the Art Institute until he stood just across the street from it. The real Art Institute! Not the brain of cybernetic organism, not a bauble in a jungle tree, but the actual thing.

Not quite yours, Tria reminded him.

Killjoy.

Kal walked through New Millennium Park, then backtracked to Michigan Avenue and walked up it until he reached the canal. He turned right and found Navy Pier exactly as he had remembered it as a child, except of course as an adult everything seemed proportionally smaller. Still, he walked the long, lakeside arcade and got lunch from a hotdog stand in the lakeside plaza near the Ferris wheel. No money, just like Earth.

The lack of nanotechnology created certain disparities that were hard to ignore. There were trash cans for one thing, and the street lights, which on Earth were powered by nanotech lumens, were glass bulbs here. But in terms of mood, Irth felt just like home.

Fashion seemed a dead match for Earth, with other young men wearing t-shirts and jeans, just like himself. Arcade goers operated computer pads with holographic interfaces. Children played in the plaza as the water lapped up against the pier.

Kal...

Oh, Tria, isn't it wonderful? This is so much like home! A home with no nanites. A place I could belong!

Kal, I've noticed something in their language.

What's that?

Well, they're not speaking Earth English at all. Besides the surface similarities, it's got very different grammar. Also, I've found some derogatory words... a lot of them.

Geez, Tria, I didn't know you were such a prude.

Kal rolled his eyes and watched a small boy carry an ice cream cone through the plaza alongside his mother and father. The boy gazed about with wide, happy eyes.

Fine, Kal. Have you been paying attention to anything here besides architecture and technology and clothing?

What are you getting at, Tria?

How many same-sex couples have you seen since you got here?

Kal looked around the crowded plaza, paying attention to couples for the first time. Everywhere he looked, there were husbands and wives, boyfriends and girlfriends. Couplings of the kind Kal would be interested in were conspicuously absent.

You mean they still have homophobia? Like the twentieth century on Earth?

I can't tell you exactly how bad it is, just that this lexicon seems to have an awful lot of words with a negative connotation for gay people. In fact, I can't find any words for gay people that aren't *derogatory.*

Kal leaned back on the bench and crossed his arms. Was this a mild form of culturally accepted bigotry, or were they interested in purges and eradication? Were genetic scans and gulags just around the corner?

How are the nodes? Kal asked.

Fixed. I sent a few nanites into the metaxia and back, and they seem to be working fine.

Kal felt cheated. Even if not exactly his home, it had seemed the kind of home he'd wanted. An Earth that was just like his own, sans nanotechnology. No nanogenic radiation to make him ill.

He sighed.

Okay, Kal thought. *I'll go find an alley. Let's get back to the metaxia.*

Um, Kal.

Yeah?

I feel bad even mentioning this, especially knowing how dangerous this world might be. I'd totally understand if you don't want to go explore it.

What did you find?

There's something else about the lexicon. A huge number of words related to genetic engineering and cloning. There's even the word 'psychorelocation.' It means moving a mind from one physical organism to another.

So they have the technology both to build you a body and move you into it?

Yeah, I think so.

Whenever he had visited an Earth inhabited by humans, Kal's trick of finding the library had served him well. Irth was no different. He hadn't even had to ask directions. The Chicago Public Library stood on State Street and Congress Parkway, just where he'd left it. Irth's was just like modern Earth's: a tall spire of glistening glass, twisting as it climbed, Chicago's new signature style.

Amongst its shelves, he searched Irth's recent history, peeling away the thin veneer hiding the differences between this reality and his real home. The crucial difference turned out to be something called Dogma, which had usurped and supplanted the Western religions of Judaism, Christianity and Islam in the early eighteenth century, the high point of the Enlightenment. It could not be called a religion since it had no social institutions, no deities, and no mythology. It was merely a list of rules for society, just under one hundred in all.

Flipping through Dogma's pages, Kal found the source of their persistent homophobia: item number seventy-one, 'a man shall engage in sexual activities only with a woman, and a woman shall engage in sexual activities only with a man.'

The desire to remove religion's toxic social institutions made a certain kind of sense to Kal, but he had a hard time reconciling that the people of Irth hadn't also realized the folly of supplanting one arbitrary list of rules with another. Number seventy-one wasn't the only strange one. Number thirty-five was 'humans shall not imitate the behavior of animals.' Or number sixteen, 'one shall not jump down from any place higher than eight meters from the ground.' Or number eighty-two, 'no person selling wares may display their prices visually.'

He and Tria shared a laugh, thinking of what retail must have been like before they'd gotten rid of money.

Though Dogma seemed at least open to *additions.* Number ninety-one had been added only a century ago: 'robotic and computer components smaller than one micrometer square are forbidden.'

You know, Kal, Tria thought. *I'll bet a lot of these rules aren't even followed today. I mean, look at this one. 'No eating squash on alternating Wednesdays and Fridays.'*

I know, it's just ridiculous, right? Their legal system can't possibly enforce these... can they?

Kal searched another two floors until he found the legal history section. First, he looked up crimes pertaining to sexual acts. Fortunately, it seemed that it hadn't been illegal to *be* gay in the PanAtlantic Union for the last hundred and fifty years. The most common legal events concerning homosexuality were divorce hearings where it came out that one partner or the other had been having same-sex encounters on the side. There were laws preventing same-sex couples from entering into legal marriage, which Kal balked at. The last of those had been abolished from Earth's remaining countries just before he'd been born.

He found no evidence of anything like forced extermination. And apparently a crusade to end so-called "heteronormalization rehab" half a century ago had been successful.

Kal closed the last of the enormous legal tomes, closed out the interfaces of the three library pads, leaned back, and breathed a sigh of relief.

It's late, Tria thought.

Yeah, let's get going.

Kal gathered up all the books and computers and dumped them onto the nearest reshelving cart. He went to the restroom for privacy and had his nanites forge him some appropriate identification.

He then went to the front desk, asked a librarian about youth hostels, and she directed him instead to a hotel.

He lay on the bed and looked at the ceiling, intermittently gazing out his twentieth-story window at Chicago. It looked so much like his. It was hard for him to believe that culturally they were so different. He wanted to believe that they would embrace him with open arms. Maybe he could be part of gay rights activism on Irth, like the brave individuals of the twentieth and twenty-first centuries on Earth he'd read about in his history books.

Tria's hologram activated, and he sat down on a chair next to the bed.

"Did you find out how to build a body?" Kal asked.

Tria nodded.

"No go?"

Tria's lips quivered, and he looked at the wall.

"You'd need at least an undergraduate degree in biology to qualify for an internship that will lead to a job in the biomedical facilities where they do psychorelocation."

Kal thought about that a moment. There were a lot of documents his nanites could help him fake, but at eighteen years old and without much knowledge of biomedical technology, he'd have a hard time convincing any facility that a nanite-constructed undergraduate degree was real. It was that, or use his nanites to do some terrifically unethical things with Irth technology.

An idea occurred to him, and Kal's face lit up. "Tria, I could just go to college! I'm the right age for that, right?"

"Well, yeah, but…" Tria looked out the window.

"What's the problem?"

"Well, let's see." Tria began counting on fingers. "You're being chased by a psychopath. The cats need feeding. You still need to help Jeikl take Gelkur refugees to Ydora. And mostly…" Tria paused and looked at the floor, tapping his foot. "I can't ask you to do that for me. I don't want to live in a place like this for, what, seven or eight years? And I can't imagine it will be good for you either."

Kal crossed his arms. "First, we haven't seen evidence of that psychopath in months, and we still have no idea how to track him. Second, I can still feed the cats and help Jeikl with Irth as my home base. And you don't know what it will be like. College is supposed to be the best time of your life! This is a singular opportunity."

Tria shot him a look. "I think you're getting in over your head. Again."

"I can't believe you of all people are urging me to leave this place."

Tria put his hands on his hips and took a step closer to Kal, eyeing him suspiciously. "I know what's in your head."

"What?"

"In your mind, you've got yourself joining some kind of gay rights activist group. Then you'll meet some sexy swimmer stud, who will sweep you off your feet, and you'll both ride the waves of social change into a prosperous Irth future."

Kal grinned and looked guiltily at the ceiling.

Tria shrugged his shoulders, shook his head, and stared out the window again. He turned to face Kal. "You won't ever be happy here."

"Maybe that's true, maybe it's not. But don't I have to try? I promised I'd help you! You deserve a normal life just as much as me."

"I don't want my normal life at the expense of yours."

"And if this is something that I want to do?"

Tria gulped, then nodded weakly.

"Alright then," Kal said. "I guess I need to find a college."

After another day of research, Kal discovered that Seton College in the north Chicago suburbs had excellent undergraduate programs in both biochemistry and psychology. After a few interviews with the counselors, he handed over his forged documents, including ID, high school diploma, and documents showing his parents to be professors on sabbatical in Africa. Not long afterward, the admissions department accepted him into the class of 2182, on the condition that he worked hard to catch up on the month he'd missed.

The lounge of Seton's admissions office had a nineteenth century English feel to it. Kal sank into a large armchair with a huge cushioned back that rose up over head. He passed the time talking to Tria in his mind and tinkering with his pad.

"You must be Kal."

Kal looked up. A young man stood over his chair, probably a sophomore or junior. He had wispy, brown hair, broad shoulders and a strong chest that showed through his tight T-shirt. Kal hesitated a moment, just looking, then stood up and shook the young man's outstretched hand. He couldn't help but let his gaze linger, just a bit.

"I'm Mark."

Kal's smile fell when he heard the trepidation and unease in Mark's voice and felt the handshake pull away too soon. Mark's awkwardness and disapproval bowled through Kal, taking him aback. None of his peers from Earth had reacted this way upon meeting him.

Mark produced a pad from a bag and shoved it towards Kal. Kal took it meekly and turned it on. A map of the campus burst from its surface.

"Come on, I'll show you around." Mark strode out the door of the admissions office, and Kal followed.

Mark talked about nothing but the campus the entire time. He took Kal through the student center, with its mail room, cafeteria and bookstore. Mark took him back outside, and they passed the humanities building, the library, the biotech building and the computer science building. The library and biotech building in particular were brand new, all pristine stone and metal and glass. The older buildings appeared well-maintained, not to be outdone by their newer counterparts.

"You have a major in mind yet?" Mark asked.

"Biology and Psychology. Dual major. How about you?"

Kal watched Mark tense up at the question. What was up with this guy? Had Kal said or done something wrong?

"Computer science."

"Cool. I was hoping to take some comp sci if I have time."

"And this over here is called the slough," Mark said, pointing to a small, brownish lake, butting up against the path they were following.

"The map just says 'pond'," Kal said.

"Yeah, but everyone calls it the slough."

Kal looked at the water, dead and still, and agreed that the name seemed fitting. It sat in stark contrast to the lawns and plazas and modern buildings, a festering blemish on an otherwise well-kept campus.

They walked the length of the slough and began climbing a hill at its end. At the top, they passed through a cluster of townhouses.

"Once you're a junior, you can live in one of these or off-campus if you want," Mark said.

Beyond the townhouses, they passed into a large grassy plaza. Two very long buildings wrapped around it, nearly a complete hexagon, broken only by the concrete path running directly through the middle of them, dividing the structure in two.

"That's Easterlin," Mark pointed to his left. "And that's Westerlin, where your dorm is."

Beyond the plaza, Kal's eyes fixated on a group of about a dozen guys playing football shirtless in the field beyond the dorms. Kal's attention shot to Mark, whose face was twisted up in a glaring scowl. Kal's bemused smile fell to a frown.

"You going to come see your dorm room or what?" Mark sneered.

A wave of emotions rushed through Kal. He wasn't used to this kind of treatment at all. He realized he was looking at the ground, and decided he didn't like that he was doing that, so he turned his head up and met Mark's gaze.

"Yeah, I'm coming."

They walked into Westerlin through a set of glass double doors and passed through a series of lounges. Students sat about in chairs and sofas, chatting, guys and girls both. Some played board games together while others studied. Another group was shooting pool at the far end of one room. He and Mark passed all of them, then entered a long hallway lined with doors. Each door was numbered, starting at 100 and climbing steadily higher.

"This is Naseth wing," Mark said.

He led Kal to door number 116, near the end of the hall, and they stopped.

Mark knocked.

The door opened, and a young man appeared. The main lights were off in the room, and he glared out of the darkness at them through red, bleary eyes. He'd clearly been sleeping, although it was past ten. He wore nothing but track pants. He was very skinny, almost no muscle on him at all.

The smell of marijuana blasted into Kal's nostrils, and it was everything he could do not to pinch his nose.

"This is your new roommate, Kal," Mark said, then turned to the roommate. "They called and told you I was coming, right?"

"Mmm," the young man nodded. "I'm Sten."

"Kal." He shook Sten's droopy hand.

Before Kal could thank Mark for the tour, however glibly, he realized that Mark was already striding down the hallway, away from them both. Kal couldn't help but check out Mark from behind as he walked away. As much as he'd hated how Mark had treated him, he couldn't pull his eyes away. Kal grimaced, not enjoying the unusual mix of attraction and revulsion one bit.

Sten had already returned to the room's interior and lay down on his bed. Clothes, books, a pad, papers, even bits of food littered the room. Sten's chest of drawers sat half open, tufts of clothes protruding. Lining the walls on Sten's half of the room were pictures of scantily clad and nude women, illuminated green and blue by a pair of lava lamps atop Sten's desk.

"Make yourself at home," Sten said.

"Thanks. I'll do that." Kal threw his backpack down on the floor next to his bed.

Kal decided to put the events of the day behind him. He made his bed and hopped into it, trying his best to ignore the smell of pot that permeated the room. He considered asking Sten if it was alright to open the window, but decided against it. Ruffle as few feathers as possible, he thought.

He crawled into bed and pulled out the college-issued pad Mark had given him. He was going to have quite a first day. Psychology 101 at 9AM, Introduction to Biology at 10:30 and English Writing after lunch. He pulled up the holographic map of the campus and cross-referenced his course schedule. Three buildings in close proximity to one another glowed green, and Kal committed them to memory.

He smiled. Mark and Sten might be gruff and off-putting, but that wouldn't be true of all students. He'd make friends here soon, just like he had at home. Socializing had always come easy to him, and he was confident that he'd build a group of confidantes before long. Just like Earth.

His eyes lit up at his next thought. He'd missed one element of his home for so long. After four years and seven months of swimming alone in Felis's Lake Michigan, he'd finally be able to join a swim team. Kal pulled up the Seton College Swim Team web page, found the coach's email and let him know that Kal would be coming to practice the next morning, bright and early at 5AM. Kal couldn't wait.

He turned when he heard a clicking sound, and furrowed his brow as he watched Sten use an antique lighter to ignite the joint stuck between his lips. Kal reminded himself that there was no nanotechnology here and that such a lighter might not be an antique.

"Want some?" Sten asked.

"No thanks," Kal said. "I'm going to swim practice tomorrow."

"Swim practice?" Sten raised an eyebrow. "Are you sure *you* want to be on the swim team?"

"Yeah..." Kal replied. "What do you mean? Is there something wrong with the swim team?"

"No, nothing wrong with them. I mean, don't get me wrong, I don't mind sharing a room with you so long as I don't get any midnight surprises, but the swim team guys... they won't be so—"

"What the hell are you talking about?!"

"Forget it." Sten exhaled smoke upward, and it clouded on the ceiling.

Tria, Kal thought, *please tell me there's a Dogma rule against—*

Nope, Tria thought. *Dogma's perfectly cool with marijuana. So's your beloved PanAtlantic Union, by the way.*

In college dorms, even?

That one I can't answer. You only have the most basic info about Illinois colleges and universities in your pad.

Kal frowned and turned back to his college-issued pad. He downloaded all his textbooks, course syllabi, and decided to read the rest of the evening, doing his best to ignore the smell until his eyes grew heavy, and he fell asleep.

Kal's pad woke him at 4:30 the next morning, much to Sten's obvious discontent. He stirred in his bed, pulling his pillow over his head.

Kal put on his racing suit, a pair of sweat pants, and a Seton College hoodie he'd picked up from the student center the day before.

He made sure Sten wasn't looking, then pulled out his own pad and made it invisible. He slid it into his backpack very quietly, watching Sten, then pulled it over his shoulder and left the dorm.

The mornings were only just becoming brisker. The Midwest's stiflingly hot and humid summer was giving way to fall, which would persist for only a couple of weeks, the whole of October if they were lucky, before giving way to five months of frigid winter.

Kal walked down the hill past the slough, back the same way Mark had taken him the previous afternoon. The athletic building lay clear on the other side of the campus, beyond the academic buildings, the student center, and even the soccer field.

When he reached the student center, Kal noticed a figure rounding the bend, not far in front of him. He had on sweat pants and a jacket as well, but Kal recognized that physique. It had intrigued him yesterday as well. Where was Mark going at this hour?

Mark turned down a concrete staircase leading to the base of the soccer field.

Okay, so maybe he was going to another morning sport. Or maybe he just had a girlfriend off campus and was coming home.

Two more guys approached from across the field, and greeted Mark, joining him.

The three of them rounded the field, heading directly for the athletic center.

Let them be going to lift weights, racquetball, basketball, anything except the swim team, Kal thought.

They entered the athletic center through large, metal doors. Kal approached and followed them inside.

The athletic center was huge. Windows in the lobby overlooked the pool, where a handful of swim team members were already doing laps. His adrenaline rushed at the sight. An actual pool where he could do flip turns! He hoped his form hadn't gotten rusty.

Kal found the sign pointing to the locker rooms, descended a flight of stairs, and found a pair of doors. He opened the one clearly marked for men. The voices of other swim team members resounded as he entered, then came to an abrupt halt as he rounded the concrete divider and entered the locker room proper. Kal gulped, and Sten's warning came rushing back to him all at once.

"Hi," Kal tried.

One young man scrambled for a towel and wrapped it furtively around his waist. He turned his back to Kal and proceeded to put his suit on underneath it. Others stopped what they were doing and just stood, scowling at him.

Mark stood in a corner, his glare malevolent.

Kal bit his lip, turned, and exited the locker room. He wandered the lower floor until he found the coach's office. The room, windowed on all sides, had one door leading into it from the hallway, and another leading out into the pool.

Kal knocked on the exterior door.

An elderly man, probably approaching his seventies, opened it and looked down at Kal.

"Hi. My name's Kal Anders. Are you Coach Strating?"

Kal extended his hand, and the coach shuffled his pad under his arm before shaking it. "Got your email. Welcome to Seton."

"Thank you."

"You have swim experience?"

"Nearly every day of my life for the last ten years. I've been ocean swimming for the last four, so my flip turns might be rusty, but I'm confident I can get caught up soon."

"Good." Coach Strating turned to his desk and began tinkering with his pad.

Kal took a step into the office. "Coach, I'm afraid I'm having a problem with the team."

"Oh?"

"I'm getting a lot of hostility from them. All I did was walk into the locker room and say 'hi.'"

The Coach looked up, his eyes catching Kal's. "You don't want hostility? Don't provoke them."

"Excuse me?"

"You think I can't tell?"

"Tell *what* exactly?"

The Coach caught his face in half a sneer, then composed himself. "We have your kind on the team. It's simple. You're welcome to practice with us, to go to meets, and I'll keep you perfectly safe so long as you don't give your teammates any excuses. Don't touch them or look at them, and we won't have any problems."

Now it was Kal's turn to sneer. He marched out of the office and the sports complex, all the way home to his reeking dorm room. Through watery eyes, he composed a letter of complaint to the dean of the college about the swim coach and threw himself into bed.

He lay in silence, punctuated only by the occasional snore from Sten, until eight, when he dragged himself away to the cafeteria to get breakfast before his first class.

Kal arrived in the cafeteria early. Only two pairs of students sat eating. As the room filled up, the other students sat in the most fascinating configuration. It was barely perceptible at first, but by the time he was finishing his cereal, a pattern had clearly formed. Each new person or group was sitting as far from Kal as humanly possible. He found himself at the center of an ever-shrinking circle of empty seats.

What the hell was this? He looked at his clothes and his backpack and shook his head. There was nothing external to distinguish him from the other students. What was it then? Some behaviors or mannerisms, maybe? He'd never given thought to such things before. And as fascinating as this phenomenon was sociologically, Kal didn't enjoy being at the receiving end of this particular manifestation of Irth's bigotry.

He finished up his breakfast as quickly as he could, grabbed up his backpack and rushed to his first class, Psychology 101.

He found the building without trouble, as well as the classroom. He arrived early, taking the first seat, and quite happily busied himself with catching up on the previous month's readings until he noticed the same pattern of seat-taking in the cafeteria recurring as the classroom filled.

He rolled his eyes and sighed in exasperation. All the motivation and excitement he might have had for the material drained out of him. He jabbed at the 'off' hologram on his pad and put his head in his hands.

The professor entered and began his lecture, ignoring Kal and the small circle of empty chairs around him.

Kal, Tria thought.

Yeah?

C'mon. Let's leave. You don't need to put up with eight more years of this.

I suppose you're right.

"You're late, Ms. Knutsen," the professor said.

A young woman with short, brown hair strode gracefully into the classroom. She eyed the small circle of empty seats around Kal, rolled her eyes, then glared at her classmates. She very purposely sat herself down next to Kal, made direct eye contact with him, smiled, and turned on her pad.

Interesting, Kal thought.

Tria retorted with a mental sigh.

Kal could barely pay attention to the psychology lecture, his mind rumbling with possibilities about who this 'Ms. Knutsen' could be and what made her tick. She must be aware of the social anathema Kal's mere being invoked, but she didn't seem to care.

"Hi," she said.

Kal perked to attention. Lost in thought, he hadn't realized that the fifty minutes of class had already elapsed. The others students were already filtering out of the classroom.

"Hi. I'm Kal."

"I'm Vivian."

A passing student glared at them and nodded to his friends. "Look at that. Queen of the fags found a new homo friend."

Vivian turned to him. "Stuff it, asshole."

He and his friends laughed with one another as they left. Kal frowned, watching them go.

"Hey," Vivian said, looking him in the eyes. "Believe it or not, there are lots of people on campus just like you. You're not alone."

Kal blinked at her. He had never thought otherwise. Was he supposed to believe that other gay people didn't exist or something?

"I know," he said, a bewildered expression surely plastered across his face.

"You... know?"

"Yeah. I mean, of course there are other gay people. What I can't fathom is why it matters when people decide where to sit down, or who's swimming next to them."

"Swim?" Vivian's eyes perked up. "You mean the swim team?"

"Well, I tried to go this morning, but the guys in the locker room were so horrible, that—"

Vivian began nodding her head, like she'd heard all this before. "Alan and Ben are on the swim team."

"Alan and Ben?"

"Two of my friends in the Seton LGBT Alliance."

"LGBT?"

"Lesbian, Gay, Bisexual and Transgender."

Kal blinked. "We have an alliance? Like some kind of political entity?"

Vivian laughed. "No, nothing that grand, I'm afraid. It's a kind of social group. For LGBT people and their allies. A safe place where everyone can be themselves."

Kal smiled. "I think I'd like to go."

Vivian extended her hand, and Kal shook it.

"But first," Kal said, "tell me more about how Alan and Ben actually manage to be on the swim team."

"They arrive and leave before the other guys."

Kal frowned. "That doesn't seem right."

"It's not," Vivian said. "But at least Strating is better than the last coach. That guy wouldn't even let them on the team. And they tell me they're not allowed to look at the straight guys. Always at the time clock or down their lane."

"*Their* lane?"

Vivian nodded sadly. "Coach Strating thinks he's doing them a favor. He wants them on the team for their contribution to the meets, but he'll only protect them from just enough harassment that they'll be able to keep swimming. Alan and Ben protect each other. I'm sure they'd love to have you go with them. Safety in numbers."

Kal nodded. "I think I'd like that."

"What's your next class?"

Kal pulled up his pad. "Biology."

"I have German next. You want to meet for lunch? I can text Ben and

Alan and see if they want to come."

"Sure," Kal beamed.

"See you then." Vivian left the classroom.

See? Kal thought to Tria.

Tria scoffed.

Kal followed Vivian out of the room and exited the social sciences building. They parted ways, heading for opposite ends of the campus. It was a warm day, but windy. Light danced through the branches of trees, their leaves just beginning to turn yellow and orange and red.

This place isn't all bad, Kal thought. *And it looks like I've found a way to be on the swim team after all. And an LGBT Alliance! This is perfect. I'll join this world's freedom fighters and push for social change. I'll bet some of them are cute, too.*

Tria thought nothing in response. His presence merely flitted away, and Kal frowned in irritation. Couldn't Tria understand that Kal was doing this for him?

Kal entered the biosciences building and sat down, resuming the catch up on his studies. The students filed into the classroom, and Kal did his best to ignore their encircling behavior.

After class was over, he checked his pad and found a message from Vivian. He read it over, then proceeded to the main cafeteria, where he spotted her, accompanied by a blond-haired guy in a T-shirt and shorts, and another with dark skin and black, curly hair, who fondly reminded him of Vik.

"Kal," Vivian stood up and gestured to the blonde-haired boy, "this is Ben." Then to the other, "And this is Alan."

Kal smiled and shook their hands, then took a seat.

"I heard you guys are on the swim team."

They nodded their heads, less enthusiastically than Kal had expected. He received only the vague hint of a smile.

"Vivian told me that if I joined the swim team, I'd be swimming with you guys."

"He's legit?" Ben said to Vivian.

"Excuse me," Kal said, directly to Ben. "What does that mean?"

Ben raised an eyebrow, almost menacingly.

Alan turned to him. "Forgive my bluntness, by why don't you try to pass?"

Kal gazed back in appalled horror.

"Alan!" Vivian's expression fell.

"Well," Ben said. "Can you really blame us? Remember Greg?"

"Who's Greg?" Kal tried, grasping at straws to understand how he'd managed to derail this discussion.

Alan ignored him, continuing to direct the conversation at Vivian. "I don't tolerate that asshole coach and the rest of the team so I can be turned around and stabbed in the back by a poser."

Kal took a deep breath. "Someone explain 'pass' to me. Please."

"If you wanted to," Ben said. "You could successfully pretend to be straight."

"Why the *hell* would I do that?" Kal said, then looked around at the rest of the cafeteria. He gulped. Now that he thought of it, trying to 'pass' might actually be less painful than being genuinely himself in this place.

Kal's countenance fell. "If it sucks so much being on the team, why do you bother?"

Now it was Alan's turn to frown. He took a deep breath, and turned to Kal, his volume low and face solemn. "My parents started me swimming when I was five, and I loved it. They couldn't keep me out of the water. I swam, and swam, and swam. I asked them about the swim team and when I got older, I joined. First grade, second grade, third grade, those were all fine. In fourth grade, the torment began. But I persisted. I wanted to keep swimming.

"One day, in sixth grade, I was practicing my dives in the deep end. I would dive in, swim underwater to the ladder, climb it, get out of the pool, and repeat.

"After one dive, I had just grabbed the ladder, some three meters beneath the surface, when I felt something heavy hit me on the head. I felt dizzy and disoriented. I managed to climb out of the pool, and three girls were standing with crossed arms. I asked what had happened, and they just scowled back. I looked down into the pool and saw an unopened can of soda lying on its floor. I reached up, touched my forehead, and brought back a hand covered in blood.

"And then, I'll never forget this, one of the girls looked at me and said, 'oops.' Just 'oops.'

"They laughed at the blood streaming down my head, and I called out to the coach. She walked away from me. I chased her halfway around the pool shouting to her that I was bleeding out of my head. Finally, I caught her, grabbed her arm, and shouted in her face that I was bleeding *from my head.*

"She shrugged and told me to walk myself into her office. Where the first aid kit was.

"I ended up needing six stitches. When I asked the coach what would happen to the three girls, she said, simply: 'Nothing. We can't make up special rules just to suit one person's whims.'

"That was the day I quit the swim team. I didn't swim a day in junior high or high school. When I got to college, I heard about Coach Strating's willingness to let us join the team, to keep us safe enough that we could contribute to the team's meet scores. And I decided I'd rather put up with his bullshit than never swim again for the rest of my life."

Kal realized that he was staring at the curved scar across Alan's forehead, and he immediately looked down into his eyes. He took a deep breath. "I'm not out to hurt anyone, or betray anyone. I'm not interested in 'passing' either. I just want to swim."

Ben and Alan shared a look, then nodded approvingly at Kal. Apparently, he was in. Tentatively.

"Lunch?" Ben asked casually, and Kal balked. Was this story of Alan's *common?* It was almost as though Ben had heard it more than once already.

Alan nodded.

Kal couldn't believe them. Alan and Ben just got up and took their place in the line leading into the cafeteria kitchen. Kal gawked at Vivian, who smiled weakly, and shrugged.

She stood up too, and he followed her into the lunch line in a daze. Ben and Alan were talking about the first meet of the year, which was coming up in a month or so, and whether or not they'd be ready, but their conversation seemed as though it was happening a million miles away from him.

He couldn't get Alan's story out of his mind. Missed all of junior high… and high school. Well, Kal was familiar with that. But only because he'd been on an alternate Earth. And he'd had his ocean. And his cats. His missed them now. He'd go and feed them as soon his afternoon class was over.

"Meet us tomorrow at four in front of Westerlin," Ben said.

"Sure," Kal said, still in a daze.

"Sorry. That could have gone better," Vivian said. "You might see some more suspicion in the LGBT Alliance at first. Some new members have turned out to be Dogma evangelists in disguise. It's rough for morale when one of those slips through."

She walked Kal back to his writing class, then later back to Westerlin.

"Oh, and, um," Vivian said as they approached his dorm. "Do you smoke pot? You know that can't be good for swimming, right?"

Kal laughed and explained his roommate situation.

When he got back to his room, Sten wasn't there. Kal opened a window, then crashed onto his bed and pulled up his school pad.

Hey, Tria thought.

Hey, Kal thought back.

This isn't a healthy place, Kal.

Alan survived his high school and he swims. I can survive college and an internship to get you your body.

I don't want you to do this to yourself.

I can't leave when I know the answer is here—the thing I promised I'd do for you. It's here, Tria!

Silence. Tria's consciousness flitted away without another word.

Kal rubbed his hands across his face. Maybe, with the way they treated him here, it wouldn't be so unethical to steal their technology after all. He laughed a little, realizing how ridiculous that was.

Sitting up in bed, he turned on his pad, intending to do his homework. He was surprised to see a new email from the dean, and he opened it.

Dear Kal Anders,

Thank you for taking the time to communicate your concerns about Coach Strating to me.

I have carefully considered the information you have provided, communicated your concerns to Coach Strating, and I can assure you that he is acting in the best interests of his team.

Seton College has a vested interest in recruiting all capable athletes into our diverse athletic programs. We believe that the Seton Col-

*lege Swim Team is a safe and welcoming environment for all students
who wish to participate.*

*Should you have any further concerns, please do not hesitate to
contact me.*

Sincerely,
Dean Hill

He threw his school pad onto the floor, curled up into his bedsheets,
and went to sleep.

∞⌒∞

Kal woke up the next morning at 3:45 to the sound of his alarm. Sten
rustled in his bed. He'd probably only just gotten to sleep.

He put on his swim suit, a pair of sweatpants and a hooded jacket, just
as the previous morning. He pulled on his backpack and walked out of the
eerily silent Westerlin Hall.

Ben and Alan met him at the front of their dormitory, and they began
their walk down the slough path toward the athletic center.

"Where you from, Kal?" Ben asked.

"I grew up in Chicago."

"What part?"

"Logan Square."

"Nice neighborhood," Alan said.

"Thanks. I like it there. How about you guys?"

"Rockford," Ben said.

"Milwaukee," Alan said.

"Was it hard growing up in the city?" Ben asked.

"Not particularly," Kal said. "Should it have been?"

"I've heard some of the Chicago schools are really bad."

Interesting. On Earth, Chicago had the fourth best school system in
the entire PanAtlantic Union, which included not only North America,
but also most of Europe and parts of Northern Africa.

"I don't know about others," Kal said. "But I think my school was
pretty good."

"Well, I'm glad you survived," Ben said.

"We've gotta stick together," Alan said.

"Wait," Kal said. "*Survived?*"

"Don't tell me you haven't heard." Ben said. "How every so often a gay Chicago schools student will get beaten, or worse?"

Kal was feeling lightheaded again, and let Ben and Alan's conversation drift away from him while he lost himself in his own thoughts. Irth seemed to get worse every time Kal thought it couldn't. Perhaps the reason that he had found no legal evidence for his suspicions was that incidents of violence had been quietly swept under the rug. Ignored. It was almost too much.

Alan dropped into an explanation of how lucky Kal was not to have been beaten within inches of his life. By the time they reached the athletic complex, Kal was almost ready to run off to the nearest secluded place he could find and escape to Felis. But thoughts of swimming seduced him inside, and the moment he dove into the water, all of his worries washed away.

Lake Michigan's waves had been fun in their own way, but it was nothing compared to race practice, the kind of zen that could be achieved in a pool that rocked only with the waves of other swimmers, with walls that you could curl up and kick off from in the opposite direction, and time clocks to measure how quickly you'd achieved a sprint, down to the millisecond.

Kal lost himself in the water and the routine, achieving a kind of harmony he hadn't experienced in years. He lost himself in it, forgetting all about Alan's story, the contracting circles of empty desks, and the letter from the dean.

Kal ended a set, stood up, and watched the rest of the swim team filter into the pool. They returned his glance with glares.

Crap.

He turned his eyes back at the holographic time clock hovering above the concrete edge of his lane.

Wait.

He stopped that train of thought, revolted at his behavior. He wasn't allowed to look at other guys?

This was stupid. No, this was beyond stupid. It was obscene. Certainly the straight guys were checking out the girls from time to time, and vice versa. There was nothing wrong with him doing the same. He was perfectly capable of restraining his desires the same as they were capable of restraining theirs.

Kal began his next set fuming and pushed off the wall wrong. It was a lousy start to a lousy set. His trance had been broken.

Immediately upon finishing the last set of their workout, Alan and Ben hurried out of the pool. Kal stood for a moment, befuddled. He didn't dare look, but he could hear the rest of the team still splashing alongside him. He wished he could do some extra sets. It had been common on his old swim team for him to do more exercise than was on the coach's list, to push himself extra hard. But he couldn't do that here. He wanted to avoid confronting the rest of the team in the locker room more than he wanted extra exercise, so he pulled himself up out of the pool as well, and followed Alan and Ben.

He passed through his morning classes as though sleepwalking. He paid attention to the lectures and caught up on past homework between courses. He did his best to ignore the other students. Occasionally, he'd hear broken fragments of conversations as he passed them.

"... fag..."

They spoke the horrible word with extra volume, then swallowed the rest of the sentence, consciously or subconsciously telegraphing their hate, he wasn't sure.

Kal met Vivian for lunch in the cafeteria.

"How's it going?"

She sure was cheery. Kal felt emotionally drained. But famished. He'd missed that part of swimming laps too.

"Fine." He stuffed down a hamburger angrily.

"You don't look fine."

Kal threw his food down onto his tray and finished chewing. "How do people put up with this? All this awful hatred?"

Vivian eyed him. "Where are you really from, Kal?"

Kal sighed. He doubted very much that this world contained any places free of homophobia's reach. "Somewhere very far away. It has to do with my parent's research. Can't really talk about it. I mean, I knew things here were bad, but I had no idea. I mean, that whole thing about not *provoking* other guys on the swim team with my *eyes*, you know what that's all about, right?"

Vivian nodded meekly. "Yes, it's so that the closet cases on the team—sorry, the guys who are just *passing*—can ignore their real feelings."

"Exactly! I mean, I might only be taking psych 101, but you don't have to have a PhD to guess at what kind of emotional disorders could arise if that goes unchecked."

Vivian smirked. "You must have seen some very interesting cultures. You're a conundrum, Kal. Most people your age can't look at things the way you do. I think it'd be good for the group to get to know you, hear about how different things can be."

Kal leaned in and spoke more softly. "Are they all like Alan and Ben? Just kind of... getting by?"

Vivian bunched her lips up and nodded. "Group's tonight, by the way. 7PM in the Easterlin basement."

"Is that safe?"

Vivian smirked. "The Easterlin residence hall manager is an ally. She patrols the first floor herself on meeting nights, paying special attention to the basement entrance."

Kal nodded. "A little kindness goes a long way."

Vivian outright smiled. "I tend to agree."

Kal grinned and realized that he was feeling better. The situation didn't feel so hopeless after all. He finished up lunch and went to his final class refreshed. Afterward, he found a quiet place in the library to study. He'd made good progress on the first few weeks of class he'd missed and was confident he'd be caught up in the next few days.

He kept his eye on the clock, and left when 6:30 rolled around. He exited out into twilight. The days were getting shorter.

Few students meandered about the campus quad. Most had probably already retired to their dorms, engaging in evening extracurriculars or preparing for parties.

Kal yawned. If it weren't for the LGBT group, he'd have gone to bed.

He hurried down the deserted slough path, glancing occasionally at the idle pool of brown water. He heard a crackling from the trees at his right and jumped to attention, scanning the dark hillside.

Taking in his surroundings fully, Kal realized that the slough path did not leave its travelers with many escape options. The slough lay on one side of it and a steep hill covered in trees on the other.

Another snap of twigs.

Kal took off into a sprint.

He felt something hit the back of his head, but only lightly. His au-to-defense nanites buzzed, and he ran faster. A heavy, stone something clattered to the ground behind him. Up the hill he ran, into the West-erlin-Easterlin grove, but he didn't let that slow him down. He ran into Westerlin, careened through the lounges, ignoring the startled looks of other students, ran down his hall and threw open his dorm room door.

Sten and two young women sat in the center of their room around a bong.

Panting and gasping, Kal threw down his backpack, sat on his bed and put his head between his knees.

"Dude?" Sten said, not moving. "Would you mind? You're kind of ruining the mood."

Kal giggled a bit. Then he laughed. He threw up his arms. "I think someone just tried to murder me, Sten!"

"Why would someone do that?" One of the girls asked vapidly.

Kal narrowed his eyes. "I'll give you three guesses."

The three of them turned up their faces in scowls.

"Gross!" the other girl said.

"Why you gotta be this way, Kal?" Sten grabbed up his bong and put it into his backpack.

Kal couldn't believe this. "You're *mad at me* for being the target of a *hate crime?*"

"You know, you could just act normal, not all... you know."

Kal stood up with clenched fists. "It's called 'gay'."

One of the girls shook her head while the other looked to be on the verge of fainting.

"C'mon, ladies." Sten glared at Kal as he escorted his girlfriends out of the dorm room.

Kal punched his bed and exhaled deeply. He considered notifying the authorities about what had happened but decided against it. He remem-bered the email from the dean. The whole system was set up against him. Everywhere he turned, people were disgusted by him and everything he represented. Though laws existed to protect minorities, the writ didn't matter if no one actually enforced it.

He pulled up his pad, his real pad from Earth, and ran the cultural analysis subroutines. There they were, staring him right in the face: the small dip in equitable relations, the spike in sexual repression, and the inordinately high frequency of mental instability among otherwise healthy adults. All just off from baseline.

They'd solved so many other social problems, just like Earth. Why not this one? Why not the one that affected him so acutely?

He looked at the clock. 6:54 PM.

Resolute, Kal got out of bed, concealed his real pad, and stuffed it into his backpack. He strode out into the Westerlin lounge, taking a look around the plaza created by the hexagon of dorms, lit up by the multitude of windows surrounding it.

He strode outside, head held high, across the plaza to Easterlin. He wouldn't cringe or hide. His attackers would have to show their faces in the highly visible quad to get to him, he decided. He passed without incident.

The inside of Easterlin was a bit newer and a little bit cleaner than Westerlin, and it definitely had been designed and built at roughly the same time, a near mirror of his dorm.

Kal walked into the basement, where other students sat in a circle of chairs. Vivian smiled when she saw him. Ben and Alan smiled and nodded to Kal, too.

Kal took a seat, and they began.

"Everyone, this is Kal Anders," Vivian said. "He's starting the semester a bit late and just arrived here."

Friendly smiles erupted around him, the only large group of them he'd seen in—he didn't know how long. Kal smiled back.

Vivian started by encouraging the young man next to her to talk, a meek, timid boy, skinny and with glasses. He had tufts of wiry brown hair and looked as though he might break if you accidentally bumped into him.

He talked about worrying that his parents might find out about his 'problem,' he called it, and pull him out of school for therapy because they 'thought that way.'

The next guy talked about how, when his father had found out he was gay, had kicked him out of the house and told him never to come back.

Another guy's dad had tried to push him off the roof of a building.

A young woman had been torn away from her first love, a girl in her art class, because their relationship had been discovered.

As the other students went on, and Kal heard story after story, he realized there was a very important part of his childhood he'd taken for granted—the ability to live his life as he was, and have society accept all his individual traits as standard or 'normal.' These students were dealing with something wholly new to him—a society that hated a group of its members for *being*. It could not tolerate them as they were. These poor souls were seen by the majority of society as aberrations, inhuman. Their loves and lusts were some kind of toxic fallacy in others' minds, something to be ignored at best and beaten at worst.

Kal realized that everyone was looking at him and that it was his turn. He opened his mouth, but no words came out. What could he say to them? What meaning would his experiences have for them? He had grown up happy, free of oppression. What good would that do?

"I— I don't really know what to say," Kal started. "I've done a lot of traveling, and seen a lot of cultures. I don't have direct experience with the kind of bigotry present in this culture—"

It hit him all at once. That was it. That was his story.

"Let me tell you about this culture I saw once, though. They're in... the jungles of South America. They call themselves the Ydorans."

Kal looked around. Was this acceptable? The other Seton College students leaned in, many had wide eyes. Even the shy kid with the glasses was looking at him with interest.

"So, first of all, they don't wear much. It's really hot there all year round. They wear a little thing around their waists that look like a swim racers and a sash over their chests. Now here's the thing. At first I thought it was that men were supposed to wear the sash over the left shoulder, and women over the right. But then I figured out I had it wrong. It's about sexual orientation. Left shoulder means you're interested in women, and right shoulder means you're interested in guys."

The guy with the glasses adjusted them. "They announce their sexuality to everyone? And that's okay?"

Kal nodded. "Yup."

"Do they have boyfriends and girlfriends? Marriages?"

"Hmm... Boyfriends and girlfriends for sure. I'm not sure about marriages, but I think they do. I'll watch for that the next time I'm there."

"Did you have to wear the same kind of clothes as them?"

Kal smirked. "Yeah."

"Didn't you get eaten alive by bugs?"

"At first, yeah, but they had a kind of lotion that kept the bugs away."

"Lotion? Aren't they primitive?"

"Not exactly. In some ways, you could say that. But they have electricity, medicine, implements for generating light and heat, all of that. They've got different ideas than we do about what constitutes an acceptable application of technology."

This animated the LGBT group even more, and Vivian had to start mediating questions. The mood of the group lightened. Vivian nodded at Kal, a wry smile passing over her face.

Many questions and answers later, Kal gave up the floor and let the young woman beside him take her turn.

He felt as though a great weight had been lifted. Despite everything that had happened that day, he just might make Seton College work after all.

Tria stopped by just one more time, the night of the first LGBT meeting group.

Do you really want to stay here, Kal? Someone's made an attempt on your life.

Didn't you see what happened at the group though, Tria? I can make a difference in their lives. I can help them see that their culture is wrong about them. That it's not their fault for being who they are, because that's what they think. And most importantly, I can help you.

Tria left him alone after that.

Kal fell into a familiar routine. Wake up, swim, classes, sneak away to Felis, feed cats, return to Irth, study, sleep, rinse, repeat. Punctuating his new schedule were weekly trips to Gelkur, usually on the weekend, in order to ferry ValYou refugees away to the Ydorans, who were more than happy to accept Gelkur's huddled masses.

Kal hardly saw Sten at all, except in the morning, asleep in his bed, but when Kal came home, he was consistently greeted by a cloud of marijuana smoke instead.

The few times that Sten was there, they would exchange brief greetings, and that would be all. Sten seemed happy to ignore Kal, and Kal returned the favor. Sten at least respected Kal's swim schedule. He never attempted to party in their dorm room. If Sten had friends in the room when Kal returned home, Sten and his friends invariably left.

Vivian, Alan, and Ben became his surrogate family. They often ate lunch together, and most importantly, Kal never went anywhere after dark without at least one of them by his side. He was never the target of violence again.

October drifted away, and November followed in its wake. With it came a new punctuation to Kal's schedule: the swim meets.

Even at twelve years old, Kal had been thinking toward his future swim career, in junior high, high school and eventually college. He had thought that his friends at twelve would be comrades and allies throughout, at least up through high school. This was nothing at all like that. Instead of comrades, he was surrounded by ferocious beasts, ready to pounce, should Coach Strating rescind his protective ward.

Kal spent the swim meets studying since there was no socializing to be had. He, Ben, and Alan would find a private area with tables and desks and go about their school work, entering the pool only when it was time for their heats.

Not how Kal had imagined swim meets at all.

Just after Thanksgiving vacation, which he spent on Ydora, Kal returned to Irth to discover that Ben had not returned to Seton. Alan refused to talk about it in detail, which only made Kal worry more. He and Alan continued swimming, but when the University of Iowa meet rolled around, Alan declined to go. Alan used his schoolwork as an excuse, but Kal knew that Ben's disappearance had shaken him greatly.

Kal decided to go anyway. So far, the other team members had gone out of their way to ignore him, so long as he followed all of the coach's rules. He'd not heard one epithet the entire time he'd been on the swim team, which was more than he could say for his experiences walking around the Seton College campus.

Despite the team's attitude, the act of swimming was the most gratifying part of his college experience. Kal lost himself in the water and the adrenaline rush of the races. The worst part followed the best. He'd pull himself out of the water after a race and remember the cheers and excitement of swim meets on Earth as he his friends would celebrate their best times and their shared victory. Emerging from the pool after such a heat on Irth, Kal experienced no camaraderie, no excitement. In this, he was still alone.

One morning in late November, Kal climbed into a bus and rode with the rest of the team to Iowa City. He realized then just how much he missed Ben and Alan. They'd been his strongest support network so far. His feelings for them weren't romantic, they were something stronger. Fellow warriors, in a sense, struggling against injustice together, struggling just to be allowed to survive.

The Iowa pool was big, its sporting complex particularly expansive. The splashes and shouts of young men and women echoed from all directions.

The races proceeded.

After coming in third in one heat and fourth in an IM, Kal reported his times to Coach Strating as quickly as he was able, and then ran to his towel and grabbed his backpack from the stands. He threw the towel around his waist and exited the pool area.

Someplace quiet, he thought. *Somewhere I can study.*

He walked through hall after hall of the sports complex trying doors. Every single one was locked.

He'd tug at the handle, and the door wouldn't budge. Over and over.

Two halls later, nearly ready to give up and return to the pool, he pulled at a door, and its handle clicked. Kal stumbled back, then caught himself. He pulled the door all the way open, fumbled for the wall panel, turned on the lights, and looked around the small classroom. It had ten desks for students and one larger desk at the head of them all.

Kal was startled to see Mark sitting atop the teacher's desk, wearing only his racing suit. Kal noticed a towel and Mark's backpack beside the desk.

Mark's face flushed red, and he snarled at Kal.

"Hey, sorry," Kal instinctively looked away. "I was just looking for a place to study."

Mark scoffed.

Kal turned and reached for the door handle.

"No, wait," Mark said.

"Hmm?" Kal turned around, looking at him.

"Lock the door."

"Why?"

"Just do it."

Kal hit the button on the door frame and the panel at the door changed from green to red.

"What are you doing here?" Kal asked.

"Waiting," Mark hopped off the desk and walked toward Kal. There was something new in his eyes, and Kal noticed it between gazing over Mark, his strong chest and beautiful abdominal muscles. Kal had never been allowed to look at him directly until now, and his body was even more amazing than Kal had imagined.

Kal's brain finally shuffled through the hormone surge and the realization hit him. "You were waiting for someone, weren't you? From the Iowa team, right?"

"He's not half as hot as you." Mark pulled Kal's towel off and threw it onto the floor.

Another surge of raw testosterone slammed into Kal's brain, muddling proper thought as Mark ran his fingers down Kal's neck, his chest, down to the string of his racing suit, where he untied it with a simple flick of the wrist. Kal bristled, swimming in an ocean of liquid pleasure, each stroke a wave of euphoria.

"Turn around," Mark said. Kal didn't, so Mark pulled him around and held Kal against his body. He pulled down Kal's suit.

No, Kal heard himself think. The voice in his head sounded distant, drowned out amongst a flood of sensuality.

No, my first time won't— can't be like this.

"NO!" Kal swung around and pushed Mark away.

Mark stumbled backward and scowled, then scrambled to retrieve his suit. "What the hell's wrong with you?"

"What's wrong with *me*? You've been nothing but an asshole to me for two months! Pretending to be straight. *Passing*. And now you want to have sex with me, just like that? Look at yourself! This is romantic to you? An encounter with someone you barely know in some closet of a classroom? You don't even know that guy from the Iowa team at all, do you?"

"This is what we get, Kal. It's this or nothing at all. And I don't know about you, but I'm no monk. Now take your shit, get the hell out of here, and if you breathe a *word* of this to anyone else, I will end you. My family has connections. I know people that can get you arrested. Remember that."

"You're disgusting." Kal put his towel back on, grabbed up his things, slammed at the door panel to unlock it, and ran away as fast as he could.

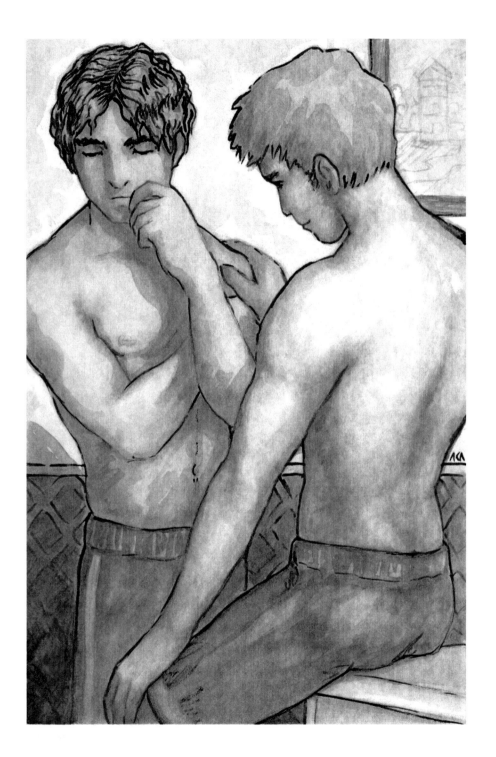

He careened down the hall, half running, half stumbling, not caring where he ended up. He grabbed at locked door handle after locked door handle. Finally, he found an empty bathroom. He secluded himself inside a stall and bawled his eyes out.

Kal? Tria thought. *Stop this. Leave this world, please. I'm worried about you.*

Tria, I need some time. Thank you for coming, but I just need to be alone right now, okay?

Kal felt solemnity from Tria as he left, off in the nanites to wherever it was he went. Those damn nanites. All this technology and he couldn't fix himself or Tria or even Irth society.

This place wasn't and never would be Earth, no matter how hard he tried.

∂❧∂

Kal opened the door to his dorm room slowly. Sten sat in a circle with two girls, all of them with joints hanging out of their mouths.

"Heya, Kal." Sten grinned through his stupor.

"Hi, Sten."

"This is Mary, and this is British—"

"Bridgette," the girl said. Mary giggled.

"This is Bridgette."

"Sten—" Kal tried.

"And I've discovered," Sten rambled on, "that Mary and Bridgette have very open minds. They don't care about Dogma, or politics, or rules, and they want you to join us for a bowl of—"

"Get out," Kal said.

Sten stared at him, stupefied.

"I haven't asked you for a single thing while I've been here," Kal continued. "I haven't bothered you about all my clothes smelling like pot, or about the perpetual heap of garbage on your side of the room, or about how you changed my interface to display naked women on startup—"

"Sten," Mary pushed at Sten's shoulder. "Not nice."

"Was just trying to help him, is all…" Sten mumbled back.

"Now I'm asking," Kal continued. "Give me ten minutes alone in this room."

"Whatever it is that's bothering you, wouldn't it be more fun to chill out together first over a bowl?"

"No. Alone. Now. *Please.*"

Sten scoffed, then motioned his exasperation to Mary and Bridgette, who left the room leaving their bowls of hallucinogens on the floor. The door slammed shut behind them.

Kal sat down on his bed and activated his pad. Tria appeared, sitting across the room from him on Sten's bed. It was good to see him. Kal smiled, but the smile was short-lived.

"I'm sorry, Tria."

"Kal, it's okay."

"No, it's not. You're in this mess because of me. Because I was dicking around on worlds I shouldn't have been. And I've been dicking around even more since then—here, Glinn, Spenfa, and others."

"Kal, you, we, are eighteen. We're human. Remember, I started from you. And I know how I'd feel if our roles were reversed. But Irth is destroying you, Kal. Even worse, it's destroying *us*. We make a good team together, exploring the metaxia, don't you think?"

Kal smiled and nodded. Tria walked to where Kal sat and wrapped his virtual arm around Kal's shoulder.

"We'll fix us both. Somewhere else. Okay?"

"Okay." Kal sniffled.

He picked up his backpack and fired up the metaxic nodes. His hand hesitated over the button. With a strong jab, he pressed it and watched his Irth dorm room fade away into swirling blue.

Ludo

Realm #7298, "Strof"
November 30, 2178

"COME ON, come on."

Kal fidgeted with his pad. Slivers of alternate Chicagos whisked past him. The edge of his bubble rippled, charging through the metaxia as fast as his nanites could take it. He glanced down at the pad interface again, at the red window with the message: 'Felis nanite perimeter breached.' If only the bubble could move faster without tearing apart space and time.

Tria stood beside him, working at his interface. Kal found himself annoyed at Tria's calmness, and reminded himself that he had none of Kal's memories. He did not share Kal's bond with the cats.

An excruciating three minutes later, the bubble finally peeled away. Kal found himself on the beach, and he shivered. The lake lay behind him, a frigid, churning, gray mass. He glanced at the charred remains of his treehouse in the distance. That, at least, though depressing, was just as he'd left it.

"Kal…" Tria pointed to a nearby sand dune. The dust devils were still there, passing over it in successive waves, each tracing out the exact same path.

Dust devils in November? How was that possible?

What had been light indentations had become stark lines in the sand, forming enormous words: 'Hello, Kal.'

The miniature whirlwinds persisted, fortifying the message against the other elements.

Tria pulled up his interface. "There aren't any nanites in the dune or in the air around it, Kal. Those dust devils are just… happening."

Kal pulled up his own interface to confirm Tria's analysis. As he puzzled over this, a gust of cold wind howled across the beach, and Kal pulled up the hood of his jacket.

His eyes went wide with realization. The cats. Where were the cats?

"Daisy? Engrie? Charles?" Kal took off away from the sand and toward the woods. He should have heard their cries by now. Waves of fear rushed through him. He crashed into the underbrush of the forest.

"Jumper? Boson? Max?!" Kal scrambled as quickly as he could through all of their favorite play and rest areas. Tria's hologram flickered in and out of the periphery of the pad's display range as Kal surged through the forest.

A horrible howling erupted. It was all of the cats, the entire pride of fourteen, yowling in pain all at once. Kal stopped only briefly, a wave of anxiety passing over him, and he took off toward their cries.

He rounded a corner and found them. Shock and horror overtook him. All fourteen cats of the pride were jammed into a ball of themselves. They were not piled on top of one another, but genetically fused. Someone had used nanites to splice them into a single organism. Max's head protruded from Higgs's back, while Jumper's rear emerged from Engrie's side.

Kal flew into a blind rage. He whipped out his pad and summoned every last nanite at his disposal. He called up the DNA resequencer, a program whose only acceptable function was correcting genetic damage, and he dropped the pad to the ground. The resequencer interface was enormous, wrapping entirely around the programmer.

His hands raced over the buttons and windows while the cat ball edged toward him, howling.

"It'll be okay guys," Kal called out, tears streaming down his face. "I'll fix this. I can fix this."

"Kal..." Tria reached out toward him.

"Not now!" Kal yelled, and Tria backed away.

After five minutes of operating the resequencer, Kal had isolated Engrie's and Catface's respective genetic profiles. He double-checked his work, and then checked it again, making absolutely sure the code was correct.

He pushed the button.

The ball of cat shimmered, and Engrie and Catface fell away free. They ran and cowered behind the trees, looking back at the blob of their family in fear. They cried out to their imprisoned comrades, and the ball writhed toward them in response.

The work got easier as Kal proceeded. The more cats he separated, the easier each cat's genetic profile was to distinguish. Kal wiped at his face every so often. The ball got smaller. More cats ran free. Finally, he separated Max from Daisy—the last two—and he ran toward Max. Max picked him up and swung him onto Max's back. He scratched Max behind the ears and hugged his neck. Max mewed and purred.

"I'm so sorry, Max. I'm so, so sorry."

Rage coursed through him, stronger than ever, and he struggled to contain it. He reminded himself that hatred and fear, jealousy and revenge, these were the destroyers, the unhealthy emotions that meant the difference between civility and barbarism. But this time his invisible assailant had gone too far. It wasn't a world full of strangers or brand new friends who'd been attacked. It had been his cats.

Kal climbed down Max's side and snatched up his pad.

Tria tapped his foot, his arms crossed, and stared at Kal sternly. "There were coordinates for a realm in the genetic data of the… cats. It's a realm on your grid. 7298. No name."

"Nanogenic radiation…?"

"Off the charts. You'd be unconscious in… fifteen minutes, maybe. Dead in twenty."

"It's an invitation…"

"Kal! Listen to me!" Tria approached and clasped at Kal's shoulders. Kal tried futilely to push Tria's hands away.

"Listen, damn it! This is someone who's impersonated you and framed you for genocide. He made an attempt at another realm but didn't kill anyone, just ruined your date. Then he put a virus in your pad so you couldn't tell anyone on Earth what he's doing, and *then* he genetically violated your cats, but he didn't kill them, Kal!"

"I told you, Tria. Life, liberty and biomaterial integrity! Genetically violating an organism is a worse crime than killing them."

"*Exactly*. Whoever did this isn't out to kill people or destroy societies. It's about *you*. He wants to ruin your adventure. So before you go running off to a death trap world, are you absolutely sure you don't have any idea who's doing this?"

Kal crouched to the ground and put his head in his hands. He mentally ticked off of all the people he knew for the hundredth time. He thought of school, of other students, of teachers, even friends of his parents. He could think of no one. Absolutely no one.

"I really, honestly, don't know," Kal looked up. "I was twelve. My teachers liked me. I wasn't bullied. And I definitely didn't get into fights."

"We can go back to Earth," Tria said. "You'll probably end up in a coma while they figure this out. I'll probably end up in a computer or stuck in nanites or something. It's the safe way out."

"Or we can go to 7298."

They stood in the glade for many long, silent moments. A cold breeze passed through the trees, their branches wiry and bare.

"I'm scared," Tria admitted.

"Me too," Kal said.

Tria slowly nodded his approval.

Kal reinstated the protection field around the cats, whatever good that would do, and he fired up the metaxic nodes.

Clouds churned across a dark sky. Thunder crackled above amidst occasional bursts of lightning. Buildings lined the streets, hulking behemoths, stripped down to their frames.

The surface of this Chicago was covered in a layer of silver goo up to Kal's ankles, a goo of nanites, unimaginable numbers of them. The silver sludge climbed the skeletal pillars of the buildings, creeping and oozing over everything.

Kal recalled the horror stories of what Earth would look like if someone were to remove the auto-replication control algorithms from nanites. Seeing the reality of such an occurrence sent chills up his spine.

He coughed and slammed a fist into his chest. Wasting no time, he began immediately down the street, the silver goo repulsed from his feet as he went. Kal's nanites and the nanites of this world waged a microscopic war all around him. The two sides could spend an eternity disassembling one another given an unlimited supply of light.

"I'm doing what I can." Tria manipulated the interface as they walked, and Kal recognized the holographic windows of medical programs. "I can use your nanites to help relieve the symptoms, but of course, I'm only buying you a few minutes."

"Thanks." Kal scanned the city with his eyes, looking for clues, but all he saw were the desiccated skeletons of the buildings, illuminated intermittently by lightning bursts. Another rumble erupted from the swirling clouds.

Kal quickened his pace, but intersection after intersection yielded no signs of anything but the corpses of buildings and the omnipresent gray goo. He knelt over and hacked again. He took long breaths, struggling to restore his breathing.

"Kal!" Tria said. "Over there. Two blocks away."

Kal ran as fast as he could, but each step seemed to make his chest feel tighter and more constricted.

He reached his destination sweating profusely, and darted around, at first disappointed not to see anything particularly interesting.

A reflection of light caught his eyes. Kal looked at the ground and discovered a pair of nanotech goggles, lying just at the edge of the intersection. They were protected by nanites, too. The sludge maintained its distance from them the same way it did from Kal.

"Oh my..." Kal stumbled back, coughing.

"Goggles?" Tria asked. "What do they mean?"

Kal bit his lip. "I know who those belong to."

West Chicago Regional Swim Club
Earth, 2172

Ludo pulled himself out of the pool. At least, he tried to. He'd watched the other boys push themselves up with both hands, then pull a leg up to get out the rest of the way, but his legs refused to cooperate. He couldn't lift either his right or his left leg high enough. He had to swim to the ladder at the edge of the pool and climb out, and that involved dodging other swimmers.

Ludo gulped. At least there weren't many other swimmers still doing laps today. Most were already in the deep pool doing cannonballs off the high dive.

He ducked under the lane line and passed through the first adjacent lane without any problems, but as he passed through the next, a sharp jab hit his side and he fell into the wall. Another swimmer popped up out of the water.

"I'm really sorry," Ludo said.

"Sorry I hit you," Kal said. "You alright?"

"Yeah! I'm... fine." Ludo started to swim away as fast as he could. His side hurt, actually, but he didn't want to make a big deal out of it.

"Your turn for the inner tube today, right?"

Ludo turned and saw Kal smiling. "Yeah, it is."

"Okay, but cannonballs tomorrow," Kal said, and he took off for another set. Probably doing extra.

It took Ludo more time than the other kids just to finish the basic set. He had, on occasion, cut sets from his routine in order to get out of the pool at the same time as everyone else, instead of twenty minutes later. But today, Coach Judy had told him that he would only be allowed to take his turn using one of the team's six inner tubes if he completed the whole thing. She'd watched him cross each set off his list.

He climbed out of the lap pool and went to the storage closet where they kept the inner tubes. Of course, there was no limit on how many inner tubes the nanites could make, but wastefulness was shunned, and it was agreed that six inner tubes could be used safely in the deep end, and thus they stored exactly six inner tubes in the storage room. Ludo grabbed the last one.

He smiled in delight. It had been over two months since he'd been allowed to use one. The last time his turn had come up, he'd been sick, and before that, he'd not been able to finish his sets. He set the inner tube carefully into the water at the edge of the deep end and climbed slowly into its center.

He pushed off the wall with his feet and let his head fall back. The tube drifted out into the pool. No more exercise. No more strain. Just bliss.

A force from below jolted him from relaxation, and he flew into the pool. He scrambled up to the surface.

"Nick!" he yelled at the boy in his inner tube. "Nick, it's my turn! I finished all my sets."

Nick yawned and stretched, making a show of enjoying himself at Ludo's expense.

Fine, I'll do it to him.

Ludo dove into the water and swam downward as far as he could go. He looked up through his nanotech goggles' air bubbles and sighted his target. He placed his hands above his head and kicked as hard as he could, rushing up toward the surface. His hands crashed into Nick's back, and... Nick didn't budge. Ludo beat at Nick's back with his fists, and still, Nick remained immobile. Ludo screamed underwater in frustration.

He swam to the edge of the pool, climbed out, and pointed at Nick.

"Inner tube thief! And now you've used nanites to stick yourself to it! Coach Judy, Nick's abusing nanites! You're not even supposed to be programming yet, jerkface."

Coach Judy strode toward Ludo. "That's a serious accusation."

She pulled a pad from the wall. Her face grew sterner as she poked at its interface. "No, there are no programs registered to Nick in the pool, on the surface of the inner tube, or on Nick himself."

Nick stuck his tongue out. "Yeah, you're just weak Ludo."

The other swim team members laughed.

"You... you stupid—!" Ludo raged.

"Ludo!" Coach Judy said. "Nanite abuse is a very serious offense. You can't accuse people of it just because you're upset about something else."

"He stole my inner tube! I did *all* my sets!"

"That may be, but I think you need to take some time away from the pool and think about your accusation."

"But Coach Judy—!"

"Enough!"

Ludo stalked to the bench at the side of the pool and threw himself onto it. Coach Judy took the inner tube away from a reluctant Nick and ordered him into her office. Ludo pulled his goggles over his eyes and shuddered.

He was facing the lap pool now and watched Kal, still swimming. Kal approached the wall, flipped, glided underwater, then broke through the surface and began cycling his arms once more. Ludo watched Kal swim back and forth for many minutes, the kids in the deep end shouting joyfully all the while. Twenty-eight laps later, Kal hit the wall, stood up, took a few deep breaths, and pulled himself out of the pool.

Ludo watched as Kal counted the number of inner tubes in the deep pool with his eyes, then finally spotted Ludo on his bench. Kal smirked inquisitively and walked toward him.

"Hey," Kal said. "What happened to the inner tube?"

"Coach Judy took it away."

"You want to do cannonballs?" Kal asked. Ludo shuddered.

"Hey Kal," a boy called out from the deep end. "Let's do cannonballs!"

"Just a minute," Kal called back.

"It's okay..." Ludo mumbled. "Go ahead without me."

"You sure?"

"Yeah."

"Is there something you want to talk about—?"

"No."

"Okay, but come on over for cannonballs when you're feeling better, okay?"

Kal walked off toward the deep end.

Ludo turned his face away from the other swimmers and pressed a button on his goggle strap. The nanotech bubble dissipated momentarily and the tears that had built up inside splashed onto the bench.

He pressed the button again, reinstating the goggle forcefields.

He knew he shouldn't feel this way. He knew he should like Kal. Kal was always nice to him. Kal would spend time with him. Kal invited him over to his house. None of the other kids did that. They called him weak and annoying and lame. But, for all that, Ludo hated Kal most of all. He hated how good Kal was at swimming, how everyone liked Kal. Not like himself, the butt of every joke, the target of everyone's ire.

He knew he shouldn't feel this way, but he couldn't help it. He just did. And one day, he promised himself, he'd be strong enough to do something about it.

$$\infty\!\!\diagup\!\!\infty$$

"A boy on the swim team when I was twelve," Kal said, his voice raspy. "His name's Ludo."

"How do you know they're his?" Tria asked.

"Look at the nanite forcefields over the eyepieces. They're opaque. Ludo used to do that because he didn't want the other kids to see him crying. He's the only person I've ever seen do that."

A rhythmic clomping sounded in the distance. Kal and Tria both turned toward it.

"But why would he want to—?" Tria started.

"I have no idea. He was sad a lot. He bruised emotionally pretty easily. But I can't imagine that humble little kid wiping out whole worlds."

The clomping grew louder.

"Maybe we should leave." Tria's hologram nudged Kal.

Kal leaned over to cough again, which built into a full-on fit of wheezing gasps.

"Kal!"

Kal pulled himself upright. "If that's Ludo, I want to talk to him. Otherwise we leave, okay?"

Tria nodded.

A behemoth of metal rounded the corner. Kal took a step back and gasped. The monstrosity stood four or five meters tall, it's body all silvery and fluid, shimmering against the bursts of lightning. Its legs and arms were enormous, its torso small. It had no head, just two glowing, blue spheres that wobbled atop its body.

"TARGET DETECTED," a deep, mechanical voice boomed from it.

"I'm guessing that's not Ludo," Tria said.

"My curiosity is sated," Kal rasped. "Get us out of here."

"Three steps ahead of you." Tria pushed a button on his interface and the electric, blue sphere crackled around them.

"TARGET IS ATTEMPTING METAXIC DISPLACEMENT," the behemoth droned. Kal watched it take up a fighting stance, its hand stretching out toward him and his brother. A spray of green goop erupted from its outstretched palm and rushed toward them.

Kal threw up his hands in front of his face as his partially-formed metaxic bubble exploded all around him, fireworks of blue sparks mixed with the spray of green slop. Heat seared his skin, and he felt himself being thrown backward.

He pulled himself up from the ground, covered in green goop. The gray ooze on the ground was getting closer to his skin. His nanites could protect him from the gray ooze, or from the green sludge, or they could make a metaxic bubble, but doing all three had left them stretched thin. Kal pushed himself off the ground, trying to wipe all of the horrible, goopy substances off himself and his pad. Another coughing fit overwhelmed him. Pain seared through his chest. The clomps of the behemoth grew nearer.

"Okay, Kal," Tria said. "I've got some focused electromagnetic pulses programmed. Nothing unethical about destroying some nanites, right?"

Kal nodded his consent, clutching his chest and unable to stop coughing long enough to speak.

Tria pointed and air rippled in three long streaks, shooting from his fingertips. The first impacted the golem at its left leg, the second its right shoulder, and the final one its eyes. The beast's left calf and right shoulder disintegrated on contact with the beams, causing its right arm to fall off and splash into the nanite goo. But the wobbling, blue eyes absorbed the burst entirely and continued bobbing and weaving. It remained unnaturally upright, supported only by a single, off-center leg.

"Run, Kal," Tria said. "Just get away as fast as you can."

Kal wheezed, his face flushed, and his chest on fire. He looked back as he ran all the same, watching as the behemoth's eyes flared and metaxic bubbles opened over its left leg and right arm. They dissipated, revealing new limbs, replacing the ones Tria had destroyed.

"No..." Kal wheezed and toppled into the gray goop on the ground. It was so close to his skin now. He could hear the behemoth lumbering toward him.

"New plan," Tria said, and his hologram flickered off.

Kal closed his eyes and gasped. He felt something grab his leg and pull him up off the ground.

"Open your eyes, Kal," a voice said. That voice. Deeper, much deeper than he remembered, but recognizable.

"Ludo..." Kal could barely get the name out. His former friend stood below him, the boy Kal had known six years ago, now approaching adulthood as well. Black hair, deep brown eyes, long face. And something had changed about his face. The left half of it morphed and rippled like the surface of water.

"I wish... I could say... it's good to... see you," Kal said.

Ludo held a pad of his own and tapped at its interface.

Pain seared in Kal's chest, blood rushing to his head, making him woozy. The metallic monstrosity clutched his leg still, and he hung suspended in the air. "What happened...? I thought... we were friends?"

Ludo jammed his pad onto his jeans and looked up at Kal. His eyes, especially the rippling one, seared with a fervor that Kal didn't recognize. The kid he had known all those years ago had gained some direction alright.

"I was in the hospital with you, you know. I used to talk to you. I imagined you heard me the whole time. They told me that sometimes people in comas can hear you talking to them. I guess you didn't."

Kal interrupted him with another coughing fit, but Ludo just kept talking.

"I got this just after your disorder kicked in." Ludo pointed to his face. "Boy, did I feel stupid when they shipped you off to an alternate Earth. You know what I've learned, Kal?"

Kal was still busy coughing, but he eyed Ludo between painful gasps for air. Maybe if he could keep Ludo talking, he'd give up the monstrosity's weakness or Tria would figure something out.

"I learned that even though life isn't fair…" Ludo gesticulated to everything around him. "…it doesn't have to be. Unfair, that is."

Kal shook his head, gasping and groaning.

Ludo just continued. "Some people are good at sports, some are bad. Some people are intelligent, others dim. Some people lead full, happy, productive lives. *Others* experience misfortune, ridicule, sudden illness—"

Kal wheezed and kicked at the monstrosity's arm with his free leg.

"I'm going to make the universes fair, Kal. All of them."

Kal glared at Ludo incredulously through searing coughs. The world felt hazy. He could feel consciousness beginning to elude his grasp and struggled for every moment he could possibly hold Ludo's attention, keep him talking.

Ludo laughed, a maniacal laugh that didn't suit the meager little boy that Kal remembered, who had seemed so kind and innocent.

"Well, it all starts with my metaxic golem here. Nanites used as nanites should be used. To create fairness."

"You mean… kill people," Kal sputtered, and the exertion only made his world hazier and the coughing worse.

Ludo rolled his eyes. "Whatever. I'm done with stupid rules from an unequal, unjust society. You were sent off into the metaxia while I was left on Earth to die alone! No more, Kal! No more fun adventures through all-possibility. Really, if you're so wonderful and awesome, why is it you can't even remember to do the simplest, most obvious of things? You don't even realize what you've forgotten to do, do you? Disgusting. No appreciation of just how lucky you are. I guess you just don't care. You deserve every bit of this. Every last bit."

Ludo picked up his pad. "Goodbye, Kal. Oh, and if you do manage to survive this, do yourself a favor. Go back to Felis and stay there, or you'll just end up making things worse for yourself and everyone else."

Kal gasped and panted through the wind and the crackling blue electricity of the metaxic bubble as it formed around Ludo, whisking him

away.

The golem grabbed Kal's torso with its free hand and squeezed. Kal cried out in pain, but his throat felt constricted, and instead of his voice, only a gasping wheeze emerged. He could feel his nanites failing, the pressure of the golem's crushing grasp slipping through.

Tell me you've got something, Tria.

I don't know what to tell you, Kal.

This is it then?

Don't talk like that.

What do you want me to say? Kal's chest scorched. Pressure crushed him from all directions, and he ached all over.

I don't know! Tria thought back. *Tell me how to make a metaxic sphere that's immune to golem spray. Tell me that snapping my fingers can send this abomination to another world.*

Okay, then, I'll tell you— Kal stopped mid-thought, and his mind raced to uncloud itself. Could it be that simple? Yes, maybe it was. *Tria... a metaxic bubble... the eyes. It's the eyes! Remember when you destroyed its limbs? Its eyes flared, and it regenerated itself with metaxic bubbles. Its eyes must be... some kind of, um... permanent connection to the metaxia!*

And I could sever that connection with the metaxic nodes! Tria's hologram appeared on the ground below.

"Hi there!" Tria waved up to the golem. The behemoth looked down at him with its swirling and bobbing blue eyes. It swiped at Tria with its free hand, but the image of Tria was only momentarily disrupted with each grasp. Tria continued his programming as the golem swung futilely through him.

Tria pressed a button on his interface, glanced up at the golem, and smiled. A sphere of blue sparks appeared, enveloping not Kal, not any of the golem's limbs, but the golem's two blue eyes. Kal felt himself falling through the air, and his body crashed against the pavement. He groaned as more pain shot through him, and he gasped for breath.

The golem's eyes slammed against the periphery of the sphere of blue electricity, trying to escape. Each time they hit the edge, a spray of blue sparks repelled them inwards.

The bubble resolved around the eyes, fizzling away, off to whatever alternate Earth Tria had targetted. The metal frame of the golem melted apart, its limbs dissolving to the ground and joining the mass of silver goo covering the surface of the planet.

Kal lay in a pile of the green and gray glop, panting and gasping and groaning in pain. It hurt so much he could barely keep his eyes open. Tria approached with his interface and smiled. He pressed a button and the horrible world disappeared into swirling metaxia.

∞⟨⟩∞

Kal opened his eyes, glimpsing the whorls of all-possibility and the intermittent shards of alternate Earth landscapes. It was getting easier to breathe. He closed his eyes once more.

Tria?

Yeah, Kal?

Ludo's planning something, and if he escaped Earth, I'm not sure there's anything Fermilab's going to be able to do about it.

And you do want to do something about it? Even after everything that's happened?

Yeah. We'll still look for a way to fix me and fix you, but finding Ludo and taking him back to Earth come first. I know I promised you, but—

I agree.

Really?

Yeah. But only on one condition.

What's that?

You get some sleep now so the nanites can fix you up.

Kal laughed, which caused a small coughing fit. *Thanks, Tria. You were awesome today, you know that?*

It was fun, actually. A nice break from linguistics textbooks.

Glad I could give you a real challenge. I'm going to get some sleep now, Tria. Good night.

Good night, Kal.

Kal closed his eyes.

Acknowledgement

The creation of Voyage is a story all its own. For brevity's sake, it will suffice to say that the novel began as a series of posts on a fantasy writing forum that my friend Matt Adams roped me into in 2000, when I was still in high school. I insisted on creating a science fiction character to live in the forum's fantasy universe. When I was asked to explain Kal's weird nanotechnology that allowed him to appear fantastical, as well as what he was even doing in that universe, my resulting answers established the fundamental concepts underpinning the Voyage universes.

Those initial forum posts led to me to write down more of his adventures offline, until the stories piled up into a novel. Over the years, the ideas piled up into so many stories that one novel was no longer enough to contain them all.

I'm indebted to both Matt Adams and John Loos. Their early involvement and feedback has helped make the Voyage worlds as rich as they are today.

I dawdled for a long time on Voyage, just collecting ideas and writing short stories. I never felt that it could find a real home in the traditional publishing world. In 2012, the e-reader market exploded, and the barriers to publication dissipated along with them. As a result, I decided to publish the Voyage series on my own.

I've been extremely fortunate to have received critical feedback from so many to people, to help me draw out my characters and make my alternate worlds more vivid. I'm indebted to everyone who has contributed their time and energy to Voyage's development.

Aubry Andersen has also helped draw my characters in the literal sense, lending her significant artistic expertise to this project. Aubry's detailed illustrations and skillful graphic design endeavors have brought richness and vivid imagery to the worlds of Voyage that I could never achieve with words alone.

I would also like to thank WJ Davies, Jc Farnham, Dyane Forde, Elizabeth Guizzetti, Mark Gyscek-Strauss, Jason Wade Howard, Nathan Procter-Jones, Madison Keller, Mariann Krizsan, T.A. Miles, and Max Zaoui for all their feedback and support.

And of course, none of this would be even remotely possible without the ceaseless support of my partner Alex, my fuzzy русский.

Thank you all.

Also from Fuzzy Hedgehog Press

The Winter (Isaac the Fortunate, Part 1)
by A. Ka

www.fuzzyhedgehogpress.com

Release Dates

Below are the original release dates in 2013 for the individual episodes of Voyage: Embarkation in electronic book format.

Prologue & Setting Sail	February 11
Longing	February 14
Just a Game	February 18
Tria	February 21
Corporeal	February 25
Norselands	March 14
Duality	April 11
Benevolence	May 9
Nanogen	June 6
Unpossible	June 27
Requiescence	July 25
Liberty	August 22
Taboo	September 19
Ludo	November 21

Voyage Along the Catastrophe of Notions continues with
Volume Two, Voyage Windbound.

Individual Voyage Windbound episodes will be available in
major ebook formats throughout 2014.

Visit www.fuzzyhedgehogpress.com for more details.